Kwarq

Lyqa Planet Lovers

Nikki Clarke

This is a work of fiction. Names, characters, businesses, places, events and incidents are either the products of the author's imagination or used in a fictitious manner. Any resemblance to actual persons, living or dead, or actual events is purely coincidental.

Cover Art: Alex Campbell

@alexdrawl

Follow and Get More Nikki

Lyqa Planet Lovers and Soulmates of Somii (in reading order):
   Kwarq: Lyqa Planet Lovers Series 1
   Bati: Lyqa Planet Lovers Series 2
   My Lyqa Valentine: Lyqa Planet Lovers Series 2.5
   Sol: Lyqa Planet Lovers Series 3
   My Alien Captor, Nyo: Soulmates of Somii Prequel 0.5
   Kyr: Soulmates of Somii 1
   Ah'dan: Lyqa Planet Lovers Series 4
   Qim: Lyqa Planet Lovers Series 5
   Something Lyqa Christmas
   Malcolm and Dinar: A Hosa Empire Love Story

Black Valley Wolves:
   Nothing but the Wolf in Me
   For My Wolves
   A Wolf is a Wolf

Third Street Conjure Boys:
   Jinx: Third Street Conjure Boys
   Lure: Third Street Conjure Boys
   Abra: Third Street Conjure Boys
* * *

Black Girls Off World:
    My Alien Threshers
    My Alien Invader, Fi'r
    My Alien Thresher Nial
    Women of Rhy'n Vella Series

Monarchs of Midaan:
    Gaad's Plan: Monarchs of Midaan Quickie
    My's Way: Monarchs of Midaan Quickie

Speculative Quickies:
    Taste: A Vampire Quickie
    The Battle Prince's Prize Bride
    Lick: A Vampire Quickie
    The Girl: Wake the Girl

Contemporary:
    If There's Still Time
    Tempting Mr. Reality

Visit my website and join my mailing list for updates!
    www.nikkiclarkeromance.com

Join my Facebook Readers Group to chat with me and other Nikki Clarke readers!

To my partner, whose only advice to me has ever been,
"you should do it."

Say It Like A Lyqa

- Lyqa : Lie-kuh
- Kwarq : KwahR-q (Hard R, Q is a click in the throat)
- Bati : Pah-tee
- Ah'dan : Ah-Dahn (breathy H both times with a noticeable pause between syllables)
- Quth : Kooth (K is a soft click in the throat)
- Mahdi : Makh-Di (H is a little harsh)
- Li'aht : Lee-aut
- T'nai : Teh-Nye
- Maq'ti : Mock-Tee (CK is soft click in the throat)
- Qim : Keem (K is a soft click in the throat)
- Qiton : Kee-tahn (hard K)

PROLOGUE

KWARQ

"Ay, they feel bad."

My brother Bati's face screws into a grimace. He exhales forcefully through his nose, and his nostrils fan wide to push out the brassy air. The sensation he speaks of is a thick, soupy agitation that rides the exhaust-filled breeze. I feel it, too. It prickles at my skin, causing the muscles in my neck to tighten. I roll my head in an effort to discharge the tension.

A man shuffles by. The thin, woven fabric of his outerwear undulates in the city's hawkish winds. His eyes are sunken moons—idle, withdrawn, and focused on some unseen destination. When his jacket brushes over the skin of my arm, there's nothing. No connection. No warm exchange of energy. Any feelings the man has are being well contained. Except for bitterness. This feeling is like its own atmosphere around him.

And it's not just him. A sea of people careen down the gray, cracked sidewalks of this city on Earth called Chicago. Every set of eyes is downcast. Clothing is pulled up over their ears against the chilly air. I can't help but view the stiff material as a symbolic exoskeleton against their kinsman.

"I can't believe this is a prime *ta'ani maul* destination. It kind of just feels like a big ball of angry." Bati shifts closer. His eyes bounce from one bitter face to another. "Everyone's so tense and wary. It's like they're all waiting for something bad to happen."

I look away from Bati's troubled expression and survey the men and women moving past us. "You chose it. We could be on Qiton, basking in their sun, completing a leisurely *ta'ani* near the ocean."

Bati snorts. "I completed that *ta'ani* when we were barely out of childhood."

The wispy, lyrical pitch of our native tongue hums in the grating cacophony of beeps, grinds, and twangs. The sidewalk is wide and walled by decorated storefronts. I press closer into Bati's shoulder to evade the crush of movement.

To our left, sunlight reflects off the glass of a storefront window where a woman stands smoking an electronic pipe. Her pale skin is speckled with bright red spots across her cheeks and nose. Braided strands of hair hang about her shoulders. Lips as red as human blood kiss the tip of the pipe, and two indents form in the sunken hollows of her cheeks. A dense, blue-tinged mushroom of smoke plumes from between her lips to mask her face before being carried off on the breeze.

"I've done some research on humans. They don't react well to the unfamiliar. We should be careful of speaking our language."

"Why?" Bati looks around. "Humans speak a variety of languages."

"Yes, but many of our sounds are foreign, unlike any heard on Earth. There's no way someone overhearing us won't be alarmed." I nod discretely in the direction of the smoking woman just as her black rimmed eyes narrow on us.

"Don't be a bore," Bati drawls with a heavy sigh. "No one is listening. Think of it as a challenge to blend in with these angry, wretched humans. I think maybe we need a challenge. *You* need a challenge."

I grunt and the breath produces its own little cloud beneath my nose. My muscles shiver beneath my skin, but not from the frigid air. The heedless surge of humans continues around us. The wind lifts their scents to form a cyclone of bitterness that fills my lungs and is quickly absorbed into my blood to be carried through my body.

"Perhaps, I need for you not to drag me across the galaxies on some stupid child's game," I bark.

I flinch at the unfamiliar edge to my voice, just as Bati's eyes enlarge in shock.

"I would say that's a good start, brother." The joke is meant to cover his hurt, but it seeps between our touching arms. "I want this to be fun, but if you are truly opposed, please forgive me. I only meant to celebrate with you."

I huff out the bitter air clouding my senses and run a hand over my face.

"No, forgive me. It's difficult for me to close myself off from their negativity. It's making me irritable. I should not have spoken to you that way. *Ma'h qitah.*"

I face my brother and wrap my hand around his neck, gripping the tightened cords between his shoulders and bringing our foreheads together. I hold him there, executing the formal gesture of apology until I feel his hurt lift away.

"Get a room and get out the middle of the sidewalk, you jerks!"

A man shoves into us, knocking me off balance. I break from Bati and twist around, a low growl rumbling in my chest. My lips pull back, exposing my teeth to the chilly air. The man's eyes widen as he stumbles back, tripping over his feet in his haste to move away from me. When I turn back to Bati, his forehead is drawn in concern. He eyes me cautiously.

"Perhaps this isn't a good idea," he begins carefully. "Let's go back to our pod. We can get a refund on this quest and go to Qiton instead."

Bati's worry pierces my haze of anger. I pull in several deep breaths, forcing myself to calm. People are beginning to stare. The woman with the pipe pulls a cellular phone from her pocket and angles it in our direction. I don't know why

I'm reacting this way. I've never felt so tense in my life, but I need to keep myself together.

"No, let's continue. We just got here. I'll adjust. I ask your forgiveness if I act out of character again."

Bati shifts uneasily, turning his head from one side to the other.

"I don't know, we're already drawing looks. I think you were right. The people seem uneasy with us."

I shake my head. "No, we look human enough. Our differences are too small to cause alarm. We just have to relax. I have to relax."

"We're too tall."

I survey the tops of people's heads as they move past me. Now this is true. And it's not just that we're tall. We're big. We tower over the humans and take up space.

Gazes linger as people pass. The human females, especially, tilt their heads this way and that, trying to make sense of what we are. Trying perhaps to understand the symmetry of my and Bati's features or our largeness or the energy we give off.

"It will be fine. We just have to be careful of how we present ourselves."

I shake my body out, relaxing the rigidness of my posture in hopes of appearing less unfamiliar. Bati clasps my arm and gives a short nod of understanding.

"We'll be careful. This will be a good thing. I can feel it." His grin is mischievous. His bright blue eyes flash once again in his dark face. "I don't know if you've noticed, but the females of this planet expel a much nicer energy."

"They do, but it's a strange energy. They're cautious. Almost afraid. Perhaps it's because all of the men are so aggressive. I scent their fear, but there is an openness as well."

"Mm. It's warm when they pass. As if they want to be close, but also think we may hurt them."

I nod my head at his assessment of this contradiction of the human female. "It's odd."

"It is."

I catch this energy on a nearby woman. She stands at the corner near the street, watching us with a furrowed brow. She approaches and then retreats before finally edging closer and stopping a foot away. Her lips turn up in a half-smile. She raises her hand in greeting.

"Are you lost? Do you need help?"

She enunciates the words carefully, the way one would if speaking to a child. Her nervous, brown eyes shift between my brother and me.

"We are well, thank you."

Her eyebrows shoot up a second before a bright red flush spreads over her cheeks. She mumbles and hastily walks back to the corner. She glances back then turns away, quickly, her hand coming up to fan at her face where little clouds of air appear in front of her mouth.

"She was aroused," Bati says. A wide, excited grin spreads across his face.

"Yes, I could tell," I return dryly.

"Maybe there's a chance to have some fun after all." His eyebrows wiggle up and down, and I glance away.

"We came for the *ta'ani maul*, Bati, not to fool arou—"

The remaining words deteriorate in my throat. I'm assaulted by an overwhelming feeling of pleasure. It's tender and sweet and surges through me, assertive and pure, to flush out the negative energy of the city. I go rigid with the intensity as I'm held captive by the sheer magnificence of such an unfamiliar sensation. I focus on the source of the scent which floats from the street where a bus is just passing by.

I see her. Just the side of her face. The mud speckled window of the bus obscures most of her features, but I can see that she's soft and delicate looking. A dark cloud of coiled hair shields me from what I know is the most beautiful face I will ever see. Her energy is a thick thread between us. It stretches through the metal structure of the bus to attach itself directly to my heart. I follow the trail as the bus chugs down the street, inhaling deeply of the woman's intoxicating scent. It isn't until the bus has reached the end of the block that Bati's alarmed voice seeps through the cloud of lust in my brain.

"Brother, what are you doing?"

"What?"

I shake my head as the trance recedes. I can still feel her, but she isn't the suffocating presence of a moment ago. Bati grips my shoulder. His cheeks pulse a dull red.

I follow his gaze down to where they're trained on my lower body. I'm hard. Extremely so. My cock strains against my thin traveling pants. It thickens more than ever before and urges me to follow the presence of that woman.

I cup my crotch and let Bati lead me to a bench.

"Did you feel her?" My excitement is a vibrating energy beneath my skin.

Bati pushes me down and settles beside me. He glances around in search of the source of my distraction.

"The older woman?"

I shake my head. I can't rid my mind of the purity of her energy. It feels so complete. So perfect.

"On the bus. The woman with the curled hair. It was so intense. How could you not feel it?"

"Brother, I don't know what you're talking about. I've felt many women since we arrived, they are much more open, but I didn't experience anything just now."

I try to make sense of what I'm feeing.

"It was thrilling."

Thrilling is a good word. The only thing I know that can

compare to the purity of the experience is the connection I have to my mother, or maybe Bati, who I shared a womb with and grew with. But those are familial emotions. This is different and *more*. It calls to the sexual part of me and settles over me like a warm hand. It's almost like…

"Maybe it's the *leht*."

Bati snickers as he speaks the words I'm thinking, and as soon as he does, I know he's right.

"It is."

My brother's eyebrow arches up and his mouth turns down disapprovingly. "Brother, I was kidding. Everyone is so miserable here, you probably just felt her joy."

"No. She's my *lehti*. I cannot explain it, how it *feels*. Even now, she could be miles away, and she is still here." I tap my chest just over my right pectoral. It's tight, the connection between me and the woman a tangible thing. Like a string being pulled too tight. In this moment, I know that it doesn't matter how far away she is, I will still feel her. I also know now that even if I wanted to leave, I could not.

I stare at the humans shuffling by a few feet away. They are miserable like Bati has said. It seems almost a miracle that something so pure as I felt could exist in such a place.

"To think. My *lehti* resides on this planet so many galaxies away. Here, of all places." I cannot fight the truth of it.

Bati, too, nods in understanding. We both know that it's pointless to question the *leht*.

"The *leht* knows no bounds, brother. If she is meant for you, there's no denying it."

"I have no intention of denying it." I feel the truth of this to my first heart.

"I knew this trip would be good." Bati nudges my arm, and his eyebrows jump when I look at him.

"I must go to her."

"You must, so I will leave you, brother." He rises from the

bench. "Find her, but keep in mind that we do not know the ways of humans. She may not experience the *leht* as you do. She may not connect."

"I know, but I have to try."

He nods. There's worry behind his assent. If I'm honest, I also wonder if this will end as it should. As it must.

"Send word when you're returning. Should I have our parents prepare for your arrival?"

"Absolutely."

Bati's smile shines brightly.

"At least you're confident." He grips my shoulder in a firm squeeze. "Good luck."

Bati cuts swiftly through the crowd. His long gait startles people out of the way. I stand and watch him make is way down the street. He'll be back at his pod and home in an instant. While I'll be here, trying to convince the beautiful human woman who passed me on the bus to love me.

I walk back to the curb, inhaling deeply of the thick, smoggy air. She's still there. Her sweet presence hasn't faded a bit. I turn in the direction where the bus disappeared and start to jog. She's mine, and I'm not leaving without her.

CHAPTER 1

KWARQ

"This movie is stupid."

My voice is too low to be detected by the humans around me, but after an hour of watching this travesty of a film, I can hold it in no longer.

I've been on this planet for two months, and in that time, I still can't believe how ridiculous human movies are.

I shovel a greasy handful of popcorn into my mouth just as the young teenage human on screen shivers and jerks before leaping out of his skin and transforming into a large, shaggy wolf. I shake my head when the beast cranes its neck to release a tortured howl.

That's just not good science. How in the universe would someone burst out of themselves to become a wolf, only to become a human again? Shifting may be an interesting idea, but it's not actually something one sees in the universe.

Humans have many interesting ideas. Their ability to imagine the most outlandish and amazing things has been their greatest strength as a species. However, when it comes to inter-planetary mingling, it hasn't helped very much.

Humans have simply thought of too many absurd scenarios for other beings to initiate contact with them safely. They've made themselves nervous with the doomsday stories and movies. Tales of creatures sweeping from the sky armed with laser beams to slaughter them. It's too risky. Humans don't have much that other species could want, so most other beings stay away. Some still venture here for sport. And the rare visitor comes for some nefarious purpose.

Nefarious. Lovely word, terrible meaning.

I love the human languages. All of them. They tell so much about a people, good or bad. The word nefarious, for instance, does not exist in my culture. We do not, as Webster says, have people or intentions that are "extremely wicked or evil." Evil is a pointless concept where I come from. I guess one could say we have evolved without the need for it.

A roar blares through the large screening room, and I focus back on the film. In this story, a young woman falls in love with all kinds of fantasy beings. A vampire. A werewolf. A fairy of some kind. I'm not really paying attention. I'm listening. As Lyqa, my hearing is better than any animal's on this planet, and right now, it's tuned into the wistful breaths of the woman sitting across the isle from me.

I still don't know her name, but I've followed her for the past two months, and I know she loves these kinds of movies. She loves any kind of movie, but she particularly enjoys movies about love. They move her. She sits through them, letting happy sighs float from her mouth. I peek at her from the corner of my eye. Her eyelashes shimmer with unshed tears. I can smell their salty reverence.

"Oh, no."

Her voice is an anguished whimper as the wolf is felled by an arrow. She clutches her hands to her chest. Her eyes are wide with fear, and it makes me smile. We all know he's not dead. Even I know it's a tactic to create suspense, but my *lehti* is consumed by anticipation. Her chest rises and falls heavily as we wait for the wolf to leap to its feet and reveal that he is unharmed after all.

"Thank god."

Her relief is barely audible, but I hear it. Just as I feel her longing. It crashes over me, warm and intense like a solar pulse, as it does every time I'm near her. I turn back to the screen, but my mind is across the isle. I don't know if I can wait much longer before revealing myself to her. To see if she feels what I've been feeling since she passed me on that bus two months ago.

AMINA

"You know, you must really like movies."

Movie Bae nearly jumps out of his skin. He's so caught up in the movie that he didn't feel me slide into the seat next to him. It's really not that great of a movie. Some cheesy, supernatural teenage love affair shit, but I'm a sucker for a sappy love story even when it's cliche'.

"I've seen you before, right? I think we go to a lot of the same movies."

His mouth opens and closes, but nothing comes out. Suddenly, his expression tenses and he leans away.

"Uh...," I stall, not really knowing what else to say now that I have his attention. I've been low-key crushing on this man for the past couple of months. I've felt more and more compelled to say something to him. I don't know why. I just feel like we should talk.

At first, I thought our shared movie interest was a coincidence. But lately, I've realized that Movie Bae is there every time I go to the show. Sitting right across from me, eating a big ass bag of popcorn. This seemed like a great jumping off point for a conversation a moment ago. Now it just feels weird. My shoulders hunch in embarrassment, but I attempt a smile anyway.

"Was that a dumb question?"

Movie Bae still doesn't respond. The only way I know he's even listening to me is from the rapid movement of his eyes as they dart across my face. He's so fine. My heart wobbles as the sharp, swirling yellow of his eyes locks on mine. Not hazel. I've seen hazel. His eyes are yellow. The only variation in color is a feather of shimmering amber at the edges. They're bright and shining and wild.

I squirm under his intense stare. It's not just the strangeness of his good looks, which are both familiar and confusing. There's something about him that speaks to me. The moment his eyes meet mine, I feel I could burst into the sizzling pop of a fire cracker.

My heart is going crazy. Movie Bae's eyes flick down to the space between my boobs, and I press a hand against my breastbone afraid that he can hear it.

And still, he hasn't said anything. He's taking deep breaths that huff forcefully out of his nose. It takes me a second to recognize them as the exasperated sighs of someone who doesn't want to be bothered. A cringe snuffs out my bit of excitement. I get it. I don't exactly come to the movies to socialize, either. Keeping my back hunched over so I don't block the screen for the people behind us, I stand up.

"I'm sorry. I didn't mean to bother you." I don't meet his eyes before I scuttle back across the isle. His gaze is hot on me as I settle back into my seat and fold my body in as much as I can. His eyes are two bright flames in my peripheral vision. I will him to look away, but he doesn't. He keeps staring. I huddle further into my seat and wait for the movie to end.

An eternity later, the movie ends, and I have no idea what happened. Did that silly little tenth grader win the battle to save her supernatural boyfriend? Is she really in love with her werewolf neighbor? I don't know, but I do know that Movie Bae is still looking.

Before the credits even roll or the lights come on, I'm out of my seat. I rush up the isle to the door in the back of the theater. The searing burn of mortification is trying to twist its way out of my body, and I wrap my coat closely around my middle to stamp that shit out.

Why did I even talk to him?

I half jog to the exit at the end of hallway and launch myself against the release bar, stumbling out onto State Street.

It's late. I really didn't think it would take so long to tell a story about a high schooler who's in love with a dog. Now I kind of wish I would have picked a movie at a decent time like most sensible people. Unfortunately, I love a late show.

For one, I can always find a seat. For two, I don't have to worry about people blabbing through the film. The only major downfall is once the movie's over, I still have to make my way home. At night. On the number four. All the way to the Southside.

I walk quickly and make it to the end of the block in no time. When I turn the corner, my feet automatically falter.

"Shit."

The block is dark and deserted. Two streets ahead, a few people are illuminated beneath the flickering yellow light of my bus stop. But between me and them, there's nothing but the shadows of the South Loop. The next bus is the last for the night, so, unfortunately, I can't wait for people to happen along and make the walk less scary. I square up and take a deep breath.

"Alright, Amina, you gotta catch the damn bus, so just go," I mutter, suck in another brave breath, and start up the street.

Look, I'm scary. I have no problem admitting it. I put on a brave face, but on the inside, I'm cowering in a corner. That's why when I catch the sudden movement of a stray cat huddled by a dumpster in an alley, it takes all of my effort not to scream and tear down the street. Still, I move quickly, making a conscious effort to keep from appearing too frantic.

"If you look scary, people will try to scare you."

It's a constant reminder. I conjure a bit of confidence and walk at an easy stride. Nothing is going to happen. I've nearly managed to convince myself when I hear the soft, even paced footsteps of someone behind me.

KWARQ

She's scared. Her fear is a thick fog in front of me. I follow it, keeping an eye out for any danger. When I pass the mouth of an alley, a frail, skittish feline slithers beneath a garbage receptacle.

"If you look scary, people will try to scare you."

I smile and snort out a low chuckle. My poor *lehti*. She's so brave and also so afraid of nearly everything.

Everyday, I watch her move about this city with her head held high, forcing herself to appear courageous. At the same time, I smell every bit of her apprehension. Although, I've come to realize that my *lehti* tends to scare herself more than respond to any actual threat that may be coming her way. Not that it matters. I'm here, and I won't let anything happen to her.

I know the moment she hears me because her scent turns acrid. Fear is bitter to the nose. Like anger, it takes over quickly and sours any good feelings that were there before. As I trail her, her usual light, sweet feeling is sharp. Her heart beats fast across the nearly ten yards between us. Her legs move at a regular pace, but the jerkiness of her steps signals she would rather be running.

I let my steps lag. A half block from her bus stop, her heart settles and she relaxes. The nervousness leaves her stride.

I don't like it when she smells like fear. Earlier tonight, she smelled like the light rain of the day before and some sweet oil she uses in her hair. Now all of those lovely scents are being overpowered by her desire to reach safety.

I wish I could tell her that she doesn't have to fear me or anyone. That I have followed her every single day for the past two months to keep her safe. That I sit in the cafe across from her place of work and drink bitter coffee for eight hours a day to make sure she isn't hurt or accosted in some way. Then at night, I sit in my rented room a block from her apartment and feel out to assure myself she sleeps comfortably. I wish I could tell her these things, but unfortunately, I missed my chance when she sat next to me earlier.

She caught me off guard. I've kept a comfortable distance from her all of this time, afraid of scaring her, but also waiting for the best opportunity to reveal myself. Finally having her that close was overwhelming. She smelled shy and nervous, but there was also playfulness and anticipation. It was amazing. The scent had filled my nose and shot straight down to my cock.

I was unable to form an appropriate response to her question with the blood rushing to my lap. In that moment, I was glad her sight in the dark isn't so good. I know Lyqa men and human men are nearly the same anatomically, but I imagine that even on this planet an unwelcome erection is a threatening thing for a woman. I could have howled like that ridiculous boy in the movie when she apologized and went back to her seat, but I was also glad for the moment to collect myself. I will do better next time. Now that I know what to expect.

Up ahead, my *lehti* reaches the corner and looks both ways before dashing across the street. In the distance, cruising slowly closer, I see our bus. She has only just made it.

I side step into the shadowed entrance of a closed shop as the bus pulls to a stop. The few people waiting file in line to board, and my *lehti* steps up last, disappearing from view.

I still can't believe she spoke to me. She sat next to me and spoke to me, even though I know how she hates it when people talk during films. I've heard her deep sighs of annoyance when someone answers a cellular phone or leans into a seatmate to loudly comment on what's happening on the screen.

The doors to the bus close, and the driver pulls away from the curb. I have a split second to decide before I'm sprinting across the street to cut them off. I plant myself in the path of the bus, waving my hands in the air until it comes to an abrupt, skidding halt. On the other side of the windshield, the driver's eyes bulge from their sockets.

I walk calmly to the closed doors. The driver trails me until I stand at the entrance. He doesn't open the doors right away. He only stares at me through the glass. I nod my head, indicating I would like to board, and he finally pulls the lever, prompting the doors' hydraulics to fold in with a loud expulsion of air.

"I apologize. I did not mean to cause you danger, but you are the last bus, and I did not want to miss it." I step aboard, ducking under the short roof.

The man's large eyes roam over me as he pushes out a shaky laugh. "No problem, brother. It's cool. You just scared me a bit. You're fast as hell. You run track in high school?"

I don't know what track is, but I nod. I've found this is the safest thing to do when someone is trying to justify those things about me they can't explain.

"Woo, man, you must have. I thought Usain Bolt had jumped in front of my bus!" He cackles loudly, and I smile in reassurance while digging into my pockets for the transit card that I have loaded with the replica American money I make in my pod.

I swipe my card through the electronic payment pad and turn to the inside of the bus. My eyes find my *lehti*. She's sitting near the back, staring out of the window. Her eyebrows are drawn in concentration, even though I know there's nothing on the deserted streets that could be of particular interest.

I feel out to her as I make my way through the isle. She isn't scared anymore, but she is on edge. It's late, and even though I'm watching her, I know there are any number of legitimate dangers for a young, human woman to watch out for.

In my short time on Earth, I've noticed many troubling things about the way men and women interact. The female humans of this planet are in a constant state of nervousness, and after careful study, I've realized that it's because the males are inclined to accost them both verbally and physically at every moment. They yell things to them on the street, even when it's clear that the woman is not interested. Even when her feelings are so obvious that I cringe with the awkwardness of it. Men grab and poke women. The eyes of girls are terrified as they move about the city, desperately avoiding the gazes of men, the same way one would a rabid animal. This is a reality I find sickening and shameful. It is a reality I don't like my *lehti* existing in. It is a reality I would remove her from if she asked me to.

She turns suddenly, her gaze meeting mine, and her expression brightens. A smile pulls at her mouth just as the muscles of her face tense to keep from showing it. Nervousness colors her scent along with something close to embarrassment. Why should my *lehti* feel shamed?

She fills more and more of my vision. When I'm two seats away, she lifts the purse from the seat beside her and settles it in her lap. She holds my gaze. Her shy smile is warm and inviting.

Twice in one evening, my *lehti* has surprised me by extending an opportunity for interaction. First, she disregarded her own movie etiquette by speaking to me during the film, and now she's offering me a seat. My eyes scan the rest of the bus. It's nearly empty, I could sit where I choose. The brief moment in the theater when she settled in next to me, arresting me with her lovely energy, comes back, and I want to feel that again.

I've just decided I will take her offer when her face changes. Her eyebrows pull down, and her lovely mouth tips at the corners. She's so expressive. She can show happiness, sadness, and excitement in a moment's turn. I wonder what's wrong right before I realize that, in my daze, I have walked past her row. I pause, not sure if I should turn back or continue down the isle. My feet shift forward then back, until I have no choice but to reluctantly settle into a seat just behind and across from her.

Again, that feeling of embarrassment is there, even stronger than before. I realize now that she must see my failure to respond to mean I'm not interested, but she couldn't be more wrong.

CHAPTER 2

AMINA

Movie Bae is breaking my heart. For like two seconds, I thought he was going to sit next to me.

It's too much like fate that he got on my bus tonight. I thought maybe it was the universe giving me a second chance to strike up a conversation, even though I'm still salty about my first attempt. And then he looked right at me. I thought I sensed interest there. Maybe not.

The darkened windows of stores pass by outside, but my mind is on the man sitting behind me. I wonder where he's getting off. Even though I deny it with one half of my brain, the other half secretly hopes we have the same stop. Maybe I haven't been forward enough. Maybe he doesn't speak English. He seems foreign. Maybe he doesn't like to sit next to people on the bus. I can understand that.

"I do not really like them, but I enjoy being in the theater."

"Holy shit!"

My heart jackhammers against my ribcage. Movie Bae's sitting right next to me. Like this dude just materialized out of nowhere. He's so close that it feels like he's everywhere.

Those deep, breathy words came from him. The delicacy of his pronunciation is at complete odds with the ferity of his appearance. Full, sexy lips peek from the low beard covering his face. The hair is strange. Both silky and thick. It looks soft. I imagine kissing him wouldn't be prickly. His lips move, and again, those soft, almost melodic sounds erupt from between them.

"Do you also like movies?"

He's asking me a question. I should answer, but my brain is on pause. I press the mental play button. I think he's continuing the conversation we never had in the movie theater.

"I guess I like them."

He seems surprised.

"In the past two months, you have been to nearly a dozen movies. You laugh. You fold yourself into your chair when you are frightened. At times you cry. Why do that if you do not like them?"

I'm too caught off guard to speak.

"How do you know all that?"

"I have seen you."

"You have?"

"I have."

He has. My mind rewinds back a week when I saw some B-rate romantic comedy. I cried like a baby when the girl got her man. The closing scene when they met each other years later, and the hero grabbed her and kissed her, turned me into a blubbering mess. Knowing Movie Bae has watched me cry at stupid teenage love stories and hide under my shirt during corny horror films makes me feel kind of vulnerable. My face warms, and I'm glad I don't actually blush.

"I do like them. I just meant it's something to do. A way to pass the time, but I do like them." My explanation doesn't alleviate his confusion. "I know, it probably sounds weird that I like to sit in a theater and cry or scream or laugh my head off. I guess I'm kind of weird."

I peek up from my lap to find him staring intently at me. He turns slightly, his large, muscular arm pressing into mine and sending a little shiver through me. He has so much presence. Even with the gentle, musical voice.

"I've shamed you, again. I apologize." He leans forward like he's going to kiss me, and I don't know why but I tilt my head back, both wanting this strange man to press his mouth to mine, and also knowing that's completely crazy because he's a stranger who's been watching me watch movies.

He grips my arms. It's a gentle touch. I don't think I've ever felt so reassured by a simple gesture, and I ease into his face as it gets closer. My mouth parts slightly when he's close enough, but he doesn't kiss me. He turns his head and presses his cheek to mine.

I can't help my sigh. His beard is as soft as I imagined. Each thick strand cradles my face. They're silky as baby hair. Yet, I stiffen. The gesture is so atypical, so intimate. He isn't just touching me. There's something intense in the contact. His deep, even breaths whisper along my neck.

"*Lehti, ma'h qitah.*"

The words swirl and caress the shell of my ear. I don't know what the hell it means, but I like it. It washes over me, and along with it, the awkwardness I'm feeling shifts into a wonderful kind of contentment. I relax into the warmth of his skin. His touch ignites a tremor that spreads like a vine up my arm, curling around my shoulders and beneath my breasts. My nipples tighten as the vine morphs into tendrils of desire. They curl down my belly, making my pussy tingle and my thighs spasm.

I jerk back, a little stunned at my response. I mean, I'm human, and the man is gorgeous, but getting wet from a hug is not the thing. I shift from the cradle of his shoulder and try to think of something to say to fill the silence that follows.

"Was that Amharic?"

He doesn't answer. He's expressionless, but I can just see the traces of a smile around his mouth.

KWARQ

She's affected by me. Being this close to my *lehti* has afforded my heightened senses a host of new experiences. Her nervousness is tangy on the smooth skin of her cheek. The soft, fluffy strands of her hair are fragrant with the sweet scent of fruit. Her heart is a fast flutter beneath her breasts. But none of these new experiences compares to the moment I scent her arousal rise up from where she presses her legs firmly together.

She gets embarrassed again, but this time it isn't with shame. This new kind of embarrassment is laced with excitement, and I can't help the smile that pulls at my mouth.

"It is not Amharic, *lehti*," I reply when she stops staring into her lap and looks at me. She has a good ear. Of all the languages on Earth, Amharic most closely reflects the breathy and sharp tones of my native tongue. I'm impressed at how agile her mind is, and even more pleased that the *leht* has bound me to her.

I want to hold her again, but I may have already overstepped my bounds in offering a traditional apology. I release her arm and settle back into my seat, keeping my body angled so that our sides still touch. It's a small contact, but I relish in it and the flood of feeling it offers me.

"Letty? Your language is called Letty? Hm, I've never heard it before. Where is it from? Sudan?"

She's so curious. I like that she wants to know about me, and instead of reacting with aversion as many humans seem to do at the unfamiliar, she tries to understand.

"No, *lehti* is something else. I will tell you later. My language is—rare. Not many people speak it here. I come from a very isolated place."

It's difficult to avoid answering her directly. Now that we're speaking, I want to tell her everything, but I must be careful.

"Oh," she ponders, and I sense her growing uncomfortable again. "I don't want to be rude. I really hate when people ask questions like this, and I'm sure you get it all the time. I promise that I'm not as ignorant as this is going to sound, but I've never really seen anyone who looks like you before. I can't really place you, not that it matters, but—what are you?"

A detect the faint cringe in her expression. Her scent tinges with shame. She is very bothered by asking me this. Even though her skin is a dark brown, warmth rises beneath it. The tips of her ears brighten.

I don't have to ask what she means. I've come to understand this thing about race on Earth. It's strange and ridiculous, but it makes her nervous, and I don't want her to be nervous.

"I am a male." I don't say man because that would be a lie, and I can't lie to her. I could never lie to her.

"I know, but where do you come from. Where are your parents from? What country? I mean, you have an accent, so what's your ethnicity?"

"What do you think I am?"

She considers me carefully, her mouth twisted up to the side.

"Um, Middle Eastern, maybe? East African? Black? A white dude with a tan? I really can't tell." She laughs and it's shy and soft. It makes my skin twitch with its loveliness.

"While I think I understand why you have asked me this, if I request that you allow me not to answer these questions just yet, will you accept it?"

Again she flushes beneath her dark skin. It's so charming, this slight embarrassment, that I have to stop myself from reaching out to feel the heat of her smooth cheek.

"I'm sorry. I'm being rude. It shouldn't matter. I was just curious about your accent. It's lovely, anyway."

She looks back out the window. Her posture is tense.

"You are lovely."

Her head jerks back to me. Her mouth parted in surprise. Maybe I'm too forward, but I can no longer keep from telling her how beautiful she is. She is the most beautiful woman I have ever seen. I don't have to wonder why my *leht* is with her. Even if my *leht* had not been with her, I still would have noticed a woman so beautiful.

Her skin is a rich, reddish brown. Her eyes are wide and heavily lidded. They make her look innocent and shy. She has a small, round nose that scrunches up in the middle when she's confused or thoughtful or finds something distasteful. It's a gesture I've come to find extremely adorable.

All of her features serve to make her appear disarmingly cute. That is, until you get to her mouth. There, her face changes into something sensual. Something that makes it hard for me not to want to kiss her.

Her lips are lusciously full and soft. Luscious. I like this word to describe her mouth. When she smiles, two little dimples appear at the lower corners. Right now, her beautiful mouth is opened so that I can just see the tips of her small, white teeth. I look at this space, wondering what she would taste like. How warm it would be in there.

"Your hair is different."

The statement blurts from my mouth, and I have to clear my throat around the awkwardness of it. I had to say something, anything, to take my mind off the tightening in my pants.

Her dark hair is an asymmetrical cloud around her head, parted and falling heavily over the left side of her face. The texture is a mixture of tight ringlets and parts that appear soft and frizzy. Around the hairline, short wavy hairs frame her face. I love it.

She reaches a hand up and pats at the cloud.

"Oh, yeah. I change it a lot."

She does. In the two months I've been on this planet, my

lehti has appeared with no less than a dozen different hairstyles. She arranges her hair in little twists that fall down her back and around her shoulders. Other times, she pulls it high onto her head into a large, curly ball. Other times still, she does something to change the texture, and it hangs in thick, straight strands down her back.

Mostly, she wears her hair the way it is now, loose and curly. She leaves her house in the morning while it's still wet and dripping around her shoulders. My favorite thing to watch is the slow change as it dries and shrinks in on itself before forming a tight curly crown.

Without thinking, I reach out and finger an errant curl sticking out from the rest. The feel of it between my fingers is both soft and textured, a simple complexity I can't help but find appealing.

My *lehti* jerks her head back. Her eyes flash with anger. I pull my hand way, realizing my mistake.

"I should not have touched you without your permission. I am sorry."

I automatically reach for her to apologize, but she angles her body fully away from me. Her expression is a hard scowl. However, she's not angry. What she's projecting is disappointment. I don't know what I have done, but I immediately realize it is something very wrong.

"I'm not a fucking dog."

Her words are laced with defense and insult. This declaration means nothing to me, however. Of course, she is not a dog.

"You are not," I return, but my confirmation only vexes her further.

"You can't just touch my hair—pet me like I'm some animal. I'm a person. It's hair like anyone else has hair. What did you think it would feel like?"

She's hurt, and I don't know why, but I feel it's important

to her, so I want to understand. I try to insert this sincerity into my voice when I respond.

"I do not think you are an animal. I think you are a beautiful woman. I did not touch your hair because it is strange to me. I merely wanted to touch you. But this was wrong of me to do without your permission. *Ma'h qitah.*"

I repeat my earlier gesture of pressing our cheeks together.

Some of the tension leaves her body. I feel better knowing she is no longer displeased. I don't like that I upset her. I will have to find out why my touch offended her.

"You know you're still touching me without my permission, right?" Her tone is teasing. I pull away, realizing she is correct.

"I am sorry, again. It is a gesture of apology in my culture."

Her eyebrows pinch, and she tilts her head to the side as she often does. "In your culture, you apologize by touching each other?"

"You apologize by showing you are sorry and correcting the mistake. When you wrong another, you throw off their energy and displace their happiness. We touch to give that energy back. It is not enough just to say you are sorry, you must correct it. By feeling my remorse, you can calm your troubles and right your energy. Every *ma'h qitah* is personalized to the receiver. It shows sincerity and respect. I will only ever offer this precise gesture to you."

She stares at me for a moment, blinking slowly. "Wow, that's pretty intense for a simple apology."

"Wronging another is a serious matter where I come from. I see that I have hurt you, although I am not exactly sure how. Still, I would offer you a proper apology. I want you to know that I am aware that I have caused you discomfort. Unfortunately, my custom seems to clash with an apology for having touched a person without their consent."

I smile at the irony of the situation, and after a moment,

her dimples flash, and everything inside of me comes to life. Her smile is a calming stroke to my soul. She may not like being touched, but I would welcome her hands anywhere she wanted to put them on me.

"That's actually kind of cool." She nods her head as if she likes the idea. "Most people here just kind of say sorry because they think they have to, you know? People don't really mean it. Anyway, I'm sorry I got so mad about it. You actually did it the right way, so I wasn't super mad. It was a knee jerk reaction."

"There is a right or wrong way to touch another's hair?"

Does human anatomy include some kind of nerve in the hair follicle? Did I hurt her?

"Well, you know, sometimes, most times, when people touch my hair it's in a weird way. They touch it like my hair wouldn't feel like hair, like it would feel like fur or something. They pet me like a dog. It's offensive. But you," she peers at me closely, "did it right. Like you just wanted to touch me, like you said. I didn't feel like a strange thing."

"You are not a strange thing. You are perfect."

She laughs. It's the same laugh she does at the comedy movies. It's loud and full. She throws her head back, and I marvel at the arched line of her neck. It's a wonder to me that so much sound can come from such a small woman.

"I'm hardly perfect, but that's a nice thing to say."

"I'm glad. I want to make you feel nice."

Her face transforms in a split second. She's wary again, and I feel a slight frustration that I continue to make her uncomfortable.

"Yeah, you probably don't want to go around saying that to other women."

I wouldn't. I would only ever say that to her. While I wish happiness on every living being, I am only concerned with how happy she is.

I don't say this out loud, however. I want to understand her so that the next time I touch her hair, she welcomes it. Instead, I ask, "Why?"

"Well, it's kind of weird. It sounds weird. Like a little stalkerish, you know?"

I don't know. "What is stalker-ish?"

She chuckles a little and rolls her eyes in a way that makes me think she finds my ignorance appealing. I'm glad. I will ask all of the questions if it will help me get closer to her.

"A stalker—it's a noun—is a person who's obsessed with another person and follows them around and watches them. Sometimes they try to hurt them because they're psycho. Sometimes they think they're in love and want the other person to love them back, but mostly it just ends in them trying to hurt them because they're psycho. So stalkerish means when you say stuff like that, it sounds like you may be the kind of person who follows someone around because you might want to hurt them."

As she describes this kind of person, it's not lost on me that this is essentially what I have been doing for the past two months, following her around, watching her. The only difference is that I would never hurt her. Ever. And I don't *think* I am in love with her. She is everything to me. Even as I think it though, I imagine telling her this would indeed sound "stalker-ish."

"I only meant, I like it better when I am not offending you," I clarify. "Even if I do not know you well. However, if you would allow it, I would like to introduce myself."

"You're kind of weirdly respectful," she says, peering intently at me again.

"Are people here not respectful?"

I ask, but I know they are not. I have seen the way people behave toward one another. I have felt their constant animosity. I have seen the way the men treat the women.

She makes a sound like she's sucking in and blowing out air at the same time.

"Uh, no, not really. Most people are kind of fucked up."

"I would never be fucked up to you, and I do not intend that in a stalker-ish way," I add when she looks at me warily again.

She laughs and rolls her eyes before sticking her hand out between us.

"Amina."

Amina. Her name settles over me, beautiful and delicate. It suits her. I want to respond, but I can't. The moment she names herself, I feel something that I knew would happen eventually but could never actually imagine. My heart begins to beat.

It's exhilarating. My body is assailed with an intense flow of oxygen. Everything is clearer. My already sharp senses feel sharper. In the moment my heart begins to pound in my chest, hers pauses for the barest second. Her free hand goes to her breast just then, her brows draw down.

"You have a beautiful name, Amina."

I finally take her hand. It's small but strong. She grips my much larger one as best she can, giving it two firm pumps.

"I am Kwarq."

CHAPTER 3

AMINA

"Kwarq, that's different. I like it. Kwarq, like quirky?"

He frowns like he doesn't know what that word means.

"Quirky means interesting in a strange way. Maybe a bit weird, but good weird."

"Ah, I see. Perhaps my parents knew this when they named me. I am sure many who know me would consider me somewhat strange in a good way. So, yes, Kwarq like quirky."

In our few minutes together, the man formally known as Movie Bae has shown himself to be really quite sweet. A little weird, but still, I've let my fuck-off face lapse more with him in the past twenty minutes than I have in my entire life.

I roll the sound of his name around in my head. Kwarq. It's cute. The way he says it comes with all of these little breathy sounds. The short 'a' is surrounded by air. The q at the end is more of a click from somewhere in his throat. I do my best to repeat the sounds when I say it again.

"Nice to meet you, Kwarq."

His face lights up.

"Your pronunciation is beautiful, Amina. I can tell you have a way with language and a very good ear. Not many people would have guessed Amharic."

"I thought it wasn't Amharic."

"It is not, but the sounds are similar."

"Oh." I want to ask him more. "So tell me something."

He isn't as caught off guard by my request as I expect him to be. He continues to smile that easy smile.

"What would you like to know?"

I want to say, *Everything!*, but I settle for something less awkward.

"What did you think of the movie?"

"It was terrible."

He makes a sound in the back of his throat and shakes his head. I don't know that I was expecting glowing, Ebert-worthy commentary on how great the film was, but I wasn't expecting him to straight up shit on it either.

"Then why did you see it? You don't seem like the teenage love drama type."

"What type do I seem like?" He's doing that thing again where he looks closely at me like my response is the answer to the existence of the universe. I shrug my shoulders to shake off the tingling caused by his stare.

"I don't know. Maybe a shoot 'em up kind of guy. Or a war movie type. You seem like a blow shit up kind of movie guy, but then I think most men are blow shit up kind of movie guys."

I laugh but break mid chuckle when he makes a face. A kind of seriousness falls over him that is more intense than before.

"I do not understand or love war." His voice is low and rough. "I am not this shoot them up kind of guy. I am not like most men, and I would not have you think I am. I value love in all of its manifestations. I will always celebrate it. This war thing you humans are so fond of is...." He makes a face that shows clearly just how disgusting he finds the idea.

"Wow, I didn't mean to offend you. I just meant the movie seemed a little silly. Even you admitted it was a bit ridiculous."

"It was, but it is important that you understand this about me. That you know I am not this kind of man."

"I get it, trust me," I say with mock chastisement, and he

nods like he's satisfied with my acceptance. "You're a little odd, you know that?"

"Why?" Again, he's completely sincere in his desire to hear my answer, and I'm finding that this kind of rapt attention isn't completely unwelcome.

"I don't know. Most guys don't go on about loving love. That's actually something I would say."

"As I said, I am not most guys, but I am glad that we share this feeling about affection."

He flashes that grin, and my heart flutters. It's been doing that on and off for the past few minutes. For a moment before, I thought it had stopped for a second. It kind of scared me, but it passed almost as quickly as it happened. It was probably just gas. I ate a lot of popcorn at that movie.

The conversation lulls. He's looking ahead, but it feels like he's relaxed a bit. His arm rests slightly heavier against my side.

"You never answered my question. Why do you go to the movies if you don't like them."

His eyes shift over to me, and they are so bright yellow that it's distracting. I still can't believe how yellow his eyes are. The little bits of brown that creep at the corners of his irises are like waves crashing against a setting sun. It's beautiful and arresting.

"I do not go to the movies because I like them," he says and shifts his eyes back to the front.

"Oh, what are you like a reviewer or something?" Nobody goes to that many movies just because.

"Of sorts."

"Okay, what does that mean? Do you have a blog?"

"No. I go to the movies because I am waiting for something."

This dude is being real mysterious for no reason. He doesn't seem to be doing it on purpose, but come on. *I go to the movies because I am waiting on something*? I nudge my arm lightly into his.

"Are you a spy?"

He examines my face. I wink, exaggerating the gesture, and his mouth tweaks up at the corner.

"Spies waiting for things to be delivered to them in movie theaters, I think, is something that only happens in the movies."

"Oh wow, sarcasm. We're making progress."

The little tweak turns into a big smile. I mentally roll my eyes. The last thing I need is some hot stranger dude getting funny ideas. I like him so far, but I've known less attractive men to try to jump into my pants at even the slightest hint of what could be misconstrued as flirtation.

"I was only kidding. Don't get any ideas."

"I already have too many ideas. If you knew how many, I think you would be surprised."

"Well, don't get any ideas about me."

"Why not?"

Just that quickly, he's back to being serious.

"Because you don't know me, and I don't know you."

"Are you opposed to the idea that we could get to know one another? That I could know you, and you could know me?"

I hesitate, a little caught off guard by the question, and also a little unsure of my answer. Do I want to know him? I do. That was my whole reason for speaking to him in the theater in the first place. That draw I felt. I still feel it, even more so now. We seem to be very much in tune with each other. But you can never know from first impressions. He might really be a stalker serial killer. They say Ted Bundy was charming as hell.

His sunset eyes stare back at me, waiting. I want to lean into him. The pull is almost like a physical rope between us.

"I mean, I guess, you seem nice enough, but you never know. I could get to know you, and you try and take it the wrong way."

"How is there a wrong way to get to know someone?"

"You know, I just don't want you to think that just because I talk to you that means I'm trying to do anything with you."

"Do anything?"

Goodness, is this dude from another planet?

"Yes, do anything. Like fuck. Have sex. I'm not. I just think you're cool."

The recording of my stop sounds out and the bus jerks to a halt. Just like that, our ride comes to an end. Even with the last few moments of borderline creepsterness, I would have liked to talk more. I don't want to seem desperate, though.

"This is me," I say and stand, waiting for him to move his knees so I can pass into the isle. Instead, he stands, too, moving to the side so I can step down to the rear exit. I push the touch sensor and the doors swing open. I hop down onto the wet, leaf covered ground. The urge overcomes me to turn and step back on, ride for a few more blocks, see if maybe we can exchange numbers. I know I can't though. It's dangerous enough walking the half block to my house. I'm not stupid enough to increase my chances of getting kidnapped.

Still, walking away from the bus feels so wrong, and my spirits slump as I start off down the sidewalk. I haven't taken two steps when I hear the sound of someone step off the bus behind me. I don't have to turn to know who it is. My heart thumps.

I take it back. Please don't let this man follow me home.

KWARQ

She probably thinks I mean to follow her home.

"Do not worry, I am not being stalker-ish. I merely passed

my stop and must walk back."

She's preparing to rush away but turns back when I speak. I catch up to her, and she takes a few cautious steps away from me, keeping space between us. Her face is wary as she watches me step in stride behind her.

"Why didn't you get off?"

I shrug. She's more at ease when I don't appear too interested. "I enjoyed talking to you. I did not mind getting off later and walking back the few blocks."

"But how did you know I wasn't getting off at the end of the line?"

"I would not have minded even walking from the end of the line. I usually walk home from the movies, anyway."

Her mouth falls open. Her full lips look soft. The desire to kiss her is immense.

"You *walk* all that way? That's like sixty blocks!"

I can only assume this is not a normal distance to walk for a human, but then I have observed that humans are not nearly as active as many other species I have met. They are active for sport, it seems, but not as a daily way of life. Even on my planet where technology is thousands of years ahead of Earth's, we still enjoy using our physical bodies as much as possible.

"It is good exercise," I respond when she continues to look astonished.

"How long does it take you? I've seen you at midnight showings. It must take you hours to get home. I wouldn't get home until dawn if I had to walk all that way."

"It does not take me long," I answer vaguely. "Also, it gives me time to think."

"That's a lot of thinking. I guess I could walk that, if I had to, but I'd be too scared to do it this late at night. I'd probably get snatched."

The idea of someone trying to harm my *lehti* makes my

skin twitch. I can almost feel the instinct to protect crowd my brain and drive out any rational thought.

"You can walk when and wherever you like. There is no person on this planet that would do you harm, do you understand? You do not have to be worried about being snatched or any other form of harassment." My voice is rougher than I have ever heard it. My English is so heavily accented by my sudden emotion that I am surprised she can understand me.

She makes that in-out air noise again and rolls her eyes, turning her head back to the front. "You are clearly not from Chicago."

"I am not," I confirm, honestly.

"Obviously. If I walked home in the middle of the night from downtown, I would definitely get snatched. Hell, I'm surprised I haven't been snatched walking the half block from the bus stop to my house. Now that I think about it, you could be about to snatch me." She waves her hand dramatically in my direction. "That's how much I will totally get snatched if I walk around in the middle of the night like you do."

I know she's joking , but I don't like that she is so sure of her vulnerability. I don't like that she doesn't realize that I'm protecting her. I don't like that I can't tell her this because she will certainly see it as "stalker-ish."

"Amina." When she turns to me, I step close. Close enough for her to see my face clearly. To see that I'm serious. "Believe me when I say there is no place on this Earth where you are not safe. No place. Now go home."

We've reached the corner where she must turn to reach her apartment. I nod in that direction. She looks down the street and then away.

"I, uh, actually don't turn until the next block. You can go ahead. I'll be fine."

She's lying. She must still believe that I am a threat to her. I find this bothers me more than it normally would.

"I am not trying to follow you home, *lehti*. I just want to assure myself that you make it there safely. I will watch you until you reach your home, and then I will leave. I promise."

"How do you know where I live?" Her eyes narrow on me. A part of me wishes she wasn't so nervous all of the time, but I know it's probably a good way to be when one lives on Earth. I may be here to prevent her from being snatched, but I'm sure other women are not so fortunate.

"I do not mean you harm. I am not a stalker. I live in this area. I have seen you go that way before."

"Before when?"

"Before before." Frustration enters my voice. It is not with her, but the circumstances that dictate her wariness of me. I step a little closer. Our connection is like a living thing between us. I can hear our synchronized hearts—mine heavier and louder—thudding in perfect rhythm. I feel out to her, letting my protection settle around her. After a moment, the wariness fades from her eyes, and she turns back to look down the dark, deserted street that leads to her house.

"You'll wait and watch me until I get all the way to my house?"

She sounds relieved. Now that she's convinced I won't hurt her, she is eager for the security my presence offers. This pleases me. I want her to lean on me. She should know she can look to me for protection.

"I will wait until you are safe in your home."

"It's at the end of the block. You don't mind waiting that long?"

"I will wait as long as it takes for you to get there. I do not mind."

She looks down the dark street again. The cover from the trees lining the sidewalk blocks out most of the light from the street lamps above.

"Do you mind, maybe, walking me down there? You can say no if you want to," she rushes, but I am too happy at her request to care that she would think she could ever trouble me.

"I will walk you if it will make you feel safer."

She gives the street one more nervous look.

"It really would."

I nod, and we turn and set off toward her house. I walk a little ahead of her, so she can see that I make no threatening movements, and keep a few feet between us.

"So, how long have you lived in Chicago?"

I look back to find her walking slowly behind me. She grips the straps of her handbag, hugging it against her side. I turn away and focus on listening for any danger.

"Two months."

"Oh, that's not long at all. Where did you live before?"

"I had never been to this place before then."

"You've only been in America for two months?"

I nod. Of course I mean the planet, but it's not a lie. I have stayed in Chicago this entire time.

"Wow, not to sound ignorant, but your English is really good. Did you learn it before you got here?"

"I would never think you are ignorant. In our short time together, I have realized that you are a very clever, insightful, curious woman. But, no, I did not know your language before I arrived."

I hear the almost imperceptible sound of her stopping, and I turn. For the second time, she gapes at me in astonishment.

"You're telling me that this conversation we've been having is only two months of English speaking for you? Are you some kind of language genius?"

I smile and roll my eyes in imitation of her frequent gesture.

"I am of adequate intelligence, Amina. Where I come from, I am what you would call a linguist. I am used to learning other languages."

She looks impressed. "What we call a linguist? What do you guys call it?"

"In translation?"

She nods.

"*Meshqa'an.*"

"Oh, I love that!"

She laughs that full laugh that I love. I smile, too, knowing I have put her at ease and made her happy. We still stand in the middle of the sidewalk. I reach for her arm and realize immediately I have touched her again without her permission. But when I go to release her, she shifts, joining our palms.

"It's okay. You can hold my hand. Besides, if anyone sees us, they'll think we're a couple and be too afraid to mess with us. You're pretty scary looking."

I look down at her, surprised and somewhat injured.

"You think I am scary looking?"

She makes that face again that means what I am saying is strange.

"Uh, no, I think you're gorgeous, but I'm sure you know you're fine. And please," she holds up the flat of her hand when I start to speak, "don't act like one of those obviously gorgeous people who pretends like they don't know they're gorgeous. It's annoying to all us average folks. But I just meant that you look like you can bench press a grown ass man. That's usually pretty scary."

I smile because her assessment of my ability to defend us is correct. Just as her self-assessment of her beauty as average is completely ridiculous.

"I will not be like those people if it annoys you. I am aware that I am an attractive male. Even on my planet, many females have tried to, how do you say, 'date' me. I am pleased that you find me attractive. I think you are the most beautiful woman I have ever seen. You are not average. You are perfect."

She narrows her eyes and her cheekbones rise in an odd smile.

"Ah, see you almost had me and then you had to go all stalkerish again," she says as she shakes my hand off. I can better tell when my *lehti* is not serious, so I chuckle and hold my hand out for her to take again.

"I will not stalk you unless you ask me to, Amina."

CHAPTER 4

AMINA

I wish it took longer to reach my apartment. I low key tried to walk slow, but Kwarq's legs are so long that I end up nearly jogging to keep up.

It's crazy, but walking hand in hand with him is the most natural thing I've ever felt. His large hand covers mine like a warm glove against the cool, fall air. The grip is strong but not too tight. An all-consuming sense of security fills me, and I'm stunned by the sheer freedom of the feeling. It makes it hard to let go when we reach my house. Our arms stretch between us as I shuffle my feet at the gate.

"Thank you for walking me. That was very sweet."

He nods.

"Of course. I would have you feel safe walking home."

I don't think I've ever known someone to so sincerely desire for me to be okay. I wait for him to let me go and leave, but he doesn't. If anything, his grip tightens a little. The pad of his thumb brushes back and forth across the back of my hand.

"When I see you again, may I speak to you?"

He's so serious, and it's such a strange thing to ask that I laugh. This Kwarq *is* kind of quirky.

"You can definitely speak to me if you see me again."

"When I see you again," he corrects, and I pull a face, but before I can tease him, he adds, "In a not stalker-ish way, of course."

He drops my hand. It's a reluctant release. I mean, if he wanted to hold my hand for another hour right in front of my house, I'd let him.

"Well, I guess I'll go in now. Thank you again."

"You do not have to thank me for keeping you safe, Amina. Now go. You are tired."

I am tired. It hits me as soon as he says it, and I'm stifling a wide yawn while I fish into my purse for my keys.

I find them and unlock the gate. When I close it between us, I instantly hate the barrier. I back away, never letting go of his gaze, until I reach my door. I step into the hallway, but peek back out to see that he's still there, watching. I wave. He raises his hand back then makes a shooing motion for me to go inside.

I dash up the steps, letting myself into my apartment as fast as I can. I fling my purse to the floor and go straight to the window where I pull back the curtain, hoping he's still outside.

The yellow of his eyes sparkle up at me. He's staring right at my window, almost as if he was waiting for me to appear. I smile and wave again, and he does the same. He repeats his shooing motion and brings his hands together to cradle them beneath his head in the universal pantomime for sleep. I nod and wave again before turning.

The curtain falls and I step away, but I'm antsy and excited. I want to see him one more time, so I step back, pulling the curtain to the side in hopes of catching him before he leaves.

He's paused with his back to me. It looks like he's waiting for something. A sliver of light casts shadows across his back. Even from my second floor window, I can see the well-formed muscles beneath his t-shirt. I try to commit each bulge and ripple to memory as I wait for him to leave.

He moves, and it's like time stands still for the briefest moment before he's a blur, and I'm only left with the impression of him where he was standing. I scream, then smother it with a hand over my mouth.

* * *

"Holy, shit."

If I thought my heart was racing before, right now it's going for gold. I scramble back into my apartment, suddenly feeling too vulnerable at the window. No person can move that fast. No human, anyway. I try to figure out what I just saw, but my mind has crossed a threshold of reality and it can't turn back.

He disappeared, and I don't mean he walked quickly away from my house. He disappeared, and I don't know what that means. I pace around my apartment trying to make sense of it.

Hours later, I've only managed to work myself into a nervous, excited mess. So many crazy ideas run through my head, each one more insane than the other. Vampire? Alien? I can't allow myself to believe the first one, no matter how much I love a good supernatural movie. The second one, however, starts to take root as I lay in bed, too nervous to sleep.

The idea sinks in as I cocoon myself into a pile of blankets. The radiator in my apartment is on full blast. I'm hot, but I need the security. Each layer of blanket feels like a shield against the boogieman who I foolishly let walk me home. How did I not realize that something was off? In the cloud of my mind, wandering little things start to come back to me. Things he said during our bus ride that were odd, but passed through my subconscious because their implications were too crazy to consider.

This war thing you humans are so fond of...

I am aware that I am an attractive man. Even on my planet, many females have tried to, how do you say, "date" me.

His face flashes through my mind. All tan, sun-kissed skin and strange features. That silky beard. Yellow eyes piercing so closely into mine. Against my better judgment, a little tingle runs through me when I think of how he touched me. When my brain conjures up a memory of his smell, earthy and dewy, my pussy gets a little wet. An excited shiver runs through me. I squeeze my legs together beneath the blankets.

I should be scared. I won't lie, I'm shook, but the universe suddenly seems so awesome and vast. I'm struck by a realization that makes everything I've ever known seem small and basic. I bolt up in bed, sweating from my fortress of blankets and the thrilling terror of this new understanding. An understanding becoming sharp and all too real as each second passes. A hysterical chuckle erupts from my mouth. I can't believe it.

"That man is a damn alien."

KWARQ

I step away from the shadows of a tree outside of Amina's apartment where I've been waiting for the past three hours for her to fall asleep. I know she saw me, or saw as much of me as she could when I turned to run from her house. At the speed I was moving, I would have appeared as nothing more than a blur.

It was careless to move at that speed in the open. I usually keep a pace comfortable for average humans. I took a chance since it is so late, but unfortunately my *lehti* does not listen very well to instruction. I should have known she wouldn't be able to resist one last look. I could hear her heart and it beat with the same anticipation as mine. I no more wanted to leave than she wanted me to.

That's what drove me to risk running home. I couldn't wait to reach the cover of my room where I could finally relieve the ache in my cock. For the hour I was with my *lehti*, all I could think of was tearing off my pants and finally letting myself get as hard as I've wanted to be all evening. From the moment she sat next to me in the theater, I've been waging a mental war to keep my body from showing just how much I want her.

It was careless. I heard the rustle of curtains and her sharp cry of alarm the moment I took off. I doubled back and stood just beneath her window. The sounds of her shock and disbelief rang through my ears just as the heavy thud of her heart echoed in my chest.

She paced her apartment for a long while, mumbling to herself about vampires and other ridiculous creatures. She laughed quite a bit, almost madly, and I worried for a moment that this small revelation of my true self was too much. I worried that I had broken her. The only reassurance I had was the slight edge of excitement beneath her alarm. For a faint moment, I even thought I smelled her arousal, but shortly after, she fell into a deep, exhausted sleep.

I give her window one last look then turn and jog at a quick human pace to my apartment. I'm barely through the door before I yank open the stiff sides of the blue jeans humans love to wear and jerk out my cock. This style of fabric may be popular on earth, but my large, Lyqa frame means I spend much of my time feeling unbearably constricted. It's worse when Amina is near.

My cock springs heavily out in front of me, throbbing and painfully hard. I don't waste any time. I take it in hand and give it three, quick pumps, groaning loudly at the relief. My memory recalls that brief scent of Amina's pussy. I know she was wet. It was the same smell as her arousal on the bus. The sweet, tangy scent rests on my tongue and I pump harder, bracing myself on the back of the door. The image of her full, soft lips fills my mind. How she drags the plump bottom lip through her teeth when she's contemplating something. How she pouts them when she's doubtful. I imagine her on her knees, taking me deep into her mouth, those lips like little cushions around my cock.

I keep jerking as these images flood my mind. I can't even consider what it would be like to be inside of her, that's almost too much to bear. It's enough to think of her mouth on me, drawing me deeply, warm and soft.

My balls draw up tight, and a thick jet of milky white cum shoots onto the door in front of me. My muscles spasm as my release continues for several long moments. My groans are loud and ragged, almost feral. Something inside of me feels like it's coming apart, and just as the last stream of semen erupts from my cock, a violent shiver rushes through me, bringing me to my knees.

I hunch over my legs, breathing heavily as I wait for the intensity of my release to pass. I finally stand. The floor and entire lower half of the door is covered with my semen. It's alarming. I've taken myself in hand many times since I've been on this planet. Sometimes it is the only way I can bear to be in the same room with Amina and not turn into one of the savage human men. I would never do that to her. I would never force my attention. However, I've never come this hard. Something is different. It seems the *leht* has already started preparing me for joining with her.

I get my only towel from the bathroom and wipe up the mess. How I will address what Amina witnessed when I see her again? Perhaps I should pretend she was mistaken. It's late and dark. Who is to say that what she saw was real? I shake my head, dismissing this idea almost immediately. Lying to her, or making her feel she's insane does not sit well with me. If she's going to be mine, and she is if she will have me, she will have to know what I am eventually.

Perhaps this mistake is a good thing. She was shocked, but

my *lehti* is a smart, sensible woman. She nearly reasoned herself into acceptance of the possibility I am not of this world by the time she went to sleep. I smile when I recall her words before she finally succumbed to exhaustion.

That man is an alien.

She's so interested in everything. The more I'm around her, the more pleased I am that my *leht* is to her. There's no need to lie. When I see her next, if she asks me what I am, I won't pretend to misunderstand what she means. I'll answer her truthfully. I'll tell her about the *ta'ani maul* and my brother's gift. I'll tell her how she stole my senses when she passed me on the bus, and how my first heart now only beats for her. I will tell her all of these things, and hope that she accepts me, because I will stay on this planet forever if it means that one day she will.

CHAPTER 5

AMINA

Shit. Shit. Shit. Shit. Shit.

Kwarq's on the bench in front of my job as I turn the corner from the subway. The moment my eyes land on him, my heart pauses then starts to beat a quick, battering rhythm in my chest.

He's wearing the same dark blue jeans as before. He has on a t-shirt, even though anyone with a lick of sense is wearing at least a jacket. I mentally shake my head. That should have been the first give away. Who the hell walks around in a damn t-shirt in the middle of October in Chicago?

I ignore the fact that his shirt shows all types of ripples and bulges beneath the thin fabric. His large, muscular arms flex against the back of the bench. I force my eyes away. I will not lust after the fucking alien man. I will not.

"Jesus Christ, Amina. Get it together," I tell myself and walk confidently toward my job.

When I near the entrance of the building, he rises from the bench and starts toward me. I pick up the pace, dipping into a group of people going inside. I duck my small frame into the middle of the crush and out of sight. Once I'm well inside the building, I glance back.

He stands just on the other side of the glass doors. Even from where I stand, I can see his frown, but there's no mistaking that his eyes are fixed on me. I wait to see if he's going to follow me in, but he doesn't. He just stands there with his hands at his waist. His large, booted foot taps against the sidewalk. Maybe he is a vampire, and he can't get in without my permission. Some of my tension eases because if that's the case, he's gonna be waiting out there forever.

I'm already late for work, so I force myself to turn away from the sight of his tall, hunky frame. I hop through the elevator doors just as they're about to shut, and half expect to see Kwarq speed inside next to me. When the doors shut without any surprises, I breathe a sigh of relief. This alien is not going to get me today.

The usual bustle of a busy day crowds out my anxiety. I go to my office and unwrap myself from my layers of outerwear then turn on my computer before settling behind my desk. As soon as the operating system loads, an alert pops up on my screen. I have almost three dozen marketing requests waiting in my inbox. As much as I would like to obsess over the alien who followed me to work, I can't. Unless he's going to abduct me tomorrow, I need to focus on my job. I set about distributing the requests to the appropriate assistants and push Kwarq out of my mind.

"Are you okay? You keep rubbing your chest."

"Hm?"

I pause my hand where it's pushing firm circles into my sternum. There's nothing wrong with my chest. That is, it doesn't hurt, but my heart is beating really fucking loud. At first, I thought it was someone thumping on the wall, and then I was sure it was a bucket boy outside, but the sound has been too steady and too persistent. It took me a moment to realize it was a heartbeat, and since I am the only person in my office, it has to be mine. The funny thing about it, though, is that it almost sounds like it's coming from *outside* my body.

"You got heartburn? I have some antacids."

One of the marketing assistants, Kelly, stands in my doorway holding a stack of proofs. She reaches into the pocket of her blazer and holds out a roll of the chalky tablets. I shake my head.

"No, it's not heartburn. I just feel weird. I think my heart is beating too hard or fast or something. You can't hear it?"

Kelly's mouth turns down. "No, I don't hear anything. Maybe you're just anxious."

I nod and reach for the proofs. She hands them over and leaves, but I see her shaking her head as she goes back to her desk.

Maybe I'm just anxious. Of course, I'm anxious. I've been trying to focus on work, but all I can think about is the fact that there's probably a stalker alien waiting for me outside.

Lunch time rolls around, and the fact that I didn't have time to eat breakfast catches up to me. I jump from my desk and head down to the lobby deli where I usually get my lunch. I'm standing in line trying to decide between a tuna melt and a grilled cheese when I remember Kwarq.

First, my heart starts to thud, and it's louder and heavier than it's been all day. It still has that out of body quality. I thump my fist against my sternum and glance around to see if anyone else is trying to figure out if there's a damn bass drum in my chest.

"You do not have to be afraid of me, Amina."

I jump and spin around, knocking into the woman in front of me. She sucks her teeth, but merely steps ahead, putting some space between us.

"Please, *lehti*, you will harm yourself if you do not calm down."

You're an alien! my brain screams, but my mouth can't work to say it. The thudding gets faster, and I dip out of line and to the side as Kwarq looms in front of me, matching my movements.

"Dude, get away from me."

I'm surprised at how scared I sound. In fact, the terror ripping through me is almost disabling. My heart feels like it's about to burst from my chest, and this only happens when Kwarq is near me. I try to move away, but my feet struggle to carry me to the door like I want them to.

Kwarq stops moving and raises his hands in front of him.

"*Lehti*, please. I promise I will not harm you. I am here for you. You do not have to fear me. I would like to explain what you saw last night. I will not lie to you."

I'm shaking my head before he finishes. The urge to run away, to just get away, makes me take another step toward the exit. He takes an answering step, and I throw my hands up. My tiny palms make a pathetic shield against the width of his broad chest.

"I'm serious, get the hell away from me."

Kwarq's face shifts, and if I didn't know better, I'd think he was sad. I don't care. This sad alien isn't going to get me today.

"If that is what you wish, I will leave you alone."

I nod. "Yup, that's what I wish."

He sighs and takes a step back. I resist the insane urge to close the distance back up. I don't want to be close to him. I'm supposed to be trying to get away.

"Then I will bother you no longer, my *lehti*."

He turns and stalks away. The other patrons of the deli part with startled movements as he moves to the door that exits onto the street and disappears around the corner.

I exhale and it's loud and shaky. A few people stare at me. Some with concern. Others with annoyance. I look out to the street again just to make sure he isn't still lurking around. When a few minutes pass, I get back in line. By the time my turn to order comes, I've lost whatever little appetite I had. I walk away and go back to my office.

I don't see Kwarq again after that. He isn't waiting for me

when I leave work. When I go to the movies later in the evening to clear my mind, he isn't sitting across from me as usual. As I look at the seat he usually occupies, I feel a little shitty. Almost like I miss him a bit, which is stupid because he's an alien.

KWARQ

The last time I saw Amina at the deli, she nearly fainted in her fear of me. That was difficult, knowing that I inspired that much fear in her.

Later, I reminded myself that she is human, after all, and if I have learned anything about humans, it is that they are ridiculously paranoid when it comes to others. At times, rightfully so, but most times, it is merely enough to be different than what they are expecting to inspire fear. I know it is this paranoia that fuels my *lehti*'s aversion to me. Before she knew what I was, she was open, even eager to know me. Now I have been forced, once again, to retreat to the shadows and watch her from a distance.

I watch her from the back of the theater. She turns her head to my usual seat again and again. When I feel out to her, it isn't fear or anxiety I scent. It's longing. Maybe there's a chance to gain her trust once she has had an opportunity to reason with herself. Even if it is a small chance, I will be patient and wait to approach her again. I hope that when I do, she will be open to listening to me, and her fear will not keep us apart.

"What the hell do you keep sighing about, Mina?"

We're on the subway train. Amina is in the car behind me with a woman who shares enough of her phenotypical features that she can only be her sister. The woman's light brown skin shimmers under the yellow train lights. She's taller and thinner than Amina, who is several inches shorter and more roundly built. Amina's sister is also beautiful, but not nearly as arresting as my *lehti*.

Their backs are to me, but I have no trouble hearing them.

"Nothing. Just something happened, and it's messing with me."

Amina sounds weary. She tilts her head to rest on her sister's shoulder.

"Aw, what is it, sis. You get rejected by Movie Bae?"

Amina lifts her head to glare at her sister.

"What, no! And he's not my bae."

"Mm, hm. That's not what you said before. I thought he was fine and all that? Did you talk to him?"

"I sure did, and if I told you what happened, you wouldn't even believe me."

"Yeah, okay. You're talking to the woman whose baby's father got deployed overseas for the last year of his military contract, decided me and his kid weren't worth the trouble, and never came back once he got out. This dude is chilling in Japan right now, speaking full ass sentences of Japanese on social media and hasn't said 'boo' to us three years. Try me."

Amina puts her head back down, and releases a deep sigh.

"It's not that serious. He seemed cool at first. He's just not my type."

Her sister's shoulders shrug. "If you say so."

They're silent after this. I keep my ears on them but turn my face to the front to watch the passing tunnel. My *lehti's* words were a lie. Even as she spoke them, her heart sped up in excitement. She may not like it, but she feels the *leht* just as I do. I told her I would leave her alone, and I have, but that doesn't mean I won't still try to reach her. I have to. There is no part of me that can turn away.

CHAPTER 6

I feel him before I see him. My heart does that funky little skip again, which I've come to associate with his presence, and then ratchets up to a nearly scary level. Over the past few days, I've looked for him in the faces around me. I expected to see his tall, golden face watching me over the crowds. A part of me wants to see him. A part of me misses him. But now that he's near, I tell myself not to panic. I'm safe. There are probably fifty people in this train car, and unless this dude is about to expose the existence of aliens to all of Chicago rush hour, then I shouldn't have anything to worry about.

But still, I *feel* him. It's not just my heart. It's like my entire body is in tune to his. He's not in my head, but it's like he's in my cells, or something. I inhale sharply at the thought. What if he's been sneaking into my apartment when I'm asleep and doing things to me? Creepy, TV abduction things. It's clear now he's been following me. All that stuff about seeing me in the neighborhood was crap. What if he's been visiting me when I don't know it. What if he's trying to stick me into some alien version of the Sunken Place?

Hysteria sets in, and my chest collapses with the short, quick breaths of a panic attack. I press my hand between my breasts and try to take a deep breath, but it's the Red Line right after work. Every side of me has a person pressed against it. It's like the air is being sucked out of me. I turn around, anything to find some space, but I end up stepping on the toes of the man behind me. He scowls and shoves me back.

"Watch where the fuck you're stepping!"

His voice is sharp and hostile, but I'm too busy looking for an exit. I can still feel Kwarq somewhere on the train. That echoing thud outside of me is louder or closer, I can't tell which. I look down at my chest to make sure my heart is still where it should be.

"What are you doing? Wait until the damn stop. There's no place to go!"

Train guy stands as a barrier between me and escape. I lower my head and duck beneath his arm where he's holding onto the rail, but he shifts, blocking me in. Everything goes blurry. I want to tear at my skin, to get out whatever Kwarq may have put inside of me.

"Please, I need to get off. I'm going to be sick," I mumble out, still trying to get around him. I tilt back, and the person sitting behind me braces me with their hands then tries to right me, but the train jerks and I end up pitching forward into train guy again.

"What the fuck!"

I flinch. I can't seem to get my brain to work right. Everything is going very quickly and I can't catch up. I focus on standing still and inhale until my lungs start to burn. With each breath, the car comes back into focus, my chest loosens, and my brain starts to work again.

The first thing I see is train guy glaring at me. He raises his hand to point his finger into my face.

"You need to learn to say excuse me. That's how people get hurt."

I blink. My head is still a little muddled, but not that muddled.

"First of all, get your fucking finger out my face. Second, I wasn't feeling good. It was obviously an accident. You don't have to be an asshole about it. Why would I just step on your foot for no reason?"

"I don't give a shit if you were about to die. Learn some fucking manners."

"Wow."

I'm not surprised. I've had worse said to me. I wish I could show him my manners, but I'm not stupid. I glance around the train car, and a rapid succession of heads shift away when they see me looking. I'm on my own if this goes too far. I sigh and turn my back to the man.

"Yeah, you better shut the fuck—ahhh!"

I whip around, my fist up to defend myself, and I'm met by train guy's bulging blue eyes. His face isn't a mottled angry red anymore, but an unnatural shade of purple. His mouth hangs open. His tongue, filmed over with thick, white saliva, jerks against his teeth. Around his neck is a large, golden hand. The veins stand out beneath the skin. My eyes travel up, past the straining forearm, the bulging bicep, until they come to rest on Kwarq's face.

His skin is vibrating. It's like the cartoons when music plays too loud and frequency lines appear on all the surfaces. Like he's about to jump out of his body.

His eyes are little, hard jewels in their sockets, and these little jewels are fixed on train guy.

He barely moves, aside from that rippling beneath his skin. Train guy struggles. His fingers slip and scratch against Kwarq's golden skin, and Kwarq doesn't flinch. It doesn't take long before train guy goes limp. His protruding blue eyes roll back in his head. His hands fall away from where they are trying in vain to free his neck and hang limply at his side.

I'm stunned. I want to tell Kwarq that he's going to kill this man on the Red Line in Chicago in the middle of rush hour. Already, people scramble to angle their cellphones at the scene. I imagine the headlines, "Crazy, might be black alien attacks man on train."

I shake out of my trance and grab Kwarq's arm with both hands. I yank around his elbow, trying to collapse the rigidity of his hold. Kwarq doesn't so much as glance my way. He's a statue. I pull again, letting my legs collapse so I'm hanging off his arm like it's a jungle gym. Still nothing.

"Kwarq let him go. You're going to kill him."

KWARQ

I'm going to kill this man. I've never killed anything in my life. I don't even eat flesh. Even the small mosquitoes that plague this planet and make me want to scratch my skin off leave my presence unharmed and filled with my blood.

But this man. I felt his anger when my *lehti* fell into him. Something was wrong. She was having some kind of attack. I could see the wild look in her eyes from the connecting train car. It scared me. Our hearts began beating in rhythm the moment I stepped onto the train, and hers was beating much too fast.

Despite my agreement to stay away from her, I tried to reach her before she hurt herself, but the crowd was too dense. Had I moved any more forcefully, I would have risked harming someone.

And then this man yelled at her. Amina yelled back, and I felt a moment of relief that she was well enough to respond. When she turned, the man bent over her, his posture threatening. After this, I don't know what happened. All I know is the *leht* surges forth, and the desire to do whatever I must to protect her takes over.

And now I'm going to kill this man. His hands fall away from my arm, and I know this is the point when I must stop or he will perish. I consider it. The way some people treat others on Earth is appalling. It's something that shouldn't be allowed. It almost feels irresponsible for me to let him go. I imagine I would be doing this world a favor.

"Kwarq, please. You're going to kill him. We have to go."

Amina's urgent voice penetrates my focus. I turn my head and see her wide, nervous eyes shining up at me. I jerk back to the front of my mind and relax my hand, dropping the man to the train car floor. He groans and coughs, dragging in ragged breaths of air. A few people step forward to help him, but many step out of the way when he reaches out for assistance.

I stare at him and wonder what would have happened to Amina had I not been here. Would he have hurt her? The urge to leap back on him is fierce, but I'm being pulled away. The doors to the train slide shut in front of my face, and I watch his struggling figure through the dirty glass. The train pulls off, and he meets my eyes. His are frightened and wide. Mine hold every bit of warning I can muster that he never threaten a woman that way again.

I'm outside. I don't remember taking the stairs, but someone leads me away. I look at my hand and see a smaller brown one tucked within it. Amina.

Her skin is warm, despite the cool air. She moves quickly, weaving in and out of the people on the street until we come to a small shop. She pulls me inside and guides me over to a table in the corner.

"Sit down here."

I follow her instruction, but when she turns to leave, I rise again.

"I'll be right back. I'm just going to get us something to drink." She points at the service counter. I eye her warily. I can almost imagine her dashing out of the shop as soon as

I'm in my chair, screaming down the street about aliens. Almost. Deep down, I know my *lehti* would never do this. If she wanted to be away from me, she would simply tell me go away. Alien or not. Still, the thought brings a fresh wave of panic to my already shifty form.

"You will return? You promise?'

She stares as if trying to decide whether she will run out screaming after all. Finally, she nods.

"I promise. I'll be right back. You can see me from here."

She doesn't wait for me to accept her promise. She turns and walks away, and I force myself to do as she says and stay in my seat. However, it's only a few moments later that she's back holding two cups. She sets one down in front of me. The clear surface of the water trembles from her shaking hand. Steam rises from the other cup. Amina holds it between her hands like a weapon.

"I didn't know if you wanted coffee, or could have it. I'm not sure if, how your—uh, body—deals with caffeine." She looks down at my arms. "You seem to be a bit on edge already."

I follow her eyes down to my arms. My skin quivers. It's not subtle. When I focus, I feel it. Like I could turn into a puddle or burst into pure matter at any moment. When I meet Amina's eyes again, they're wide and nervous. Her hands grip the cup so hard, the cardboard begins to collapse.

"My *lehti*, I will not hurt you."

I put my hand over hers. She flinches, but I persist, covering her wrist. I have again touched her without her permission, but I can't stop myself. My nature takes over. I need her to feel my intentions. I would only ever keep her safe. I would never hurt her.

The moment we touch, my skin settles. The vibrations ease to a pleasant hum in my muscles. We both start at the sudden change. I jerk my hand away and immediately begin to shake again. The woman sitting next to us looks up from her book, and Amina slaps her hand over mine, stopping the shake before the woman can notice.

"Why does it stop?" She leans forward to whisper. Her hand rests lightly over my skin. I'm no longer shaking, but her fingers tremble where she touches me.

"You calm me. My anger made me unstable. My kind is not used to such emotions. I am sorry if it frightens you. It is just my need to protect you. It is the *leht*."

She frowns. "The what?"

I shake my head. I can't explain it here. There are too many people. There is too much to say.

"I can only tell you in private. I promise I will not hurt you. Can we go somewhere private?"

She shakes her head and pulls her hand from mine. We both wait for the vibration to return, but it doesn't. Whatever overcame me has passed.

"No. If you gotta tell me something, you tell me here. I don't feel comfortable being away from people."

Her eyes shift away, and I know she means she doesn't feel comfortable being away from humans. I don't like that she automatically assumes that because I am different, I am a threat. It is a very human way to think, but then, I have to remind myself again that she is human, my *lehti*, and she carries a lifetime of culture from which to draw.

"It is not like the movies, all lasers and abductions. I am not here to hurt you. You have to feel that I would not hurt you."

She leans forward, her expression suddenly panicked and furious.

"I do feel it!" Her voice is a harsh whisper when she speaks. "You did something to me!"

I frown to match her expression. Her smell has turned acrid again.

"I did nothing to you, my *lehti*."

"What is it? Some kind of experiment. Did you," she swallows, "implant something in me?"

I laugh. She's so serious. I may have underestimated how much she likes the movies she goes to see.

"*Lehti*, your movies are really foolish. I did not come here for some kind of invasion or abduction. I am alone. I was with my brother, but he went back to our home. I promise, I have done nothing to you."

She eyes me warily but settles back into her chair. I liked it better when she was leaning forward. Her light jacked is unbuttoned. The deep V of her shirt shows the swell of her breasts. Against my better self, my eyes linger there as she speaks.

"Then what's going on with my body?"

My eyes dart to her face. "Your body? Are you sick?" My panic increases. The vibration resumes. My skin flinches with the little spasms.

"No, my heart has been acting funny. Skipping, stopping. Or like now, it's beating like a billion miles a minute. It didn't do that before I met you. And quit it!" she nods down to my trembling arms.

"I cannot stop it."

I turn my palm up on the table. She stares at it for a minute before sighing deeply and slapping her hand down on mine. It stops the tremble immediately.

"There is nothing wrong with your heart, Amina. It is the *leht*, which I will explain to you in private, but do not worry that you are ill. You are fine. You are synchronized to my first heart, so when I am near, our hearts must adjust to keep the same beat."

I can see she struggles to understand my meaning. Humans deal a lot in metaphor. The heart is often used as a symbol for love and courage. In my species' case, matters of the heart are quite literal. Our hearts do in fact "skip a beat" when we are in the presence of the one's we love.

"Is that supposed to be romantic or something?"

She isn't smiling, but she also isn't afraid anymore. I smile because this is better.

"I *am*, in fact, a romantic, so if it can be, then yes."

"I thought you were a linguist."

"I am a romantic linguist."

Her mouth twitches. Her beautiful lips pout as she resists the desire to laugh. She looks like she's about to give in, but instead she brings her hands up to cover her face.

"I can't believe I'm sitting here flirting with an alien."

Her head snaps up and swings quickly from side to side.

"I can't believe I said that out loud."

"I am not worried. I would hear if anyone was alarmed."

She looks at me skeptically again. "What do you mean, you'd hear it? You have like super hearing or something?"

"I do."

It's best to answer her plainly. We can discuss details later.

"And you can move really fast?"

"I can."

"And you're super tall."

I smile. Now that we are calm again, I'm reminded of how incredibly adorable my *lehti* is. So charming and clever.

"I am only tall here because you are all so short."

She makes that disbelieving sound with her mouth.

"We have Shaq."

I chuckle. "You do, my *lehti*. You have Shaq."

"He's taller than you."

I shrug my shoulders. "And better at basketball, but that is only because it is not a sport that is heard of where I come from."

"If you've only been here for two months, how do you know about Shaq and sports?"

Curious Amina is back, and I want to tell her everything. I will answer all of her questions, but even I am not foolish enough to think our conversation will go unnoticed for too long. I stand and open my hand to her. She crosses her arms over her chest and stares at my open palm, the indecision clear on her face. Her mouth twists up as she considers it.

"I can answer all of your questions, just not here. If you come back to my apartment, I will tell you everything you want to know."

She leans forward and whispers, her voice so low no one else could possibly hear it. She's so clever.

"Is apartment code for spaceship. Did you just invite me back to your spaceship?" She lifts her hands next to her head and waves the first two fingers of each up and down every time she says "spaceship."

I laugh again. This is good. Even her disbelief is better than her fear.

"No, apartment is code for my apartment. I live on 51st and Cornell. Come."

Another pause. I wait patiently because I can smell her excitement. She's interested. Finally, she stands with an exaggerated sigh and flops her hand into mine.

"I swear to god, Kwarq, if you try to abduct me, I will fight you."

CHAPTER 7

AMINA

Don't ask me why I'm walking around Hyde Park holding hands with a damn alien. Just don't. Don't ask me why this alien lives on 51st and Cornell in a studio apartment. Don't ask me why I'm about to go this alien's apartment to talk about him being an alien, and don't ask me why I'm just the teensiest bit turned on by him. I don't know.

Maybe it's because the whole time we walk, he rubs little circles on the back of my hand. Maybe it's because the moment I slapped my hand into his, this little tingle ran up my arm and has slowly been spreading through my body, so that each step is torture between my legs. I don't understand it. Maybe it's this *leht* thing he keeps bringing up. Even though I don't know what the hell it is.

The truth is, I'm kind of curious. Out of all the people who could have come across a tall, fine, yellow-eyed alien, I did. The blerd in me is silently going crazy. I'm walking around Hyde Park holding hands with an alien. And he's fine and sexy as hell. I may be in shock, but I'm not oblivious. There's something going on between us. It's weird if I think about it, but he hasn't been shy about his interest in me. The dude almost choked a man to death for yelling at me. That part was kind of scary, but really, train guy was an asshole, and it felt nice to be defended for a change.

The little bit of excitement cuts the lingering fear my rational mind is holding on to. What if he can do really cool shit like teleport or has one of those food rehydrators like in *Back to the Future*. I just want to rehydrate a pizza. That's all I want. And obviously the cure for cancer, obviously. Altruism and all that. But first, I want to rehydrate a pizza. I feel a squeeze against my hand. Kwarq's smirking down at me.

"Be patient, my *lehti*. I will tell you everything you want to know."

I have a stupid grin on my face.

"I can't believe you're a fucking alien."

He snorts. "I am only an alien here because humans don't know any other words for those who are different."

"Yeah, that's kind of true." We aren't the most welcoming bunch. "So are you going to tell me all kinds of cool, alien shit?"

He chuckles and gives my hand another squeeze.

"I will tell you whatever you want to know, my *lehti*."

"Do you have a spaceship?"

"Of sorts."

"Can you teleport?"

"Of sorts."

"Can you rehydrate a pizza?"

Kwarq laughs and releases my hand to pull me against his side. He leans down and nuzzles his face into my hair. It's an unusually familiar gesture, maybe too familiar, but it's nice, so I don't remind him of the whole personal space thing.

"Oh, my *lehti*, you will be so disappointed. It is nothing like the movies."

It really isn't. I'm more than surprised when we enter his apartment through the front door like the rest of humanity and stand awkwardly in the elevator to his floor. His apartment is at the end of the hallway, and while he fishes around in his snug, slightly too short jeans looking for his key, I shuffle from foot to foot. The awe is starting to wear off. What the hell am I doing here?

Kwarq finally pulls out his key and fits it into the lock like he's done it a million times before.

The inside of his apartment is sparse. And by sparse, I mean empty. The space is small, just a single room big enough to fit a bed and a few pieces of furniture, but none of those things are here. There's a cheap sheet spread on the floor near the only window. Next to it is a small pile of clothes. Beside that is a neatly folded towel.

Kwarq steps into the room, and I follow, a little less enthusiastically. I'm looking for the pizza rehydrator or a telecommunicator or damn space suit. A little laugh erupts from me as I realize how silly I am. This man isn't an alien. He's just some dude. With my luck, he's probably a hotep or some shit.

"I, uh, I'm going to go home now."

I move to leave but Kwarq turns back and there is such genuine confusion on his face that I pause. I really don't know what's going on here, but this does not look like the home of a visiting alien. Kwarq follows my eyes around his apartment. He smiles and takes my hands.

"You are disappointed by my home?"

"Uh, no. No." I stumble. "I just, uh, realized that I have something to do..." my lie trails off, and I don't meet his eyes.

Kwarq laughs. It's an amused sound. Almost like he's laughing *at* me. I pull my hands back as he kind of doubles over, holding his stomach. I'm more than skeptical now, but that skepticism quickly turns to embarrassment. He played me. I can't believe I thought he was an alien. I'm too old for this shit. I feel so stupid. I turn to leave, but before I can even move, Kwarq shifts, and becomes a golden blur in front of my eyes.

"I would not lie to you my *lehti*. I am what you think I am."

A little scream erupts from me as I spin around to face the door. Kwarq is there when he was just standing in front of me a moment ago. He's still smiling. I take a step back.

"Oh my god. I can't believe it."

"Why, because I do not have a laser gun or a floating bed?"

"Dude, you don't have a bed at all."

He laughs again. "I do not have a bed because I do not need one. I am not going to be here long."

This brings me down. I don't know what's going on, but the idea that Kwarq is going to one day just disappear and go back to wherever he came from bothers me.

"Why are you here? I mean, this is so crazy. How did you even get here?" I'm overwhelmed. I don't know whether to run out the door or stand here and listen to him.

"I came here with my brother."

"You have a brother?" My mind races. I'm trying to keep up.

"I do."

"And you came here with him?"

"I did."

"Why?"

"For *ta'ani maul*."

"Ta'ani—what?"

He laughs. He's too happy. I feel like I'm going crazy, and he's acting like this is the best moment of his life. Maybe he's like the witch in the gingerbread house, and now that he's gotten me here, he's gonna eat me.

"It is a scavenger hunt for my people. A recreational activity. They happen all over the galaxies. My brother got it for my birthday."

"It's your birthday?"

"It was."

"Oh, happy birthday."

He nods, and I don't know why I'm saying any of this. Maybe I just need this conversation to feel normal, even though if I think about it, it's not that strange. He's an alien. But even aliens have birthdays, right? Still…

"You've been following me." I know it's true. He all but admitted it before. Why wasn't I listening before?

"I have, but not in a stalker-ish way."

"Is there any other way to follow someone? I feel like I should go."

"May I have your permission to touch you?"

"What?"

He opens his arms and waits for me to let him come close. I don't know why, but I nod my head. Maybe it's because he asked and didn't just grab me. Maybe it's the way his yellow eyes soften as he waits patiently for me to give my consent. My brain knows it should be afraid, but I don't feel it. In fact, I feel safe and calm. Kwarq pulls me into his arms. He leans his tall frame over and presses his face into my hair.

"My *lehti*, please do not be afraid of me. I will never hurt you. I am not here for any nefarious reason. If you will sit down and let me explain, I hope you will understand."

Everything about him holding me like this feels right. My mouth responds before my brain can chime in.

"Okay, but you have to tell me what *lehti* means, first. You keep saying it, and you might be calling me your servant or something."

My voice is muffled against his body. I put my hands against his stomach and gently push away, but not before I note the panel of muscles along his abdomen. Jeez.

He steps back and lets me put some distance between us.

"I will explain what the *leht* is if you have a seat and stop thinking about running away."

"How do you know I was thinking about running away? Can you read my mind, too?" I peer closely at him and try to fill my head with a bunch of bizarre images to see if there's any reaction. Instead, I can only think about what he would look like without his shirt on. I grow warm, my body tingles and a shiver runs through me. Kwarq's nostrils flare slightly, and his mouth quirks up at the corner.

"I cannot read minds. Not even yours, but I wish I could if only to know what has gotten you aroused."

I blink.

"Can—can you smell me?"

"I can."

"Ew." I pull a face, and his smile widens.

"I assure you, my *lehti*, there is nothing 'ew' about it. It is the single sweetest scent I have ever smelled in my life. Right before the way you smell when you are laughing and whatever it is that you put in your hair."

I'm flattered. I don't know if I should be, but I am.

I mentally snap myself out of it. This dude is an alien. He's talking about loving the way my pussy smells, and I can't just be all up in his apartment getting gushy over it. This is crazy. And as if he really can hear the battle going on in my mind, Kwarq rolls his eyes and sighs heavily.

"Stop guessing about what I can tell you to ease your mind. Sit so we can talk."

I glance around the nearly bare room. "Sit where?"

He folds himself down cross-legged on the floor. He's pretty flexible for such a big guy.

"Down here with me if it suits you." He looks nervous for a moment. "I did not think that you would end up here. I should have made an effort to make my home more presentable for you, *lehti*, I apologize."

He raises to his knees, which puts us basically at the same height, and pulls me down so he can press his cheek to mine like he did on the bus before. It's such a lovely gesture, really, and I immediately feel guilty for making him feel like he has to apologize to me.

"No, I'm sorry. I shouldn't make you feel embarrassed about your home. That's rude."

I don't know what makes me do it, but I lean forward and

take hold of his face. The yellow of his eyes flickers as I lean down to press my forehead to his, holding it for a moment, nuzzling our noses together in the same comforting way he did a moment earlier.

Something happens. It's almost like every emotion I could ever imagine is triggered inside of me, and I want to cry, but like good cry, and I want to scream with joy, and I want to laugh. I'm almost consumed by this sudden feeling of happiness and safety. I sink into it.

"My *lehti*." Kwarq's voice catches. His eyes are intense. The yellow is a little fire that swirls and flickers as he looks at me. "It means 'my beat'."

"Huh?" The moment breaks.

"*Lehti* it means 'my beat'."

"Oh."

He smiles again. "You are disappointed?"

"What? No. I mean, it's probably just something that's lost in translation. I guess I imagined something a little…softer. Like sweetheart or honey."

Kwarq sits back and pulls me down to his lap. One arm comes around to hold my hip. With the other, he lifts my hand and places it against his chest. When I go to pull my hand away. He holds it firm.

"You have my permission to touch me." I let him press my hand flat against the hard space between his bulging pecs. "Do you feel that?"

I nod my head, but I don't have to. I can hear it. The sound of his heart is like an echo in my own body, and my eyes widen when I realize that *this* is the sound I've been hearing. But then I realize too that there is another thump beneath his chest, and it's only slightly off rhythm to the other one. It is also weaker. I probably wouldn't have noticed it if I wasn't touching him.

"Do you have two hearts?"

"I do."

He's patiently letting me absorb this alien anatomy lesson.

"What do they do? Why is one so loud?"

He does that patient little smile again. He's trying to put me at ease before he really blows my mind.

"It is not loud. It is an echo. Only you can hear it."

"What? Why?"

"Because it is yours."

KWARQ

She doesn't want to run, at least.

"I do not mean that metaphorically," I clarify when she looks at me skeptically. "All the men of my kind are born with two hearts. One, the second heart, is small and functions as yours does, supplying oxygen through blood to the body. The other, the first heart, lies dormant until the moment we meet the person who makes it beat for the first time. We call this moment, the *leht*, and the person who makes it happen is your *lehti*, your beat."

"What does it do? The other heart, the first one? Why does it only beat when you meet someone?"

"Not just someone. The one you are meant for. Your partner. It also supplies blood to the body. Blood for one's *lehti*."

She makes a face. "What do you mean, for one's *lehti*? Like, you share blood? Like some weird vampire shit?"

I roll my eyes again. I have become very fond of this gesture I learned from her. It comes in handy.

"No. It supplies blood in service to one's *lehti*. It supplies blood to a very specific part of the body. It beats to provide pleasure."

Her eyes widen as my meaning becomes clear. She pulls her lips in, but that doesn't stop her dimples from showing.

"You're telling me that you have an entirely separate heart for the sole purpose of getting your dick hard?" Her eyes widen more. "Wait, you do have a dick, right?"

"I do."

I'm please to know she cares. I hope this means she is entertaining the idea of being with me. Because it definitely means I'm finding it very hard at the moment to keep from showing her just how my first heart works.

"But it is not just to make me aroused. It also provides the energy I need to protect you and provide for you and connect only to you."

"You keep saying 'you.'" Her expression is confused.

"Because you are my *lehti*."

"I am?"

"You are."

Her eyes shift back and forth in their sockets before settling back on me.

"Okay, and what does that mean?"

"It means that if you will have me, you are mine."

"Your what?"

"My *lehti*."

"Yeah, but what does that *mean*?"

Our hands are still pressed over my hearts. I lean close to her until our foreheads rest together.

"Listen. What do you hear?"

She holds completely still. A faint tremor runs through her.

"I hear your heart."

"Just mine?"

She shakes her head.

"Mine, too."

"They beat as one. Whenever we are together, they will connect to each other in this way. Do you understand?"

"Not really."

"It means that from the moment you passed me on that

bus two months ago, I have been here for you. The moment you became known to me, my first heart has beaten only for you. I have only stayed here to watch you, protect you, and wait for this moment when I could tell you all of these things. The moment when I could ask you to be mine." I wait and let my words sink. "I, of course, mean all of this in as not stalker-ish a way as possible."

"You watched me for two months?"

"I did."

"But not because you're a stalker?"

"Not because I am a stalker."

She frowns as she peers up at me, and there is such disbelief in her expression.

"Then why?"

"Because I love you."

I don't know what to expect, but it isn't for her to lean forward and press her full, luscious lips against mine. I don't move, not even when she turns into me, wraps her arms around my neck and twists her head to the side, licking along the seam of my mouth. She presses soft kisses to my lips, giving attention to each one.

I let her continue in this way, pressing her lips against mine with varying pressure. She licks against the seam again like she wants me to open my mouth. I keep my mouth shut and concentrate on keeping my cock from rising. My first heart beats madly. It's already trying to get as much blood to my cock as possible. I will it to slow down. At the same time, I will her to give me what I need, so I can respond like I want to.

"Why aren't you kissing me?"

Her voice is soft and nervous. I can tell she's being brave right now. She's giving in to what she feels, even if it's at war with her mind. I swallow, my throat dry with the emotion of finally being in this moment.

"You have not yet given me permission to." I hope she does soon. Otherwise, I will have to stop her, and I don't want to do that.

She pulls back, and I miss the feel of her against me almost immediately. She's smiling.

"Kwarq, you can kiss me."

CHAPTER 8

AMINA

I think Kwarq is the only male who could ask to lick my pussy and make it sound so…respectful. It's pretty sexy.

I can't lie. I really want to let him show me just what he can do with his gray, creepy tongue. I'm attracted to him. I'm also so wet it's embarrassing. I'm pretty sure he can smell me. He's taking deep breaths, groaning a little each time. I want to say yes, but the whole tongue surprise has me wondering about other differences between him and human males. He said he had a dick, but that could mean anything now.

"Um, maybe we could talk about a few things first." I'm not quite meeting his eyes. He gently turns my face.

"Do not be embarrassed, my *lehti*. I will tell you anything you want to know."

I swallow and brace myself. It's probably best to just blurt it out.

"Is your dick normal?" I groan and cover my face with my hands. "I don't mean normal. I just mean, is it comparable to a human male's?"

A slow smile forms on Kwarq's face. He chuckles.

"It depends on what you mean by comparable."

I'm getting nervous. I don't think I can take too many more surprises. I'm willing to give it a shot, but what if there's something really weird waiting for me down there. What if it's not down there? What if he has like a weird tentacle thing? What if it shoots acid instead of sperm and he disintegrates my pussy? What if he implants something in me? As every possibility forms in my mind, I get an intense case of the heebie jeebies.

Kwarq sighs deeply and lifts me off of his legs. I frown, worried that I may have killed the moment. I guess having a woman look like she's about to puke while thinking about your dick is a definite mood killer. I ease away from him. He rises in front of me.

"Stop scaring yourself. I will show you if you want to reassure yourself that we are compatible."

His hands are at the buckle to his jeans. He's all business. There's nothing suggestive about his offer to show me his junk. I suddenly feel very nervous. I want to know, but do I?

I nod, and immediately he begins to unbuckle his jeans.

"Wait!" I throw my hands up to stop him. "Give me a minute. What if it's too different and it scares me? I don't want to offend you."

Kwarq sighs again, but it's not in frustration or even impatience. It's almost as if the idea that I'm so worried about offending him is what's bothering him.

"*Lehti*, I have been to dozens of galaxies. Until a few days ago, you were not even aware there was life on other planets. Until two hours ago, you were not even sure about what you suspected. It is completely understandable that you would be nervous. I will show you if it will put your mind at ease, but if you think it will scare you, I will not do it."

He's so considerate. Any human man would have totally whipped it out by now, whether I asked or not. I mean, what's the worse that can happen? A dick is a dick is a dick, right?

"Is there anything terribly strange going on down there?"

His mouth twitches again. "I do not know what would be strange to you."

"Well, you know what a human penis looks like, right?"
"I do."
"Is it anything like it?"

"It is."

"In what way?"

He fights another smile. "It has a head, shaft, and testicles."

"That's it?"

He nods. "That's it."

That doesn't sound so different. His hands are still on his button. I take a deep breath and nod firmly. "Okay, show me."

He makes quick work of his buckle, probably more for my benefit. Like ripping off a bandaid. He pulls apart the zipper and lowers his jeans down his hips then stands with his hands at his sides waiting for my reaction. Too bad I can't speak. I can barely move. I'm struggling to get my mouth to close from where it's dropped open.

Comparable my ass.

KWARQ

The hardest thing I've ever had to do is bare myself to Amina to put her mind at ease. It's not hard because I don't want to do it. It's hard because I'm trying my best *not to get hard*.

Her eyes widen as she takes in my semi-erect cock. It hangs heavily over the front of my jeans. The head is swollen and tight. The tip has turned a deep bruised color from my first heart's efforts to prepare it for intercourse. I'm barely breathing. It's all I can do to keep from getting completely erect and scaring her to death. I'm sure she has already convinced herself that something ridiculous will happen when we copulate.

Copulate is not as good a word for what I want to do with her. Fuck. I want to fuck her. Fuck is a good word.

She's impressed. My chest flares with pride that she finds me satisfactory. She licks her lips, and I focus on the wall above her head when my cock twitches.

"You're huge." She sounds both excited and worried. I should put her mind at ease.

"I will fit, my *lehti*."

I've researched human female anatomy. The vagina has amazing stretching abilities. It may not be comfortable for her at first, but it will fit, and I will do my best to give her pleasure.

The scent of her arousal fills the room. She shifts, and I hear the wetness squishing between her thighs. Help me.

"Can I touch it?" Her voice is an awed whisper. My eyes drop down to hers. They're still fixed on my cock, but they rise to my face and the desire I see in them almost breaks the careful dam of control I've constructed.

"You never have to ask my permission, Amina. You are welcome to touch me in anyway you want as my *lehti*."

She nods and scoots forward on her knees until she's a few inches from my body. Her hand hovers over my cock, suspended and trembling in the air. I'm no longer able to control myself. I rise, filling with the blood being furiously pumped by my first heart. My cock swells and thickens until it meets her hand, and she flinches with the contact. Her eyes widen and fix on my increasing erection.

"Oh my god."

She looks terrified, but she smells excited.

Her hand settles lightly over my shaft. The energy pulsing between us is tingly and electric. I feel the imaginary sparks all along the length of my cock and throughout my body. She grips me as best she can. My hands fist at my sides when she experimentally pumps along my length.

"Amina." I groan low in my throat. It's the best feeling I've ever felt. She holds me with confidence, her grip tight but gentle.

I watch transfixed as she leans forward until her mouth is nearly touching me. She pauses and glances up to gauge my reaction. Her eyes are questioning. I can barely breathe. This is a moment I've imagined almost every night since I first saw her. It is the image of my dreams and my fantasies. How could I ever deny her?

I nod. "You never have to ask."

My voice is strangled and rough. The breath I'm taking catches in my throat when she presses her full, soft lips to the head of my cock. I grab her around her arms to anchor myself as my legs threaten to collapse.

The tip of my cock beads with a milky drop of semen, a testament to my need for release. Even these small touches are too intense. I move to pull away, but before I can, Amina's tongue darts out to catch the drop, and my entire body jerks. My legs finally give out, and I shift away from her and sink to my knees.

"Amina, have mercy on me please. I won't be able to contain myself."

"You're sweet."

Her voice is full of wonder. I look up from where my head has been lowered in an attempt to gain control. Her fingers are pressed to her lips. I drop my head back to my chest. This is nearly too much.

"Thank you."

"No, I mean it. You taste really really good."

I don't know what to say. I focus on breathing. I focus on maintaining control.

"You have my permission, Kwarq."

My head jerks back up. Amina waits with intense anticipation. The scent of her arousal is so thick that I can taste her on my tongue. It's not enough. I want to really taste her there.

I pull her into my arms. The sight of her so close is the most beautiful thing I've ever seen. Her smooth, dark skin, the thick fringe of her eyelashes, her thick coiled hair. Her mouth parts, and the tip of her short, pink tongue is just visible. I want to kiss her. I want to sink into all of her warm places.

"I have your permission, even with my creepy, long tongue?" I smile to let her know I'm not offended by her discomfort with my anatomy.

"Are you my *lehti,* too? I mean, is there another word that I should refer to you as?"

I shake my head. "I am your *lehti.* Always."

She smiles, and it is the second most beautiful thing I've ever seen. "Then, you never have to ask my permission, Kwarq. You're welcome to touch me in anyway you want."

Hearing her recite my words back to me is like a ray of light through my spirit. I sink into her mouth, stroking my tongue through the warmth. Making sure to give what is comfortable. She moans when our tongues touch, and I feel it, too. It feels so perfectly right. She feels so right.

Now that I have her permission, I want to toss her onto her back and sink into her. However, a sudden realization has me reluctantly pulling away.

"I do not have a bed, *lehti.* I should have prepared for us better. I am sorry. We can wait—,"

Amina lunges at me, pressing her mouth back to mine. Her hands fist in my shirt and yank it up my chest.

"I don't care about the bed. I want you. I don't care."

I can't tell her no. I'll remedy my living quarters later, but now I need her. I need this to bind her to me once and for all. I ease her away from me.

"Let me undress you."

I remove all of her outer garments. Her shoulders shimmer beneath the light of the setting sun peaking through the windows. I fumble with the fastening to her undergarment, and she takes over with a chuckle, unclasping the band with an expert hand and tossing it aside.

"It's called a bra. It's the devil."

I don't care. I'm too busy taking in the sight of her full, beautiful breasts. Her nipples are taut and erect. The areola have constricted to form two enticing targets. Unable to resist, I lean forward and flick my tongue out at one tight, dark nipple.

"Mm."

Amina's head lowers to watch me through half-closed lids. I lock onto her warm brown eyes and give her another lick. This time, she sucks in a sharp breath. I take hold of her breast, testing the weight in my palm. She fits perfectly into my large hand. I plump the flesh, presenting her nipple before closing my mouth over it.

Her high-pitched gasp is met by my own low groan. Her skin is sweet. Lingering notes of flowers and water stick to my tongue. I swirl the tip before drawing more. She grips my hair, tugging me closer.

"Kwarq."

I love the sound of my name in her soft, dusky voice. She says it properly. The vowel is light, the last consonant a short click in her throat. I don't think I've ever heard my name said in such a pleasing way. Having her say it while I pleasure her is even better.

I move to her other breast, drawing firmly on the nipple, learning what she likes. My *lehti* likes a sure touch. When I wrap my hands around her soft waist and lift her to my mouth, she cries out, arching her back in surrender to my control.

Her legs twitch, perfuming the hair with the dizzying smell of her pussy. I continue to lavish her breasts, alternating between gentle, swirling licks and strong, pulling sucks. I leave faint purple marks along her skin. They satisfy something primitive in me. The desire to claim her as my own.

I treat each of her breasts in turn to a firm suck, letting her tight, little nipples plop out of my mouth and making her gasps echo off the walls of my apartment. The reverberating sound triggers a rush of blood to my cock and sends my need spiraling to a point of urgency. I can't wait to have her completely anymore.

I straighten and set her away from me. She follows my movements as I arrange her discarded clothing into a reasonably comfortable padding. I cover the mound with my single sheet and smooth it down.

"Come." I hold out my hand, and she takes it without hesitation, rising to her knees and scooting over to our makeshift bed. I ease her onto her back so she's laying before me, her skin shimmering, her heart echoing my own immense need.

I slide my hand beneath her hips to pull down the small scrap of fabric that's the final barrier between us. When she's finally bare, I sit back and take it in.

I can't believe Amina would not be considered the most beautiful woman in the universe in this moment. Her legs are curvy and toned. The flat plane of her belly is still feminine and soft. The muscles show beneath her tight skin, but there's a lushness to her that makes me want rub my face all over her body.

My eyes fall on the neat, trimmed patch of hair covering her pussy. Her scent is overpowering now. I gently take hold of her knees and push them apart. Her stomach spasms and curves inward. She's shaking.

"Are you scared?"

Her chin taps her chest with a jerky nod. I run my hands along her legs, hoping to sooth her before I stand between her parted thighs. I'm still fully dressed. Perhaps seeing me without my clothes will calm her. She has so many crazy ideas about what it's going to be like to lay with me.

I undress quickly. Excitement makes my muscles twitch as I stand above her, giving her an opportunity to see me. To see that she has nothing to fear.

"You're beautiful," she whispers.

I cover her, giving her just enough of my weight that my skin touches every part of her that it can. She's so soft. Beneath the scent of her arousal is the faint smell of flowers and sugar. I flick my tongue out and taste the skin at the hollow of her shoulder.

"I know this will be different for you," I tell her. I have not forgotten that she doesn't experience the *leht* as I do. She does not yet have the surety of our joining that I do. She does not yet *feel* what I feel. "Before we join, I would tell you that I love you, my *lehti*. You are now the most important being in my life. More than my parents, more than my siblings, and more than myself. I will always protect and provide for you, and I will never lie to or hurt you. Ever. You are mine, and I am yours."

I kiss her then because her eyes get glassy and wide. The melancholy expands, pushing in on her desire. I kiss all of her that I can reach. Her cute, flared little nose, her smooth, round cheeks, the dimpled corners of her mouth. I continue down one side of her neck then follow it back up, tracing a path along her jaw to the other side. I plant a trail of kisses down the middle of her chest, lingering briefly to suckle at her nipples until she moans lustily and fists her hand at my temples, pushing her chest into my mouth. Only then do I continue down to her belly.

"You're so soft and round, here," I tell her as I run my lips and tongue over every bit of skin I see, dipping into the small recess of her navel. Every part of her is sweet.

"I think that's called I haven't been to the gym in six months."

I flick her hands to the side when she tries to cover herself.

"I think it is called beautiful and sexy. I will remind you of this every day until you believe it."

She squirms and giggles when I kiss the hollows of her hips, so I do it again and then again. I love the sound of her soft, pealing laugh. As I get closer to her pussy, my skin begins to shake with vigor.

Her sweet scent fills my nose when I reach the juncture of her thighs. Amina jerks and releases a shaky moan. Using my nose, I nudge my way between her folds, covering my face with her wetness. Her pussy drips with her desire, but I need to prepare her more. I also need to satisfy the burning urge to feel and taste her on my tongue.

"Kwarq, please."

I stick out my tongue—my long, creepy tongue—and drag it between her folds.

"Ah!" Her cry is shocked and piercing. I curl the tip of my tongue to catch the swollen bud nestled at the top of her slit and she lurches up, her chest heaving.

"Oh, my god Kwarq. I can't."

I chuckle.

"Do you see, now, my *lehti?*" I drag my tongue through her folds again. She screams and her fingers curl against my head. She bucks her hips up just as she pushes against my head to hold me away, but I need more. I unfurl my tongue to its full length and flutter it along her pussy lips, causing her to release me and fall back to the floor, grabbing at the sheet as if it will save her.

"Do you see now," I taunt again, "why my tongue is so long?"

CHAPTER 9

AMINA

Do I ever fucking see. Every firm swipe of Kwarq's tongue sends me into a spasm of pleasure that doesn't seem to stop. One wave blends into the next only distinguished by a crest of pleasure so intense I think I'm going burst out of my skin. My orgasm lingers on the edges of it, threatening me with an intensity I'm almost too afraid to submit to. I try again to push at Kwarq's head. I manage to push him a few inches away, but that damn tongue doesn't stop.

"Ah, Kwarq, I'm going to come, it's too much," I plead and make one more attempt to escape the sweet torture of him going down on me.

He shakes my hands loose from his head and nuzzles back into my pussy, lapping noisily. His nose caresses my clit as his tongue swirls around my folds. Suddenly, I feel him at my opening and then he presses his way inside of me, curling his tongue up to run it along my sensitive walls.

I choke on the scream that erupts from my throat as a thousand stars burst inside of me. It's edged with a tingling almost painful sensation, but it's pure pleasure. I open my eyes when my orgasm peaks, expecting to see some kind of light or flame shining from my body.

When I finally come down, my throat feels dry and raw. I've been screaming. I blink. Kwarq's smiling, pleased face comes into my line of sight.

He's hard and shimmering golden above me. His dick rests heavily against my abdomen, and I feel a slight sense of apprehension at what's to come. As if sensing my unease,

Kwarq ducks his head and presses a soft kiss to my mouth.

"You are amazing when you orgasm. Do not be nervous. Your release will help you to take me, but it will still be uncomfortable at first. Tell me if I hurt you."

I only nod. Mostly because I still haven't gained control of all of my faculties after that orgasm, but also because despite his reassurances, I'm nervous as hell. My legs shake against his hips, the width of which are spreading me so wide that my joints ache.

He kisses me deeper, his tongue tangy with the taste of my pussy. He eases back and reaches between us to position himself. I take a deep breath.

He's hot and hard at my opening. The head of his dick settles against me, and it already feels like too much. He must see the shock on my face because he runs his free hand along the thigh that's gripping his waist for dear life and gives me a gentle peck on the lips.

"Relax, *lehti*. I will go as slowly as you need me to. We can do this."

I nod again, and he nods in return before easing his hips forward the tiniest bit. I tense, expecting discomfort, but it only feels like pressure. The head breaches me, and I feel stuffed. I shift my hips to adjust to the feeling, and he sucks in a deep breath. His eyes are pinched shut. The hand on my thigh squeezes.

"Do not move. I cannot go slow if you move. This is—it is incredible."

I breathe through it as he works another half inch inside of me. The fullness is now edged with a twinge, and I resist the urge to move again.

Kwarq's sweet, minty breath huffs into my face as he eases out of me and then presses in more insistently. A sharp, stinging pain radiates through my pelvis, and I stiffen, prompting Kwarq to still as well. He's breathing like he's run a marathon. The vibration beneath his skin is on one hundred.

"I will stop if you need me to."

"No."

I want this. I also in a weird way want the pain. It's not unbearable. It's not even unpleasant. It's edgy and erotic. I feel like he's claiming me in some basic way, and it's turning me on.

"It's not bad pain. I like it. Don't stop. Keep going. Give me more."

He moans, and it almost sounds like regret, but his hips raise a little higher and he presses in, forcing another inch inside of me. I cry out and wrap my feet beneath his ass. I press him further, steeling myself around the stretching of my body.

"*Lehti.*"

The endearment is pushed through gritted teeth, but he continues to work into me in short gentle strokes.

"More."

I use my feet again to push him further in, and he sinks a little deeper. The pain is dull now, and all I'm left with is the feeling of being so full of him that there's no where else to go. I press him down and thrust up until I feel him hit my cervix.

"Oh my god!"

Another savage orgasm rips through me when he's finally inside. My body jerks, and my pussy clinches against the thick length of his dick where it's stretched me to a delicious brink. I open my eyes. Kwarq stares down at me, almost appearing to be in pain.

"Are you okay? Does it still feel go—"

My question is cut off by his mouth slamming down on mine. He pushes his tongue inside to tangle with mine at the same time his hips jerk up and slam his dick down into my pussy. A delicious burning sensation accompanies the pleasure of him stroking along my walls, and I have to pull away to breathe through it.

"Too hard?"

His voice is a carefully contained growl. He seems barely in control. Seeing his restrained passion makes something kinky rise in me, and suddenly, I want to see just how much he can bring it.

"Oh, my *lehti*," I say with all the sweetness I can muster. I know he likes it because the yellow of his eyes blaze. "Fuck me harder."

KWARQ

Fuck is definitely the word for what we are doing. Amina's sweetly worded request sends me into a craze. I raise my hips and flex them down hard through the tight passage of her pussy, giving her as much as I can until she flinches in discomfort. She's so warm and tight. Her pussy gushes around my length, so that plunging into her body feels like being surrounded by the wettest softest silk. Every nerve in my cock flares to life as her walls constrict and spasm along my length.

""Kwarq." She keeps moaning my name. Desperate little cries that are both plea and praise. Each murmur puts a little fissure in my control, and I have to stop myself from pounding into her. She wants it hard, but her body can only take so much. I cup beneath her knee and lift her leg, hooking it over my elbow. Her body stretches for me, opening wider, and I thrust harder, immediately filling the space.

"Uhn!" Her little grunt as she takes my cock is a tender moan of pleasure.

"Yes, my *lehti*. Do you like that? Am I giving you what you need?"

"Yes!"

Amina lifts her hips when I slam down again, giving her just a little more. I have finally managed to seat my entire cock. Being enveloped so completely by my *lehti* is a sweet torture that's nearly my undoing.

"Tell me how it feels, my love."

"Good."

It's not enough. I need more.

"Words, my *lehti*. I am a linguist. I like words. What does my cock feel like inside of you." I pull out until I nearly leave her body before pressing back in a smooth, firm stroke. Her back arches when I bottom out against her womb, and she gives a throaty moan.

"Fuck, Kwarq. You feel so good. So fucking big inside of me. Stretching my pussy."

Her words cause something in me to snap, and I increase my speed until it's almost beyond the point of human ability.

My sense of touch is just as sensitive as my other senses, and I feel the tissues of her pussy swelling around me. Our sounds are stickier with the thickening of her juices. It tightens her passage, increasing my pleasure as I struggle through it, but also, I know, beginning what will soon be discomfort for her. As if underlying this point, Amina hisses through her teeth before clenching around my cock on another orgasm.

The force of her passage gripping me is so strong that I lift back from the warmth of Amina's body, needing to see the place where our bodies are joined. I continue to piston through her tight, warm tissue. My hips ache with the force of my thrusts, and I train my eyes on the sight of my cock disappearing and reappearing into her body.

"*Lehti*, you are so beautiful. You take my cock so well."

She is. The deep brown flesh of her pussy is puffy and bright with her arousal. It drags along my cock every time I retreat, sucking me back in, gripping the marble length of my shaft and pulling my waiting seed from my testicles.

"My *lehti*," I lean back in to suckle her nipples, and she moans. Every moan, every gasp brings me closer to the release I so desperately want.

I slow into deep, easy strokes. I'm barely holding on. My balls draw up tight against my body as I sink deeply into her again. The image of my sperm covering the floor when I took myself in hand last fills my mind, and suddenly I want my semen where it belongs. Inside of my *lehti*, coating her, absorbing into her body. I know that many human women take pills to prevent conception. I also know that Amina is not taking anything. I would smell it. Instead, she smells fertile, and I want to give her all of me.

"I am close, Amina," I rasp out as I work her pussy in quicker and quicker movements. My cock grows further in preparation to release, and her body's resistance increases. She whimpers a little, and I know the time has come to let go.

"Come." Her voice is a soft, tense cry.

"Can I release inside of you, Amina?"

I wait. My hips are a blur as they slap loudly against her, my breath harsh. My release is right at the edge, insistent and painful. Her chin knocks against my shoulder as she nods her head frantically.

"Yes, cum inside of me."

Her consent breaks the hold on my control. I press deep, angling her knees wide so I can wedge right against her womb. The flood of semen that I've been holding back shoots from my cock, straight into her waiting pussy. I start at the loud, feral growl that issues from my throat as I pump a steady stream of my seed into her, until it seeps from between our bodies.

With one last body jerking spurt, I collapse onto her, spent and so full of contentment that I can't catch my breath. She's mine. Even if she decides not to keep me. It was worth it just to feel her this one time.

91

CHAPTER 10

AMINA

I can't move. I don't know what I was expecting, but the body numbing sex Kwarq just hit me with was not it. He's so serious and formal, I imagined all tangled limbs and breathy sighs. But that's definitely not what happened. It was good. Probably the best I've ever had. No, it was absolutely the best I ever had, but it wasn't making love. This man just fucked the hell out of me.

Everything was so much. I mean everything. First of all, the man has stamina. When I told him to fuck me harder, I maybe should have said 'fuck me ever so slightly stronger' because he went in. Then he came in me for like two minutes nonstop. I'm so full, it feels like I have to pee, but from *there*.

I don't know why I said he could come in me. I was caught up in the moment. Caught in the feel of him stretching me, the teeth clacking thrust of his hips, that edge of pain that made me flinch every time he sank into my body, all of the things he kept whispering to me. It was primal and raw, and it felt good and right. But now I'm wondering if that was such a good idea. Who knows what his nut is going to do to my body.

Kwarq's breath is deep and heavy against my neck. I would think he was asleep if it wasn't for the slight tugging in my scalp where his fingers twist around a curl. He spreads his fingers wide along my head, rubbing through my sweat dampened coils.

I let him rest his weight on me for a moment longer before

the necessity to breathe makes me have to shift beneath him. Immediately, he raises to his elbows.

"I am sorry, my *lehti*. I am hurting you." He brushes his cheek along mine before pressing a light kiss to my lips.

He eases back, slipping from inside of me, and I wince as he drags through my tender tissue. The moment he's away from my body, I'm hit with the full aftermath of our love making.

Everything hurts. Where a moment ago I felt the best bliss of my life, now I feel like I've been tossed down a flight of fucking stairs.

My hips cramp in protest when he lifts his pelvis from the cradle of my legs. I bring my knees together and rock them to my chest.

"Mmm," I groan as I try to work out the stiffness. I'm flexible, but not *that* flexible. I hold still and assess the most obvious casualty of sex with Kwarq. My cooch.

My pussy throbs like there's a pulse down there, the inside tight and hot. Almost like I've had a dick the size of my arm pounding into me for the last half hour. Kwarq watches me with a worried expression.

"I think I may have been too vigorous with you. You will be sore."

He was very vigorous, but I don't regret it. Not even when my back catches from the hard floor as I sit up.

"It's okay. That was amazing. It was totally worth—what the hell?"

A thick flood of milky liquid gushes from my pussy. I glance up in horror to find Kwarq looking embarrassed. It's not an expression I've seen on him before. His skin pulses a dull red. I'd laugh if this wasn't so gross.

"I don't usually release that much. Only since the *leht* has it been so plentiful."

Plentiful is a few teaspoons. At least a cup has oozed from

my body.

"Okay, why?"

"To increase our chances."

"Of what?"

"Of having offspring."

My eyes jump to his face. Right. I let him come in me. And because he's an alien with a super smart, evolved body, naturally it would do its best to make sure I get knocked. Naturally. Well, it's a good thing I'm human and he's...not.

"That can't happen, right? You and me. Cause we aren't the same species."

Kwarq frowns like I'm not making sense.

"We are not the same species, but we are compatible, Amina. We will have young."

"We will?"

He sniffs the air like he's checking to make sure a chicken in the oven isn't burning. A second later, his mouth breaks into a wide smile. His face brightens. The yellow of his eyes goes soft and gushy. I don't like it. He takes my hands and kisses the backs of them.

"We will. My seed has breached you, *lehti*. We have conceived."

Wait, what?

I pull my hands from his and scoot back out of the puddle of semen like it really is acid.

"Uh, what do you mean, we've conceived? We just had sex."

"It only takes once, my *lehti*."

"Kwarq, I'm serious. Don't play."

Maybe alien sense of humor is different than human, but this isn't cute like the tongue thing. This shit isn't funny.

Kwarq tries to reach out to me, but I scoot further away. He stops and stares at me with a puzzled expression.

"Amina, I do not play. My species' conception is

immediate. I am able to scent it even now. My seed has connected with your egg. You have conceived."

"What are you talking about? How?"

"How I have explained. I did not think you were opposed. This is why I asked if it was okay to release inside of you. When you said yes, I thought..."

He stops because I'm shaking my head.

"I didn't think it was going to be instantaneous!"

I jump to my feet and back away. I feel strange. The ache from his penetration is intense now. I move gingerly, causing more cum to seep from my pussy. I'm panicking.

"*Lehti*, of course we will have a child whenever we come together and you are fertile. We do not have to, but if you make the decision to allow me to release inside of you, it will happen."

He's saying things that kind of make sense, but I'm not listening. I'm thinking about the thing that's growing in my womb right now, that he can apparently smell.

"You could tell I was ovulating?"

"Of course. I have a very good sense of smell."

I'm not so impressed by his amazing spidey senses right now.

"You knew I would get pregnant? Why didn't you say anything?"

"I did. I asked you if you wanted me to finish inside." He's so calm. It's like I'm the one who isn't making any sense.

"Yeah, I thought that was because you didn't want to give me space gonorrhea or something!"

His jaw clenches in irritation. "We do not have these diseases where I am from, and I would not copulate with you if I knew I had them. I am insulted that you think I would."

Kwarq has never expressed anger toward me, but there is an edge of annoyance in his tone. I don't see why he would be annoyed, though. He's not the one knocked up with an alien baby. Oh, god, I'm knocked up with an alien baby.

I back away. Kwarq stares. The pool of cum is right at his feet. It slowly spreads until it touches his toes, and my stomach rolls.

I turn and rush past the kitchen until I find the bathroom. I get the lid up on the toilet just as the acid spray of my breakfast erupts from my mouth. I bend over the bowl, jerking violently as I empty my stomach. After while, my stomach begins to ache as it tries to release what's no longer there.

"The sickness will pass, *lehti*. It is bad for the first day after conception, then it is better." Kwarq's large, warm hand settles on my back. He rubs between my shoulder blades in slow, firm circles.

I spit and lift my head, holding my curls from my face with one hand. "This is morning sickness?" I can't believe it. I almost won't believe it.

"It is a sickness that happens with the attachment of the fetus. Our gestation is somewhat more rapid than yours. I do not know how your body will adjust, but this is normal, and it will pass."

And here I just thought I was grossed out by the alien baby invading my body. I sit back from the toilet and look down at my stomach. Despite having puked up the meager contents of my belly, I feel full. Almost like I do when I drink a lot of liquid.

"I feel strange. Something's wrong."

Kwarq kneels beside me in an instant, his face all worry. The earlier annoyance is gone, like it was never even there.

"What are you feeling?"

"What are you a gynecologist, too?" I snort out.

"I am trained to birth young, yes."

Of course he is.

"I thought you were a linguist."

"I am."

"And a gynecologist?"

"More like what you would call a doula on this planet."

I roll my eyes. This dude is too much for me right now.

"What are you feeling?" he persists. "I would make sure everything is going as it should."

He's talking like I'm five months pregnant and not five minutes. It's throwing me off. Still, I should probably know if a gray-tongued alien spawn is going to come bursting out of my chest in a minute.

"I feel full. Like I'm holding a lot of liquid in my stomach, but lower."

He nods, and his face relaxes in relief.

"That is normal. The liquid is in your womb. That is the remainder of my release."

"It's your cum?"

"It is."

"Is it going to come out?"

He shakes his head. "It is there to protect and nourish the baby."

"Like amniotic fluid?"

He nods. "It will merge with your fluid and surround our baby."

Our baby. I little tingle goes through me. I'm pregnant. I don't even know what to say. A few hours ago I was almost too scared to sit across from this alien man in a coffee shop, and now I'm going have his baby.

KWARQ

There are new smells to my *lehti*. One is the pure, clean scent of new life—our young—which is now taking root in her womb. The science of us both, blending, forming into something of its own.

The second smell makes my first heart ache with sorrow. It's disgust, and it's rolling off of Amina in sharp, stinging ripples. She is repulsed by our child.

Her distress is like a stab to my chest. It wars with my own elation over our joining and the resulting conception. In my dreams of starting a family, my *lehti* and I would come together joyfully, and any resulting offspring would be celebrated and welcome.

I'm saddened this isn't the case, but there are too many things I need to tell Amina about what will happen from now for me to dwell on it. She sits across from me on the bathroom floor, her face a mask of shock, and I hate that I must distress her further. She needs time to understand and to decide. I would never try to take away her right to choose, and whatever she decides, I will support her. But it is a choice she must make soon.

"I can't have an alien baby."

I flinch at her description of our child. I know what she's imagining. A slimy, worm-like creature fighting its way from her body. Something foreign and unrecognizable bursting from beneath her skin, clawing out from inside of her. I cover her knee with my hand, and when she doesn't shy from my touch, I smooth it over her thigh to comfort her.

"You do not have to have the baby if you do not want to. We can terminate."

Her eyes leap to mine. There's confusion there. It makes me feel guilty and ashamed. Somewhere deep inside, past my own desires, I know that when Amina agreed to let me release inside of her, she wasn't agreeing to this. I wanted it, and now she's forced to carry the burden of this difficult decision.

"How am I supposed to terminate this pregnancy? Am I just supposed to go down to my local clinic and get it done? What if things don't look like they're supposed to? What if it's strange or they detain me because they think I have some kind of disease?"

These are crazy questions, but I understand why she's asking them. Even if I'm sad that we won't have a child, I'm glad that I can put her mind at ease.

"We do not have to do it here. I can take you to my home planet to perform the procedure. It is quick and painless there. We are more than equipped with the technology to do it. Not all Lyqa women desire offspring, and mistakes happen."

Our child is not a mistake, but if this is not what she wanted when she agreed to let me come inside of her, then it is my fault to be responsible for.

"Lyqa? Is that what you are?"

Maybe having a regular conversation will calm her down. If she knows more about me, perhaps she will feel less afraid of what has happened.

"Yes," I nod, "I am Lyqa."

Her brown eyes narrow, and her head pulls back on her neck.

"Lyqa. What kind of being is that?"

"We are humanoid of sorts."

"What do you mean, 'of sorts'? What does that mean?"

"It means I am Lyqa, Amina. Nothing more."

"You keep saying that, but what the hell is a Lyqa?"

"It is a being like a human. There are some differences as you have noted. Heightened senses, a larger physique, an increased instinct." I already know what I say will scare her, but I want to be honest. As expected, her eyes widen further.

"Instinct? Like an animal?"

"We are all animals, *lehti*."

"Stop doing that! You know what I'm asking. Are you part fucking dog or squid or something?"

I resist the urge to roll my eyes. I don't think my *lehti*

would appreciate my impatience. Humans and their imaginations.

"Amina, I am not trying to alarm you. I am not an animal in the sense you are thinking. My people do have an instinctual part of ourselves that is, I could say, more in tune with our senses than humans, but we are neither feral beasts nor shape shifters. Do not worry."

Amina's dark skin has been slowly turning an ashen, gray color. She's still, so still that I worry she's having an attack like the one she suffered on the train earlier. I squeeze her thigh where my hand rests and she gradually refocuses on my face.

"Is my baby going to be human?"

Despite the fear in her voice, my heart lightens and fills with hope. Maybe her mind is not made up. Maybe she is considering carrying our child.

"Our baby will be part human, yes, and part Lyqa. He or she will be beautiful and normal. My *lehti*, we are different, yes, but not so much that you have to be afraid. However, if you want to terminate, I will support you. There is always time to have a child," I add this last part quietly. It is important that she knows this is not a deciding moment for us. I am with her always, until she turns me away from her heart.

"I don't know." Amina buries her face in her hands. Her cloud of hair bounces about her shoulders when she shakes her head. She is worrying too much. Again I feel the guilt of having impregnated her. This is too soon, and yet we do not have a lot of time. I must impress on her the urgency of her decision. I don't want to, but I must.

"I would never seek to pressure you, my *lehti*, but you will have to decide soon. As I have said, our gestation is slightly different than yours. Things will progress—quickly. If we are to terminate, it must be tonight."

Her eyes lock on mine, wide and full of panic again. "What do you mean tonight? How am I supposed to do it tonight?" She jerks her knees up to her chest, causing my hand to fall from her leg. She folds herself against the base of the bathtub, out of my reach. She looks horrified. "Are you—do you do that, too?"

I shrink back at the thought. While I do not shame a woman for her choices with regard to conception, I could not be the one to terminate my own fetus. I have not the skill nor the heart for it.

"No, I would take you to my home."

"How are we going to get there tonight?"

This is not the time to explain the complexities of space travel, but if it will put her mind at ease, I will do my best.

"Without going into too great detail, space travel is not as difficult as humans think. I am able to fold space in time in a precise measure, so I can get us to my home very quickly. Would you like to go?"

I wait. Almost hoping she takes too long to decide, and we miss the opportunity for termination. It is a selfish thought, but it would be a lie to say that the moment I scented her conception, my first heart didn't swell with pride and love for my *lehti*. I can imagine nothing more beautiful than watching her belly get round with my child. But her safety and emotional wellbeing are more important. So I wait, and when she finally nods her head, I try not to let my disappointment show.

"I will take you now. You do not have to prepare. I can have you back before tomorrow."

CHAPTER 11

AMINA

I'm in a damn spaceship. It's like a suped-up space version of a smart car. Two large, padded high-backed chairs are fitted flush against the back of the pod, and a lighted panel sits just below the wide, transparent window in front of us. There's just enough room for me and Kwarq. I almost laughed when I followed him out to the alley behind his apartment building and saw that he had it parked out back. No kidding. It was in his landlord's garage. Apparently, he rents it for an additional charge each month. I could only shake my head wondering how that conversation went.

How much to rent the garage?

Thirty bucks a month.

Cool, I need it to store my spaceship.

Now I'm settled into one of the cushy seats. Kwarq is in the other, fiddling with the numerous controls on the dashboard.

This is surreal, and by surreal, I mean insane. When he maneuvers us above the city, my insides lift then slowly lower back down. I grip the arm rests to focus on keeping my stomach from rebelling.

"Won't people be able to see us?" We're high above Hyde Park. The perfectly square roof of his apartment building is getting smaller and smaller until it looks like a little Lego piece.

"Do not worry. Our cloaking technology is too advance for any of your monitoring systems to detect us."

My mind races with expectations. Things are happening too fast. I feel like this moment could be an example of me making all of the right decisions or a prime circumstance where I make a bunch of wrong ones that are going to lead me somewhere crazy. Crazier than being in a spaceship with a fine, tan alien man with a ginormous dick who just knocked me up.

"This will feel strange. Something like being on an amusement park ride. Do not panic." Kwarq's voice is gentle. He has been this way since I decided to go with him. Calm and reassuring, but his eyes look sad.

"Have you been on an amusement park ride?" I latch on to the only familiar part of his warning. It's easier than acknowledging that I'm actually in a spaceship headed toward an alien planet. Let's talk rollercoasters and the Floor Drop.

"Of course, I have. Last month, you went to Great America. You closed your eyes on every ride. It will feel similar to that."

Right. Kwarq has spent the last two months following me around. If I were a smarter woman, I wouldn't be willingly engaging in interstellar travel with my stalker. But then, I wouldn't have slept with and be knocked up by my stalker, either. I brace myself, digging my nails into the soft material of the chair until the joints of my fingers ache.

"If it will make you feel less afraid, you can close your eyes now."

I do. I squeeze them until every bit of light is blocked behind my eyelids. I squeeze them until it feels like my eyeballs are going to suck into my head. I hear a beep and the sound of Kwarq's nimble fingers tapping against the panel just before the pod gives a jolting lurch. My back lifts from the seat for the briefest moment and floats back down. That familiar sinking feeling enters my stomach. I clutch it with one hand and immediately move my hand away. I don't want to think about what's going on in there.

"We must wait to dock, but we are here."

I crack open one eye. Everything outside the pod is calm. We're suspended in the sky. In front of us, a row of crafts hover in a line as they wait to pass through some kind of check point. A small, square booth sits in suspension ahead of us. It almost resembles highway toll booths back on Earth. Except I'm not on Earth. I'm on another planet.

"Holy shit."

Kwarq chuckles beside me and continues to tap away at the control panel. Now that I think about it, all the cool shit I've been waiting to see from this alien encounter is right in front of me. Kwarq's little pod is like something from old school *Star Trek*. A series of holographic images and data streams float across his side of the screen, too quickly for me to try to make sense of, but then again, I'm only barely looking.

Like everything else today, this moment has yet to feel real. I sit quietly beside Kwarq as we get closer and closer to the station until we're next in line. He pulls up to the booth.

At the window, an expressionless woman dressed in a bright red uniform holds out her hand. I blink. She looks so... human. Like Kwarq, she's tall. Even sitting down, her torso is long, but other than that, her face is that same odd amalgamation of human features that I find so fascinating.

Her skin's olive. Her round green eyes are surrounded by rows and rows of dark auburn lashes. She blinks them slowly as she regards us through the open pod door. A puff of coppery-red hair that's almost my own kinky texture curls out wildly to frame her face. If she was on Earth, she'd be a hipster folk singer or super-model or the chick that sells artisanal jelly made from pinto beans at the farmers market. It's all too normal. I find myself shrinking back into my seat, afraid that she's going to suddenly sprout fangs, leap through the window, and eat me.

She says something in Kwarq's language, and I'm surprised to hear her husky, melodic voice. The words flow from her lips in an almost sensual way.

Kwarq responds with a long stream of Lyqa. He gestures with his hands, making circles and shooing motions. At one point, he presses his hand to his chest before taking my hand.

"I told her that I came from *ta'ani maul* on Earth. There, I connected with you, my *lehti*. I have explained that you have mistakenly conceived and we are coming to terminate. Our stay will only be for tonight."

I'm so glad I don't blush, but I feel my face warm when the woman ducks her head and peers closely at me. She inhales and one slender eyebrow raises before she turns away and begins to move her hands over a panel inside the booth. I drop my eyes to my lap.

"Did you have to tell her why we're here? It's a little embarrassing."

Kwarq frowns and squeezes my hand.

"You do not have to be embarrassed, *lehti*. It happens. We do not consider this something to be ashamed of."

They may not consider it shameful, but that doesn't stop me from squirming in my seat when the woman takes my information, fits me with a tracker-like wristband, and sends us along.

As we pull away from the booth, I keep my eyes on my lap, mostly because I'm still in too much shock to risk a look at what's around us. I can't escape everything I've ever seen in a movie or read in a book. Images of wild, creature-filled jungles and cold, metal metropolises float through my head. I'm freaked the hell out, but I'm also tempted to peek and see if I've landed on Pandora or Mars.

"I will park here. My family has automatically been notified of my return. I do not want you to be alarmed when they come to greet us. If it concerns you, I will greet them first and send them back to our home. Then we can go and have the procedure."

Before the words are out of his mouth, Kwarq's door flies open, and there's a flash of dark blue and gold as he's yanked out of the craft. A scream rips from my throat, and I pull my legs up into the seat to escape whatever's coming for me. I brace myself for the cold constriction of a tentacle or the piercing burn of a pair of fangs. My heart kicks up, trying to beat out of my chest. Am I about to die?

I squeeze my eyes shut and cover my face. If I'm about to be eaten by a huge slug, I don't want to see it. Strangely, the maternal instinct to protect the life inside of me makes my hand move to my stomach in a gesture that I hope is comforting to whatever is in there. *Please, just don't let it hurt,* I ask in a silent prayer to the universe.

I curl into an even tighter ball as I wait for whatever has gotten Kwarq to get me next. The moments tick by slowly, but nothing happens. It's probably only been about five seconds, but it feels like an eternity. The sounds of crafts and movement and people is suddenly loud in the silence.

"*Lehti*, it is okay. It is just my brother."

Kwarq's gentle voice expels the all consuming terror that grips my body, and I risk a peek between my fingers. He's leaning into the craft, and right beside him is a face that resembles his, except…darker.

"Whoa."

Kwarq is all tan skin and strange ambiguous features. His "brother," whose features are exactly the same, is the darkest black I have ever seen.

I once knew a Sudanese man who had the richest, bluish-black skin. It was lovely and smooth, almost surreal in its flawlessness. The man beside Kwarq is this color, but darker. It's different, and familiar, and really really sexy. I stare openly at him until I'm able to swallow around the sudden dryness in my throat. I need a moment to absorb this new layer of alien.

"This is your brother?" I can see it. They do look alike. Exactly alike. How is that even possible?

"He is."

I relax but cross my arms over my chest just in case I need to return to my protective huddle.

"Same mother, same father?"

Kwarq chuckles. "Same womb, same time."

I don't have to see my face to know that I look like a gaping fool. They've got to be shitting me.

"You're twins?"

Kwarq's eyebrows flinch in confirmation. His brother, who's been watching our exchange with an amused smile, crouches down and leans across the inside of the craft.

"I am sorry, my *sa'aih*," he says to me in softly accented English. His voice sounds just as delicate and breathy as Kwarq's. "I did not mean to frighten you."

I'm still curled up in the seat, but he manages to maneuver around my knees to take gentle hold of my arm. I sit in stunned silence as he leans in and presses his jaw to my temple. He holds it there briefly, and just like with Kwarq, I can feel his warmth. It instills a sense of calm and safety in me, pushing out the anxiety. He isn't going to hurt me.

"Bati, she does not like to be touched without her permission." Kwarq's gentle instruction comes from outside the pod along with something else in their language, and Bati pulls away hesitantly. He leans toward me and then away again until I realize he wants to apologize, but that would mean he has to touch me again.

"It's okay. I'm sorry I screamed. I didn't know what was happening. I'm so nervous. This is all new to me. I'm scared."

I want to cry. It hits me hard and quick, and before I know it, a sob bursts from my throat. My vision blurs, but not before I see Bati reach for me before pulling away, looking nervously to Kwarq for guidance.

"Amina has conceived tonight," I hear Kwarq inform his brother around my sobs. "The hormones are settling heavily on her. She has already had the initial sickness. I will see to her. Can you send mother and father home? We will not be here for long."

I roll my tight, swollen eyes at Kwarq's insistence on telling everyone with ears that I'm pregnant. Bati's face brightens at Kwarq's initial announcement, but then he sobers, glancing over at me.

"She will not stay for the birth?"

Kwarq shifts uncomfortably, leaving a heavy silence before he responds.

"It was an unintentional conception. I was not as careful as I should have been. I have brought her here to terminate, then I will see her back home."

Again there is a pause. Kwarq leans in to whisper to his brother who nods solemnly and looks back in at me.

"I apologize again for scaring you, my *sa'aih*—Amina." The slight bow of his head is respectful. "It has been good to meet you. I will leave now."

He walks off. His footsteps clang along the short metal landing that extends from the pod down to the ground. I still haven't looked around, but I let my eyes float over the outside of the pod now, and I'm surprised to see that we're parked at the curb of a large, open terminal in some kind of transport center.

In front of our pod is a stopped craft. Two Lyqa males, both tall and graceful, embrace on the curb beside it before one rushes inside of the terminal. Several Lyqas move to and from the transport center. Overhead, a sleek, reflective bridge arches between two buildings. Everything is so regular. It's difficult to spot something foreign to make the moment real. I almost want to believe that I am not on a strange alien planet. By the look of things, this could be any airport back home.

"Amina, we do not have much time. If you want to stay for a while after the procedure, you can, but we must hurry."

I remember why I'm here. My brain doesn't seem to want to catch up to the last few hours. It's back on the Red Line trying not to step on train guy's toes.

I let Kwarq hand me out of the craft. All manner of Lyqa pass by us, and the first thing I realize is that Kwarq wasn't lying. Everyone is tall. Way taller than me. A few Lyqas look my way, but no one lingers too long on me. Out the corner of my eye, I think I see a short bright pink figure, but before I can get a good look, Kwarq speaks quickly to an attendant, a youngish looking male with long, silky blond hair and honey brown skin, before rushing me out of the terminal.

"You're just going to leave your pod here?"

"It is not my craft. I rented it for the trip. I was returning it. I have secured another reservation for our return, do not worry."

I am worried, but not about that. I'm worried that Kwarq seems different, more distant. He rushes me through the street like we're late for something.

I glance to my right as we beat a path along the sidewalk and see what looks like a large puppy. Its shaggy coat hangs heavily on its body. It shuffles along the road, and as it moves, I see that its legs are thin and boney, the two-toed feet have long sharp claws at the end.

I recoil and skitter to the side, bumping into Kwarq, causing us both to lose our footing for a moment.

"It is just a local animal. They do not hurt anyone. Try not to panic."

The comfort of his tone is undercut by that same sense of urgency. He quickly rights me and hurries me along.

* * *

A few minutes later, we come to a bright blue building. As Kwarq rushes us to the entrance, I arch my neck to check it out. It's made from some kind of opaque glass. Everything about it is round. The floors look like donuts stacked on top of each other. There are a few Lyqas standing outside in long, priest-like robes.

"This is similar to a hospital on Earth. We can have it done here."

I pause even though Kwarq seems anxious to get inside. There's too much happening.

"Wait, I need a minute. Just hold on. I can't think. How do I know it's okay to let them operate on me? What about payment? What if something goes wrong? What if I get some alien disease?"

I'm being really human right now, but I can't help it. I need to feel like I understand what's about to come, and I don't. Kwarq sighs again, and this time, I detect a little bit of impatience when he responds.

"We do not charge for healing here, and even if we did, as your *lehti* and the one who brought you here, I would not expect you to provide any compensation. I will, of course, cover any expenses of your stay. Do not worry about disease. There are very few things here that we cannot cure. But we *must* hurry."

He doesn't just seem hurried, he feels nearly panicked. This feeling propels me forward. Maybe something is wrong, and he just doesn't want to tell me.

KWARQ

I would laugh at the dazed look on Amina's face if I weren't so worried about the change in her scent. The early mixture that signaled her conception has taken on a more distinctive smell. It worries me because that means she is farther along than I thought.

I move us through the building quickly, but Amina keeps pausing to take in this or that thing. A group of physicians walk along side a hovering healing capsule. Inside, the patient is in a calm, sleep-like stasis. Amina cranes her neck and nearly trips over her feet trying to see inside, and I only narrowly stop her from crashing into it.

Healing centers and travel ports are the mostly likely places to see non-Lyqa species, so when we pass a short, gray being with tall pointed ears and a thick, fleshy neck, she gawks, her hands gripping at my shirt in alarm. I gently ease her away, while putting myself between her and the confused Krccɔian.

Amina continues to gape at everything, rushing close to things that seem interesting and then pressing her face into my side when things are too unfamiliar. It takes us several minutes to get to the maternity wing of the healing center. I guide her straight to the desk where a young, Lyqa woman is reviewing something on a holoscreen.

"My *lehti* has mistakenly conceived, and we would like to terminate," I tell her in our language. She looks up with a smile and gestures to the small machine beside her.

"Can the patient put her arm in here so we can assess her, please?"

"Amina—"

I turn, but she's no longer beside me. I spin around. Panic is a cold fist in my chest before my brain kicks in. Nothing will happen to Amina here. Even if she is lost, she is safe. That alleviates my worry, but not my urgency. I must find her. We are almost out of time.

AMINA

I hear it, and it's like hearing English for the first time when you're in a room full of people who don't speak English. It's the moment you're the only Black girl in a new hire session and you spot that one other ethnic person across the room, and you think, *thank god!*

It sounds just like a human. The reedy, lamb-like wail. I step away from the desk where Kwarq is talking to the receptionist and follow it. It's coming from a small bassinet sitting just inside a room a little ways down the hall. I look around to see if someone will stop me, and then I tip toe through the door to find a Lyqa woman resting in a bed.

She has the tired expression of a woman who has just given birth. Her body is limp against a stack of pillows. Her chest rises and falls in deep, exhausted breaths.

She turns when I enter, and I shrink back at being caught creeping into her room. Before I can duck out, she smiles and waves me in.

"Um, hi." I wave. She frowns but nods kindly. Maybe she doesn't speak English. I point to my eyes and then to the bassinet. She smiles and nods again before turning away and letting her eyes drift shut. These people are really trusting. I could be a baby-snatcher for all she knows, but she's all, go ahead, have a look.

I inch a little closer to the cradle, listening to the familiar sound of a fussing infant coming from within.

Unease constricts my chest as the baby comes into view. I can't imagine what I'm going to see, but I brace myself for the worst while at the same time telling myself that it can't be that bad. After all, all babies are cute. Even baby sharks are cute.

Trembling, I finally get close enough to peer over the edge. "Awwww!"

It's just...a baby. My eyes travel from the downy shock of thick hair to its two wrinkly little feet. If it weren't for the strange mix-up of features, I would think this was a human baby. Its little legs pump as it continues to grunt out its displeasure. A small cloth diaper is tucked beneath its belly to allow room for the remaining umbilical cord still attached to the navel. It's all so normal that I'm overcome with relief. Until this moment, I imagined the thing inside of me to be just that, a thing.

"Look at you. You're such a cutie." I cluck my tongue and make kissy faces as I regard the small, wiggling being.

There are a few differences. For instance, this kid is big. It has the chalky, wrinkly skin of a newborn, but it's probably the size of a four or five month old human baby. The round little face is scrunched up in anger, and I lean down to coo at him, hoping to soothe him a bit. When I look up, his mother is watching at me with a curious smirk. She says something in her language.

"Uh—"

"Nah'ah lehti, qa'ahni tahl qih'an."

Kwarq's deep melodic voice sounds out behind me, and I turn to see him looking down affectionately at me.

"She asked if you were trying to talk to him," he explains with an amused smile. "I told her this is how one comforts babies in your culture."

"Oh." This kid is kicking up a fuss, but his mother doesn't seem to be in a rush to address it. "Is she just going to let him cry?"

Kwarq shrugs.

"She can sense what is wrong. They have *lehti'an*, the bond between mother and child. He is fine. Just testing his new state."

"Oh." The bond between mother and child.

I look back down at the baby boy, who has quieted. He's a soft, sable brown, even though his mother is the palest Lyqa I have seen so far. His jet black hair is straight and plentiful. He looks like a little wookie. When his eyes open and fall on me,

I notice that they are bright and—yellow. They shimmer in the dim illumination of the room, and I can't help but wonder if that's what Kwarq and my child's eyes would look like.

"*Lehti* we are almost out of time."

I ease away, but take one last lingering look at the little boy before waving to the mother, who regards me with a mixture of curiosity and amusement. She nods back.

Kwarq leads me back to the reception desk. The woman working the station smiles and gestures to a machine situated to the right of the desk. It looks like the blood pressure machines at the pharmacy I used to play on as a kid when my mother was grocery shopping.

"You must put your hand in, Amina." Kwarq's voice is gentle and patient.

I do as he instructs and let my forearm rest in the tube. A bright green light shines over my skin, and I think about the shining little eyes of the baby down the hall. How his tiny fisted hands pushed into the air. How his mother rested easy knowing, instinctively, he was okay.

They have the bond between mother and child. I know by now that Kwarq does not speak in metaphor, which means this bond he speaks of is a real thing. I wonder what it's like. My connection to Kwarq is unreal, and all it does is make our hearts beat together. I can't imagine what it would be like to be connected on such an profound level with someone I've carried in my body. I'm human. Would I even have the bond? This *lehti'an*.

"Kwarq, if I don't do this, what will happen?"

I think I see a glimmer of hope on Kwarq's face before it's gone just as fleetingly. He takes my hand and pulls it to his chest where he holds it like it's his most prized possession. His grip is tender and almost reverent.

"I will care for you until you give birth, and I will love and care for you and our child after."

It's said so easily. Like this is the most natural thing in the world. Like three hours ago we weren't strangers on a train, and a week before that we weren't strangers in a movie theater. And yet, I believe him, and regardless of how strange and sudden it is, I want this too, just like I wanted him to make love to me a few hours ago. There's something in my spirit that calls to this Lyqa man, and I can fight it, or I can let someone take care of me for a change. I'm still apprehensive, but I believe Kwarq when he says he'll make sure I'm okay.

"Do you still want to do it?"

Kwarq's whispered question breaks through my thoughts. He wants this, too. He will support any decision I make, but he wants it. I shake my head.

"I want to keep it."

Kwarq's sensual, full mouth breaks into a wide, toothy smile. He brings my hand from his chest to his lips and kisses the back before turning to the woman behind the desk. He excitedly rambles off something in his language. I can almost feel the pride coming off of him. The receptionist turns to disappear through a door directly behind her. She returns, carrying a large, covered basket which she passes off to Kwarq before holding her open palm out to me.

"She needs to see your wristband," Kwarq supplies when I look questioningly at him.

I hold my arm out, and she runs a short wand over the band before tapping something into the keypad on the desk. Her head jerks in a short nod then she looks up from the screen to me.

"Congratulations."

"O-Oh," I stumble, surprised to hear the breathy English word come from her mouth. "Thank you."

Kwarq executes his own abrupt head nod and says what I am assuming is an appropriate response. He lightly grasps the woman's arm then leads me away with a possessive hand at my back.

"How does she know English?" Kwarq pulls me against his side and maneuvers me back to the entrance.

"She is a public servant. She is equipped with a learning implant that allows her to adapt to the language of anyone she may need to assist."

"Wow."

That's pretty cool. A learning implant sounds kind of badass.

"Can I get one of those? Is it expensive?"

Kwarq's mouth twitches in amusement as he glances down to me.

"You do not have to worry about expenses, my *lehti*. I have said I will take care of you. The implant is somewhat invasive, I would not recommend it right now, but if you would like to receive a device that will help you with translation, I can arrange it."

"But is it expensive? If it's some crazy luxury, never mind."

He rolls his eyes. It always looks funny when he does it. Unlike my causal flicker of eye lid, Kwarq's imitation of my gesture is precise and slow. He's such an alien.

"It is not a luxury. In fact, I can fit you with one myself later."

"Is this where you tell me that you're a linguist/doula/implant specialist?"

Kwarq's deep, rumbling chuckle vibrates through my body where we touch.

"No, this is when I tell you I am a linguist, which means I deal with languages. You want a language translator. I believe that falls in my realm of expertise."

I keep forgetting that Kwarq is a real person. He has a profession. He's kind of legit.

"Oh, right. Well, if it's not too much trouble."

"It is not."

We fall quiet until we're outside the healing center. We loiter a few feet from the doors, and I turn to him, needing to clarify my earlier misgivings.

"It's not that I didn't want this baby. I just wasn't sure if I was ready. I was scared. I still am," I admit. He listens patiently. "Three hours ago, we were sitting in a coffee shop, and now you're telling me that I'm pregnant, and I just can't wrap my brain around it. But if this is really happening, if I'm really going to have a baby, I want to try. I mean, I want us to try and figure out how it will work. *If* it can work. You're an alien, for goodness sake." I cover my face with my hands and groan. "I'm sorry I keep saying that. I don't know what I'm thinking or feeling right now."

Even though he told me not to be ashamed of my initial decision to terminate—and I really wasn't, just terrified and confused—I know that it wasn't what he wanted. I didn't miss the pleasure on his face after he smelled my conception. He was like a kid on Christmas.

"Thank you for being here for me in all of this. You could have left me back home to deal with it myself. I know this is your whole culture and what makes sense to you, but it has to be hard for you, too. I'm not Lyqa. That has to be a little strange."

"It is not strange," he replies without hesitation, and the sincerity of it sends a spiral of warmth through my body. "From the moment I saw you, you made complete sense to me. I will never question you, my *lehti*." He lifts my hand and places it on his chest where I feel the strong thud of his first heart. "I will never question this. You are my reason for living. Your happiness is more important to me than anything. Even having offspring."

His words trigger the prickle of tears in my eyes. I'm feeling something dangerously close to love. It seems unreal that in the space of one day, I have found a man who is solely committed to my happiness and have literally started a life with him. It's almost too good to be true. Optimism makes me want to go all in on this, but a lifetime of cynicism has taught me that it's best to walk into these situations with my guard up.

We stand quietly for a few more minutes. My hand is still pressed to Kwarq's chest as he stares at me like I hang the moon. It gets awkward and I ease my hand away, missing the contact almost immediately. When I tentatively hold my hand out to him, he takes it.

"So what do we do now? Do you still have to take me home right away?"

He shakes his head.

"You have been permitted the equivalent of four Earth months here."

"Ooh, I have a Lyqa visa. I bet no one else on Earth can say that."

"With the option for residency should you desire it."

He says this last part carefully. I nod but put that little tidbit aside for another day. I can't think about leaving Earth to reside on another planet right now. One thing at a time.

"You can, of course, go home whenever you want in that time," he adds quickly.

"Okay. So what about now? Do you guys have hotels on this planet? Or do you have an apartment here where we can stay? How does this work?"

For the first time since we've been here, Kwarq smiles a real smile. It's big and boyish.

"I do not have an apartment. In my culture, we live in extended dwellings with our immediate family."

"So what does that mean?"

His smile get's wider.

"I am taking you home."

CHAPTER 12

KWARQ

Amina has made me happier than I ever thought I could be. It would have been enough just to have her, but now she has decided to gift me with not only her partnership, but with our children.

I keep to myself the fact that by the time we made it back to the reception desk, it was already too late to perform the procedure within the optimal range of safety. I was prepared to petition for an exception. Anything for her until she was ready.

I'm glad I didn't have to, and it's what she wants. Watching her with the infant in the healing center warmed my heart to a point where it had been nearly impossible not to toss her over my shoulder and take her some place where I could convince her to give this a chance. However, it is never my intention to force my *lehti*. I would only have wanted her to come to this decision if it is what she truly wanted.

I now get to take her to my home. I get to introduce her to my family as my *lehti* and introduce her to the culture that our children will share.

Amina's scent has changed. The swirling mix that signaled her conception has taken on two distinct smells. This is only a mild surprise. Among my kind, twins almost always produce twins. My father is a twin. His twin, my uncle, has twins, my cousins. I'm overjoyed at this realization, but I will wait to tell Amina. She has had enough surprises for the day.

"Where is your home?"

Her small, warm hand grips mine tightly as we walk

through the nearly empty streets. It's considerably late at night. Lyqa days are longer than Earth's, but most of my people have retired to their homes by now. I'm curious to see how my people will respond to Amina. Not many humans have been to our planet, but we are an accepting people. I suspect my kinsfolk will be curious about her, but she is in no danger from anyone here.

"It is a short walk. Perhaps about twenty Earth minutes. Is that okay? We can take a transport if you like."

Humans don't walk as much as Lyqa. Amina doesn't know it yet, but her body will begin to feel the effects of her pregnancy soon. She will be more tired than usual. Perhaps she is already feeling exhausted.

"It's okay, we can walk. Honestly, I've been kind of scared to look around. I keep feeling like something crazy is going to happen. Like something is going to try to get me."

I laugh. She's so cute. I love that even when she may appear ridiculous, she is honest.

"Nothing crazy will happen to you while I am here. Nothing will get you. We are the dominant species on this planet, as you are on yours. However, my people are warm and kind. We are very in tune to the feelings of others. While we are not perfect, we try not to intentionally hurt one another. It would hurt us more to do so."

She looks at me sideways, her expression disbelieving.

"I don't know if the guy on the train back home would believe that."

Her reminder does not inspire even the least bit of shame in me. "He was trying to harm you. As I have said, my people are kind but not stupid. We do not tolerate the abuse of others, and *I* will never tolerate anyone attempting to harm you."

When her small hand squeezes around mine, I look down to see her smiling up at me, though her expression is tinged with the sadness I have come to expect.

"Thank you for protecting me. No one has ever done anything like that before."

This pains me. She is so convinced of her vulnerability.

"You do not ever have to doubt your safety. I love you. I will not let anything happen to you."

She nods and then clears her throat.

"About that. Can you, maybe, stop saying that?"

I'm puzzled. She looks embarrassed again. That little bit of red colors her dark skin.

"Saying what?"

"That you love me."

I stop. She halts, too, and I turn to face her, but she won't look at me. Her eyes are on her feet. She shuffles back and forth.

"Why do you ask that I not declare my love for you? Is this something that is not done among humans?"

"No, it's not that. It just makes me uncomfortable."

She can't see my confusion because she's looking everywhere but at me.

"Amina, look at me, please. Why does it make you uncomfortable to know that I love you?"

Sighing, she finally meets my eyes. I see the discomfort she speaks of. It is a thick scent coming off of her.

"I just don't like it when people throw around those kinds of words. It was sweet before. I thought you were just being hyperbolic. And I get that I've made your heart beat and now you think you have to be with me. You've been great, I would even say you really care about me, but it's a little hard to believe that you suddenly have this great love for me."

"Why is it hard to believe?"

"Because you don't know me!" Her voice rises in frustration, and I try to focus on her energy to better understand this reaction. Beneath her discomfort, there is cynicism and fear. The same emotions I detect when I tell her she is beautiful.

"Why do you think I must know you to love you?"

"I mean, I don't know. How can you love someone without knowing who they are? What if I'm a horrible person? What if my insides are rotten? What if I just suck as a human being?"

These are all ridiculous notions. I don't try to hide what I think of her suppositions from my expression.

"I have been inside of you. I would have noticed if it was rotten in there."

She sighs heavily, and her shoulders drop.

"I'm serious, Kwarq."

"I am as well. I have been *inside* of you. I felt you with every part of me. Our hearts beat together. You have welcomed me into the most sensitive parts of your body. I have witnessed your pleasure and been the recipient of your passion. You are not rotten. You are not a horrible person, though I suspect that many people have been horrible to you. Furthermore, you do not suck in any way that is undesirable."

She rolls her eyes at my teasing, but her expression softens.

"However, if it makes you more comfortable, I will refrain from speaking of my love for you until you feel I have earned the privilege."

"Kwarq, it's not that, it's just—ugh!" she lifts her free hand and buries her face in the crook of her elbow. I have come to realize that when my *lehti* is angry or unsure, her first instinct is to shield herself. It makes me think she is used to being attacked, and I don't like that. She never has to censor herself with me.

"Do not worry, my *lehti*. You have not offended me. These things take time. I promise I am not bothered by your request."

This is not completely true. I'm bothered at whatever has happened to bring her to this place of being wary of accepting love from me. But I am also patient. I waited two months for the opportunity to speak with her back on Earth. I can wait for her to have faith in my love.

AMINA

I'm such a weirdo. I should probably be thrilled that someone has declared their love for me, goodness knows men weren't clambering to do more than waste my time back on Earth, but I can't give in so easily. I'm not setting myself up to be a sucker. I've been a sucker before. I've probably been a sucker more than most because deep down I really believe in this shit.

I want a family. I want a man who loves me. But I can't lay up with the first alien that comes my way. If Kwarq's first heart, or whatever, had not bound him to me, would he really have given me a second glance on his little visit to Earth? Probably not. I can't be all dreamy and tell myself that's not the case. I have to be smart about this even if I just want to climb into his arms and let him love me like he wants to.

I shake these thoughts out of my head and focus on the new world around me.

Along the sidewalk where we stroll, several different peeps and chirps echo from the bushes beside us. Some sound familiar, like crickets and cicadas, others are so otherwordly that I get the shivers just hearing them and step a little closer to Kwarq to be safe.

Kwarq leads me through the paved streets with an easy familiarity. The houses are similar to adobe houses back on Earth. They're square and at least two or three stories tall and built into the foliage that seems to sprout from everywhere.

Many have several wings and take up large parts of the long blocks we walk. Everything is so familiar, and yet I'm very aware that I'm in a foreign place.

The smells are unlike anything I have ever experienced. They're more complex. Things are spicy and pungent and sweet. My head is lighter, and I have to wonder if I'm taking in more oxygen.

It's quiet. Like deathly quiet. Aside from the creatures in the bushes, which are loud, there are no traffic or other sounds. The chaos of the travel port is gone. It's eery and comforting at the same time.

"We are here."

We stop in front of one of the adobe houses. It's one of the larger ones we've passed. The structure extends up three stories. A set of stone steps leads from the sidewalk to the front of the home where a deep porch wraps around the side. Several patios extend from the front. It actually looks pretty fancy.

"It's beautiful," I whisper. Speaking any louder feels wrong.

"Thank you. For the next four months, it will also be your home."

Kwarq moves to take the steps leading up to the large, ornate wooden door, and I pull on our joined hands to stop him. He pauses, his foot midair, and looks back at me.

"Is everything okay, *lehti*?"

He sounds so patient, so ready to please me. I want to do this for him. I can do this. He's with me. I'm safe. Nothing's going to happen. Strangely enough, I'm a little apprehensive that his parents are going to take one look at me and give Kwarq the "what are you thinking" look.

"No, I'm okay. Just nervous," I explain and try to give him my best smile.

"If you are uncomfortable—"

"No, I'm fine, really. I want to meet them. I always get nervous when I meet someone's folks. Plus, you know, I'm not even from this planet. I usually only have one worry when I date a guy outside of my race. Now, I gotta worry about being human, too."

Kwarq frowns and steps back down in front of me. When I don't meet his gaze, he nudges beneath my chin with his hand until I do.

"You are worried your being human will upset my parents?"

"That and other things."

"Like what?"

"Uh, being Black."

Kwarq's scowl deepens as he tilts his head to the side. "You think my parents will be surprised that I am *leht* to a woman who looks like you?"

The intensity of his stare makes me dart my eyes around before settling back on him. He waits patiently for my response. This is such a weird conversation. Nothing is ever as easy as Kwarq makes it seem. Back home, these situations can be a fucking minefield. Some folks are cool, but you get the wrong family, and you're being asked not to drink out of the good cups.

"I don't know. I just don't want to put myself in an awkward position, and I don't want to freak your parents out. It's happened before, trust me."

"You believe my parents will freak out because you are Black?"

"Maybe."

He leans down close to my face. I don't know if he's about to kiss me or what. His eyes flicker. The yellow is a warm glow. Having him this close throws my senses for a loop. His fresh, spicy smell swirls around me. His minty breath is intoxicating.

"Amina…"

"Yes." I can barely speak. My entire body suddenly feels very warm. I really wish he would kiss me.

"Have you seen my brother?"

I burst out laughing. My cackle echoes in the quiet of the block. Once I start, I find I can't stop. I bend over, holding my stomach as I try to get myself under control. When I lift up, Kwarq's smiling down at me through the tears that fill my eyes. I wipe at my face as my cackles subside.

"We shall have to make her do that more often, brother. She has a beautiful laugh."

"Oh shit."

I quiet. Behind Kwarq is a very tall, very handsome male. He's at least half a foot taller than Kwarq. His skin is a deep, reddish brown. Almost more red than brown. He looks like Kwarq and Bati, although his features are more blunt than their sharper ones. His nose is flatter, with slightly flared nostrils. He has the same sharp cheekbones, and slightly droopy, yellow eyes. His hair is the darkest black I have ever seen and hangs long and curling about his shoulders. He shares the twins' strong jawline, and the slight chin indentation that I've noticed through Kwarq's short beard and on Bati's bare face. Also like his brothers, the man's smile is wide and toothy.

Kwarq turns to his brother, and they take hold of each other's arms, leaning in to press their temples together.

"We missed you, baby brother," the man says after releasing him. He turns to me and nods.

"If I have your permission, I would like to greet you, my *sa'aih*. It would require me to touch you."

I groan inside. Bati has clearly spread the misconception that I am completely opposed to physical contact. Great. Now their first impression of me is that I'm some contact-phobe who doesn't want babies.

"Of course," I say as I shoot Kwarq a nervous look. He smiles reassuringly.

I stand still as his brother steps forward and takes hold of my waist. It's an oddly intimate touch, even though it doesn't feel creepy or even sexual. Still, having such a good-looking man put his hands on me in this way has an effect. A tingle runs through me.

He reaches beneath my hair and cradles my neck, pulling me close to him. I'm stiff so I fall forward and catch myself by taking hold of his waist. His jaw presses against the side of my head and his cheek rests against my hair. We stay this way for a moment, and gradually I relax. It's a sweet embrace. Even if it is causing some embarrassing things to happen in my lady parts.

He eases away but keeps his hold on me. I smile, but it's wobbly and nervous.

"I am Ah'dan. This one and Bati's elder brother." He nods his head back at Kwarq.

"Amina," I croak out and then clear my throat. "It's nice to meet you."

"And you, my *sa'aih*. Did your procedure go well?"

I get warm with embarrassment and shift out of his grip. He lets me go, but frowns in confusion. Kwarq frowns, also, and steps around his brother to my side, placing a hand at my back.

"I asked Bati not to mention it."

Ah'dan's eyes stay on me as he answers.

"He only told me. He said nothing to our parents. Although," he leans his head down to catch my gaze, "it is nothing to be ashamed of. These things happen. What matters is that you are happy and safe."

"Yeah, thanks," I mumble. I swear, I never thought I would find myself in the position where I was experiencing too much consideration.

"Besides now that I am close enough to scent you, I see that you decided to carry after all." He looks to Kwarq, who's still holding the basket the receptionist at the healing center gave him. He says something in Lyqa, his smile growing wider. Kwarq's eyes flick to me, but he only nods tersely and mumbles something in return. Ah'dan doesn't reply, but when he turns back to me, his expression is mischievous.

"Well, congratulations and congratulations," he says and turns back to the house. "Come you two. Mother and father are waiting up to greet their new *dahnai*."

Kwarq takes my arm and we follow Ah'dan up the steps. They're almost too tall for my short, human legs, and by the time I reach the top, I'm winded.

"What's a *dahnai*?" I huff out as we follow Ah'dan through the tall door.

Kwarq takes my hand again and raises it to his lips to kiss the back.

"Daughter."

CHAPTER 13

KWARQ

Amina's hand quivers as we step through the door. I hold her firmly to reassure her of my earlier promise that there is nothing surprising waiting for her here. She steps close, but does not hide behind me. She's being brave. Pride swells in my chest. She always impresses me, my *lehti*.

My parents stand in the entry way. Normally, they would rush to greet me, but now that I know Bati made Amina's discomfort with unannounced contact known, I believe this is only for her benefit.

Amina's sigh as her eyes fall on my parents is audible. She was no doubt expecting two beings with tentacles or acid spitting fangs. Instead, my non-tentacled, non-acid fanged parents stand with patient smiles across from us.

"*Dahni.*" My mother steps forward. I release Amina's hand and meet her half way, sure to stay in front of my *lehti* as I sink to my knees and lift the hem of my mothers dress to kiss it. She places her hand on my head, holding it there as we experience the *lehti'an*. After a moment, she steps away, and I rise to my feet.

"Kwarq, you have returned home, finally. I thought perhaps you meant never to come back."

My father says this in our tongue and moves in front of me to clasp me behind the head and bring his temple to mine. Through his touch, I feel his worry as well as his curiosity. In fact, the entire room is awash with curiosity. It radiates from everyone, including Ah'dan, who is never curious about anything.

My parents look to Amina, who's standing awkwardly behind me. I move back to her side.

"Amina, it is good to meet you, my *dahnai*. Please feel welcome in our home." My mother looks as if she would like to move forward to greet Amina properly, but she holds herself back, clasping her hands in front of her. My father inclines his head, politely.

"*Dahnai*, I am Quth, and this is my *lehti* and partner Mahdi. We are so very happy that you and our son have found each other."

He also steps forward, but I raise my hand, respectfully, halting his progress.

"Father, Amina does not like—"

"Oh for goodness' sake, Kwarq, you're making me seem so damn rude!"

Amina pushes past me and walks up to my mother. Standing on her toes to compensate for the height difference, she wraps her arms around my mother and pulls her into a hug.

"It's really nice to meet you, and I just want to say that I don't mind if people touch me. I just mind if men touch me without my permission. They tend to take liberties."

My mother's tinkling laugh fills the entryway as she squeezes Amina back. She inhales over Amina's shoulder, and her eyes spring open to meet mine. She has caught the scent of our young. She looks at me questioningly, and I shake my head in a subtle request that she not mention it.

Mother releases her, and her eyes are wet. She is a feeler more than most. I should have known the news of our conception would touch her the deepest.

My mother steps out of the way, and my father hesitates. Amina saves him from figuring out what to do by wrapping her arms about his waist in an equally affectionate hug. He looks down at her head and then back at me. His smile is wistful. I know he, too, can sense her pregnancy. He chuckles and squeezes her back.

Amina steps away from my father and plants her hands on her hips. Her shoulders lift and drop heavily as a loud, shaky breath erupts from her mouth.

"Woo, now that's out of way, let me just say, I am so glad you guys didn't try to eat me."

AMINA

Kwarq's mother is beautiful. I see now where Bati gets his looks from, and I see why Kwarq thought my nervousness about meeting his folks was misplaced.

We're sitting in their living room. The space is large and open with a fireplace and plush cushions situated around a low communal table. Kwarq's mother has brought me some kind of fruit drink. I take a sip. It tastes like red Kool-Aid.

Mahdi's holding Ah'dan's head in her lap, gently stroking his hair back from his face. Ah'dan, however, is staring at me. His drowsy eyes linger on my face. It's a little awkward, but with the constant physical contact the people of this planet engage in, staring must not be a big deal. Still, I avoid his gaze and study his mother. She's asking Kwarq questions about his time on Earth.

Like Bati, her skin is a rich black, but it's tinged with the reddish undertones of Ah'dan's skin. Her hair is an almost ashen blonde, like Kwarq's, and like his, it's thick, but curls about her head wildly.

I let my eyes stray to his equally handsome father. Bati joined us shortly after I met Kwarq's parents, and I came to the conclusion that his whole damn family is just really really good looking. His dad is basically an older Kwarq with Ah'dan's hair. His is also a very dark black and straight. It hangs around his ears and forehead boy-bandishly, lending a charming, playful quality to him.

In turn, my eyes move from Quth, back to his beautiful wife, to gorgeous Bati, quickly to Ah'dan, who's still staring, and then to Kwarq, who's lap I'm sitting on. His arms are linked around me protectively. It's so strange to look at them. It's almost like someone took every human phenotype and played pin the feature on the Lyqa. In this context, my lingering sense of being out of place disappears. It suddenly has no place here, and I'm really relieved.

"Lehti."

I blink away from the side of Kwarq's face and glance around the room. Five sets of eyes are glued on me. Kwarq's mother wears a knowing smile, and one glance at Ah'dan lets me know he's still being a creeper. I look at Bati. To my surprise, he winks and grins widely.

"What? I'm sorry. I'm still taking all of this in."

"I was wondering if perhaps you were hungry?" his mother says.

"Your stomach is making noises," Kwarq supplies quietly.

I look down at my middle, and almost on cue, my stomach lets out a loud growl. How many hours have passed since I puked my brains out in Kwarq's apartment on Earth? One? Five? Do I need to account for space travel when determining how long it's been since I've eaten?

"I'm sorry. I haven't had a chance to eat today."

Everyone's eyes immediately shoot to Kwarq, and he shifts uncomfortably beneath me. Even Ah'dan scowls at his brother over my shoulder. His mother sucks her teeth and rambles off a quick bit of Lyqa that I can only assume is a scolding. Kwarq's doing that pulsing blush. An odd desire to protect and defend him overcomes me. I don't like that they're ganging up on my man.

"It's not his fault," I say. "Everything happened so fast, today. I was pretty sick earlier. Don't be too hard on him."

Kwarq's mother smiles at me but her eyes shoot to Kwarq with the silent admonishment only a mother can show.

"They are right, my *lehti*, I should have been more careful with you. I have been remiss."

Remiss. This man and his overindulgent use of the English language. I roll my eyes and turn back to the room. The fact is, I am pretty hungry. If anyone wants to feed me, I'm down. As long as it isn't something weird.

"I could eat," I say, finally responding to his mother's initial question. "Kwarq also hasn't had anything all day."

Again, his mother sucks her teeth and rises from the cushion, letting Ah'dan's head fall without ceremony. He shoots her a glance and huffs, but she ignores him.

I wait for his mother to bring us food, and I can't help but feel apprehension. I'm a brave eater. I don't shy away from much, but this is another planet. There haven't been too many crazy surprises since I've been here, but am I really ready for Lyqa cuisine? I mean, really?

"Do not worry, it will not be anything with tentacles or fangs."

Kwarq's voice is an amused murmur in my ear. He wasn't kidding about the super hearing because Bati hoots and Ah'dan snorts. Even his father smiles. I guess I can rule out any ideas of privacy during our stay.

"Tentacles I can do. Octopus is delicious. Anything weirder than that, and I can't make any promises."

Ah'dan snorts again. Kwarq smiles and nuzzles my neck.

"It will be neither of those things. Lyqas do not eat flesh."

"You're vegetarians?"

"More like vegans. There is no part of the animal that we consume."

I expected them to be chowing down on raw meat. I guess, I really don't have to worry about anyone eating me.

Kwarq's mother returns with a large platter piled high

with various vegetables and several different kinds of fruit. The familiar scent of vinegar reaches my nose. She also carries a small plate piled high with bread. Bread. Thank god.

She sets it in front of us and waves her hand over it.

"Please eat as much as you can."

I hesitate with my hand over the platter. Kwarq reaches around me, picks up one of the veggies and takes a bite. It has the distinct, satisfying crunch of a pickle. Maybe it's the preggo in me, but I suddenly really want a pickle. As if reading my mind, he passes me the remainder of the one in his hand. I take it, bringing it to my nose to sniff discretely. I smell vinegar and spices. Tentatively, I take a bite, more worried that it may be poisonous and I'll drop dead in two seconds flat.

I hold the small bite in my mouth, waiting to see if I feel anything bad. When nothing happens, I start to chew, slowly at first and then more comfortably.

This. Thing. Is. Delicious.

It's like Korean pickled radish and the best artisan dill pickle on planet Earth. I devour the rest of it and grab another, my hunger hitting full blast. Kwarq's hand knocks into mine as I reach for the last one, and I swat it away and snatch it up for myself. Someone chuckles. I stop shoveling food into my mouth. Everyone's watching me.

"Kwarq, let your *lehti* have what she likes. Clearly the babies enjoy it."

I pause with the pickle half-way to my mouth. Kwarq chokes on his mouthful.

Did she say 'babies'?

I can't seem to make my eyes blink. Kwarq rushes to say something in Lyqa and his mother gasps, bringing her hand to her mouth as if to take the words back, but I know what I heard. I turn slowly to look at him, and he looks sheepishly back.

"Please don't tell me that I'm having some kind of Lyqa litter."

My voice is a tight, low whisper that I know everyone can still hear. I don't really care. I'd rather not offend anyone, but apparently I would have to mime in order for that not to happen.

Kwarq executes his customary slow, exaggerated eye roll.

"No, my *lehti*, you are not having some kind of Lyqa litter. I keep trying to tell you. We are not dogs or squids. It is not—"

"Like the movies, I know, but your mother did just say babies."

"She did."

I wait for him to elaborate, and when he doesn't, I prompt, "And?"

"You are having twins. It was highly probable. For my kind, twins will almost always have twins."

I remember something and turn to look at Ah'dan. I'm not exactly sure I like him. Even if he is kind of adorable.

"Thank you and thank you," I say dryly. He doesn't respond, but smiles like he actually gets my sarcasm.

Everyone is still watching me, particularly Kwarq, and I feel like he's waiting for me to flip out or something. I probably should, but at this point, nothing is really a surprise. Meet an alien at the movies? Sure. Have amazing sex? Why not. Get knocked up and taken to an alien planet? What's so crazy about that. Find out you're pregnant with twins? Of course. Even if I wanted to freak out, I'm too tired to even attempt it. Instead of answering, I open my mouth and yawn really long and loud. It's kind of rude, but I'm taking some liberties. This day has been stressful.

"*Dahnai*, you must be exhausted. It is well past the evening hour. How about we all go to sleep?"

Kwarq's mother is doing the mother thing, and I let her. She helps me to my feet. I wobble and Kwarq steadies me.

"Thank you for welcoming me," I say to her. Mahdi hugs me before one by one, Kwarq's brothers and father give me a round of quick embraces. Ah'dan repeats his earlier embrace, and I glare at him when he steps away. He only laughs and ruffles my hair, which I don't think anyone has actually ever done to me before. It's kind of endearing. Maybe I do like him a little.

I'm too sleepy to look around as I follow Kwarq through the long, cool hallways of their house. We reach a tall, heavy door, similar to the one that leads outside. Kwarq pushes it open and guides me in inside.

"This is my apartment," he says quietly, even though it doesn't seem like anyone else is here. "We will live here until you are ready to go home."

I nod. Kwarq takes my hand and pulls me through a smaller living room and to a bedroom off to the side.

"Yes, a bed!" I gasp out when my eyes fall on the huge, platform bed in the middle of the room. Kwarq lets out an exasperated sigh behind me.

"Amina, of course we have beds."

I turn back and give him the side eye.

"What do you mean of course you have beds?"

"*Lehti,* my people can travel across galaxies. Did you really think we slept in the dirt like animals?"

I turn back to the bed and snort. "I thought we were all animals? Plus, how would I know? You were sleeping on the floor with a sheet."

The corner of his mouth turns up, and my overwhelming sense of sleepiness disappears. Suddenly, I'm hot. My inner thighs clench as I take him in. The light fabric of his shirt whispers over his muscles. They bunch and ripple with every of his slight movements.

My eyes slide lower. Behind his thin drawstring pants, I can see the thick bulge of his dick. Even flaccid, he's impressive. I gulp as I'm overcome with the desire to feel him inside of me again. To feel the delicious ache of us coming together.

CHAPTER 14

KWARQ

I stand by the door to my bedroom and watch as Amina pulls down her jeans, leaving her in a fitted t-shirt and panties. She stretches her arms over her head, and from the side, I can just see the slight bulge of her new belly. Our babies are in there.

And Amina is here. In my home. In my bedroom, about to crawl into my bed. Any nervousness she was feeling appears to be gone. I'm still amazed she didn't react when she learned she's carrying twins. I'd expected shock and perhaps anger that I kept it from her, but I guess in the context of the day's events, it is not as startling.

Amina makes her way to the tall edge of my bed and pauses to consider it. She lifts her leg then drops it before planting her hands on the side as she tries to figure out how she will comfortably navigate it. She's so small. Even taking the steps was tiring for her. I move away from the door and go to her, taking her by the waist. I lift her, again surprised at how slight she is, and toss her onto the bed.

"Mm," she mewls as she wiggles her body. "This is a really comfortable bed."

"I'm glad." My voice is strangled. Amina lays on her back with her legs open. My eyes fix to the impression of her pussy behind her thin scrap of panty. My cock twitches just as my first heart begins to speed up.

"Do you know what would make it even more comfortable?" she purrs, and I want to groan.

"What?" I'm ready to give her whatever she needs.

"You in it with me."

She's being flirtatious, and my body responds immediately. This is an unexpected contrast to her previously anxious state. I scent the air and detect heightened pheromone levels. She's very aroused.

"I would tell you that how you are feeling is a result of your pregnancy. The babies are making you—happy. This may not reflect how you truly feel."

She sits up and rolls her eyes in the way that she does, and I find myself doing more and more.

"Kwarq, I'm still a mess, don't worry. I haven't forgotten that I'm knocked up on an alien planet with your insanely beautiful parents and hot brothers, and your fine, charming ass. I'm just trying to make the best of an unexpected situation."

"Okay." As long as she isn't afraid, I will accept it. Her eyes shift to the side before training back on me.

"So, I think I've forgotten something, and I might need you to remind me."

My confusion is accompanied by a frown.

"Remind you of what?"

"Of why your tongue is so long."

A slow smile spreads over my face just as a distant but distinct hoot of laughter sounds out somewhere else in the house. I am really going to strangle Ah'dan. Amina's eyes widen before she falls back on the bed, covering her face.

"Are you serious? How the hell did he hear that?" She rolls to her side, closing her legs and groaning. "Ugh, never mind."

"I must apologize for my brother. He is an ass." I feel the loss the moment she closes her legs, shielding her pussy from me. "It does not mean that we cannot have sex."

Amina looks up at me from beneath her hands with a look of horror.

"Kwarq, I'm not going to do you in this house where

everyone has fucking spidey hearing. I think we've established that I am not exactly quiet."

She's whispering. Her voice is low and harsh. I fight a smile and resist the urge to explain just how the Lyqa aural system works. Her attempt at being quiet is actually more likely to be heard.

"My brothers should not be listening," I say slightly louder than necessary, and hear the faint snorts in response from elsewhere in the house. "I think that unless they wish to embarrass you, they will mind their business."

A sly smile spreads across Amina's face. Even she knows after this short time that intentional injury in any form to another being is a grave Lyqa offense.

"That's right, babe, you shame them."

"I will shame anyone who tries to keep me from you." I kneel at the bed and take gentle hold of her ankles to pull her to the edge. She squeals, and the scent of her arousal grows more intense.

"Are you sure it's okay?" Her knees press together.

"It is okay, but I will only do it if you want me to." I reach one of my hands between her spread feet and run my fingers lightly over her pussy. "Although, I must admit that I want you very badly, my *lehti*. I also think you need this."

She shivers, a slow moan escaping her mouth as she throws her head back. I continue to stroke over her panties. The fabric becomes more and more soaked with her wetness.

"Kwarq, it's too much, do something."

"I will help you, my *lehti*, and you can be as loud as you want."

I remove my hand from between her legs. She lifts her hips for me, so I can slide her panties off.

The smell of her hits me hard, and I groan as it overwhelms my senses. I part her knees until they lay flush to the mattress. The light of the room is dim, and her pussy glistens in the soft glow. I slide my hands beneath her bottom, lifting her to my face. Her legs shake, and her breath huffs out in anticipation as she waits for me to pleasure her. My cock rises to its full length, wedging against the mattress.

My first lick is slow and precise. I run the full length of my tongue through her slit, curling it under when I get to her clitoris.

"Ah!" Amina lurches off the bed. Her startled cry is loud and sharp in the room.

I lick her again. I wiggle my tongue along the inside of one of her pussy lips. Amina twitches, her moans muffled in her attempt to remain quiet. I treat the other side to the same attention before I press my face close, trying to get as much of her as I can.

"You taste so good, Amina. So pure. So delicious." I continue to lap at her, bathing my face and catching every bit of her arousal.

Amina's entire body shakes, signaling the proximity of her orgasm. I press my tongue into her entrance, and she loses the battle to remain silent and cries out.

"Kwarq, I can't be quiet." Her voice is needy and desperate. I want to give her what she needs.

"Then don't, my *lehti*. Let me hear you. Let me hear how good it feels."

I swirl my tongue inside of her, extending it along her passage in imitation of the thrust of my cock. I run my hand over her clit just as I flick my tongue up along the sensitive underside of her passage.

"Kwarq!" Her back arches off the bed as her orgasm rips through her. She clenches around my tongue, and I continue to lave her inside, drinking her down until she collapses against the bed.

I roll my tongue from inside of her and lean back from the bed. My cock juts out painfully. I release it from my pants, stroking myself to relieve the pressure.

"Fuck you're big, Kwarq," Amina breathes out. She moans and runs her hands down her stomach to cup her pussy. I'm not sure if it's to keep me out or impatience to have me filling that space.

"I am big, *lehti*, but you take me well. You were made for me."

She nods, and I'm happy that she agrees. "Can we have intercourse if I'm pregnant?"

Amina watches me work a firm hand over my cock. Her gaze on me is enough to send me to the edge. The tip of my cock beads with semen. I pause my hand and regard her. Her legs are still splayed. Her curly hair is wild around her head. She's removed her top, and the tight, dark peaks of her breasts beckon me to taste them.

"Are you still sore?"

She shakes her head. "A little. Not really."

"Then, of course, we can have intercourse if you want."

Her lips curve in a playful smile. "Are you sure you won't flood them out?"

I manage a short chuckle. I'm too tense for much more. I want her too badly. I'm just waiting for the moment she says that I can have her.

"I am sure. It is good for the babies for you to receive more of my semen. It will reinforce your womb."

"Seriously?" Her little eyebrow raises suspiciously.

"Seriously."

Amina leans back and opens her arms to me. I rise from the floor and cover her. The initial contact of our bodies sends a surge of energy through my body that nearly has me releasing on the spot. I settle onto her, giving just enough of my weight, and nuzzle my face between her breasts, licking at her warm flesh, running my tongue over the straining tips.

"I need you now," I whisper. I want to take my time, but I

can't. The need to be inside of her is almost painful.

Amina reaches between us, and I lift my hips so she can fit me against her opening. The heat of her body sears the head of my cock as I press forward. She mewls and hisses out a little breath while I continue my slow, steady entry into her warm passage. She's still so tight, her tissue swollen from our earlier joining. I reach between us and stroke over the tight bud of her clitoris, and she softens, gasping out her pleasure. The increased wetness eases my way. I pause when the head of my cock breaches her. My entire body shakes with the effort.

"Are you okay?"

"Yes," she moans out and it's impatient and needy. She wraps her legs around my thighs and presses me forward. I push another few inches into her.

"Kwarq, more. All of it."

She holds her lush bottom lip between her teeth as she tries to lift her hips to take more of me. I lean down and suck the tempting little pillow of flesh from the grip of her teeth into my mouth. At the same moment, I raise my hips and sink all the way to her womb with one, powerful thrust.

"Ah!"

Her cry is part pleasure and part pain, but she grips me tighter as I start to work her in deep, quick strokes. The tight walls of her pussy clench around me. I push beyond her resistance, feeling every drag of my cock through my entire body. My skin vibrates as satisfaction surges through me.

"You're shaking again." Her voice is an awe-filled gasp that whispers hotly against my neck.

"It is you. How deeply you take my cock. How perfectly you feel around me. It is everything. Everything is you."

She mewls softly and pulls me closer. "More."

I comply, angling my hips to hit her sensitive underside and strengthening my thrusts. A slick sheen of sweat forms between our bodies. The slap of my pelvis meeting hers is sharp.

"My *lehti*. I am so close," I murmur next to her ear as another jolt runs through me. My skin is a constant hum. My hips work in furious time to get her to where she needs to be.

Her knees dig into my torso, signaling the approach of her orgasm. She opens herself to me, surrendering to the pummeling of my cock. Her eyes squeeze shut, and her mouth opens on a silent cry that I can still just hear.

"Come for me."

It's a whispered command accompanied by a sharp thrust of my hips. I lower my head and swirl my tongue around one of her nipples before drawing it into my mouth and sucking firmly.

She cries out, moaning my name over and over. Her head thrashes back and forth across the mattress. I don't slow my thrusts until her pussy finally eases its clenching. Only then do I slam my hips down, wedging my cock at her womb, and give her my seed.

When I finally stop pulsing inside of her, I drop my head to the bed and pull in a long, ragged breath. Amina's chest brushes up against mine with each of her answering inhales. She's so still, so quiet that I think she may have fallen asleep. I press a kiss to her temple.

"We were so damn loud." Her voice is sober, the passion having lifted. I raise my head to see her slowly shaking her head back and forth. "So. Damn. Loud."

My answering laughter echoes throughout the house.

AMINA

"I'm not leaving this room."

"*Lehti*, you do not have to be embarrassed. We do not care about these things." Kwarq tries again to lift me from the bed.

I hold fast, grasping the edge for support.

"I am *not* leaving this room. Not today. Not ever."

I have no idea what came over me last night. No, wait, I do. Raging Lyqa pregnancy hormones. Even now, I can feel the tingling edge of desire pulsing through me. A part of me wants to reverse the tension of our joined hands and yank Kwarq down on top of me. I resist the urge. I already can't show my face outside of his apartments again.

"Besides, I probably couldn't walk out of here if I wanted to. You destroyed my pussy."

Kwarq flinches and pulses red. "I am sorry, my *lehti*. I should have let you recover. I should have known that it was too soon."

He's so serious.

"God, dude, I'm kidding. I mean, you did almost fuck me to death, but I'm not complaining. Actually, the ache is kind of nice. It reminds me of where you've been." I wiggle my eyebrows, and his mouth twitches then slowly spreads into a smile.

"I also will be thinking about where I have been for the rest of the day." Almost absentmindedly, he runs a hand over his crotch, and I bite down on my lip to keep from moaning.

"Yeah, well, I'm going to be thinking about it in here because I'm not leaving this room, babe."

He lifts his hands in surrender. "Very well, but will you at least let me bring you some food. You must be hungry."

I am hungry. Actually, I'm starving. The handful of pickles I ate last night have come and gone. I need some real food. I won't admit this to Kwarq though because I feel like his protective instinct would compel him to toss me over his shoulder and carry me out of the room.

"I'll eat," I agree casually, even though the very thought of food has me nearly salivating, "but I'm not—"

"Leaving this room. Not today. Not ever. Yes, my *lehti*, you have said."

Kwarq shakes his head and leaves. The heavy door to his apartments shuts a moment later, and I jump from the bed and toss on the short-sleeved tunic he was wearing last night.

I step out into the living room. It's smaller than the family room in the main wing of the house. But like the other room, large cushions are arranged around a low table in front of a fireplace. The furnishings are minimal, but there are a few decorative items scattered about.

On top of the table is the large basket the Lyqa lady at the healing center gave to us. I heft it into my arms. It's heavy. I settle onto a cushion then lift the thin cloth cover to see what's inside.

"Oh!"

It's a baby basket. On top are a dozen neatly folded cloths. They're made from the same thin, super soft material of Kwarq's clothing, but when I lift one up, it's a tiny tunic with short sleeves and leg cut outs. I lift each one, oohing and ahing, before setting them aside.

Next are cloth diapers. They look just like the ones on Earth, but they feel strange. The fabric is springy and almost spongelike, but they're still whisper soft beneath my fingers.

At the very bottom is a stack of fabric. I lift one and it rolls open to reveal a long, roomy dress. It's beautiful. The hem is embroidered in swirling loops and star bursts. The fabric is similar to jersey, but it's softer, insanely soft. I can only imagine what it feels like against the skin. There's one in white with gold threading. Another is a deep purple with silver embroidery. The last one is royal blue and is so lovely my mouth falls open.

The fabric of this last is slightly heavier than the others. It falls in billowing pleats of fabric from the fitted single strapped bodice. I can't help but wonder what it's for. It seems too fancy for every day.

The dress billows as I hold it up. A warm breeze rushes over me, and I turn to the open patio door behind me. After arranging the items back into the box, I stand and walk out onto the stone balcony.

CHAPTER 15

KWARQ

"What's wrong with our tongues?" Bati opens his mouth to stick out the aforementioned appendage and angles it up in front of his face, causing his eyes to cross. Ah'dan smacks the back of his head, and Bati's teeth chatter down. He winces and pulls his tongue back in.

"Human tongues are shorter, thicker, less agile," I say. "Apparently, on Earth, the only things with tongues like ours are animals. She said it was strange. If you give too much during kissing, it can be uncomfortable."

I sift through the box of my mother's recipes. I want to feed my *lehti*, but I also want her pleased with the food I prepare.

"We are animals." Ah'dan reaches past me to pull out three recipe cards. "Here. She is sure to enjoy these."

I take the cards and scan them. They're my favorite dishes. One is the pickled root she enjoyed last night. The other two are stewed in sweet and spicy sauces. Ah'dan is right. She will enjoy these.

"Yes, but for some reason, humans are offended by acknowledging their place in the animal kingdom. They see themselves as higher than a more basic beast," I return.

"That is strange. How does she pleasure you with a tongue so small?" Bati jumps back in.

"Yes, brother. Please educate us on the abilities of Earth women," Ah'dan smirks. I roll my eyes.

"My *lehti* is perfect, and I assure you, her small tongue is more than capable."

Ah'dan grins wider and shifts closer.

"Did she scream when she saw it?"

"My tongue? She did. It was actually quite funny. She covered her eyes and refused to look at me until I promised not to show her again."

He laughs. "Not your tongue, brother. Your cock."

I shake my head as Bati hoots. As usual, my older brother is being ridiculous.

"If she did scream, it was in pleasure."

"Hm. Still, she's so small," Bati returns. "I have researched human male anatomy. Our cocks are significantly larger. How did you not damage her when you joined?"

I don't know why my brothers are suddenly so curious about human copulation, but I answer truthfully.

"It was—uncomfortable—for her at first. She is small, and —tight." I have to swallow. My cock stiffens at the memory of Amina's body clamping around me last night. I was not exaggerating when I said I would think of it all day. It hasn't been far from my mind, and this conversation with my brothers isn't helping. "But she is able to take me. I would not join with her otherwise. I would never hurt my *lehti*. It is pleasurable for her. She releases every time, several times."

"Well, she sounded pleased enough last night." I turn to Ah'dan, frowning.

"Don't be crude." Surprisingly, my skin begins to vibrate. I don't like the idea of anyone enjoying Amina's pleasure. She is mine.

"It's not crude to acknowledge the pleasure of a woman," Ah'dan returns, unfazed by my annoyance. "You should be proud that you have such a responsive *lehti*. She's lovely. As your brother, I'm pleased that she's pleased."

I grunt in response, but my annoyance recedes. It's hard to be upset when anyone praises Amina.

Bati's head cocks to the side. "She's pleased by something now. I can hear her sounds of joy."

I perk my ears and, indeed, I can hear Amina sighing and laughing at something. The sounds warm my heart. I almost want to go and see what it is that has brought her such joy, but I begin pulling down pots and pans to prepare her meal.

"Amina is not used to being so exposed, brothers. You embarrass her when you listen. You can ignore it, so please do." Lyqa hearing is good, but we do not have to hear everything. We can choose to block some sounds out. My brother's nod, and I, too, close my hearing off, leaving her to her joy, and concentrate on feeding her and our children.

AMINA

The air outside on the balcony is fragrant and moist. The humidity levels are much higher than they were last night, and they are definitely higher than they are on Earth. A thin film of sweat beads out on my upper lip, and my hair lifts around my neck and ears as it absorbs the moisture. I inhale deeply and again I'm hit with how different the smells and sounds are on this planet.

The wall of the patio is tall for me, but it would probably just hit the waist of most of Lyqas. I stand on my tippy-toes to peer over the edge. Just as I do, a large, winged bug flies up from below the patio straight at my head.

"Ah! Ohmygod!" I yelp and duck back behind the stone wall.

The thing that just tried to kill me is a cross between a large wasp and a dragon fly. Oversized double wings flutter from the sides of its bright green triangular head and yellow bulbous body. It darts erratically around the patio, hovering just above my head. I stay low until it flutters off. It's cricket-like chirps get fainter and fainter, letting me know when it's out of range.

Cautiously, I rise up to my full height. I peek over the

ledge, and that's when I realize that the air and ground around me are swarming with all kinds of flying, crawling and hopping creatures. They all seem to move about in a non-threatening way. I watch them closely, curious and also cautious.

Many of the creatures look like some variation of Earth animals, except the colors are brighter and more intense. The textures are also off. Birds appear furry or shaggy. Bugs have feathers. Below, a graceful Lyqa woman walks a scaled animal. It looks like something out of a nightmare, but it yelps happily around the woman's legs.

I follow her down the sidewalk, beneath the house, and I'm surprised when she gets to the front and steps up out of view to the door. A second later, a musical tinkle sounds out from somewhere above me. It's the doorbell.

I wait to see what happens. The bell sounds out again. I go inside to the door of Kwarq's apartments and pause. I should at least make sure someone hears it.

"Yeah, right, Amina. You're just being nosy," I snort under my breath.

Ah'dan heard me and Kwarq from across the house last night. I'm pretty sure everyone can hear the damn doorbell. I really just want to go and see who this woman is.

I look down at myself. I haven't showered yet. My hair is a poofy mess around my head. The insides of my thighs feel sticky, and when I run my tongue over my teeth, they're slimy and filmed over. I'm kind of gross right now. I'm pretty sure I'm a little bit musty. A quick scrub at my eyes dislodges the crusted over residue of sleep.

Still, I'm nosy. And when I say nosy, I mean the curiosity is nearly eating me up. I have to know. I don't care if I look like shit. And when I think about it, Kwarq is taking a really long time with that breakfast. I should probably go and see what's up with that.

I step out of the room and train one of my ears to the hall. The doorbell rings out again, making me jump. When after a few seconds, nothing happens still, I start making my way down the hall, hoping she doesn't leave before I can get to it. Why has no one answered? Did everyone leave? Where's Kwarq?

It takes me some time to find my way to the main house. I was tired and unfocused when Kwarq led me through the house last night. I make a couple of wrong turns before I finally see the front hall. The ornate wooden door is taller and heavier than I remember. I stand in front of it just as the bell sounds again. I can hear the high pitched yelps of the woman's pet on the other side.

"Shit."

I don't really like Earth pets on a good day. I'm not sure I'm ready to have an alien dog jumping all over me.

"Uh, can you leave your pet outside?"

I speak loud enough to hear through the door. If the woman is Lyqa, I'm sure she can hear me. The yelping stops. I wait for some kind of confirmation that I won't open the door only to have some scaled chihuahua gnaw on my leg.

"Kwarq?"

The voice is soft and musical. The pitch is almost child-like in its delicacy.

"Uh, no, I'm his uh—his friend. Hold on."

I turn around helplessly, hoping to see someone coming down the hall to deal with this. The foyer behind me is empty. I look back at the door and listen. I don't hear the animal. In fact, it's almost too quiet. Thinking, she may have left, I risk it and pull on the heavy door latch. It swings open, lighter than it looks. It wasn't even locked.

I only open it a crack. A wet sniff draws my eyes down to the large, wide eyes of her pet. Its tiny slit of a mouth o's as it looks up at me.

"Kwarq?"

My eyes jump from the scaly dog and meet the confused gaze of a Lyqa woman.

Mono-lidded, blue eyes, fringed with thick, dark lashes stare back at me. Her round, tawny face is framed by a mass of long, black springy curls that hang over her shoulders.

Like all Lyqas, she's tall. I tilt my head and take a step back to see her more comfortably.

As soon as I move, she slides into the house. I breathe a sigh of relief when her pet stays on the step outside. I close the door, turning to the woman, who's standing well into the hallway now.

She's kind of stunning. Now that I can see all of her, I'm taken aback by how pretty she is. The thin bandeau top she's wearing shows off her lean, toned shoulders and sculpted stomach. Her boobs are small and perky beneath the scrap of material. Loose yoga pants sit low on hips that flair out in a graceful curve from her itty bitty waist. I tug on the end of Kwarq's shirt, which covers most of my three-day stubble legs. I don't like this chick, but I can't even be a hater and pretend like she isn't nearly perfect.

We stare at each other, both of us not knowing what to do, but both also clearly checking the other out.

"Kwarq?"

Seriously, is that the only word she knows? What does she think if she keeps saying his name, he's just going to magically appear? I want to say, 'I get it, you're looking for my man,' but I don't because of course she's looking for him. I mean, of course she is.

"Um, let me see if I can find someone for you."

I raise my hands in front of me, pushing them out in the sign for her to stay put. I'm not sure what guest etiquette is on this planet, and I hope that I'm not being rude. Well, I kind of hope I'm not being rude.

The woman's eyes flicker down to my hands and she frowns, taking a quick step toward me. I take a step back. Whoa. She moves in that fast, creepy Lyqa way. My back hits the door, and she stops, looking more confused.

"Yeah, let me get someone for you."

I skirt around her, and she turns with me, watching as I scuttle from the hall to the living room. It's empty. I look back, and I'm only half surprised to see that she's followed me. Okay. She clearly doesn't understand a word I'm saying. Maybe she thinks I'm leading her to Kwarq. I don't need to know who she is to know this is about to be awkward as hell.

I'm relieved to see Kwarq standing behind a long island in the middle of the kitchen.

His tall frame is bent over the island, sleeves rolled to his elbows. He doesn't look up when I enter. Steam hovers from several pots behind him, and his usually straight, thick hair is damp and curled adorably over his forehead. His brows huddle in concentration.

My gaze lingers on the muscles of his forearms. They bunch and roll beneath his skin as he spoons food from a pot. Savory smells fill the large space, and I forget for a moment about our house guest and focus on the plate of food Kwarq is serving. I'm starving.

"Kwarq, babe, someone is he—"

"*Kwarq! Ma'ah lani!*" The woman rushes past me. She moves quickly. So quick I worry she's going to knock into him, but to my surprise, he turns and catches her just as she flings herself against his chest. His arms go around her back, and she wraps her legs around his waist, squealing and pressing her forehead and nose to his.

"Uh..." I'm not sure what to do. I don't know if Kwarq even realizes I'm here. The woman murmurs softly in Lyqa as her fingers comb through his beard. This is weird.

I almost expect a camera crew to jump out at any second and say this is some big Lyqa joke. I imagine a bunch of tall, Lyqa teenagers in backwards trucker hats, leaping from the bead covered entrance to the pantry, high-fiving each other and yelling that I've just been 'punq-ed.' I mean, I really hope this is a joke or the Lyqa way of greeting one's sister. A really creepy, incesty way of greeting one's sister.

Yeah, it's not. The woman pulls away and immediately leans in to press her lips to his. Kwarq jumps, but then presses into the kiss. I get a glimpse of gray, swirling tongues between their mouths. I keep waiting for him to jerk away, but he doesn't. Instead, he moves one hand to her back and holds her still against him.

So, I ran off to an alien planet with a hot alien dude whose weird, heart problem has decided I'm his soulmate. Only to find out that *lehti* is really just Lyqa for side chick.

The sloppy sound of saliva signals the end of their kiss. Kwarq presses his forehead to the woman's for a brief second. A deep, satisfied sigh issues from him before he finally lets her slide down his body.

I probably should have done something by now, but my brain doesn't seem to be working in its usual mode. Instead of being consumed by the desire to turn this kitchen into an episode of *The Jerry Springer Show*, I'm just really hungry.

I pick up the plate of food that's been abandoned on the counter. I assume it's for me, but even if it's not, I'm taking it. Just because I've realized I'm being played, doesn't mean I have to starve. And I am really really hungry. Like hungrier than I've ever been in my life. It feels like a living sensation in my body. I suddenly want to eat everything.

"I, uh, I'm just going to take this and leave you two alone."

Kwarq turns to me. His eyes flare. Is he freaking out because I busted him face fucking his little girlfriend or does he think I'm going to flip the fuck out? I should be flipping the fuck out. And also, there's a broccoli looking pile of vegetables on the plate that's dripping with a sauce I can't wait to taste.

"Amina."

I raise my eyes slowly from the dark, red sauce to meet his bright yellow gaze. "Yup, it's me. I'm here."

His eyes flicker quickly over my face. I can barely look at him, but I also can't look away. My gaze keeps straying to where his arm is wrapped around the Lyqa woman's waist. And there's a pile of root vegetables on the plate that is calling my name.

"*Lehti*, I would explai—"

I shake my head. "Nah, I'm good. I'll just take this back. That is unless you two are going to need the room. You look like you need a room."

This sad little quip is the only bit of shade I can muster at the moment.

"There are many rooms in the house we can use. You do not have to leave," Kwarq replies seriously, and my moment of triumph is cut short.

"Right. Well, have fun," I snark out and stomp out of the kitchen.

CHAPTER 16

AMINA

I walk quickly through the living room, kicking aside cushions as I go, and down the hall. With every step, I listen for the sound of Kwarq coming to get me, but he doesn't. Not even when I sigh dramatically and mumble about cheating ass fuckbois. I know he heard that shit.

After a few minutes of making wrong turns, I finally make it back to his apartments. The humiliation crawling through my body makes my hands shake as I set the plate down on the table next to the baby basket. I stare at it, feeling my humiliation intensify the longer I look at the items I was so charmed by earlier.

Anger slashes through my hunger, and I lash out, slapping the basket to the floor. The beautiful, blue gown lands near my foot. I snatch it up and throw it as far away from me as I can then turn to my plate of food.

Somewhere in the back of my mind, I know I should be more concerned with the fact that Kwarq is probably giving that long-legged, Halle Berry-looking Lyqa bitch the D somewhere in this house, but the smell of the food hits my nose and I'm in instinct mode.

Everything vegetable on the plate is roasted or stewed. Some are covered in a dark glaze. The pile of peas is smothered in a thick yellow cream. I reach for one of these first and plop it into my mouth with my fingers. I didn't even get utensils. I don't care. An image of Kwarq lifting that woman onto the island before burying his face between her long legs flashes in my mind just as the sweet, slightly spicy taste of the pea explodes in my mouth.

"Mm!"

I sound like a commercial. My eyes close and my head drops back in pleasure. This. Is. Delicious. Like finger licking good. And since I don't have a napkin, that's just what I do. I drag my tongue up my thumb to catch all the sauce that's dripped down my hand. I suck shamelessly at my fingers. I don't care. I'm eating for three.

Right. I'm eating for three, and I have a babies' father who was just tonguing down his girlfriend or wife or lover or some shit in the kitchen.

"Tiani isn't going to believe this shit," I mumble to myself as I reach for one of the glazed roots.

I shiver when it hits my tongue. It's tangy, almost like balsamic vinegar. There is also something herby about it. I love it. I eat three more then run my tongue across my lips to catch a bit of dripping juice.

"Oh my god, this is delicious!"

"I have never enjoyed anything my brother has cooked that much."

I don't even flinch when I hear Ah'dan's annoyingly smooth voice sound out from behind me. I turn, never stopping my hand as it shovels another piece of food into my mouth.

"I'm hungry."

"You are."

I only spare him the slightest glance before turning back to my plate. He moves in the corner of my eye and settles across the table from me. He sets aside several items that fell from the baby basket. He frowns and leans to one hip, pulling a rattle from beneath him before tossing it onto one of the pillows.

"Who is Tiani?"

These people have hearing so good I'm surprised they

can't hear my thoughts.

"My sister."

"She is on Earth?" He sounds interested. More interested than I've ever heard him sound. I don't care. These Lyqa carrots are amazing.

"Yup."

"Is she beautiful?"

"Yup."

"Hm. Tiani," he says it slowly, dragging out the syllables. "I like that name."

I nod and shove a handful of peas between my lips.

"What is a fuck-boy?"

I sputter, nearly choking on my mouthful. I clear my throat and manage to swallow the lump down. It travels painfully along my esophagus, making me wince. Of course he heard that. But now I know that if he heard it, that means Kwarq definitely did.

"Your brother."

Ah'dan reaches for a piece of food from my plate. I quell the urge to slap his hand away. I feel a moment of loss as I watch him toss the carrot into his mouth and begin to chew. That could have been in my belly.

"Because he fucks you?"

I sputter again. Is he trying to kill me?

"What?"

"Last night."

When my eyes widen, he sighs deeply, like I bore him with my insistence on being shocked about this whole privacy thing.

"Even if I was not trying to listen, no one in this house is deaf, my *sa'aih*," he says matter of factly.

I want to be embarrassed, but clearly, Kwarq banging girls out in this house isn't news. My heart thumps in my chest when I imagine what sounds Ah'dan can hear coming from wherever Kwarq and that woman are. In this moment, I'm supremely glad I'm human, even if the masochist in me strains just a little to see if I hear any moans or other indications of a dickdown.

"Why are you sad, Amina?"

I've stopped eating. I hold a long, stringy green at my mouth. I fold it onto my tongue but find that my earlier insatiability is gone. I'm actually kind of over food. I spit the green into my hand and place it back on the plate, not caring if it's gross or impolite. Ah'dan doesn't bat an eye. He's trained on my face as he waits for my response.

I look around for something to wipe my hands on. One of the baby blankets is on the floor nearby. I consider using it, but then find that as hurt as I am, I don't want to ruin any of the stuff I got for the baby. Babies, I correct myself.

"I'm not sad, Ah'dan. Just a little homesick. I'm probably going to see about getting back home today."

"You are not going to stay for the birth?"

I focus on wiping my hands on the hem of Kwarq's shirt. I'm not as reluctant to mess up his shit. I actually feel a slight bit of satisfaction when the juice stains dark on the white fabric.

"Well, I was only staying for tonight anyway. I just came for the, uh, procedure, but I guess since I'm doing this, there's no reason for me to be here anymore. I have a life back home, and Kwarq has a life here. It's a little awkward, you know?"

"I do not."

Of course he doesn't.

"Let's just say where I come from, it's not necessarily a normal thing for a woman to just hang around with a man and his side chick."

Ah'dan frowns further, and I already know what he's going to ask.

"What is a side chick?"

Why am I having this conversation while Kwarq is probably down the hall getting swirly, grey-tongued, Lyqa head from that woman?

"It's the woman who's not the wife or girlfriend of a man. A woman he sees on the side, usually behind his wife or girlfriend's back."

"Li'aht is not Kwarq's side chick."

Li'aht. The way he says the name makes it sound lovely. Now I hate that chick even more.

"I know. I was talking about me."

Again that frown. "You are his *lehti*."

I roll my eyes again. It's like we're exchanging these two expressions. He frowns. I roll my eyes. We probably look ridiculous.

"So I've been told, but I just don't think that means what I thought it did."

"And that is why you are sad?"

"I'm—not—sad." The words squeeze through the tight clamp of my teeth. I wish he would stop asking me questions.

"You smell sad. It is sour like swamp water. I would have you smell sweet like you do when you are laughing."

I try to smile. I don't know how to deal with sweet Ah'dan. Sweet Ah'dan is throwing me off. "Yeah, well, I haven't had a bath today so..."

His mouth turns down. He tilts his head to the side and regards me.

"You smell of my brother. That is not the sour smell, but perhaps you would like to have a bath? Maybe it will help to relieve your sorrow."

"Oh my god, I'm not sad!" My eyes blur, and I burst into tears. I'm not sad. I'm really not.

Ah'dan shifts and I feel him settle beside me. He pulls me into his lap.

"You do not have to be sad, my *sa'aih*."

"I'm really not sad. I'm not. It's just the pregnancy hormones."

The sobs that croak from my throat are ugly and loud in the quiet of the room. Ah'dan pulls me closer. I feel his mouth press into my hair as he rubs slow circles over my back.

"Please do not cry, Amina. I do not like it."

The door to the apartment bangs open. I jump and wrap my arms around Ah'dan's neck.

"What's happened?"

Kwarq's voice is panicked. I turn my face into the hard curve of Ah'dan's shoulder. He sounds like he came in a rush.

That's what she said.

Despite myself, a snorted chuckle slips past my lips.

"She is upset about being a side chick, but she says that it is just that she has not bathed and she is carrying the babies."

I could almost laugh again at how seriously Ah'dan says this. Almost. What I really want to do is cry some more, but it's probably wasted. Clearly this is all normal behavior. I'm the one taking things to heart that I shouldn't. I rub my eyes across Ah'dan's shirt and raise my head.

I'm prepared to see Kwarq standing in front of me in some state of undress, but he's still fully clothed, even though his shirt looks a little rumpled. He stands over us. When I meet his eyes, he crouches down, reaching out to put his hand on my thigh. I shift away, using the pretense of moving from Ah'dan's lap to get out of his reach. He frowns, but doesn't move to get any closer.

"I'm not sad, really. I'm just a little homesick. I'm ready to go back home."

Kwarq doesn't respond for a moment, but I feel him searching my face with a shifty gaze. "You do not wish to stay for the birth?"

"She says, no, that it is not customary for women to hang around with a man and his side chi—"

"Thanks, Ah'dan. I think I got it." I loudly cut him off. He shrugs casually then startles me by kissing my forehead before rising and leaving the room. Suddenly, I'm alone with Kwarq, and I really wish Ah'dan would come back. I just might like him after all.

Kwarq doesn't say anything when his brother leaves. He looks so distressed. I start to feel bad. I don't want to, but my rational mind tells me that I can't really hold his customs against him. He didn't ask to get attached to me on Earth. He seemed really happy to see Li'aht. And since he's been nothing but respectful and accommodating up until now, I don't think I have a right to be mad.

"I appreciate everything you've done for me. I'm just not cool with all of this. It's a little awkward. I think I'd be more comfortable back home."

KWARQ

Amina is not only sad, she feels betrayed. She pulled away from me, and I know it's because of what happened in the kitchen with Li'aht. I don't like that she saw that. She will not understand, and while I don't have an adequate excuse for my behavior, I must try.

"I know you are upset with me, *lehti*."

"I'm not upset, Kwarq, really. It's fine. This whole situation just isn't my kind of thing."

She is upset. She doesn't have to say it. I feel it. She won't look at me. Her eyes settle everywhere else in the room. Right now, she picks at a stain on the bottom of my shirt that she's wearing.

"If you would let me, my *lehti*, I will explain my behavior with Li'aht."

She turns her head, and my heart aches when I see a tear slip from the corner of her eye. She quickly wipes it away before turning back to face me. Her mouth curves into a wide smile. This smile is a lie. It's shaky and stops before it gets to her eyes.

"Kwarq, you don't have to explain. I just want you to take me home."

"*Lehti*—"

"Please—," she shouts and then takes a deep breath and continues in a falsely calm tone, "stop calling me that, Kwarq. It makes me feel weird."

Her pain makes my skin tremble. I want to hold her and make her listen, but her heart is so far away that I can barely hear its echo.

"I will not call you that if it bothers you, Amina."

"It does bother me, okay. You don't have to call me that."

"I call you that because that is what you are. You are my *lehti*. I cannot change that or how it makes me feel toward you."

"Yeah, I know that, and I already feel bad about it, so you don't have to rub it in."

She chuckles, but her attempt at a joke is also a lie. She isn't joking.

"You are my heartbeat, Amina. You should never feel sorry about this. I will never be sad about this."

She snorts out another deceptive chuckle. "Well, it does come with some useful enhancements, which I'm sure Li'aht has already benefitted from, so tell her I said 'you're welcome'."

I am confused by this message. The only benefit to my first heart's awakening is that I am much more able to love and care for my *lehti*.

"I do not know what you mean."

Her eyes are glassy, despite the strained smile that pulls at her lips.

"You know, your first heart makes your junk extra hard—

forget it. I just want to go home."

I don't want to forget it. I want her to listen to me so she will not want to leave, but I can't make her stay if she doesn't wish to.

"Allow me to make arrangements. I can return you home tonight. My family will want to see you before you leave if you wish."

She sighs deeply and doesn't say anything for a long time.

"No, that's fine. I want to see them, too. It was great to meet your family. I just think we should both get back to our lives. You know?"

I do not. I don't say this, however. I give her what she wants, and I nod.

"How long do you think it will be before we can go?"

"Perhaps a few hours. I will try to make it as soon as possible."

I stand, not wanting to leave, but I must if I am going to find a way to get her home within the time I have promised.

As I take a step toward the door, my foot tangles in something soft. There's a bit of blue material around my ankle. I hold it up. It unfurls into a floaty swirl of fabric.

It's a birthing dress. Lyqa women wear them right after they give birth. The intricate patterns contain properties to aide with emotional balance and physical recovery. A look around. The contents of the birthing basket are scattered across the room. Amina has made a mess of the gift from the healing center, but it is no bigger a mess than I have made of everything else.

Amina has not moved from her spot. She covers her face with her hands. Her shoulders jerk as she sobs quietly. The shame that crowds my heart makes me turn away. And as I leave the room, the sound of the door closing, while barely audible, is loud and final in my ears.

* * *

"You are an idiot. You know this, right?"

"I do."

"Did you do any research on human relationship customs before you revealed yourself to her?"

I spare Ah'dan a glance before I sit at our home communications station to rent a pod so I can take Amina home.

"I did."

"And yet you greeted Li'aht as your lover in front of her?"

Does Ah'dan think I don't know that I have made a mistake? One look at Amina's face in the kitchen let me know I had done something gravely wrong. I also heard her mumbled comment about cheaters, although I didn't fully understand it. It doesn't matter. I most likely am this "fuck-boy" that she called me.

"Li'aht caught me off guard. I responded out of habit. There was no passion in it."

Ah'dan shakes his head as I give my feeble excuse.

"You may as well have spread her across the counter. How could you be so careless?"

I bring my hands down onto the table a little more forcefully than I would like. I already feel helpless. Having my stupidity detailed for me by Ah'dan isn't helping.

"I would never be with another woman. Amina is the only woman I want."

"I am sorry to say this, brother, but you definitely looked like you wanted Li'aht. She is beautiful, I will admit, but so is Amina. I would not have you ruin this for our family. Your *lehti* is special."

Ah'dan has never spoken this way about anyone before. Normally, he would not be bothered to insert himself in any of my affairs.

"You think I don't know she's special? She is mine."

"She believes you don't love her. That you only tolerate her because of the *leht*."

"I know."

"Is it true?"

My skin trembles. I have never been angry with my brother. Anger is not a natural Lyqa emotion. We are not an angry species. Still, I feel the rage rise in me. It is the same rage I felt when that man threatened my *lehti* on the train back on Earth. But it's mixed with shame, and instead of being directed at Ah'dan, it's aimed at myself.

"I love her with my entire being. She is my *lehti*, but even if she wasn't, I would still love her. Do not ask me such a thing again."

As expected, Ah'dan doesn't even acknowledge the threat. He would know better than any other how love can affect one's behavior.

"We both know it isn't safe for her to give birth on her planet. Have you explained how her pregnancy will proceed? Does she know?"

I sit back in the chair and look at my brother's worried face. My sense of shame intensifies. Kissing Li'aht isn't my only mistake. I have also done a poor job of preparing Amina for carrying our children.

"I have not had the chance to speak with her," I admit. "And I don't want her to leave. I'm making the arrangements because I have given my word that I will take her, but I will try to convince her to stay, at least until the birth. Perhaps that will give me time to correct this."

"Why did you not perform *ma'h qitah* the moment you saw her?"

Ah'dan's question is laced with confusion.

"Humans do not accept apologies so easily. Trust me, I would have if I knew it would do any good. I don't think it would have been enough."

"Perhaps if you got on your knees and begged."

I snort. I will do anything to have my *lehti* stay with me. Of all of the things that could have happened as a cultural misunderstanding, this is the worst. I know my *lehti* has issues with trust. For the first time in my life, I wish that my cultural upbringing would have allowed me to push Li'aht away. To Amina, it would not only have appeared that I greeted Li'aht as a lover, I would have seemed to enjoy it.

"I have ruined things terribly." I feel the truth of my words all the way to my spirit. When Ah'dan's hand comes down onto my shoulder, it does little to settle the disappointment I feel in myself.

"She may not understand it, but I believe she cares for you."

My heart warms at the thought but then immediately aches when I think of how she looked through me in our apartments. "Maybe she did before this morning, but that no longer seems possible."

"She is going to need you in the next month," Ah'dan continues quietly. "Beg if you must beg, but do not let her leave here."

CHAPTER 17

AMINA

After Kwarq leaves, I pick up the stuff from the baby basket and put everything back as it was. I get a little sad again when I fold the beautiful blue dress.

I quickly run out of energy as I bend and rise to collect the scattered items. I probably shouldn't have eaten so much. I'm getting a serious case of the Itis. The desire to sleep overtakes me so fiercely that all I can think about is crawling into bed. It's just like when I felt hungry earlier. It was almost like nothing else really mattered, not even Kwarq face sucking with his little girlfriend. I just wanted to shove food into my mouth until I wasn't hungry anymore.

I cover the basket and go to the bedroom, jumping onto the wide, cushy mattress and falling face first. I snuggle into the sheets, which smell of Kwarq, all earthy and warm. I don't want to feel comforted by it, but I am. I remind myself again that I don't really know this man. I try my best to push aside any feelings I may have been developing.

I don't even know him. How could I possibly think that I love him in such a short time?

What I need is a nap. Just to rest my eyes. When I wake up, things will make more sense.

I have to pee. I didn't have one thing to drink before I went to sleep, but it feels like I chugged an entire gallon of water.

There's a warm hand moving in slow circles across my stomach. I don't have to open my eyes to know it's Kwarq.

His chest is a firm wall against my back. His thighs shelf

the backs of my legs. The arm that rests over my side is heavy. I can feel the thick impression of him against my ass. I settle back a little more. He smells so good. I'm going to hate leaving him.

Because I'm going to leave. He has a girlfriend, and as much as I want to be understanding of his culture, I'm not about to play baby mama to an alien and his super model Lyqa wife.

My eyes feel tight when I finally peel them open. I'd give anything to wallow in the warmth of Kwarq's arms for a little while longer, but I can't fake sleep forever. Honestly, I'd give anything for it to be a week ago. I would have stayed in my chair at that damn movie theater and never opened my mouth.

The room is bathed in a soft, late afternoon glow. I don't know how time works on Lyqa, but I couldn't have slept that long. I do feel better though. Less weepy and really rested. I actually feel a little hyped. Like I could spring up and jump on the bed. It's a strange sensation. This sudden surge of giddy energy. If I didn't know any better, I would believe that I was happy.

The hand on my stomach is still moving. I shift my head down just enough to see Kwarq's golden hand moving gently over the slight swell of my belly.

What the…?

"Kwarq?"

"Yes, my *leh*—Amina?"

"What the fuck is going on with my stomach?"

He chuckles softly behind me, and I feel him nuzzle into the top of my head.

"I have some things I must explain to you. Changes that will happen to your body. As I said, Lyqa gestation is a bit different than human's."

"Different how?"

"Well, for one, it's quicker. We only gestate for about one Lyqa month, which is equivalent to two and a half Earth months."

"Like a dog?"

It's minor shade, and the only hint that I'm still salty about Li'aht. Kwarq doesn't get it. He chuckles again. He's pretty damn happy, too. Maybe he got some from Li'aht after all. I'm only a little annoyed when even this thought doesn't really dampen my mood. Why am I so fucking happy?

"Like a Lyqa, Amina."

"So you're telling me that I'm going to give birth in two months when I get home?"

His hand pauses on my stomach, but resumes moving after a second.

"Yes, you will give birth in one Lyqa month, or two and a half months on Earth."

Okay.

"So that's why I look four months pregnant right now? It wasn't like this earlier."

"Did you feel very hungry and then very tired before?"

I remember that insatiable feeling I had this morning followed by the overwhelming desire to sleep a short time later.

"Yeah."

I feel his head move behind me in what I am assuming is a nod.

"The stages of development are often preceded by the desire for nourishment to fuel growth and then long periods of sleep while the fetus develops."

I'm listening to everything he's saying, but my brain latches on to the last part of his explanation.

"Long periods of sleep. How long was I out?"

"Most of yesterday and today."

"What!" I sit up in the bed, flinging Kwarq's hand off of

me. "You let me sleep for two days?"

I can't believe it, but then I notice something else. I'm clean. My skin smells of something sweet, and I'm no longer wearing Kwarq's dirty tunic. I'm in the white dress from the basket. It's whisper soft against my skin. I honestly can't say I've ever been in anything more comfortable. Still, how the hell did I get into it?

"Who changed my clothes?"

Kwarq sits up, frowning at my obvious discomfort at his revelation that I've been playing sleeping beauty for the past day and a half.

"I did, of course. It is my duty to care for you when you enter the resting periods."

"Wait a minute. Was I in a coma or something?"

Kwarq places his hand over mine. That feeling overcomes me again. Like his touch is giving me energy. Like it's soothing me. I feel less panicked almost immediately.

"Amina, you were not in a coma. There was no danger. Because the babies are growing so quickly, your body needs an opportunity to rest and acclimate itself. It is a necessary and expected thing. You did sleep slightly longer than a Lyqa woman, but it is to be expected. Your body is not prepared for this and is trying to adjust as best it can. But you are well. I would not let you come to harm."

He says this like he says everything. Like it's the most natural, right thing in the world. I, however, am too weirded out to be charmed by his show of devotion.

"What did you do to me?"

He looks confused.

"While I was asleep. What did you do?"

He smiles. A real smile. The adorable boyish smile that I have only seen from him a few times. His chest visibly puffs out.

"I did everything I was supposed to do. I bathed you. I

provided you with liquids and supplements. At night, I held you and spoke to our children, telling them to grow well inside of you and not be too hard on their mother until after they are born. I think, for now, causing you strife is my job."

He seems so proud of himself, and I'm touched. I want to be freaked out by the idea of him playing rag doll with me, but I'm not. I can only imagine him holding me throughout the night, his deep, musical voice whispering to the babies inside of me. Our babies. My throat tightens, and I remind myself that I can't afford to read too much into his gestures.

"I appreciate you looking out for me. That couldn't have been fun for you. I'm sure you had other things you wanted to do."

"I had nothing to do, except care for you and our babies. It is my obligation as your *lehti* to look after you during the periods of rest."

Everything he does for me is just another burden of the *leht*. I fumble with the raw edge of the sheet and avoid his gaze.

"I don't want to be your obligation, Kwarq."

"Then it is my pleasure, Amina."

I push out a frustrated breath and fling aside the sheet.

"Yeah, I know, Kwarq, but it doesn't have to be. You have a life here, and obviously this whole thing isn't going to mix too well with it. It's probably a good idea that we try and figure out the best way for me to deal with this myself."

He swallows and I look quickly away from the cords of his neck where his throat works. "You mean when you return home? Without me, how will you care for yourself during resting periods?"

"I don't know, but I'll figure it out. Maybe I can hire someone. Maybe my sister can help me."

"But it is my duty. It is not a burden."

"It's not your duty, Kwarq. I'm not your duty. I'm not

anything to you. We made a mistake. I probably should have asked more questions about your situation before I agreed to come here. I just wasn't prepared for some things."

"Like Li'aht?"

I hate hearing him say her name. I hate the ache in my chest when I think about how bright his smile was when he looked up and saw her in the kitchen. How closely he held her. The low moan that rumbled in his throat when he kissed her back.

"That and other things."

"Amina, since you have been here, I smelled your fear, the tangy smell of apprehension, and the sweet smell of your passion. The only time I have scented sadness is when I mention her name."

I keep forgetting that he's basically a walking mood ring.

"Yeah, well, finding out you have a girlfriend was a little hurtful. But I can't really be mad at you. You aren't human. You have no way of knowing that something like that wouldn't be cool with me. It's my fault for not doing more to better understand the *leht*. I thought it was more like a soulmates kind of thing, which I know is stupid, but it's just what I thought. I shouldn't have assumed."

"Amina, you have not misinterpreted the *leht*."

I chuckle softly. "I think I have."

Kwarq shakes his head and sits up in front of me. He takes my hands in his and brings them to his mouth.

"You have not. Amina, Li'aht is not my lover. She was, but no other woman has existed for me since the moment you awoke my heart."

I force myself to ease my hands from the warmth his.

"Kwarq, I know you have to feel this way, but really, I understand. And not to throw shade, but you seemed *really* happy to see her."

His skin pulses red when I remind him of his reunion in

the kitchen. I still can't believe I slept for nearly two days. Also, I really have to pee.

"My behavior was unacceptable. In my culture, we are not accustomed to rejecting affection, and I would have offended her by rejecting her embrace. I realize now that I should have risked it. I would rather that than have you be hurt by my actions. *Ma'h qitah.*"

He says this last part softly. He takes gentle hold of my arm and he presses his cheek to mine. I feel the regret through this simple contact.

"It's okay, Kwarq."

"It is not okay. I hurt you, but more importantly, I have made you want to leave me. I have made you believe I do not care for you."

I don't say anything. My throat tingles and starts to tighten, and I do my best to clear it. If I cry, it will just make him feel worse. Plus, I don't want to think about whether or not he cares about me.

The guilt knowing he's been taking care of me while I slept but also torturing himself over what happened eats at me. Knowing he would have shirked custom for me now seems a little extra. I mean, it was just a kiss. It's not like we're married or anything. I'm really just a glorified baby mama.

I sigh and reach out to rub my hand over his short beard. The hair is fine and silky against my palm.

"I'm glad you weren't rude to her. I'm sure it was a shock to her, too. I've just kind of showed up and stolen her man."

"Once I explained who you are to me, Li'aht was very embarrassed of her behavior. Had she known, she never would have come here. She would have known that we were no longer lovers."

I'm a bit surprised by this. It seems a little cold for a culture that's defined by being almost overly affectionate.

"So you guys are just through? She has no problem with

the fact that you've basically dumped her for some chick that isn't even Lyqa, let alone from this planet?"

"Whether or not you are Lyqa is of no consequence. And as for the risk that I have broken her heart as you human's say, she and I were not in a committed partnership. We were what you would call casual lovers."

My eyes widen. "You were cuttie buddies?"

His mouth quirks up at the corner. "If this expression means that we were friends who also engaged in sexual relations, then yes. We were cuttie buddies. Does this bother you?"

Kind of. A little. Hell yeah.

"Not really. I guess it doesn't matter. I'll be going home soon, anyway, right?"

My desire to leave isn't as pressing as it was a couple of days ago. Now that Kwarq's explained the situation with Li'aht, I feel like I want to stay. I don't know if I should say this though. Maybe I'll get lucky, and he'll say that he can't take me for a while.

"Yes, I can take you if you still wish to go. My mother has asked to see you before we leave. Is that okay?"

I like Kwarq's mother. She reminds me of my own mom. In fact, his whole family has been nothing but welcoming to me. Even Ah'dan, who seems like he could be a jerk if he wants to, was surprisingly comforting the other day. I feel guilty knowing I'm taking Quth and Mahdi away from their first grandchildren.

"Of course, I'll see her. I want to thank her for welcoming me into her home. Let me use the rest room, and I'll get ready."

I scoot backwards off the bed. Once my feet touch the floor, I fully feel the difference in my body. Gravity pulls everything down just a little bit heavier. My breasts are full and achy. That watery feeling in my womb is even more pronounced and only serves to make it more apparent that I have to use the restroom. I haven't peed in Kwarq's home before. I really really hope it's nothing weird. Like don't let the toilet be a communal room where Bati's gonna be taking a shit next to me or something. These Lyqa kind of like their shared experiences. And please, please let them have toilet paper.

Kwarq watches me with an amused expression, like he already knows I'm imagining all kinds of weird bathroom scenarios.

"Can you show me where the bathroom is?"

His mouth twitches, and he swings his feet over the side of the bed to stands in front of me, holding out his hand.

"Of course, Amina."

KWARQ

It's hard not to laugh at the varying emotions on Amina's face when she asks to use the toilet. I don't have be in her head to confirm that she's imagining wildly ridiculous things waiting for her in the room where we relieve ourselves.

Her energy is nervous as I lead her out of the bedroom to the room in the back of my apartments. When we get to the door, I push her forward and step away. My heart immediately begins to beat quickly in time with hers, and I cover my mouth, barely able to contain my grin. She's actually scared. My poor, human Amina and her ridiculous imagination.

I wait patiently as she bolsters her courage and pushes the door open. The moment she steps through, and I can resist no longer.

"Be careful."

CHAPTER 18

AMINA

Kwarq is such a butthead. I nearly piss myself when he issues his little warning, but as soon as the lights brighten, I realize that I seriously need to calm down. It's just a damn bathroom. I turn around and glare into his smirking face before I slam the door. Kwarq's muffled laugh is loud on the other side.

The toilet is larger than a human toilet. The tub is ginormous, but other than that, it's a regular old bathroom, if a little more spacey and high-tech looking. I clasp my hands to my chest and send up a silent prayer to the universe when my eyes land on the neat stack of toilet paper next to the commode. Thank you, Black Jesus.

I have to pee, like really have to pee. I have to pee more urgently than ever in my life. I flip my dress up and take a cursory glance inside the toilet to make sure there isn't anything swimming in there. I mean, a girl can never be too safe. Once I determine the coast is clear, I turn and plop down on the seat, nearly fall in, then steady myself with a hand on the wall as I let go of what feels like two days' worth of pee.

"Aaaahhhhh!" My deep sigh echoes off the bathroom walls, and I hear Kwarq chuckle again.

I don't care, this is the best thing I've ever felt, and I've been feeling some good stuff lately. Actually, I've been thinking that a lot about almost everything. Almost everything feels like the best thing ever. Very urgent and intense. I haven't been able to explain it.

"Why does this feel so good?" I shout through the door. I'm still peeing. It doesn't seem like I'm going to stop any time soon.

"I may have been excessive with your fluids. I could have relieved your bladder for you, but I did not think you would appreciate that just yet."

He's right, I wouldn't have. I have no idea how he would have done this, short of giving me a catheter, but I'm glad he realized that would have been taking his caring duties a little too far. That's not what I was asking though.

"No, I mean, why does everything feel so intense? Like when I'm hungry, I'm *really* hungry. When I'm tired, I'm *really* tired. When I'm happy I want to jump on the bed. When I'm sad, I want to cry forever. And this pee is the best pee of my life. Everything feels like the best anything of my life. Why?"

"Ah, I understand." Kwarq is amused again. I bet he's getting a real kick out of this. "It is because of our babies. You have the *lehti'an*, so you experience your needs as our children do, with no patience or understanding of restraint. Your hunger feels like it needs to be fulfilled immediately. Your happiness is unrestrained. Your sadness feels all-consuming. And even your pee is the best relief in the world."

Hm. Makes sense in a weird, Lyqa way. My abdomen twinges. I expect the pressure to lessen, but it actually feels like it's getting more intense. My belly twinges again, but this time it feels more like a cramp. I must have been holding this for a very long time. I hope that I haven't ruined my bladder.

"Geez, is this ever going to stop?" I mumble. A second later, the door swings open and Kwarq fills the doorway. I shriek, my hand slipping from its brace on the wall. My butt falls into the toilet just as a new gush of pee trickles out of me.

"I'm almost done. What are you doing?"

Kwarq isn't listening. He sniffs the air with an expression that is getting more panicked by the second. He drags in a deep breath, and his eyes widen in horror.

"Something is not right."

His words are punctuated by another large gush of liquid falling from me. Okay, that was kind of weird. I look between my legs. What I thought was pee is really a thick, milky liquid. It almost looks like…

"Is that your cum?"

I don't have time to be shocked or grossed out. I'm totally going to kill Kwarq if his "care" of me included him doing me while I slept. That wouldn't be Lyqa weird. That would just be universally weird and a deal breaker. Just the thought makes my skin crawl.

I don't have time to question him, however, because he rushes forward and lifts me from the toilet.

"What are you doing?"

"No, no, no, no."

He keeps saying this. He rushes me down the hall back to his bedroom. My heart's beating really fast, inhumanely fast. It's not my heart. It's *his* heart that mine is beating in time to. He's scared. It's a new emotion from Kwarq, and it fills me with terror. I feel out my body. He said something was wrong, but I don't feel different.

KWARQ

I try to slow the beat of my heart, but the moment I scent the pungent odor of my and Amina's fluids on the air, I know she is losing our babies. I focus on remaining calm, even as I'm engulfed by terror.

Engulfed. This is a good word for the panic flooding my ears until they echo with a piercing ring. There is only one thing I can think of to stop this from happening. I quickly bring Amina to my bedroom. She hasn't realized yet what's occurring, and I'm thankful for this. Her confused calm is probably the only thing that is slowing the progress of the expulsion.

I place her gently on the bed and begin to remove my clothes. When I lift my shirt over my head, her eyes widen.

"What are you doing? What's wrong with me?"

"You are expelling the fetuses, Amina." I can barely get the words out. I feel like saying it out loud will seal it as our fate. "Maybe the progress is too fast for your body, but we can stop it, hopefully."

As my words sink in, fear radiates from her. I will myself to calm more. My calm will connect to her. I take a deep breath. I hope I am not too scared to help her.

"Shouldn't we go the hospital? What can we do? Oh my god."

Her voice shakes. She cradles her belly. When her eyes rise to mine, they're wet with tears. I ease onto the bed and cover her hand with my own. We will both have to be strong in this moment. She will not understand, but this is our only option.

"I need to strengthen your womb. I am sorry, but this is the only way. We will not make it to the healing center in time."

I push her back and move to cover her, but she braces her hands on my shoulders, her eyes going wide with alarm.

"Kwarq, you seriously want to fuck right now? I'm having a miscarriage. I need to go to the hospital!"

She pushes against me and tries to scramble away. The bed under my thigh is warm and wet with the liquid coming from her body.

"Leh—Amina, please. My semen will replenish the fluids you are losing. My body is made for this purpose. Please, let me help you. I would never take advantage of you, please!"

She gasps as more liquid seeps from her. I'm about to plead further, but she grabs me by the shoulders and yanks me over her.

"Stop it, now! Do it!" Her voice is scared and urgent. I

don't waste time. I yank down my shorts, and my cock springs heavily between us. My first heart has done it's work. I'm hard and ready to release. I don't feel any desire, but something more instinctual. The instinct to protect my family. To do whatever I must to ensure they are safe.

"I will be gentle. I will try not to hurt you," I tell her as I position myself at her entrance and press my hips forward.

Amina squirms slightly as I breach her. The wetness of the expulsion seems to prevent any discomfort. I work quickly and methodically, thrusting urgently to reach the end that I feel lingering just out of reach. I focus my mind, and soon I'm releasing vigorously inside of her. I press deeply, holding her hips at an angle to keep it inside. Amina lays beneath me with her eyes shut. Her lips move, and when I listen, I hear the soft, pleading litany she's saying to our children.

"Stay in there, little ones. Please stay."

"They will stay, Amina. I will not let you lose them."

I kiss both of her moist eyelids as I continue to release inside of her. They're swollen from her crying. Her brown skin is streaked with tears.

The last jet pulses inside of her, and I relax, breathing deeply from my efforts. Her arms come around my back. Her legs grip my sides. The hard little plates of her knees dig into my hips.

"Is it enough?"

"I cannot tell. If not, I will give more." My first heart is ready. It is already beating in anticipation of aiding her. The strength of the *leht* is even more amazing to me in this moment. I pray that it is strong enough to save our children.

Amina sniffles beneath me. I hold her close, keeping as much of my weight off of her as I can. I try again to transfer some of my calm to her, and I'm pleased when I feel our hearts start to slow. her breathing eases and deepens. She has fallen asleep.

Carefully, I ease from inside of her. I wait anxiously to feel the gush of liquid that follows, but nothing comes from her body. I don't risk moving her. I pull the sheet up and ease next to her, careful not to jostle her too much or wake her. She's in a deep sleep. I can tell right away. I'm glad. Her body needs to heal. I rest my hand lightly over her stomach.

"Stay in there, little ones. Please stay." I repeat their mother's words and settle in to wait.

CHAPTER 19

AMINA

My eyes spring open. Above me, the light walls of Kwarq's bedroom flicker with shadows. The familiar earthy, spicy smell of Kwarq surrounds me. I don't move. I can't move. My last conscious thought was that I didn't want to lose my babies. It's almost like my brain stopped working mid-thought and now that I'm awake, my terror picks up where it left off.

"It is okay, Amina. You are well. They are well."

I turn my head. Kwarq's sitting on the edge of the bed. He looks a little ragged. His hair sticks up around his head. The yellow of his eyes appears dull. He looks hollow, like he's lost weight.

"They're okay?"

He smiles, faintly, and nods. "They flourish. Look."

I move cautiously, lifting my head to look down at my belly. I can't stop my quick intake of breath. My stomach sticks roundly from my body beneath the sheet. My eyes fly back to Kwarq.

"How long have I been asleep?"

"It has been nearly two weeks."

My attempts at moving gingerly are forgotten, and I sit up onto my elbows as much as my belly will allow me to.

"Oh my god. Why did I sleep so long? You couldn't wake me?"

"Carrying two fetuses is making the adjustment to a Lyqa gestation slightly more difficult for your body. We had a healer come see you. He said that is why your body tried to miscarry. It was attempting to expel what it perceived to be—alien."

I frown. *I* can refer to my kids as alien, but that doesn't mean any one else can.

"They aren't alien."

"I know, Amina," he smiles, and it's sad, "but they are not what your body is expecting."

He isn't just talking about the babies. He's talking about himself. I have no doubt that Kwarq has spent the last two weeks beating himself up for knocking me up in the first place. If there is one thing I am sure of, it's that Kwarq sees it as his duty to protect me. He may not have been what I was expecting, but he's been better to me than any man I've ever taken a chance on. That he thinks he's in some way failed or disappointed me makes my heart hurt more than I ever thought it could.

"Can I move?"

He nods and pulls the covers back, moving forward to help me. I hold up my hand to stop him.

"I can do it. Just—just stay where you are."

His face falls, but he manages to school his features quickly.

"Of course. I will not touch you, my *leh*—Amina—if you do not wish it. Of course, I will not."

I mentally roll my eyes. Kwarq is so extra.

I sit up and wait to see if anything funny happens. It doesn't. I would expect for my arms or back to be stiff after two weeks of laying down, but they feel fine. Better than fine, actually. I feel very loose and relaxed. I have energy. I move up so that I'm on all fours and crawl slowly down the bed until I'm in front of Kwarq. He sits completely still, staring at me with wide eyes. It doesn't look like he's breathing. When he doesn't move to make space for me, I gently swat at his arms.

"Move."

He complies, lifting his arms to the side in confusion. I crawl into his lap, settling myself along the hard tops of his thighs and wrapping my arms around his middle. The breath he expels is harsh and forceful over my head. A low moan rumbles in his chest, and his arms come around me, squeezing tight, almost crushing me against him.

I nuzzle closer and listen to the beat of our hearts. His beats loud and bassy over my softer thud.

Nothing makes sense. Things I never imagined happening in my lifetime have happened, and through it all, Kwarq has been with me, protecting me, caring for me. The man literally overcame abject terror to fuck me and save our babies. I can't even begin to wrap my brain around that kind of devotion. So I won't.

"I love you, Kwarq."

I do. It hits me like the truest truth. It hits me like the truth of my own existence in this vast, amazing universe. I love this Lyqa dude.

I lean away from his chest and look up at him. When I'm this close, I can see how dull his usually golden skin looks. The dark rings around his eyes. The yellow is so matte. That vibrant sparkle I'm used to seeing no longer shines back at me. I miss it. I want it back.

"Did you miss me?"

He swallows and nods, but it's just a jerky twitch of his head.

"I did."

"Were you scared?"

"I was."

"Do you still love me?"

He frowns, and I get a little nervous. Please don't let this be one of those moments where I completely misread the situation. Please don't let me have crawled up into this man's lap thinking I'm cute, and he's about to send my scary, comatose prone ass back home.

His eyes flicker across my face. I wait, not sure if I've been waiting for two seconds or two minutes. I kind of expected him to confirm his love for me right away.

"I didn't mean to put you on the spot. I'm sorry."

I move to push off from his lap, but his arms tighten around me. His brows meet tightly in the middle of his face. His full lips press together. He looks mad.

"That is not a proper apology."

He says it gently, but there is an edge to it.

"Right."

The only way I can do a proper apology is if I face him. Maneuvering in a half circle as best as I can with my belly, I straddle his legs.

I hold his face and rise to my knees to press our foreheads together. Warmth fills me. I nuzzle closer, letting my nose brush his.

"*Ma'h qitah*, Kwarq." My pronunciation is garbage, but I really am sorry.

"Why are you sorry? You have to say the offense to mend it."

This is a different Kwarq than I'm used to.

"I'm sorry that I put you on the spot and made you worry and have to take care of me for nearly a month. I'm just sorry. For everything."

"No."

I laugh. "Kwarq, you can't tell me what to be sorry for."

"I can. That is not how you have offended me, Amina."

I try to lean away but he puts his hand to the back of my head to keep our faces together.

"Kwarq, I don't know what else I've done, but whatever it is, I'm sorry."

"Do not be sorry. Fix it."

I've woken up to difficult Kwarq. Why can't he just spit it out like he usually does?

"Well, I don't know what I did, so how can I fix it? Ninety percent of what I do is wrong. It's just easier to issue a blanket apology. Trust me, I feel bad."

A low, annoyed growl sounds out. What? Kwarq, bastion of patience, is frustrated with me? I'm almost too stunned to wonder why.

"You asked me if I love you."

"I did," I reply cautiously.

"But you made me promise not to tell you that until you were comfortable. So fix it."

Kwarq finally lets me lean back. He's still frowning, but what I thought was anger, I can see is restraint and pain. I've put the brakes on every attempt by Kwarq to do what comes naturally to him. It seems so silly now. I'm not a bad person. My insides aren't rotten. I deserve love. I deserve *his* love, and I'll take it.

"You have my permission."

I squeal when Kwarq flips us over lightening fast and presses kisses all over my face.

"I love you. I love you. I love you. I love you."

Each kiss is followed by a declaration. In his deep, melodic voice, it begins to sound like a song, and I laugh. This feels good. It really really feels good.

"We definitely must make her do that more. She truly has a beautiful laugh."

I duck my head around Kwarq. Ah'dan's standing just inside the room. He smiles, and I lift my hand from Kwarq's back and wave. Kwarq doesn't even acknowledge his brother. He leans his head into the exposed crook of my neck and presses a kiss just at the sensitive area behind my ear.

"I love you, Amina."

His voice is a gentle, emotion-filled whisper. It warms

every part of me until I think I'm going to burst from happiness.

"Kwarq?"

"Yes, Amina."

"Stop calling me that."

KWARQ

"Eat more, my *lehti*."

I pull the large bowl of roasted vegetables closer to Amina just as Bati reaches for a glazed root. He frowns.

My instructions to Amina are unnecessary. She's in the grips of a hunger, and instinct drives her. She shoves piece after piece of food into her mouth, chewing slowly, her eyes closed as she savors each bite.

I have seen this before with other Lyqa mothers, but it is still a fascinating thing to witness. She is oblivious to everything around her. When a piece of food slips from her fingers to the floor, she looks so forlorn at the loss that I must smother a laugh. I'm glad our babies are hungry, and that she is strong enough to feed them.

Amina finishes Bati's plate and begins looking for more. Her eyes fall on Ah'dan's half-eaten bowl. He sighs and pushes it across the table to her.

"Thank you. God, I'm so hungry!" She reaches into the plate, picks up a long sliver of root vegetable and folds it into her mouth. Immediately, her mouth turns down, and she stops chewing. The blissful expression of a moment ago is now a mask of complete disgust. She opens her mouth and the food splats back into the bowl.

"Ugh, that's it. I'm over it."

I push the plate away, but it's not far enough. Amina scoots it across the table, back in front of Ah'dan, who shrugs and picks up the piece of food Amina spit back into the bowl and plops it into his mouth.

"Ew, Ah'dan, you are so gross."

Ah'dan cheeks raise in a self-satisfied smirk. He finishes chewing and his eyes flick to mine. His smile grows more mischievous. Bati notices and smiles too. I know what they are thinking. I roll my eyes, but nod my head. I never should have told them that story. Amina's going to kill me.

"Amina?"

She's wiping her hands on a napkin, her head bowed as she works to get the sauce and bits of food from beneath her nails. Her head pops up, and she smiles. She's so beautiful.

I let my mouth drop open at the same moment as Ah'dan and Bati. Our tongues unfurl in a synchronized roll and slap wetly against our chins.

Nothing happens. Amina doesn't even flinch. She rolls her eyes and goes back to cleaning her nails.

"Jokes on you. I'm not worried about your creepy, long tongues anymore." She looks up at me and narrows her eyes. "I know what they're good for."

Ah'dan chokes and automatically clamps down. He rolls onto his back covering his mouth, a high-pitched wail sounding from behind his hand. Bati laughs, holding his side and pointing a taunting finger at our brother.

Amina trains her eyes on my squealing brother and raises one eyebrow.

"That's what you get."

CHAPTER 20

AMINA

It's been another week since I woke up from my second bout of sleeping beauty syndrome, and I feel really pregnant. When Kwarq said I was asleep for two weeks, I thought he meant two Earth weeks, but he meant two Lyqa weeks, so that kind of freaked me out, but there's nothing I can do about it now.

I'm basically eight months pregnant. It's weird. In my head, I'm still a size six. In real life, I'm a house. I'm a fucking two-decker.

I'm also excited. Today is the first day Kwarq's taking me out of the house. Mahdi spent the first few days fussing over me, bringing me breakfast in bed, meditating with me because apparently that's a big Lyqa thing, and otherwise doing the mother thing. If I wasn't already decided on staying with this Lyqa dude, his mother fluttering over me would have definitely swayed me. After all, she's carried Lyqa babies two more times than I have, and I've had enough scares in this pregnancy to last a life time.

Overall, we've all been very careful. Every night, Kwarq "reinforces my womb" which is just the less creepy way of saying he jerks off inside of me. It's completely nonsexual, which is a little frustrating, but it's necessary.

After a couple of days of wondering, I just had to know how this reinforcement went down while I was sleeping. Kwarq was genuinely appalled that I thought he was doing me while I was comatose. Apparently, it wasn't necessary then. My body was in healing mode. It took care of itself.

While all of the coddling's been nice, I'm so anxious to get out of the house that I think I'm going to scream. I spend a lot of time on our little balcony, watching Lyqas and other beings walk by. Checking out the weird little animals. I'm not even anxious anymore about what might be waiting out there. I just want to be out.

I'm standing by the door, shuffling from foot to foot when Kwarq, his brothers, and his parents converge on the foyer. They're so damn beautiful.

His mother's long, bright yellow dress ties at the back of her neck and hangs low on her back. The skirt displays a large, tie-dye design of swirling browns and blues.

Kwarq and Bati wear similar outfits. It's so cute. Even alien twins dress alike. They have on bright blue, fitted t-shirts. The soft material molds over their solid chests. Their pants hang low on their hips and fit loose down their legs only to taper at the ankle. They look like they're about to go practice karate.

There were two seconds back when I first got to Lyqa when I thought perhaps Ah'dan had the hots for me. He likes to stare, and I'll admit I stared back. He's pretty gorgeous. But I've learned that Ah'dan just likes to be Ah'dan. So I'm not shocked he's wearing hunter green culottes, gold woven sandals that tie up to his knee, and no damn shirt. I roll my eyes. He's such a show off.

"You do not approve?"

"Please, you know you're gorgeous. I can't stand you."

He throws his head back and laughs. Bati snorts and Kwarq smiles.

"Come on now, my *dahni*, do not tease her," their mother chides and links her arm through mine. It's a little awkward. She's so much taller that she ends up mostly holding my upper arm. I cover her hand with mine and turn my back on the grinning brothers.

"So where are we going?"

"I will take you to my place of work to fit you with a translator as you asked before."

I turn to Kwarq and raise my eyebrows.

"Your job? You have a job? I was beginning to think Lyqa jobs weren't a thing."

Everyone frowns at me, and my face gets hot when I realize my mistake.

"Oh god, I wasn't trying to say that you guys are bums or anything. I mean, I just never see anyone go to work. I mean, I've been sleeping alot of the time, but—ugh!" I cover my face with my hands and shake my head. "I'm sorry. That was really offensive."

Quth gives a deep, rumbling laugh before his arm comes around me in a gentle squeeze.

"Do not feel bad, my *dahnai*. I and Mahdi are what you would call retired in your culture. We have provisions set aside to see to our comfort and the maintenance of our home. Bati is a builder. I do not know what you call it in English. My implant is not supplying the word."

I look over at Bati and frown. "You work in construction?"

"He is the person who designs buildings," Kwarq supplies.

"You're an architect?" I never would have guessed.

"If this is the word for the designer of buildings, then I am."

"Hm," I nod my head and turn to Ah'dan. "And what about you? Or do you just stand around looking beautiful?"

"I also do that, but I am an artist."

"Really?"

"Really."

"So is this just like a break time for you?"

"Our system of work is a bit different here. It is less rigid. At the learning center where I work, I conduct lectures and presentations, periodically. Bati provides plans for structures as they are needed, and Ah'dan does what he likes."

"Damn, must be nice."

Kwarq cradles my cheek. "I did not like to watch you work so much on Earth. I am glad I can take care of you now." His voice is gentle. I feel the warmth of it spread through my chest.

"I am also glad my son has brought you here where you can rest and prepare for the birth of my grandchildren without the stress," his mother says at my side. "Shall we go now? I thought after Kwarq takes you to the learning center, we could meet at the market and then see a show."

My eyes fly to Kwarq's.

"A show? Like a movie?"

Mahdi smiles at my surprise.

"Yes, a film, if you enjoy them."

I'm listening to her, but I'm staring bullets at Kwarq.

"I don't know, do I enjoy them, Kwarq?"

He has the nerve to look bored.

"She enjoys them very much, mother."

"Great! Then we will go to the market and then to see the new drama that is showing. I am excited. I can never get the boys to come with me to see a film."

As if to punctuate this point, all three of her sons groan loudly. Even Kwarq's father appears uncomfortable with the idea.

"That's so funny because I met Kwarq at the movies," I say and have to cover my smile when his mother shoots him an disbelieving look.

"Did you?"

"I sure did. Actually," Kwarq steps forward and tries to cover my mouth, but I dodge out of his way. "Kwarq was a big fan of the movies back on Earth. You must have seen, what ten, twelve movies while you were there?"

His mother glares at him. Under her penetrating gaze, Kwarq turns into a little kid. His head bows and he shuffles from one foot to the other.

"I was only there for her, mother. You know only something as irresistible as the *leht* would make me sit in a theater and watch that garbage. Earth movies are ridiculous."

I snort. "Yeah right. You know you loved them."

Kwarq pins me down with his stare.

"I love you. I would sit through a thousand terrible films to have you know that."

I love hearing him say that, and now that I've given him my permission, he says it all the time.

"Well you only have to sit through one with your mother, right?"

His mother beams and nods triumphantly. "Right."

I send Kwarq a pointed look when it seems like he's going to argue. He sighs and steps forward, dropping to his knees and lifting his mother's hem to kiss it.

"Of course, mother, I will accompany you to any film you wish to see." His mouth quirks up at the corner as he rises. "We all will."

The chorus of groans is so dramatic that his mother and I both laugh out loud.

"Is this a university?"

I tighten my grip on Kwarq's hand as he leads me through the courtyard. It looks like a quad. Several young Lyqas walk and stand about. Groups sit on benches and in the grass. More than a few heads turn as we pass. I smile at the Lyqas I make eye contact with. They nod and smile back.

"It is a kind of learning center, yes. Lyqas have a much more informal education system. More like apprenticeships. Learning of any kind is open to all who wish it. These centers are places where anyone can come to gain knowledge. One can learn and try many things if they like."

"Is that how you became a linguist/doula?"

"It is. A friend of mine was *leht* very soon after we finished our first training. His *lehti* conceived from their first joining."

"Like us?"

"Like us. He was trained as a healer and attended his own birthing. He said that the feeling of those first moments when his child entered the world was like nothing he had experienced aside from the *leht.*"

"So you took training to deliver babies?"

Kwarq's shoulders lift and drop back into place. "I would know that feeling with my own young. I would not let something so small as a bit of training stop me from experiencing such love."

My smile is immediate and unrestrained. "Wow, you really are a softie, huh? I think that's probably the sweetest thing I have ever heard any man say."

In real life, I don't think I'll ever get used to someone, especially a man, speaking so reverently about love. He's so serious, and he's not even the least bit self-conscious about his show of emotion.

"I am not sure if I am a softie, since I do not know what that means." His expression is reserved, as if he isn't sure if I'm calling him something bad.

"It means you're a sensitive person. That you're not afraid to indulge your emotions."

He frowns in the way he always does when I say something he thinks is strange. "I am not afraid to show them, no. Is this a bad thing on Earth, to be a softie?"

"I don't know. I guess it's considered a little weak. People take advantage of others who are too emotional."

He stares at the side of my face. I'm too embarrassed for my species right now to look at him. In moments like these, when I'm forced to explain our habits, humans seem pretty sucky.

"Do people take advantage of you? Is that why you were

reluctant to accept my love?"

"I mean, a lot of women get taken advantage of when it comes to love. Human men aren't really as happy about love as you are. They don't generally feel so privileged about it."

"I do not understand. Do they not want love?"

"No, they want it, but usually so they can get other things they want from a woman. They don't really value it, I guess."

Kwarq's hand vibrates in mine. I don't need Lyqa senses to know he's finding this all very disturbing.

"What could you possibly want from a woman that is worth wasting love over?"

My chuckle is more cynical than I want it to be.

"Usually, they just want to smash."

He frowns. "Smash? Hurt them?"

I laugh a little uncomfortably. "No, it means have sex."

"People call this smashing? It is such an aggressive word." He's frowning even harder now. His disturbance has morphed into genuine concern. I can only imagine what he's picturing in his mind. It's probably not too far off from what passes for sex with human men.

"Well, actually, that's Ebonics. It's a type of English dialect, but humans refer to sex a lot of different ways."

"Yes, like 'fuck?'"

Hearing him say the word in his soft, lyrical accent sends a shiver through me. It's hard not to feel something when I'm talking about sex with the sexiest male I've ever met in my life. He must feel my slight flare of excitement because his hand tightens on mine for a second. When I look up, his gaze is heated on my face. I swallow around the sudden lump in my throat and look away.

"Yes, but fuck isn't so bad. There's also screw, bone, bang, nail."

"Hm, I like 'fuck.' The others do not sound pleasurable. When you called me a 'fuck-boy' is it because you thought I was having sex with Li'aht?"

My face gets warm. I forgot all about that.

"Uh, no. A fuckboi is like a guy who isn't any good. A guy who does women wrong. I'm sorry I called you that."

I peek up at him, expecting him to look hurt, but he's smirking. He pulls me into his side.

"You do not need to be sorry, my *lehti*. I can see how my behavior would lead you to think I was a fuck-boy."

KWARQ

Amina laughs and shakes her head again.

"You're so funny when you use slang."

"Why?"

Her shoulders jerk up and down. "I don't know, you just are."

"Do I use it incorrectly?"

"Yes, babe, you do. You sound super corny."

"Is this word 'corny' also slang?"

"It's also Ebonics, which is Black people slang. It means not cool or silly."

"Black people have their own slang?"

She laughs again, and it's a little lighter than usual. The tension she usually carries is missing.

"We kind of have our own everything. Black culture is pretty unique. We have our own music, dance, language, popular culture. We've had to reinvent ourselves a lot. It makes for some interesting creations."

I find this ability to adapt and overcome so many varied circumstances admirable and impressive. I am again pleased that my *lehti* is who she is.

"Can you teach me Ebonics?"

Her mouth twitches like she wants to laugh, but she doesn't. Instead, she leans in and presses a soft kiss to my arm.

"You're so cute, Kwarq. I will absolutely teach you."

CHAPTER 21

AMINA

"Qim, you're here. I thought you were going on a vacation."

The male standing at the desk in Kwarq's office turns with a bright smile on his face. Kwarq leaves me at the door to go embrace him, and I hope to god I'm too far away for them to scent my reaction.

Like every Lyqa on this planet, so far, Qim is a cutie pie. He's got this young, multi-racial Brad Pitt thing going on, and I have to stop myself from breaking into a stupid grin when he turns to face me. His looks startled to see me, but his mouth curves back into his easy smile a second later.

"Qim, this is my *lehti*, Amina. She is from Earth." Kwarq comes back to me. He places his hand gently at my back and urges me forward. "Amina, this is Qim, my colleague and friend."

"Hi, Qim." Like Kwarq's name, the 'q' in Qim is a soft click in the throat. I carefully try to recreate the sound when I say it.

"You're Lyqa pronunciation is impressive, Amina. I have never met a being from Earth. It is a pleasure."

His voice is deep, much deeper and rounder than Kwarq's, and surprising coming from such a boyish face. He takes a step forward, wrapping his arms around my back and pulling me into a gentle hug.

Kwarq shifts beside me, and I hold up my hand before he can tell Qim not to touch me. I really want to hug this dude. He smells good, not as good as Kwarq, but good enough that I take a nice deep breath when my face gets close to his shirt.

My tight, round belly bumps against his waist, and even through our clothes, I can tell he's fit and finely built. Goodness gracious. Qim pulls back, frowning slightly.

"You smell anxious. I am not familiar with human customs. I hope I have not offended you."

"She is not offended. She finds you attractive."

My eyes widen. I hinge my head in Kwarq's direction.

"Way to put a girl on the spot, dude."

Kwarq's smirk is cool. He doesn't seem bothered by the fact that I'm kind of lusting after his friend. When I turn back to Qim, his toffee colored skin pulses a dusty rose.

"I'm not attracted to you," I rush out. "I mean, I think you are attractive. All you Lyqa are fine as hell."

"Fine?" Qim's head tilts to the side. I keep forgetting that their translators don't take AAVE into account.

"Uh, yeah. 'Fine' just means very good-looking."

He nods his head slowly in understanding. He's no doubt trying to work out the linguistic connection between whatever database of vocabulary he has and what I've just said.

"It is Ebonics, Qim, a very wonderful dialect of American English originated among Black Americans, which my *lehti* has agreed to teach me. I think it would be a very worthy contribution to the language databases of Lyqa. If you like, perhaps she can teach you, too. We can submit the collection to the association together."

Qim's face brightens and his teeth flash between his full lips. He has a little sliver of a gap between the front two. It's charming and surprisingly sexy. This dude really is super hot.

Kwarq clears his throat. I'm staring.

"I'm so sorry. I swear, I'm not trying to make you uncomfortable. I'll try to mask my responses better."

Kwarq snorts and pulls me against him. He doesn't seem jealous, but there is definitely an air of possessiveness in how he settles his arm around me. I don't mind it. In fact, I like it. He hasn't touched me in such an intimate way for a while. Since the miscarriage scare, he's been treating me like I might break if he does more than hold my hand.

"My *lehti*, I don't know if you realize, yet, but you are terrible at hiding your emotions."

KWARQ

My *lehti* is a patient, generous woman. For nearly two hours she carefully introduces me and Qim to various phrases and idioms of her native dialect. She explains the origin of sayings, constructing practical and appropriate uses for them in every day conversation.

"Ebonics is a little complicated. The greatest risk to sounding unnatural is not knowing what situations a word can be used. Then you end up sounding corny. You don't want to sound corny."

"And corny means 'uncool' or 'uninteresting,' correct?"

Qim's and Amina's heads are bent close together. His hand moves quickly over the keypad in front of them as he listens raptly to what my *lehti* says. The holoscreen flashes the English words and the Lyqa equivalent. Amina watches Qim add the phrases, correcting him when the Lyqa translation into English is incorrect.

"Yeah, if you're talking about a person. But it can also mean that something isn't funny. Or boring. So one might say, 'That dude was corny,' if talking about a man who thinks he's charming but isn't. Or 'that joke was corny,' if someone says something that was meant to be funny, but isn't. Corny has many uses."

Qim adds her explanations. I've been listening to all that Amina has said, but mostly I've been watching her. When she was in her resting period, I had many days to observe her without her shying away or becoming embarrassed. In that time of caring for her, I came to know everything there is to know about my *lehti*. All of the small intricacies that make her unique and beautiful.

Right now she's frowning. Just above the full, roundness of her cheeks, a faint bit of blood rushes to her face. She's embarrassed again.

"I feel like all of the stuff I've been telling you is bad stuff. Like ways of being mean. Maybe don't put corny in there."

Qim laughs and covers Amina's hand with his own. Her eyes flicker up to me. Every time Qim touches her, she gets nervous. Perhaps she believes I am jealous that she finds my friend attractive. She does not realize yet that the *leht* doesn't allow for such feelings. She is my heartbeat, and I am hers forever. Another handsome male won't change this.

"All language is useful, *sa'qi*. We do not judge. I am sure these kinds of words have their uses on Earth."

"Yeah, but it makes us seem so boo."

"What is 'boo'?" he asks before I can.

My *lehti*'s beautiful, cackling laugh bursts from her throat. My eyes shift up the curved line of her neck when she angles her head back.

"You guys are so funny. Boo is just a general word that means not good or satisfactory. So English is cool, but some of the meanings can be a little boo. Got it?"

We both nod. Qim's eyes seem to linger on Amina's face for a moment.

"Do you have any sisters, Amina?"

"I sure do. Two. Why?" Her brows are drawn in a curious frown.

"You are lovely. I would know if there are other women like you in the universe."

"Aw, thanks."

Her brown skin tinges with red, and she looks over to me,

her mouth pulling down in another, strange smile-frown that accompanies the scent of embarrassment. Apparently, my *lehti* feels shy when *anyone* offers her a compliment.

I take the small translation chip and go to where Amina sits with Qim, trying her best to avoid his fascinated gaze.

Human women aren't a species many Lyqa have the opportunity to interact with on any level of intimacy. I know how enthralled I was by Amina's wit and charm when I finally had the opportunity to speak with her. I understand why Qim feels the same way.

"*Lehti*, let me fit your translator. It will not help you speak Lyqa, you will need a more invasive procedure for that, but it will help to translate what you hear."

She angles her head away when I reach out for her.

"Is it going to hurt?" She eyes my finger where the chips rests on the tip.

"Do you believe I would hurt you?"

"Not if you didn't have to."

"Then come. Do not worry yourself unnecessarily."

She tilts her head to the side giving me access to the space behind her ear. I press the small square of biomaterial to her skin and hold until it bonds. Amina bravely lets me finish, although her breathing picks up slightly.

"It is finished," I say and sit next to her, pulling her against me. I lean in and whisper into her ear.

CHAPTER 22

AMINA

"I love you, my most honored and treasured beat."

The English translation of Kwarq's Lyqa is a whisper through my subconscious. I squeeze his hands where they rest on my belly.

"I love you, too, babe."

Qim watches us with that fascinated look he had earlier. I ease away from the soft kisses Kwarq presses along my neck.

"So say something to me in Lyqa, so I can make sure this thing works, properly."

"What would you have me say, *sa'qi.*"

That's what he says, but when it gets to the Lyqa part, my translator kicks in, and I hear: *respected and valued friend.*

"Wait, what does *'sa'qi'* mean?"

"Friend," Kwarq supplies at my ear.

"Uh, that's not what I heard."

"It is a rough translation."

"So what's the literal translation?"

He pauses for a moment to think about it. "Respected and esteemed acquaintance, perhaps?"

"That one word means all of that?"

"The sentiment is implied in the word, itself," Qim explains. "Does 'friend' not mean the same in English?"

I chuckle a little. "Uh, no. Friend just means friend. Like someone you know and like, a little. I guess you can have a best friend, that might be like a *sa'qi.* Or like your boos."

"I thought 'boo' meant unsatisfactory?" Qim looks confused again.

"Well, it does, but when you talk about people, your boo is like the person you love, your partner, or a friend you cherish. Like Kwarq is my boo. Or my bae, but you only use that for your lover or romantic interest."

"Aaaah!"

Both Kwarq's and Qim's voices are a chorus of awe-filled understanding. I laugh and shake my head.

"I have so much to teach you guys."

"Oh. My. God. Kwarq, this is trash!"

I don't know why I bother whispering. It's not like every single Lyqa in the theater can't hear me. We spent more time at Kwarq's office than we anticipated, so instead of meeting his parents at the market, we met them at the movies. If this travesty can even be called that. Did I say that Lyqas were extra? Because Lyqas are so extra.

"I told you," Kwarq's sing-songy whisper is a caress in the dark.

We occupy a row in a large viewing room that closely resembles an opera house back on Earth. The film being shown is displayed as a large projection at the front of the room, and it's the worse film I've ever seen. I'm talking horrible acting, terrible script, and surprisingly bad special effects. These people can transport across galaxies in an instant, but I can clearly see blood squibs during death scenes.

"You said they were bad. This is horrible! How can you even compare this to Earth movies?"

Lyqa theaters aren't nearly as dark as human theaters, so I have no problem seeing the flash of disbelief in Kwarq's yellow eyes.

"*Lehti*, you routinely paid to sit through hours of teenagers falling in love with vampires. This," he waves his hand at the projection, "is cinematic genius compared to that. And," he adds after a moment, "it is free."

A lot of things are free on Lyqa. Healthcare, public transportation, childcare, and really crappy movies. The first three are amazing. The last is a mercy. No one should have to pay for this shit.

The male lead of this "romantic drama" is dying a dramatically over the top death on the screen. He clutches at his chest, falling to his knees. My translator converts everything to English, so I can understand what's happening. I wish it didn't. In the few hours I've been able to understand Lyqa, I've realized they stay doing the most. I cringe when the dying man on the screen gasps out a final farewell to his…veins?

"It is lost in translation," Kwarq murmurs into my ear. He must see my confusion.

"Clearly."

His chuckle is loud. His mother leans over and taps her hand against the back of his head. Kwarq ducks and rubs his hand over the spot. I slap my hand over my mouth to keep from cracking up. Somewhere behind us, a shush sounds out. I duck further in my seat, although I don't have to. The seats are so much larger than me, that from the back, I'm sure it looks like mine is empty.

"You are going to have to make that up to me."

His eyes flicker like little torches in the dim light. Suddenly, the room is too warm. Aside from the little kisses at his office, it's been forever since he looked at me with anything but concern. Even our nightly reinforcements are functional and to the point.

I look back to the screen. He does the same after a moment. Slowly, I slide my hand into his lap and immediately feel him stiffen.

"*Lehti…*"

It's a low warning, but I ignore it and cup my hand over

his crotch, squeezing firmly. He grunts and shifts in the seat.

"Make it up like this?"

He immediately gets hard under my hand. The loose fit of his pants provides more than enough room for him to grow to his full length. He thickens and pulses beneath my fingers.

"I've missed you," I whisper, turning to him, willing him to look at me, but he doesn't. His jaw clenches, and his hands grip the armrests of the seat.

"*Lehti*, please."

"You are aware that we can hear you, right?"

Bati stage whispers at my other side. Of course they can. I wish for once, they would pretend like they can't.

I pull my hand back. Kwarq exhales loudly and slumps down in his seat. My heart beats fast with his. My pussy tingles against the cushy seat. Bati takes in a breath and then jerks away, turning back to the screen. In the flickering light of the projection, his dark skin pulses bright red.

KWARQ

I haven't touched my *lehti* since she came out of her resting period. In the week since, she has been stronger than ever. The fatigue that plagued her after she conceived is gone. She eats heartily and as often as she wants. I don't sense any vulnerability in her form. I feel confident that she will be safe from here out.

Watching her flourish with our children has only made me want her more. Her hormones are a concentrated signal to my first heart to make love to her. And even though every night we join so I can give her my semen, the act holds none of the passion either of us would like. Just last night, I noticed the tight passage of her pussy softening as I moved within her. She'd turned her head away in embarrassment, but had not been able to stop the soft moans that filled my ears each time I sank deep inside of her. I can't fight it anymore. I want her. She is past the point of danger, there is no need to wait any longer.

The screen flickers off and the lights brighten, signaling the end of the movie. My eyes first turn to Amina, and I'm surprised to see her wiping a streak of tears from her cheeks. My mother, too, is brushing at her eyes. I, my brothers, and father wait patiently while Amina and my mother collect themselves, each of us wearing varying looks of disbelief. Ah'dan looks appalled at their display. I can sympathize. The movie was, as my *lehti* said, trash. How anyone could be moved by such a blatant display of poor writing, directing, and acting is beyond me.

Still, both my mother and Amina sigh wistfully as we lead them out of the theater. Ah'dan and Bati go ahead. My mother links her arm through my father's, and he pats her hand comfortingly as she continues to extol the movie's sensitivities.

I take Amina's hand in mine and guide her through the isle. When we get to the exit, she leans her body into my side and expels a long, heavy sigh.

"That was such a sweet movie."

"I thought it was trash?"

"It was, but the end was kind of sweet. How can you not be moved by the fact that he died from a broken heart after he lost his love? It's sad but sweet. Every girl wants that kind of love."

Ah, yes. This is another thing I forgot to tell my *lehti,* and one she would not consider. Perhaps this is a good time to explain how the *leht* actually works.

"Every Lyqa's partner has this kind of love," I say carefully. I don't want her getting nervous and anxious for nothing.

"Because of the *leht*?" her expression is curious as she looks up at me. I still don't think she understands just how physical the *leht* is. That it is not just a feeling but a manner of existing. That once my first heart began to beat, I truly came into being.

I nod patiently. "Yes, because of the *leht*. It cannot be undone, and one cannot live without one's heartbeat."

"What does that mean?" She's making the face she makes when she knows something strange is coming, something foreign and overwhelming. I don't think even she could suspect what I am going to tell her.

"Amina, the *leht* is not just some feeling a Lyqa has for another. It was not sweet that the man in the film died when he lost his *lehti*. It was biology. Once your first heart starts beating, you cannot lose the trigger that keeps it going. If you do, you will die. We do not speak in metaphor. To die of a broken heart is a very real thing for us."

We're walking down a quiet road back to our home. My brothers are ahead of us. I can hear them discussing the stupidity of the film. My mother and father are just behind them.

All of this is happening in the periphery of my mind, however, because Amina has stopped in the middle of the sidewalk. Her expression is a mix of awe and horror.

"Are you trying to tell me that if I ever leave you, you'll die?"

"No, we do not have to share the same space or stay together, but if you were to die, my first heart would cease to beat, my body would weaken, and I would not be far behind you."

Her eyes are saucers in her round face. I feel my heart speed up a notch with hers. The anxiety that rolls off of her is a putrid cloud.

"Are you serious?"

"I am."

"But your body worked fine before you met me."

"It did."

"So why would you die?"

Her voice raises. I hear my family pause ahead of us. I try to keep my voice calm. This is a reality I have known my entire life. I am not afraid of the end that I know will follow were I to lose my *lehti*. I would welcome it. I could not imagine a universe where Amina wasn't thriving somewhere in it. I pull her into my arms and smooth a hand across the stress lines on her forehead.

"My *lehti*. Do not be alarmed. Any world where you no longer existed would not be one that I could endure. You are my heart. It beats only to serve and protect you. And while I will gladly follow you into the unknown of death, I will also do all that I can to ensure that you are safe and have the freedom to live a long, healthy life. You have made me stronger, and with my strength, I will care for you and our family."

Amina maneuvers away, pushing her hands up her forehead and over the top of her hair, pulling her face taut in a way that only serves to make her panicked expression more impactful.

"Oh, my god. This is crazy. How can you be okay with this?"

"It is just the way it is for my kind. I am not worried about it." I'm not. I know I can protect her, and if I can't, I will follow here wherever she goes.

"Yeah, but what if something randomly happens to me?"

"Like what?"

"Like anything!" Panic grips her. I feel out and try to project my calm. It doesn't work. If anything, my acceptance of the *leht* is only serving to make her more panicked. "What if I get hit by a bus? What if I slip and fall in the tub? What if I choke on a fucking piece of broccoli?"

Once again, my *lehti* conjures the most absurd hypothetical situations to justify her fear of the unknown. I know by now that I must let her worry until she sees that everything will be okay. It is useless to try and placate her with promises.

"Amina, yes, any of these things may happen. It is my job as your *lehti* to keep as many of these misfortunes from befalling you as possible, but you are right. I cannot and will not be everywhere at once. I would not hamper your freedom to protect you, but I also would not trade the love I feel for you to avoid losing you and therefore myself. I hope that one day you will feel the same for me."

Though it is not my intention, guilt crowds out her panic. She huffs out a deep breath and leans in to my chest. I hold her close, inhaling the sweet scent of her hair.

"I love you so much it scares me, Kwarq." Her voice is laced with sadness. "I didn't think it was possible to love anyone as much as I love you. I wouldn't want you to die because of me."

"Amina, I am only now fully alive because of you," I tell her, and it's the truth.

CHAPTER 23

AMINA

So, apparently, I hold Kwarq's life in my clumsy, little hands. But according to him, that shouldn't be any pressure.

It figures his biology would dictate that his very existence be reliant on me not accidentally drowning in the bathtub or tripping into rush hour traffic.

The moment Kwarq tells me about this bit of *lchti* juju, I feel like anything that could go wrong is going to. I trip like ten times before we make it home, and Kwarq assures me that it's all in my head. I try to listen to him. I tell myself that everything will be okay. Nothing is going to happen to me.

When we get home, Kwarq's brothers shoot me nervous glances all throughout our meal of roasted vegetables and stewed greens. My worry is forgotten as my babies get hungry, and all I can think about is shoveling food into my mouth. The moment I'm full, however, the anxiety hits me full force.

A billion doomsday scenarios flicker through my brain, and they all end up with Kwarq falling to his knees, gripping his chest in agony just like the Lyqa man in the movie we saw earlier. A movie that no longer seems like the sweetest thing in the world to me. Now it just seems tragic. I was right the first time. That movie was trash.

I want to reason myself around this bit of Lyqa evolution, but I'm having a hard time accepting something so absolute. It doesn't help that Kwarq is completely fine with it. I get it's all he's ever known, but still, isn't one's base instinct supposed to be survival? I love love as much as the next

Lyqa, but why does every cultural difference between us have to completely throw my entire world for a loop?

I'm in my head for the rest of the evening. Kwarq's father suggests we move to the living room after dinner. Perhaps in an attempt to lighten the mood, we watch some Lyqa sitcom on their television type device. It's funny and almost completely centered around the *leht*, as I expected. Apparently, falling in love with someone in some kind of crazy heart bond is their most compelling topic. I laugh a little bit, but then one of the characters accidentally eats a bad fruit, causing her and her *lehti* to fall into a coma, and before I know it, I'm back in doomsday scenario mode.

I know everyone can sense my tension. I'm sure I smell like a thousand nervous grandmas, whatever that smells like. We only watch one episode of the show before everyone agrees that calling it a night is the best thing to do. Before his parents go off to bed, Mahdi gives me a big, sympathetic hug and kisses both of my cheeks.

"The *leht* is a beautiful thing. I have never once worried that my life is linked to Quth's."

Of course they heard our conversation earlier. If I recall correctly, at one point I was shrieking in alarm like a crazy woman in the middle of the sidewalk. One wouldn't even have to be Lyqa to have heard me.

"Come, let us go to bed."

Kwarq has been quiet, but he isn't as nervous about my anxiety as everyone else. He's actually behaving quite normally. The moments when he threw his head back and laughed heartily at the funny parts of the show were like little glimmers of light in the gloom of my thoughts.

I follow him through the house until we get to his apartments. We left the patio doors open, and the room is cool and sweet smelling from the breeze. I expect Kwarq to lead me to the bedroom, but he passes through the sitting room and takes me down the hall to the bathroom.

I'm more than a little curious when Kwarq leaves me just inside the bathroom and turns on the tap in the tub. Steamy, lavender tinted water spills into the deep recesses of the bowl. A light, herby smell scents the room, and I move closer to peer into the water.

"I thought it would be nice to have a bath. It may relax you."

I'm distracted by the movement of Kwarq's broad, muscular shoulders beneath his t-shirt as he swirls his hand back and forth through the water. Everything inside of me flares to life as I watch his gentle, purposeful movements. Even on this planet, where everyone seems to be some strange version of attractive, one look at Kwarq sets my body on fire.

I squeeze my thighs together when my pussy starts to tingle and moisten. Kwarq's hand pauses in the water before he turns to look at me. His face glistens from the steam, but the yellow of his eyes is like ice. There is no mistaking the hunger on his face. It echoes my own rising need.

"It has been too long, my *lehti*."

His voice is strangled and gruff. In this moment, I want him more than I have before. I just want to feel him close to me. To feel the safety of his arms around me.

"Is it safe to do it like we want to? I mean, it won't hurt them?"

"It will not."

He doesn't have to tell me twice. The tub is nearly full and Kwarq waves his hand over the tap to stop the water. Plumes of steam float around us, but our gazes stay locked through the milky space between us.

"Help me?"

I barely hear my own voice, but Kwarq rises immediately

to stand before me.

"Of course."

My belly is pretty big, and I'm still getting used to it. Waking up one day the equivalent of eight months pregnant is not something that I've been able to maneuver easily. Especially when it comes to getting in and out of clingy Lyqa garb.

Kwarq reaches for my shoulder and pulls free the tie that holds the single strap of my day dress up. The light brushes of his fingers along my neck and collarbone send stinging tingles throughout my body. I suck in a breath when he peels down the bodice and cups my breasts in his large, warm hands. He holds them gently, lifting them in his palms.

"They are bigger," he comments softly.

"They are."

I expect him to pull away and continue undress me, so my cry of shocked desire is loud in the room when he leans forward and firmly sucks one of my nipples into his mouth.

"Kwarq!"

"You are so sweet. So full and soft." He murmurs between fiery flicks of his tongue. He covers me and draws me into the hot cavern of his mouth, sucking and lapping.

My legs wobble as he moves to my other breast, lavishing my sensitive skin with the same attention. I need more. I feel it taking over me. A single minded desire, and all I can think is that I want all of him now.

"Patience, Amina."

Kwarq's amused murmur breaks through the fog of lust that has taken over my mind.

"I can't. I'm horny."

He laughs, but pulls my dress over the bulge of my belly and down my hips until it pools at the floor. I'm naked beneath. Lyqa aren't a fan of underwear. I was hardly aware of it throughout the day, but now all I can think about is the warm, wet air that wisps over my pussy.

Kwarq pulls one of my straining nipples into his mouth, releasing it with a little pop, then begins a trail down my belly, leaving smacking kisses across my tightly stretched abdomen.

"My beautiful, brown Amina. Creator of my children. I love you."

"I love you, too, Kwarq."

Once he's covered my stomach, he moves down. He's barely reached the spot between my thighs where I'm already dripping with wetness before he unfurls his tongue and drags it through my slit, flicking up at my clitoris and causing me to nearly jerk out of my skin.

KWARQ

"Oh, god!"

Amina flinches violently and grabs hold of my hair, pressing me further into her pussy as I swirl my tongue through her sweet, juicy folds. Every time I get to the top, I curl the tip of my tongue and catch her tight little bud. I've never tasted anything so sweet.

My *lehti* is so wet for me. Her desire covers my face, and I lap greedily to get as much of her as I can.

My loose pants still don't have enough room for my straining erection. My first heart has picked up a furious beat, and my cock pushes painfully against the fabric. I yank my pants down my hips, freeing myself, and allowing my cock to lengthen to its full potential. I stroke my hand up the shaft and over the head just as Amina tense above me. She's so close. I am too, and if I want to release when I am inside of her, I will have to calm down.

I let go of myself and focus on bringing my *lehti* to her orgasm. Her hips roll in time with the movements of my tongue, and her breathy gasps are loud. I nuzzle my face between her slick, swollen pussy lips and press my tongue into her opening, extending it as far as it will go.

"Ah, Kwarq!"

Amina comes with a violent shudder. Her hands tighten against my head. I reach around and hold her soft, round bottom as she jerks and flinches against my mouth.

Her legs collapse, and she sags to the floor. I hold her close, rubbing along her back as her heart slows. She relaxes further and slides down my chest. Perhaps I have put her to sleep. I hate to think her orgasm was so intense that it has triggered another resting period. And if it has, I hope it doesn't last as long as the last one. The anxiety of waiting for her to awaken nearly drove me mad.

"I want to taste you, too."

This moaned declaration is the only warning I get before Amina's warm, wet mouth closes over the head of my cock. Pure magnetic energy surges through me, and I fall back, bracing myself against the cool, stone floor, and inadvertently providing myself with a better view of Amina taking me into her mouth.

"Mm."

She moans and draws her little pink tongue in a line from the base of my cock all the way to the tip. I tense, too consumed by the feel of the little bumps of her tongue along my skin to move. When she gets to the top, she stretches her mouth wide over the tip and lowers her head down. I watch with bated breath as she works inch after inch of my cock into the hot hollow of her mouth, not stopping until I hit the soft back of her throat. It's almost too much.

"Ahg! My *lehti*, please have mercy."

She doesn't. She draws me back out, flicking her tongue along my length and sinks back down, taking even more, taking me past the soft back of her mouth, until I feel the constricted muscles of her esophagus squeeze me.

"Damn, you taste good," she murmurs when she releases me again. I want to tell her that nothing could taste as good as she does on my tongue, but I can't even think.

Her movements quicken. The hand holding me at the base squeezes tighter as it jerks up and down to meet her lips. I won't last much longer.

It takes all of my effort to take hold of her soft, fluffy curls and gently pull her away from me.

"Come, get in the water."

I stand from the hard, stone floor and hold out my hand to her. My cock juts out between us, glistening from her attention. She stares at my straining length through her lashes and my body vibrates from the effort not to come on her beautiful face.

She rises and lets me hand her into the tub. We sink down into the hot water. Immediately, Amina turns to me and presses against me, bending her legs to straddle my hips.

"I want your dick in me now."

Knowing my *lehti* wants me as much as I want her is all it takes for the last of my control to slip. I palm her plump bottom, lifting her high by the tight globes until the tip of my cock rests at her opening. In one firm movement, I thrust up into her tight pussy and pull her down against me.

"Ahg!"

"Uhn!"

Our strangled cries ring out in unison. Amina's face pinches the moment I breach her, but then it softens, settling into a languid expression.

"More, Kwarq." Her gasp is sweet and needy.

I grit my teeth around the desire to come and give her what she wants. I lift her and quickly slam her back down, pushing through the resistance that threatens to strangle my cock.

"More."

I know this is the same need that makes her want to eat everything in sight. Knowing that right now she is hungry for my cock fills me with pleasure. I will do all that I can to fill her and make sure she is satisfied.

I settle into an easy rhythm of lifting and impaling her onto me. She moans out her pleasure, filling the large bathroom with cries that echo off the stone walls and ring in my ears. Still she wants more. She takes over, wrapping her arms around my neck and linking her legs at my back. She uses the leverage to lift her hips and bring them down hard to meet my thrusts. Our bodies slap loudly in the water. The vigor of our movement makes little waves slosh over the side of the tub.

"I missed you, my *lehti*. I missed this warm, tight pussy."

"Oh god, Kwarq, I love it."

She raises high and drops down, the additional weight of her belly making her fall hard on me. The ache in my balls crests. I'm on the edge of release.

"Come for me, my love. Come on my cock."

My balls are drawn so tightly to my body that it's painful. Every time her pussy grips me, I have to steel myself against the urge to fill her with my seed.

I angle my hips up just as Amina slams her hips down again. She jerks and screams, her head falling back as her orgasm rockets through her body. My shout is a sharp bark. I fill her, coating her walls and her womb with my seed. I feel the thickness of it begin to crowd me out, and I try to give her more. I give her all that I have until she starts to overflow into the clear water around us.

Amina is pressed to my chest. The hard swell of her belly pushes against my firm stomach. I ease my hold on her and lean away. She makes a little sound of protest and tries to nuzzle back in.

"I do not want to crush the babies," I whisper, but let her lean into my chest, anyway. I pull my own stomach in, giving hers more room.

"That was amazing," she sighs out, and I chuckle.

"You always say that."

"It's always good."

"We have only made love three times. Perhaps that is not enough to know if it is always amazing."

She leans away from me and her eyes are half-lidded and sleepy from our sex.

"You're right. We should do something about that."

My abating need flares back to life, and I urge it back down.

"We will, my *lehti*. I plan on making love to you every chance I get."

"That's good to know, but I mean, now."

She rolls her hips forward. My first heart goes to work.

Amina rises over me and sinks down onto my length with a splash. If possible, the feeling is better than before. Our previous lovemaking has softened her, causing her to cradle me in an even tighter embrace. As she begins to rise and fall down onto my cock, I relinquish myself to her movements, letting her take all that she needs. She is my heart. My beat. I could never deny her.

CHAPTER 24

AMINA

"Mm—ouch!"

My first thing in the morning stretch is accompanied by an achy tightening in my inner thighs and ass. My pussy is warm.

Last night was great. The upside to having my horny take over is that I have an extremely well endowed Lyqa man who can go all night if I want him to. The down side of my horny take over is that I have an extremely well endowed Lyqa man who can go all night if I want him to. Then once that horny high comes down, I feel every place he's been. Every single delicious place.

"Are you very sore?"

Kwarq's at the edge of the bed. He's dressed. He always gets up before me, and I always sleep late. I can't help it. I'm tired. Kwarq says it's the babies, and it probably is. Although I would argue that today's late rising is courtesy of the Grade A dickdown I got last night.

Kwarq's face is pulled down in concern.

"I feel amazing. I don't mind the soreness. I like it. In fact, if you're not busy now…"

I let my suggestion trail off, and Kwarq's eyes flare, the yellow flickering brightly. He stands and pulls the light tunic he's wearing over his head before tossing it to the floor. He shoves his lounge pants down his hips, and I suck in a breath when his erection comes springing up in front of him, thick and pointed right at me. I still can't believe I take all of that.

Kwarq crawls up the bed, his face determined and fierce. I

lean back when he stretches his long, hard body over mine, parting my legs so he can settle between them. He presses into me in one, steady motion, filling me completely.

His blazing, yellow eyes hold mine as he withdraws from my body and slowly eases back in, pushing through with steady determination.

This is the calmest we've ever made love. Yet, despite his gentle movements, I'm more on edge than I've ever been. My orgasm pulses behind my clit where the thick head of Kwarq's cock drags lazily at my sensitive walls. I know it's going to be intense before it even hits me. Kwarq, ever in tune to my body, slams forward, allowing me to catch it just as it peaks, and I tumble into a volcano of pleasure. It flows hotly beneath my skin, making it hard to do anything but tremble in its wake.

Kwarq thrusts deeply and buries his head in my hair. A low rumbling moan sounds out as he begins to pulse, bathing me with his release.

"I thought we could go to your home today."

I pull another single strap dress up my body. I've come to love the simplicity of Lyqa fashion. While I was asleep, Kwarq purchased several of the dresses for me. The one I'm wearing is in a bright coral color. Kwarq has explained that the fabric is infused with various supplements to keep me comfortable and help me through my pregnancy. It doesn't hurt that they are also really beautiful.

"My home? Like Earth?"

"Yes, Earth. I still have the transport arranged, and I said I would take you."

He wants to take me home now? Is something wrong?

"Oh, I didn't think we were going anymore."

"*Lehti*, I said I would take you home. I would not go back on my word."

I don't care about his word. I care about him trying to send me home all of a sudden. Is it because I'm no longer at risk in the pregnancy? Did I miss something? Does he think I still want to leave him?

"It's okay. I don't want to go now."

Kwarq smiles and cradles my cheek in his palm.

"I would feel more comfortable if you went home before deciding to stay."

My stomach flutters, and it's not the babies. This feeling is more like the urge to scream and puke at the same time. I don't know what could have happened since a half hour ago. Was it my reaction to the *lehti* juju? Is my tendency to freak out about our cultural differences too much for him?

"Kwarq, I thought things were going well. I thought you wanted me to stay with you."

Kwarq's expression is patient as I silently panic. He pulls me against him, resting his chin into my cloud of hair.

"You were never meant to stay this long, *lehti*. As much as I have loved having you here with me, I do not think it is a good idea that you just vanish from your home planet. What about your family? Your parents? It has been over two months on Earth. Your people will expect you back at some point."

Oh. My. God. My family. I haven't even thought about my mother or sisters since I've been here. Between the unexpectedly long resting spells and just enjoying being with Kwarq, it hasn't even occurred to me that I basically left my home in the middle of the night and never returned. My job probably called my mother, who's my emergency contact, when I stopped showing up for work. My family probably thinks I've been kidnapped or I'm dead.

Kwarq's right. I have to go back if just to let my family know I'm okay and alive. I'll have to explain to them how I'm showing up a month later looking almost nine months pregnant, but I'll figure that out later. I need to get home. Just thinking of my mother crying herself to sleep wondering what's happened to me makes me feel awful.

"I didn't even think about my family. I should visit and let them know I'm okay. When do you want to leave?"

Kwarq nods and he almost appears relieved. He's kind of acting like I'm not coming back. Why is he acting like I'm not coming back?

I don't actually have anything to pack. I came to Lyqa in a pair of jeans and a t-shirt, neither of which fit me anymore. I didn't even bring my purse. I left it at Kwarq's apartment. A part of me wants to be petty and pack all of the stuff I've acquired since I've been here, just to see if Kwarq objects, but another part of me is too scared. What if he's just like, "let me help you with your bags?"

I give up on the idea of the petty pack. Kwarq's suggestion that I return home is the responsible thing to do. He didn't actually *say* he wanted me to stay there. I'm just doing what I always do and reading too much into things.

I leave his apartment and make my way to the front of the house. Kwarq's voice sounds out from the living room. I can't tell who he's talking to, but it's clear whatever he's saying is serious. He sounds bummed. Maybe he doesn't want to take me after all.

"I would not have chosen her for myself. She could never compare to you. To your beauty and intelligence. She is not who I want, you know that!"

I stop in the hall, holding my breath so no one hears me. This is not the time to get busted by Lyqa spidey-hearing.

"If she wasn't your most treasured beat, would we have had a chance?"

"If I'd never passed her on the street, I would still be yours. You know our hearts are bound. I can't stop it. Help me, I can't stop it!"

"Oh, my love, we may not be able to have a life, but we will always have our love. Go to her. Do what you must."

"I will go, but she will never replace you. You are my true heart's beat."

They're speaking in Lyqa. My translator spits out the English for me. This explains why they sound so dramatic.

I've only heard the person he's speaking to once, but it would be hard to forget the breathy, musical voice. Li'aht is here, and now I know why Kwarq wants me to leave.

The pain in Kwarq's voice is so intense that it almost overrides the sharp stab of betrayal I feel. Everything he's ever said about loving and protecting me has only been because of the *leht*. Damn.

I don't realize I'm crying until I feel the tears begin to fall onto my chest. The shuffling of clothes and feet let me know that someone is coming. I hurry back the way I came until I get to the guest restroom off the foyer. I manage to close the door just as I see a flash of white cloth come into view.

"*Lehti*, are you okay?"

Lehti my ass. Apparently, all I am is a roadblock to his "true" heart. Still, I have to clear my throat before I can answer.

"I'm ready to leave. I'll be out in a moment."

Kwarq doesn't respond right away, and I don't move until I hear him shift away from the door. Only then do I sag against the sink, unable any longer to hold back the anguish I'm feeling. I never should have believed him.

If I'm honest with myself, Kwarq has never tried to deny that his attraction to me is because of the *leht*. He basically lives his entire life by the dictates of the *leht*. Everything he's done so far has been because he has to do it, because I'm his *lehti*. The man unquestioningly stranded himself on a hostile alien planet just to fulfill his stupid first heart's purpose. As I try my best to muffle the sounds of my sobs, I have to face the fact that this hasn't been the grand love story I've been imagining.

It takes me longer than I would like to gather myself. I keep telling myself that it hasn't been long enough for me to feel the way I do. I'm not Lyqa. Kwarq may be bound by the dictates of his heart, but I'm smarter than this. I should have been smarter than this.

I push away the pain that makes me want to fold myself into a ball on the floor of the bathroom. Instead, I splash my face with water, wincing when I catch my reflection and see that my eyes are too puffy to do anything about. I shrug at my reflection. Who cares anymore.

KWARQ

I can smell Amina's sadness. It is not just sadness. It's anguish. My first heart aches in chorus with hers, and I have to grip the wall to keep from bursting through the door to find out what's wrong.

When the door finally slides open, I notice several things right away.

Her eyes are red and puffy. Even beneath her dark brown skin, the capillaries are mottled and the rims of her rounded nostrils are swollen. She's been crying. She must have been very careful to remain quiet because I didn't hear her. My heart aches with the knowledge that she's been suffering alone.

"*Lehti*, what is wrong?"

My tone is careful. It must be something serious if it has managed to upset her this much. I would know what it is, so I can fix it.

"Oh, nothing. It's just the—babies. You know how it is. It's like zero to one hundred."

She tries to sound casual, but it's forced and insincere.

"*Lehti—*"

I reach for her, but she dodges my hands, letting out a weak chuckle.

"I'm fine, Kwarq. Let's go."

My parents and brothers wait to see us off. The wave of sadness that rolls off of Amina is so thick that my mother flinches when she pulls her into a fierce hug. When my mother's panicked gaze meets mine, I can do nothing more than shrug. I have no idea what's happening.

"Should we hire a transport? The walk may tire you."

She avoids my gaze and squints in the bright afternoon. She looks lovely, despite her sadness. Her skin shimmers in the sunlight.

"No. Let's walk."

"Are you sure, *lehti*?"

"I'm sure. I want to walk."

She strolls at my side, widening the distance whenever I try to step closer to her. Finally, I give up and let her keep the space between us.

My *lehti* has only been out of the house a few times, and the first time, she was shy about looking around. Now she looks at everything. She runs her hands along the leaves and feathers of plants that we pass on the road. She waves and nods to Lyqas sitting on their patios. For the short walk to the transport center, her sadness lifts, and I hope that she is just feeling sentimental about home. I also wonder about the distance she's putting between us.

Our pod sits at the curb of the rental station when we arrive at the transport center. She lets me hand her in, and it is the most contact we have had since I found her crying in the bathroom.

As soon as she's settled, she jerks her hand away. I can't even begin to sort through my confusion.

229

CHAPTER 25

AMINA

I ignore the tingling in my fingers when Kwarq takes my hand. The truth is, I'm too bulky to manage the pod by myself, so I have no choice but to let him help me.

I've been careful not to touch him. I don't want to be fooled by the magnetism of the *leht*. I don't want to feel that connection, knowing it isn't real. That it's just a force of biology.

Kwarq expertly maneuvers us to the immigration checkpoint. I'm surprised to see the same redhead from our arrival waiting in the booth. When her eyes fall on me, she breaks into a wide grin.

"Congratulations."

I'm too caught off guard to respond, but Kwarq says something in Lyqa that my translator interprets as a type of gratitude. The woman removes my wrist band, typing something into her screen before turning back to us.

"I hope you have enjoyed your stay, and best wishes on your birthing."

I nod, but my throat is tight. Everything feels too real. In a moment, I'll be back in Chicago like I never left. I should be happy, at least to see my family, but I can only feel like I'm losing the one thing that has ever made any sense in my life.

It's just like I remember. One moment Kwarq is warning me to brace myself, and the next, we're hovering over Chicago. The landscape beneath us is draped in a thick, white blanket of snow. The roads show the dirty tracks of traffic. People file about like little ants on the sidewalks below. As we lower closer to the ground, I hear the deep rumble of a train nearby.

It's surreal. Kwarq parks us at the alley behind his old apartment building. I wonder where he plans on hiding the pod, and I'm surprised to see him pull out a regular old garage opener and press it, opening the same car port he used before.

"Uh, you know that you can't just show up and use this garage, anymore, right? They probably think you skipped out on the apartment."

Kwarq glances over to me. His mouth is turned up in a little smile as he maneuvers the pod into the dark, wide space.

"They do not think this."

"Yeah, that's not how things work here. We've been gone, what, a month and a half? Two months?"

"We have."

"Right. Well, you have to pay rent here on time. If you just leave your apartment, they will toss your belongings onto the street. I'm pretty sure that's the case by now. For you and for me."

I just abandoned my life to go to Lyqa. Even though it wasn't my intention to stay, once I thought I was happy with Kwarq, I didn't even give my apartment, my things, my family a spare thought. Who knows how long it would have been before I realized that everything I knew was galaxies away. If I hadn't heard Kwarq this morning, I probably would have been content on Lyqa in La-La-Land.

Kwarq doesn't seem too concerned. I'm damn near bursting with guilt and hurt.

"Do not worry. In the time you have been at my home, I have maintained both of our residences here on Earth. When you entered your second resting period, I tendered your employment resignation and had your final compensation administered to your banking institution. Additionally, I provided funds for your building management to withdraw your monthly rental fee. I located your mother and sisters and sent them a message from your cellular phone reassuring them of your safety. I explained that you received a once in a lifetime opportunity to travel to another country and you would be back soon. Hopefully, they were calmed by this belief."

I'm too stunned to be glad that my apartment is still there and my family doesn't think I'm dead.

"Why didn't you say anything?"

We're sitting in the pod. The garage is dark, but the internal lights of the transport make it easy to see the frown that pulls at Kwarq's face.

"Amina, you are my *lehti*. I said I would take care of you. I would not just bring you to my home without ensuring that your life here would continue as uninterrupted as possible. I would not have you come back to chaos. I thought this was understood."

I thought a lot of things were understood, but Kwarq is dropping me off back home, so that is clearly not the case. I'm still grateful that he had the foresight to handle these things. I sure wasn't thinking about them.

"You didn't have to do that, but thank you. I probably should have thought about all that. I hope coming back here wasn't too much trouble."

"It was not."

His response is careful. He's staring at the side of my face. I keep my eyes trained to the inside of the garage. When it's all said and done, he's been good to me. I don't want him to see my hurt and feel guilty.

"Well, thank you for bringing me back. I really enjoyed visiting with you."

I press the door release button on my side of the pod and it hisses softly open, sliding back into the side of the transport. I turn to step down before I realize that I'm a good two feet up. The bulk of my belly makes it hard for me to counter the momentum, and before I know it, I'm sliding out of the seat toward the ground.

"Ah!—"

In an instant, Kwarq is there. He stops me mid-air, probably only a few inches from the ground. The fall wouldn't have killed me, but with my added weight and general awkwardness of movement, I would have been sporting a nice sprained ankle.

His grasp on my hips is gentle. I barely felt the jolt of him halting my fall. In the shock of my rescue, my eyes fly to his and I freeze as he holds me suspended in air like I'm weightless. The yellow of his eyes is warm and open. I wish it wasn't. I wish he didn't insist on looking at me like I hold his heart in my hands, even if I kind of do. I wish he didn't hide the anguish he feels about being *leht* to me instead of Li'aht. It would make it easier to let him go.

I wiggle my legs, prompting him to finally let my feet touch the ground. Once I'm on firm footing, I ease out of his grasp. There's too much feeling there. His first heart is loud in the quiet garage. It taunts me.

"So are you just going to settle things here at your place?"

"I will. There is no need to keep it, but I will continue to pay your housing fees if you would like."

"No, that's not necessary. I'm sure I can get my old gig back. And if not, I have some savings. Once the babies are born, I'm sure I'll find something."

I'm not sure. Actually, I'm pretty sure my life from here on out is going to be a world of struggle. And I can't even think about the mechanics of giving birth to two half-alien babies, right now.

"Amina, I am more than happy to secure your apartment

for as long as you wish. Your are my *leh*—"

"Yes, I know, Kwarq, I'm your *lehti*, your heart beat, but we're on Earth now, you don't have to do all that. No one, least of all me, is going to hold you to some flaw in your biology, so you can stop with all the first heart obligations, okay. It's not like I'm going to sue you for child support."

Our parting of ways is taking too long. I was hoping he'd just drop me off, wave goodbye, and blip on back to Lyqa. All of this is just making me want to cry. I'd rather do that when I'm alone in my apartment.

"What do you mean, 'sue for child support'."

I sigh, dropping my chin to my chest. Of course that's all he got from my little speech. I consider ignoring him, but it's probably just easier to answer the damn question.

"Basically, sometimes fathers end relationships with the mother of their children and decide they don't want to contribute to care of their kids. They don't love the mother, so they don't think they should have to care for the children. Or maybe they love someone else and they want a real family. In those cases, if the mother is having a hard time, she has to go through the legal system to make the father help. But I was joking. Obviously, you live on another planet. I can't expect you to be around to buy school supplies and take our daughters to little league." I go for a wry chuckle, but Kwarq is tight-lipped as he stares back at me.

"You think I would not care for you? For our children?"

Here we go. For a man who's pining after his ex-lover, he should be taking full advantage of this whole from another galaxy loophole.

"No, Kwarq. I know if things were different, you would take care of us. You've already taken such great care of us. More than you had to. I'm just saying that this doesn't have to be difficult. I don't know if we'll see you after this, but I just want you to be assured that I can handle it from here."

I can't handle it. Just the idea of handling it, any of it, makes me want to scream and cry and run far far away. Run to another planet. Preferably one where a beautiful, tall, golden Lyqa man loves me and wants to be a family.

I know I can't think like that. Millions of women take care of children by themselves every day. My mother did it. My sister is doing it. I can do it.

"You do not have to worry, Amina. I will be there. I will always be with you."

That's it. I can't take it anymore. I don't want him to be nice to me. I don't want him to do his duty and follow his stupid first heart. I can't get his conversation with Li'aht out of my head. It makes me want him out of my face.

"Kwarq, I'm going to go now, okay. I can't do this anymore. Go home. Go back to your real life. Go back to Li'aht."

KWARQ

Go back to Li'aht?

I don't know what's going on. My *lehti* is behaving strangely. She has been since we left Lyqa. First she cried in the bathroom and embraced my family like it was the last time she'd ever see them. Then she spoke of child support as if a father and partner does not automatically support his family. Now she's talking about leaving as if I would ever allow her to be away from me if I could help it. I don't understand what is wrong, and I don't understand what Li'aht could possibly have to do with us any longer.

"Amina, why do you think I would want to go back to Li'aht? She has nothing for me. You are my first heart's beat. You are my *lehti*. You are the only one I love. The only one I will ever love."

I'm upsetting her, and I don't understand. She turns away

from me and there is no mistaking the disgust that rolls off of her.

"Kwarq, please just stop. You don't have to lie to me anymore. You don't have to pretend."

"I do not pretend, Amina, and I would never lie to you. Ever."

Her face crumples with hurt and disappointment. She steps away from me, shaking her head. A heavy sigh fills the silence and with it her whole body seems to weigh down. I take hold of her arm, gently, and I don't release her even when she tries to pull away. Everything in me says to make her stay, but I'd rather fix what's wrong. I'd rather understand what's changed.

"Amina, please give me a chance to understand how I have hurt you."

She looks up and smiles. I have seen her smile in a dozen subtle ways, but this is the only smile that makes my heart ache. It's the smile she wears when she is expecting to be hurt. It's the smile that she cannot help when I tell her that she is beautiful. It's the smile that made her uncomfortable with accepting my love.

"It's okay, Kwarq. I know you tried, but this just isn't what you really want."

"It is the only thing I want." It is. Except, perhaps, for this moment to be different. For this trip to have gone as I imagined. Not me standing in a dimly lit garage as Amina tears my heart out for reasons I can't understand. "Why do you think I do not want you more than anything in this universe?"

"Because I heard you."

I scowl. I'm missing something, and it makes me angry that whatever it is, it's keeping Amina from me.

"What did you hear?"

"I heard you talking to Li'aht before we left, Kwarq. I know you're only doing this because I'm pregnant and because of your stupid first heart. I know you really want to be with her. So stop it. It's harder to hear you say things I know aren't true, even if it's well intentioned."

The relief that courses through me is cold and jolting. I release the breath I've been holding and pull Amina against my chest, burying my face into her fragrant cloud of hair.

"You humans and your imaginations. Amina, when will you realize that I love you more than my life? That even if my stupid first heart had not bound me to you, I would have followed you on that bus even if it went to the ends of this ridiculous, silly little planet?"

She's stiff in my arms, but I can still feel the tremor run through her as she weeps into my shirt. My poor, poor Amina. She has such wild, crazy ideas.

"Come."

I set her away from me. Her face is puffy and streaked with tears. I brush my hand across her cheeks and then lap at the salty water on my fingers. She tastes like so much sorrow, so much worry, so much disappointment. My poor, poor Amina.

"Kwarq, it's probably best if I just go—"

I shake my head and hold her when she tries to ease away from me.

"I said come. I can fix this. Although I wish I could fix your very human tendency toward distrust and wild, unreasonable pessimism."

She lets me lead her back to the pod. I take her by the waist and lift her up, settling her into the seat and closing the door so she can't try to hop back out. I go around to my side and slide in beside her.

"Kwarq, we don't have to go all the way back to Lyqa. I know what I heard. I know how much this hurts you. I never really expected this to last in the first place. It's okay."

I shoot her a quick frown and then roll my eyes. This

gesture is probably my second favorite thing about humans. Amina is my first. Even though my *lehti* loves to say that things are okay when they are clearly not okay.

I don't respond to her comment. I pull up the controls for the pod and switch all of the displays and audio to English. Then I activate the database search feature and begin to type.

CHAPTER 26

AMINA

LOVE'S TRUE BEAT.

The English letters blink in succession across the screen. Kwarq watches me expectantly. My sigh feels like it's coming from the depths of my spirit. Am I really ready for another Lyqa love lesson?

"Don't tell me, I'm your *lehti*, but every Lyqa has a true love and for you that's Li'aht? Am I wrong?"

"You are."

I frown, but Kwarq's smiling. It's probably the closest to gloating I've ever seen.

"Then what the hell is that supposed to mean? Don't tell me it's a metaphor or something. I thought your people didn't do metaphors."

"We do not," he says just as easily and then taps the panel.

The screen flashes onto a lush field covered in feathery flowers and tall, bluish blades of grass. The angle pans out and two figures appear on the screen. My eyes widen. I glance over to Kwarq and he looks slightly uncomfortable. My eyes glue back to the screen.

Holy, shit.

"I would not have chosen her for myself. She could never compare to you. To your beauty and intelligence. She is not who I want, you know that!"

Kwarq collapses to his knees, gripping his head in agony. A heavy rain falls, and his hair hangs into his flashing yellow eyes.

"If she wasn't your beat, would we have had a chance?"

Li'aht is in a flowing, red gown. Even in my stupor, the symbolism isn't lost on me. It's surprisingly subtle.

"If I'd never passed her on the street, I would still be yours. You know our hearts are bound. I can't stop it. Help me, I can't stop it!"

"Oh, my love, we may not be able to have a life, but we will always have our love. Go to her. Do what you must."

"I will go, but she will never replace you. You are my true heart's beat."

Kwarq's hands are fisted in his hair as he stares through the night sky in anguish.

I cover my mouth to stifle a chuckle. Kwarq's eyes are fixed to the screen, but his shoulder is flinched as if he's trying to ward off the horror of what he's seeing.

"Oh, shit, Kwarq, I'm so sorry. I didn't know—" I try to inject some genuine regret into my voice. I did just accuse him of betraying me. Instead, I end up laughing. I lean over, holding my belly as my cackles fill the pod. Kwarq presses the control panel and puts a halt to what is perhaps the worst movie ever made, Lyqa or otherwise.

KWARQ

I would rather have my *lehti* laugh at me than cry, so I wait patiently as she rocks back and forth in her seat, holding her round belly and laughing her beautiful laugh.

"Oh, shit. That is hilarious!"

She continues laughing, so I wait, and wait, and wait.

"It is not *that* funny, Amina."

She snickers and pulls herself upright. She folds her lips in, and her nose flares with the effort to control herself. She takes several deep breaths and then blinks for a long moment before turning to face me.

"You're right, babe. That was not that bad. It was just unexpected!" She loses the battle for calm and bursts out laughing again. I roll my eyes and lean back in my seat. Tears roll down her face. I'm only feigning impatience. She called me 'babe.' Everything is right in the world.

After several long moments, she seems to recover. She stares at the screen, where the image of me on my knees is paused, and shakes her head. Every so often, a little chuckle erupts from her.

"I just can't believe it."

"I have tried many things in my life, *lehti*. It is not uncommon among Lyqa."

She turns to me and her eyebrows raise to meet in the middle of her forehead.

"Oh, no, linguist/doula/actor I can definitely believe. But how you could even fix your face to talk about human movies when you knew this garbage was floating around the universe, I will never understand."

"What I will never understand is how you can believe that you are unworthy of my or anyone else's love."

Amina's smile drops and she looks down into her lap.

"It's not that. I just don't want you to feel obligated."

This is important. I don't want to be staring at the top of my *lehti*'s beautiful head when I say it. I reach beneath her chin and lift until her eyes meet mine. They are nervous and still so wary.

"Why does it matter if I have an obligation to you? That I feel honor and heart bound to you? Why do you think my desire to protect, provide for, and love you is a burden? Furthermore, why do you not expect this of me? I would understand."

Her eyes shift away. I gently squeeze her chin, and she locks back onto me.

"You wouldn't understand, Kwarq. It's not like that with humans."

"I am not human, and it is like that with me."

"I know, but—,"

"If you know, why do you question it?"

Her scent starts to change. Her heart speeds up, and mine responds in kind. She looks away and then back to me and away again. Her voice, when she responds, is quiet.

"Because I'm scared I'm going to love you as much as I want to, and this is all going to end up breaking my heart."

CHAPTER 27

AMINA

Kwarq is quiet for a long time. I don't risk looking back at him, although I can feel him looking hard at me. My admission has left me vulnerable. I brace myself, and when Kwarq's hand closes around my wrist, I flinch. He presses my hand flat against his chest and holds it there. Finally, I raise my gaze back to his, and he's smiling again. It's a gentle curve of his mouth.

"What do you feel Amina?"

I feel his heart. It hammers against my hand, almost pushing against his breastbone.

"Your heart."

"What do you hear?"

"Your heart."

"Is that all?"

No, that's not all. I hear mine, too. Only this time, it's just as loud and strong as his. My chest flinches with the force of the muscle's contraction, and I press my free hand to the space between my breasts. We are in prefect sync. His heart thumps into one hand at the same moment as mine does into the other.

All of the anxiety and nervousness is being pushed out by a feeling of love so all-encompassing that I want to scream with the joy of it. I get it now. I can *feel* it. I can feel his love. I can feel it pulsing into me, it's like a warm gust of wind throughout my body. It's an instinct. It just is. I can't believe I almost missed it.

"My *lehti*, do not be ashamed. If it would have taken you

two-hundred years to realize it, I would have waited that long."

He's serious. These aren't just pretty words. I know now that he would have waited as patiently as he is now for me to stop crying like an idiot. When I continue to blubber, he pulls me into his lap. I settle against the warm, hard ridges of his thighs as he presses my head into his chest, shushing me and patting my back.

"Amina, it is okay. I understand."

"I'm sorry I didn't believe you."

"Do you believe me now?"

I nod. "I'm sorry I didn't trust you."

"You would have eventually. I would have had no problem stalking you until you came around."

I angle my head back. He's smiling. The yellow of his eyes is warm and bright in the dim pod. He lowers his head, and the moment his lips sink onto mine, I stop feeling guilty. I stop everything. Or rather, everything stops as I open for him and his smooth, creepy tongue slips inside, curling around mine and sending tingles through my body. God, I love this Lyqa dude.

KWARQ

Amina's face is still puffy from her crying, but she smiles as we move around her little apartment, gathering things to take back to Lyqa.

"I don't see the point in paying for an apartment if Lyqa's gonna be my home now."

She's sorting through a surprisingly large collection of shoes. I can't imagine what person would need so many shoes, but I take the ones she tosses to me and place them into a box.

"It is up to you, my *lehti*. I do not mind maintaining a

residence for you here just in case."

She turns from where she's sitting cross-legged in front of her closet and frowns.

"In case of what? I'm not going to leave you, Kwarq, and you can't get rid of me now, you butthead."

I laugh at her strange insult because I'm sure it is meant in jest.

"You will never leave me, unless you want to."

"I won't ever want to, unless—"

My heart ratchets up. "Unless what?"

"Unless you make me watch *Love's True Beat* again."

She throws her head back and hoots.

"My love, I do not even want to watch that film again. I do not know what made my mother watch it before we left. And when I came into the living room, she was crying! Can you believe that?"

"I mean, I guess it was sweet in a way." She's considering two pairs of shoes. She tosses one into the discard pile and the other to me, then she pauses before reaching for the first pair and tossing it to me as well. "I can see why that would be heartbreaking."

I roll my eyes. "It is trash, Amina. I have accepted it. You should as well."

"Oh, I accept it, babe. Trust me on that."

Amina snorts and picks up a pair of black pointy, boomerang shaped shoes. Her mouth twists to the side as she turns them about in her hands. She reaches back and holds them over the discard pile before turning and tossing them to me. I sigh and walk over to her. I bend down and scoop up the remaining shoes, including the ones in the discard pile.

"We will take them all. You do not have to choose."

"Oh, I don't want to bring too much stuff to your house. I don't mind downsizing a bit."

I dump the shoes into the box and close the flaps with the

roll of tape Amina gave me.

"It is your house as well. You were never a guest. From the moment you stepped through our doors, you were daughter, sister and partner. If you wish to fill our entire apartment with shoes, you may."

She smiles and wraps her arms around my waist. Her hair rests over her eyes and I push it back so I can see her beautiful, brown eyes. They are urgent and flare with passion.

"Oh, my love, I will always cherish our life and our love. I honor the day you came to me. My heart, my breath, my veins!"

Amina tosses her head back, one of her hands releasing me to press back against her forehead. She holds the position, her eyes closed in rapture. After a moment, one eye peeks open, and she gives me a squeeze with the arm still around my waist. I sigh and roll my eyes yet again. She asked for it.

I drop down to my knees, gripping the front of my shirt as if I would tear it from my body. One arms stretches to the ceiling, my hand clawed and grasping for some salvation that is just out of reach.

"Oh, Amina, my love, my heartbeat. The mother of my children, the keeper of my spirit. No one will ever replace you. You are my true heart's beat. If you take your love away from me, I'll go crazy. I'll go insane!"

Her head falls back and a twinkling laugh erupts from her throat.

"Dude, did you just quote Blackstreet?"

"I did."

CHAPTER 28

KWARQ

"Kwarq!"

I thrust deep into the tight sheath of Amina's pussy, and she clamps around me, squeezing me so tightly that my cock cramps.

"My *lehti*. You're so tight and so wet."

The sound of me sliding through her dripping passage is a nuanced orchestra of arousal that only I can hear. It makes me harden even more, and she gasps, angling her hips up to receive my pounding thrusts.

"Kwarq, please, more. Harder."

I shift my feet to get leverage so I can give her what she wants, but her short bed means my legs hang over the side, making it hard to brace myself. I ease myself from her warmth, and she moans at the loss.

"Get on top and take as much as you want."

I fall onto my back beside her, my cock jutting in the air. The tip drips with my impatient release. The entire length pulses with the desire to be back inside of her.

Amina sits up and faces me, her eyes falling to my straining, slick cock. She leans forward and flicks her pink, little tongue out, lapping at the dripping tip, and I have to fist my hands to keep from erupting into her mouth.

Tentatively, she lifts her leg and straddles my stomach, letting my cock come to rest between the lush cheeks of her bottom. I take her around the hips and lift her enough to nestle the head of my cock within her dripping folds. Slowly, she sinks down, and my hands fall away.

"Ah, Amina. It feels too good."

We both shake as she lowers onto me. Her full bottom lip is clamped between her teeth. I fix my eyes on her tense face until I feel her bottom come to rest on my thighs.

"Oh my god." Amina falls forward, only to be stopped by her belly pressing into mine. Her curls fluff around her head. Her tight, full breasts swell just above my face, the nipples begging me to taste them. I flick my tongue out to its full length and swirl it around one dark tip before sucking the entire thing into my mouth. At the same time, I flex my hips up, pressing even deeper into her.

"Kwarq!" She says my name desperately.

"Yes, my *lehti*?"

"I fucking love you."

I release a tense chuckle. "Do you love me, or do you love my cock buried inside of you?"

"I love you, Kwarq. Only you." Her declaration is breathy and the feeling behind it is my undoing.

Amina raises on her knees, and drops down to meet my next thrust. She cries out when when my cock caresses her womb. We keep up this brutal pace. I can't seem to get deep enough inside of her, although I feel the end of her pussy with every thrust.

"Come for me, my love." I pump my hips up in a series of quick, deep thrusts. I angle my cock at the sensitive underside of her pussy, and the textured passage brushes my tip, pushing me over the edge just as she begins to flex around me. Her head tosses back on a strangled cry, and her hips buck up and down milking me of my release until it seeps from inside of her in a warm puddle between us.

When she's down to little twitches, she falls forward, holding me inside of her.

"That was amazing."

I chuckle.

"You always say that."

She lifts her head, her round chin balancing on my sternum.

"Yeah, but now we've done it enough that I can say with scientific surety that you always give good dick."

"Amina, my love, my heart, my *lehti*…"

"Hm?" Her eyes are closed. Her breathing has slowed and blows out in fragrant little puffs into my face.

"That's not science."

AMINA

"I don't know if this is a good idea. How am I going to explain this?" I hold my hands palm up alongside my belly, which if I didn't know any better, has grown since I woke up from my post-sex nap. At first, I thought I had slipped into another resting period, but Kwarq assured me that I was only out for an hour or so. Still, that doesn't solve the problem of how to explain to my mother and two sisters why I'm showing up two seconds from giving birth to twins when I was rocking a two piece at the beach three months ago. As usual, Kwarq doesn't seem too concerned.

"What do you mean?"

We're driving to my mother's house. I could have been knocked over with a feather when Kwarq led me back to the garage at his old apartment, thinking we were going to get back in the pod, only for him to open a second garage space to reveal a brand new fucking Mercedes. A Mercedes, because he didn't have a bed, but bought a luxury car. Of course he did.

Kwarq handles a right turn like a pro, rotating the wheel with the heel of one hand. The other rests on my thigh in an attempt to reassure me. This is all officially weird again.

"How the hell do you know how to drive?" I ask, finally

distracted from my worry.

He shrugs as he comes to a smooth break at a red light.

"The Internet."

My chin drops to my chest.

"You watched the Internet to learn how to drive?"

"I did."

"Is that also where you learned about Shaq and Blackstreet? What, did you only search the 90s?"

He smiles and chuckles, taking another turn like he's been driving his entire life. A space pod this is not. I'd be impressed if it wasn't so surreal.

"I searched generally for things that were practical, like driving and courtship rituals among humans. But I also searched specifically for things that would have been popular in your formative years. I was worried that our age difference would make it difficult to relate to one another."

I frown. Our age difference. Kwarq looks about my age. Not that I would know what that looks like on a Lyqa. He could be two hundred for all I could guess. Let me find out I'm dating a senior citizen.

"So, how much older are you than me, anyway?"

He turns briefly to look at me before his eyes go back to the road. His brows crease in a confused frown.

"I am not."

"You're not what?"

"Older than you."

CHAPTER 29

KWARQ

"Twenty-two!"

I nod. "Twenty-two."

"Oh my god. I'm a goddamn cougar."

How many times do I have to tell her? "*Lehti*, we are not wolves or dogs, and even if we were, you would not be called a cougar as that is a completely different animal."

She narrows her eyes and smirks in a funny way where her cheeks rise and fall quickly.

"Yeah, thanks for that zoology lesson, Mr. Linguist. A cougar is a slang term that refers to an older woman who seduces and sleeps with younger men."

"This is Ebonics?" Are older women romantically involved with younger men seen as predators? If so, that's ridiculous.

"No, babe. It's just regular old American English slang. Anyway, you don't care?"

I flick my eyes over to her.

"About what?"

"That I'm so much older than you!" Her scent is embarrassed. She has nothing to be embarrassed about. Once again, my *lehti* is as she likes to say, 'doing the most.'

"Amina, you are only twenty-nine."

"That's a whole decade!" The safety belt twists against her belly as she turns to face me. Her hands splay in front of her to present her point.

"Technically, you are only about five Lyqa years older than I am. If we look at it that way, I am really twenty-five. Is that better?"

She puffs out a lungful of air, but the urgency leaves her body.

"I mean, I guess. I just can't believe you didn't mention it before. How do you know I don't only date older men."

I shrug. "I would not have cared. I would have made you see the benefits of being with me."

One of her eyebrows raises. "What benefits?"

"Unfailing patience with your tendency to be entirely too dramatic."

"Seriously, that's a benefit? Coming from the star of the Oscar-worthy *Love's True Beat*?"

I cut my eyes to her, but ignore the mention of that dreadful film.

"I am strong and able to protect you from all of the psycho stalkers who would harm you. Did one thing try to snatch or eat you while you were on Lyqa? No. That was because of my superior ability to protect."

She snorts. "That's because I was asleep eighty percent of the time."

"What about the scientifically proven amazing sex?"

"Kwarq, my love, my heart, my *lehti*..." I glance over. "You win, cause that is definitely science."

"It is."

She straightens in her seat with a little huff and focuses on untwisting the safety belt.

"Yeah, well, you better be happy you give good D."

"D?"

"Dick."

"Ah, yes. If that is what keeps you with me, then I am happy for it."

She peers closely at me. Her little eyebrow raised. "You know I'm kidding right? I love your fucking guts."

"I do, and I also love you and our children, who reside in your guts."

Her nose scrunches up. "Kwarq, ew."

AMINA

Kwarq thinks he's distracted me, but I'm still worried about facing my family. When we park outside of my mother's yellow brick bungalow, I stop him when he reaches for the door.

"Just give me a minute, will you?"

He sighs, but it's not with impatience. Like all of his sighs toward me, they imply I am worrying for nothing.

"Kwarq, you realize that we are about to walk into a family of Black people from the Southside of Chicago and convince them that we are in love and expecting not one, but two, children in a matter of minutes, and, oh yeah—you're an alien. Trust me, I'm not exaggerating."

"From what I have seen, your people are refreshingly rational. I do not think it is outside of the realm of comfort to understand this. Can you trust me? I will not let this harm you or your family."

He looks so sincere. I run my hands over my face and try to shake off my nerves. I can't stay away forever. It would be even more weird to leave and show up later with a bunch of kids and a damn alien, not to mention hurtful for my family who I already disappeared on for two whole months.

"Also, days."

"What?"

"You will give birth in days, not minutes. I would say maybe five days or so. That is why I wanted to come now. You may not be able to travel for some time once you give birth."

I blink and I blink again.

"How do you know it's five days?"

"I can hear them turning. Getting into position. Do you not

feel the difference?"

I don't feel anything. This whole thing happened so fast that I've only been able to feel heavy and awkward. But now that I think of it, there has been the slight flutter of movement every so often. Holy cow. I'm going to give birth in five days. What the hell is that even going to be like?

"Come, let us go in before you begin to panic. I do not want you inducing early labor with your wild imagination."

Kwarq doesn't wait for my assent. He opens his door and gets out, coming around to open my door for me and help me rise from the car. Now that he's given me a due date, I feel rounder and more pregnant than ever. I have to pee, I'm hot, and there's an annoying pressure in my pelvis.

We make our way to the house and up the steps. My heart beats nearly out of chest, and I know Kwarq feels it because he keeps squeezing my hand in reassurance.

"Relax, *lehti*."

"You relax, my people are going to freak the hell out."

He chuckles and pulls open the metal security gate. When he reaches for the door handle, I move to stop him, but he twists and it opens with ease. What the hell?

"Amina Danae Bennet, if you don't get your narrow behind over here right now."

I cringe back out the door, but Kwarq drags me forward until I'm standing in my mother's living room. I step through and pause, too stunned to speak.

My mother stands a few feet away from me with her fisted hands perched in the curve right above her round hips. Her eyes narrow, but I can tell that she's relieved.

Directly behind her stand Kwarq's parents. They're towering, smiling figures at her back. Like sentinels guarding their queen in some twisted urban fantasy.

My sisters are perched nervously on the couch. Bati leans

against the wall between the small foyer and the living room with his arms crossed over his chest. His teeth shine brightly in the blue-black of his face. He's so fine. Whoever gets his *leht* will be a lucky woman. He looks like he's laughing at some private joke, but then I realize he's looking across the room at my sister Tiani, who's doing her best to ignore him.

My eyes search for Ah'dan and find him leaning against the fireplace looking very much like Ah'dan. His gaze is locked on me. He's still not wearing a shirt. I can't help it, I roll my eyes, causing him to smile wide.

"I know you heard me."

I snap my eyes back to my mother. She looks nervous. I probably look like something from a horror movie to her. Showing up only a little over two months since she's seen me as big as a house and with a family of aliens.

"It's okay, mom. I'm okay."

I close the space and wrap my arms around her. She stiffens, but immediately sags against me, holding me close. I hear her sniffle and it nearly breaks my heart. I pull away and see that her eyes are red.

"You know, I almost had a heart attack when this boy showed up at my house? What were you thinking?" My mother waves her hand back to Bati.

"Bati came here?"

Bati turns his head to me, but his gaze lingers on Tiani until the last second.

"He sure did. I was so worried about you. I almost called the police, but he said you were fine, and explained the— situation. I nearly jumped out of my skin when he sped around this room. Dear god."

My mother covers her cheeks with her hands like she still can't believe it. I smile and rub her arm.

"I know, it scared me, too, at first. I'm sorry I just disappeared. Everything happened so fast. I didn't even realize I'd been gone so long."

"Mm hm, I see."

She nods down to my belly, and I get warm with embarrassment.

"Yeah, Lyqas gestate a little—uh—quicker than humans."

"I see. So you're just shacking up with aliens now?"

Her eyebrow is raised, but her mouth twists slightly like she's trying to fight a smile. I relax. Everything is going to be okay.

KWARQ

Amina laughs and cries when her mother hugs her again. My parents step forward next and embrace her, which only makes her cry more.

"I thought I was never going to see you all again," she sobs when my mother releases her.

"*Dahnai*, why would you think that?"

"She heard you playing my movie before we left. She misinterpreted the final scene."

My mother's dark black skin pulses a bright blush tone. I don't think I've ever seen her embarrassed before.

"Oh, *dahnai*, I have a soft spot for my children's accomplishments. I should have been more careful. *Ma'h qitah.*"

She pulls Amina back to her, pressing their foreheads together briefly.

"No, it's not your fault. I have a habit of reading too much into things."

"Yeah, or maybe not reading enough into them. Excuse me, Kwarq's mama." Amina's sister Tiani, the tall, skinny one with the short, coily hair, she steps forward to pull her sister into a hug. She leans her head close to Amina's ear and whispers.

"So, we're definitely gonna talk about how you thought it was a good idea to take some alien D," she cuts her eyes to me briefly, "even if it is fine alien D. And you're also gonna explain why the hell his brother thinks my name is Lettie and keeps staring at me."

"He called you *lehti*?"

Amina's eyes shoot over Tiani's shoulder to Bati, just as mine do. His gaze is pinned to his *lehti*'s back. He jerks his head quickly from side to side. Amina's eyes shift back to her sister, and she smiles brightly.

"Uh, you know, it's just a kind of term of endearment. They all use it. Bati's a sweetheart, really."

Tiani snorts. "Whatever. He's creeping me out."

Amina laughs awkwardly, but when Tiani steps away, her eyes shoot to mine in surprise. I shrug. I had no idea. I guess Amina isn't the only one who will be having a sibling talk later.

Her other sister LaShay rushes over next. The scent of her excitement is sharp as she elbows her way to her sister. When she finally gets to us, she leaps forward, wrapping her arms around me in a tight, quick hug. I laugh, impressed. That was nearly Lyqa speed.

"Uh, sorry, Kwarqy, I need to talk to my sister."

CHAPTER 30

AMINA

I'm dragged off to a corner by LaShay. She wedges us in the space where the two walls meet, and it's awkward because my belly is so big. I look down. I'm pretty sure it's grown again.

"Girl, you've been running around for the past two months with fucking *aliens* and you didn't even think to take me with you? You ain't shit!"

My eyes slide back into my head. Why am I not surprised. If I thought I was a weirdo, LaShay is capital Wier-D.

"You know, I was totally thinking about how I was holding out on you when I fucked Kwarq and got instantaneously pregnant. Yeah, I wasn't."

LaShay's eyes widen. "Instantaneous?"

"Instantaneous."

"Daaaaaamn. He must have that Mount Olympus dick."

I cringe and pull her closer, but she only bumps into my belly.

"They can hear you, Shay."

She flips her hand in the general direction of the living room and twists her mouth up.

"Girl, no they can't. I'm whispering."

"Trust me, they can hear you." I raise my eyebrows to push the point, and her own eyes look like they're going to bulge out of her face. Her head rotates slowly until she's facing the living room.

Kwarq is doing a terrible job of hiding the proud smile playing about his mouth. His parents are both pulsing pink.

Ah'dan is being Ah'dan. I have the uncontrollable urge to pop the knowing smirk off his face. The only one not paying attention is Bati because he's too busy scoping out Tiani.

LaShay twists her head back to me. She could catch flies with her mouth as wide as it is.

"Spidey hearing?"

"Girl, fucking spidey hearing."

"Daaaaaamn."

LaShay walks off in an amazed daze, and I go to Kwarq, who's sitting on my mother's couch. The way he drapes his tall, muscular body across the furniture like he's been here before makes me wonder if this man is ever out of place.

"What is Mount Olympu—"

"Don't—" I cut him off, "even ask."

He smiles and shrugs his shoulders before pulling me onto his lap. He rubs his hand over my stomach. As if on cue, I feel four little knocks against my belly. It's the first time I've consciously felt our children. When my wide eyes meet Kwarq's, his smile is even wider.

"I have a surprise for you."

"You mean better than making sure my family knew I was safe? Better than sending your brother here so they wouldn't freak out on all of us?" I lean down and press my forehead to his, holding it there. "You're the best. Thank you."

"You do not have to thank me, *lehti*. And yes, it is better than all of those things, I hope."

My heart beats a little faster, and I realize it's Kwarq. He's nervous. He eases me back to my feet and rises with me, taking my hand in his and squeezing.

"Alright. Let's move to the backyard. I have some food set out for us," my mother announces and we all begin to file to the back of the house. Kwarq and I exit last, and as soon as my feet hit the deck, I stop. My hand tightens on Kwarq's as I take in the beautiful scene.

"Oh, wow." My free hand comes up to cover my mouth, smothering the gasp.

There are two white linen covered tables on the deck. In the center of each, is a small bucket of baby's breath. On each side of the steps leading to the backyard are large metal lanterns. A ring of vibrant mosses and berries are arranged around each one. A wide path of flower petals lead from the steps all the way to the end of the yard. Two even rows of seats are arranged before a tall, wooden arch draped in billowing white panels and laden in calla lilies and other flowers, some I've never even seen.

It's beautiful. It's more than beautiful. It's magical. I turn to Kwarq and am surprised to see his bright yellow eyes level with mine.

KWARQ

This is the only part of human courtship traditions that I like. The getting down on one knee. It means I can look into Amina's face and see the rims of her eyelids begin to redden and constrict. It means I can see her round little nostrils flare as her breath quickens with anticipation. It shows her I am willing to bend for her. That I will always hold her above me even as she stands as my equal.

"Kwarq?" Her eyelashes are beginning to gather little beads of moisture as she looks down at me.

"Yes, my *lehti.*"

"Are you about to propose to me?"

"I am."

A wobbly laugh escapes her. I reach into the pocket of my pants and pull out the tiny box that I've kept on my person since I learned of this strange human custom. I had the ring made on Lyqa by a renowned jeweler I met during my brief time as an actor. He crafted it from the most precious metal from the Lyqa mountains and set it with a custom jewel given to me by my mother that had been in our family for generations. It is the perfect blend of our cultures. It is the perfect symbol of our love.

I pull back the lid of the box and all of the humans gasp. Amina looks almost horrified. Panic rushes through me. Have I misinterpreted the custom? Her mother and sisters are all wearing similar looks of shock.

"*Lehti*, is this bad—"

The words are knock back down my throat by Amina throwing herself at me. I brace us with a hand around her back as her wracking sobs fill the quiet of the night.

"It's just so sweet!" She stutters and cries. I smooth my hand over her back. Her mother wipes tears from her eyes. Tiani holds a hand over her heart, and LaShay's mouth is open so wide her chin is nearly touching her chest. I ease Amina away to see that she's smiling.

"I did well?" I'm still not sure if there is something wrong.

She nods, her head jerking up and down as she swipes her fingers across her cheeks.

"Oh, my god, dude, I have no idea where you got this rock from, but you did so well."

I can see now that she's happy. Her joy radiates out to me, warm and sweet.

"May I finish?"

She laughs and steps out of my arms, going back to her feet and making a show of fixing her clothes and drying her face. She takes a deep breath and blows it out, wiggling her hands at her sides before straightening her shoulders.

"Okay, I'm good. I'm good. Go."

I love her. She's so adorable and honest. I know I will never have to guess what she is thinking or feeling. Just like when I first observed her at the movies, she laughs when she wants to laugh, cries when she wants to cry, screams when she wants to scream. It's a freedom that many do not give themselves, and I'm glad that my *lehti* feels safe enough to do so. I take her hand again, and this time it's still and sure. All the nervousness is gone, and I can only sense anticipation.

"Amina, my *lehti*, my heart, my love," her eyes shine into mine. She's holding her bottom lip between her teeth. It makes me want to kiss her, so I continue quickly since that is what traditionally comes at the end of this custom, "will you...

"...go with me?"

EPILOGUE

AMINA

Five days later...

"Amina, love, you have to stop laughing and push."

I pull my lips in tight and bear down hard until the contraction passes, then I collapse back against the cushioned side of the birthing pool.

Let me just say, Lyqa epidurals are the shit. The bomb dot com. Awesome-sausome. I feel nothing, except the uncontrollable urge to crack up. Apparently, that's a human side effect to the amazing cup of tea they gave me to help "ease and calm" the birthing process. But instead of making me all zen, it's given me the giggles.

Kwarq's positioned like an umpire between my legs. It makes me chuckle.

"Babe, you said, 'Will you go with me?'" I lower my voice when I do his part, which triggers another round of snickers. "Your Ebonics is bad."

Kwarq rolls his eyes. He's intense and focused on what's going on in my va-jay-jay. "I know, my *lehti*, you have been telling me this for the past two hours. Aside from being very amused by my misspoken proposal, are you feeling well? It will not be long now."

I wave my hand. "Eh, I feel fine. A little pressure. Anyway, I loved your proposal. I said yes, didn't I?"

"You did."

"See?"

"I do. I also see a head."

"Really? Is it curly? I bet our kids are going to be cute. Do you think our kids are going to be cute?"

I pull up to my elbows. Kwarq's fumbling and moving frantically in the water.

"*Lehti*, I am sure they will be beautiful since you are their mother, but you are crowning. It is time to push again."

I sigh and bear down.

"Yeah, yeah, I'm pushing."

The giddiness I've been feeling evaporates in an instant the second Kwarq places our first child into my arms. She's a beautiful squirming thing, and I hold tight as she slips around in my hands. It's all I can do to contain the joy that courses through my heart.

Lyqa definitely do not speak in metaphor. The *lehti'an* is real. I feel it. It's a clear emotion like I have never experienced and it blends perfectly with my subconscious. Right now, it's laced with confusion but also with trust. I feel my daughter seeking my comfort. It's such a pure thing that my eyes fill with tears that annoy me but only because they blur her beautiful little face.

Our daughter's nose scrunches much like mine does when I'm upset. I hold her to my breast, and her little mouth roots around until she latches onto my nipple.

Her eyes flutter open and immediately find my face. My breath catches. She blinks. Her long, curly lashes slowly lower over her bright yellow eyes before shining back up at me.

KWARQ

Blissful. Another lovely human word, and the only one I can use to describe this moment.

The birthing tea has worn off, and Amina rests in the bed of the healing center. Beside her is a shallow bassinet holding our two children. A daughter and a son.

I'm next to her on the bed, holding her hand. Both of our gazes fix on the squirming bundles.

"They are small," I say quietly. Amina smiles and squeezes my hand.

"They're average human size, I think. Just a little bit bigger."

"Hm." My *dahnai* opens her little mouth to yawn, triggering an answering yawn from her brother. Amina chuckles.

"They're so adorable. I love it."

I'm not sure if it was the effects of the birthing tea, but for the first time, Amina did not scared herself with crazy ideas of what would happen after she gave birth. When I first presented our daughter to her, she didn't hesitated to open her arms and pull the wailing, slippery little thing to her breast. The moment our son came into the world, she pulled him from my hands right away, pressing them both to her naked chest and initiating the *lehti'an*. She encouraged me to do the same.

"It's called skin to skin. It's good for newborn babies, and fathers can do it, too," she said before having me remove my shirt and cradle them to my body.

Holding my children close to me, feeling their trusting energy was a feeling second only to the love I have for their mother.

"They are adorable and beautiful and perfect," I confirm and kiss her soft, beautiful mouth.

"They are." Amina smoothes a hand over T'nai's thick, red curls and down her smooth, bluish-black cheek. "Kwarq, I swear, I never slept with Bati."

I chuckle. "They do look like him. Lyqa genes are unpredictable. Our children will look like all of us."

Our son, Maq'ti, shares his sister's dark skin, except his

hair is a tight cap of coils my shade of ashen brown. They both have the features of their mother, however. It's almost uncanny.

"Are they well?"

Amina's smile widens and excitement colors her scent. It's sweet and vibrant.

"They are. I still can't believe the *lehti'an*. I can feel them. It's so cool and strange, but kind of amazing. Everything is new, so they're a little overwhelmed, but okay."

"And you are happy?"

"I'm so happy."

Her free hand caresses my face. I cover it and lay the other on our son's back. The babies have managed to each wiggle an arm from their swaddles and find each other's hands. The result is a lively circle of love and warmth between me, Amina and our children.

My heart thumps a strong, even beat in my chest. Amina's keeps in steady rhythm. Beneath it, T'nai and Maq'ti's hearts patter back and forth. It's a beautiful song, and one I look forward to hearing for the rest of our lives.

The End

The daughter of a straw seller

Samanchi Ghizi
(Novel)

Esmaiel Yourdshahian Urmia
www.yourdshah.com

First edition Nov 2010-11-14
Second edition May 2022-03- 09

آثار تحقیقی:

۳۲-پدیده‌شناسی انسانی (در سه جلد) از ۱۳۵٤ تا ۱۳٦۱ دانشگاه سلطنتی بروکسل

۳۳-جامعه‌شناسی روستایی

۳٤-بررسی رخساره اجتماعی آذربایجان غربی، چاپ ۱۳٦٥

۳٥-دولتمداری شرق، دولتمداری غرب، ۱۳٦٤

۳٦-مقدمه‌ای بر کلیله و دمنه، چاپ ۱۳٦٤

۳۷- فکری دیگر (تحلیلی در مسائل تاریخ هنر و ادبیات و شعر امروز ایران) ۱۳۷٤

۳۸- تبارشناسی قومی‌و حیات ملی (جلد اول)، نشر فرزان روز ۱۳۸۰ و چاپ چهارم ۱۳۹۸

۳۹- تبارشناسی قومی‌و حیات ملی (جلد دوم)، زیر چاپ

٤۰- مبانی حسی زبان و شعر، تهران – ۱۳۸٤ نشر فرزان روز

٤۱- زبان، ذهن و معنا تهران پائیز ۱٤۰۰ انتشارات مروارید

٤۲- فکری دیگر. در انتظار چاپ

٤۳- چهل وهشت مقاله علمی و تحقیقی منتشر شده در زمینه شعر و ادبیات، زبان‌شناسی جامعه‌شناسی روانشناسی اجتماعی و پزشکی در سطح بین‌الملل در نشریات و مجامع علمی و دانشگاهی کشورهای مختلف جهان

دختر کاه فروش

(داستان زندگی دختر کاه فروش)

سامانچی قیزی

تهیه و تألیف: اسماعیل یوردشاهیان اورمیا

سریال کتاب:P2445100072

عنوان: دختر کاه‌فروش

عنوان دوم: سامانچی قیزی

زیرنویس عنوان: داستان زندگی دختر کاه‌فروش

تهیه و تألیف: اسماعیل یوردشاهیان اورمیا

ویراستاری: مهری صفری

صفحه آرایی: نرگس تاج‌الدینی

شابک: ISBN: 2-132-77892-1-971

موضوع: رمان فارسی – حکایت واقعی تاریخی

مشخصات کتاب: کتاب جلد مقوایی، سایز A5 تعداد

صفحات: ۲۸۸

تاریخ نشر در کانادا: می ۲۰۲۴

انتشارات در کانادا: انتشارات بین المللی کیدزوکادو

Kidsocado Publishing House

خانه انتشارات کیدزوکادو

ونکوور، کانادا

تلفن: ‏+1 (833) 633 8654

واتس آپ: ‏+1 (236) 333 7248

ایمیل: INFO@KIDSOCADO.COM

وبسایت انتشارات: HTTPS://KIDSOCADO.COM

وبسایت فروشگاه: HTTPS://KPHCLUB.COM

مقدمه

از گذشته‌های بسیار دور از او فقط یک نام و یک تصویر بود. به هر جا که می‌رفتی در هرخانه و مغازه و تالاری تصویر و یا بهتر است بگویم تابلوی نقاشی او با خوشه‌های گندم بر دوش و بر دیوارها نصب شده بود.

از هرکس که می‌پرسیدی او کیست؟ می‌گفت:

- سامانچی قیزیده (دختر کاه فروش است)

او آشنای همه، جزیی از خانواده و فرهنگ و زبان و فکر مردم و در نهایت سمبل زیبایی و اسطوره پاکی بود. به طوری که مردم آذربایجان وقتی می‌خواستند از زیبایی و پاکی دختری و یا بانویی تعریف و توصیف کنند می‌گفتند:

- گزلده، سامانچی قیزده (بله زیباست، دخترکاه فروش است.)

اما وقتی می‌پرسیدی اوکی بود؟ کجا و چگونه زیست؟ و اکنون کجاست؟

همه فقط یک پاسخ داشتند:

او دختر کاه فروش بود، او را کشتند.

تمام دانسته مردم از او همین بود و جز این هیچ من هر چه تحقیق کردم و جستم هیچ نیافتم جز افسوس از سرنوشت تلخ و زیبایی بی‌نظیری

که داشته و کسی نمی‌دانست که او کی بوده و چه شده؟ از او فقط یک تصویر مانده بود، یک نام و خبر روایتی کوتاه که او را کشته‌اند. همین.

در خصوص معنی و مفهوم اسم او هم اختلاف نظر بود. اکثر مردم اسم او را {سامانچی قیزی، سامان (به معنی کاه) قیزی به معنی دختر} در کل به معنی دختر کاه فروش می‌دانستند اما تعدادی از محققین و تاریخ‌دان‌ها او را با توجه به دوران پر تلاطم و ناآرامی‌که می‌زیسته و سعی در کمک و آرام کردن اوضاع شهر و آرامش مردم داشته، فردی سامان‌گر دانسته و اسم او را دختر سامان‌گر گفته‌اند. اگر کمی‌در معنی واژه‌ی سامان (سهمان) که معنی نظم و آرامش را دارد و لغتی مشترک بین زبآن‌ها ی ترکی آذری، فارسی، کردی است، تامل داشته باشیم. می‌توان تا حدی موافق بود که او سامان چی قیزی (دختر سامان‌گر) بوده. روایتی دیگر هم از گذشته‌های دور بر پایه اسطوره‌ی (زمان) در بین مردم آذربایجان هست که در تلفظ ترکی در طی گذر زمان مبدل به سامان شده است. مردم بومی آذربایجان، ترکیه، قفقاز و کردستان، کهکشان راه شیری را راه زمان و یا زمان یا (سامان بولی) گویند و اعتقاد بر این دارند که خدواند هنگام آفرینش هستی، گونی کاهی را به فرشتگانش داده بود تا آن‌ها در مسیر گذر خود بپاشند و راه و مسیر زمان و گردش ستاره‌ها را مشخص کنند و مقرر نموده بود که در هر دوره‌ی زمانی یعنی هر چند قرن زن و مردی از این راه بگذرند و صاحب دختری شوند و آن دختر، دختر زمان (سامان) و یا (سامانچی قیزی) است.

با توجه به معنی گسترده اسم (سامانچی قیزی) و اختلاف نظرهای زیاد من برای عنوان کتاب، دختر کاه فروش (سامانچی قیزی) را که بین

اکثر مردم آذربایجان متداول و پذیرفته شده است. انتخاب کردم و بر آن شدم که داستان زندگی یا بهتر است بگویم رمان او را بنویسم و سال‌ها به نوشتن آن نشستم. اکنون که نوشتن آن را به پایان رسانده‌ام. تقدیم می‌کنم به مردم دیارم آذربایجان باشد که بپذیرند و این تاکید را دارم که تمام سوژه و فصل فصل رمان آفریده ذهن من است. اگر در متن رمان به یک مقطع تاریخی اشاره و یا یک واقعه تاریخی با شخصیت‌های موثر آن در بطن جریان وقایع مورد استناد و دست مایه قرار گرفته‌اند به خاطر نزدیک نمودن رمان به حقیقت بر اساس منطق رمان است نه چیزی دیگر، چرا که رمان حاصل تخیل بر مبنای حقیقت زندگیست تا زمان و زندگی و دنیای تازه‌ای بی‌آفریند.

اسماعیل یوردشاهیان اورمیا

اورمیه- ایران- پائیز۱۳۹۲

تجدید نظر کلی و باز نویسی و کامل نمودن رمان اردیبهشت ۱۴۰۱

فهرست مطالب

فرار از تفلیس

۱

-آن‌ها تو را می‌کشند سارا، آن‌ها تو را می‌کشند. همان‌طور که پدرت را
کشتند، مادرت را کشتند، شوهرت را. روزی خواهد رسید سارا که آرزو
خواهی کرد. ای کاش به این جا به این شهر و سرزمین اورمی نیامده بودی.
همان‌طور که پدرت آرزو می‌کرد.

نسترن خاتون می‌گفت و می‌گریست و صدای گرفته و غم‌بارش در فضای
تیره و مرطوب انبار انعکاس می‌یافت. صبح بود کمی‌مانده به ظهر هوا گرفته
و ابری بود، باران ریز می‌بارید. همراه با ریزش باران دود غلیظی فضای
اطراف کاروان‌سرا و میدان مقابل آن را پر کرده بود. هر چند گاه صدای آه
و ناله و فریاد مردم همراه با صدای گلوله از ناحیه‌ای از شهر به گوش
می‌رسید. سقف انباری که آن‌ها را در آن زندانی کرده بودند کوتاه بود و

سیاه با تیرهای چوبی کلفت و کهنه و تیرک‌های چوبی باریک و حصیر دود گرفته‌ی سیاه که زیر بار سنگین سقف تاب برداشته و خم شده بودند. انگار از تحمل بار سنگین سالیان دراز خسته بودند.

سارا صدای نسترن خاتون را شنید. چشمانش را گشود و خیره به هر سو نگریست. هوای تاریک، کم نور و نمور انبار دم کرده و نامطبوع بود. دست برروی بالش گذاشت، نیم خیز شد و نشست. تلی کنارش آمد و در حالی که با نوک انگشتان شانه‌هایش را مالش می‌داد و نوازشش می‌کرد. گفت:

- بیدار شدی خانمم؟ خدا را شکر

سارا نگاهی به اطراف‌انداخت. چشمش که به یوسف خورد پرسید:

- ما کجا هستیم؟ اینجا کجاست عمو؟ مرا کی آورده‌اید به این جا؟

یوسف که نزدیک در چوبی انبار چمباتمه زده و به دیوار تکیه داده بود گفت:

- دیشب دخترم. اینجا انبار کاروان‌سراست. تو را اینجا به طور موقت زندانی کرده‌اند. ما هم خواستیم کنار تو بمانیم.

سارا روانداری پشمی را که روی پاهایش کشیده بودند کنار زد. گره روسریش را که به رنگ بنفش بود باز کرد و روی شانه‌هایش انداخت. گذاشت موهای صاف قهوه‌ای روشن مایل به طلائیش روی شانه‌هایش بریزد. پیراهنش سفید بود و بلند با حاشیه ملیله دوز آبی رنگ و یقه‌ی سرخ رنگ چین دار زری دوزی شده. او را روی ملافه‌ای سفید که روی کاه‌ها پهن کرده بودند خوابانده بودند. به زحمت از جایش بلند شد. دو روز از زایمانش می‌گذشت. بچه‌اش را که نوزادی پسر بود. کمی پائین‌تر از او در گهواره‌ای چوبی خوابانده بودند که نسترن خاتون با پایش آرام تکان می‌داد.

سارا احساس ضعف می‌کرد. ناتوان شده بود. صورت گرد استخوانیش رنگ پریده و مهتابی بود اما باز لبخند مهربانش را برلب داشت. چشمان آبی موربش زیر طاق کمان ابروان با وجود درخشندگی رنگ و حالتی از ضعف داشتند. تلی کمک کرد که از جایش بلند شود و به کنار پنجره‌ی کوچک انبار برود و بیرون را نگاه کند. جلو در انبار دو مرد مسلح مشغول نگهبانی بودند. وقتی متوجه او شدند کنجکاو با چشمان مات اما ترس گرفته و حیا زده چشم به او دوختند. وسط میدان جلو کاروان‌سرا تل آتشی دود گرفته می‌سوخت. دسته‌ای از جیلوهای[1] آشوری همراه با سربازان روس و چند گرجی مسلح با قیافه و چهره‌های متفاوت اما اکثرا با ریش و سبیل بلند در حالی که با صدای بلند حرف می‌زدند و می‌خندیدند به سمت غرب میدان دروازه غربی شهر می‌رفتند. چند سرباز روس نزدیک نارون کهنسال و بلند میدان ایستاده بودند و به مرد ساز زن دوره گردی که زیردرخت نارون نشسته و مشغول کوک سازش بود. نگاه می‌کردند. درخت نارون شاخه‌های بلندش را به هرسو کشانده وگسترانده بود اما برگ نداشت. بعضی از شاخه‌هایش در میان دود و مه غلیظ گم شده بودند. هوا گرفته و

---

[1] جیلوها طایفه‌ای از آشوریان مسیحی ترکیه بودند و در کوه پایه‌های شهرهای نزدیک مرز ایران سکونت و زندگی عشیرتی داشتند که با شروع جنگ جهانی اول هم زمان با کشتار ارامنه در ترکیه به ایران پناهنده شده و در شهرهای سلماس و اورمیه سکنا گزیدند اما بعد از چند سال با حمایت و تحریک نیروهای روسیه و انگلیس و گرفتن اسلحه از آنها همراه با گروهی از آشوریان و ارمنیان محل سر به شورش و جنگ و قتل و غارت نهاده و ادعای حکومت و کشور مستقل مسیحی در منطقه را نمودند. شورش جیلوها که باعث کشته و آوارگی ده هاهزارنفر و ویرانی و قحطی شد در تاریخ و خاطره مردم محل به سال‌های قحط و بلوای جیلولوغ معروف است.

ابری بود، باران ریز می‌بارید. باد می‌وزید، همراه با وزش باد و ناله و انفجار گلوله، صدای بهم خوردن مهیب و سخت چیزی سنگین انگار سنگ بر سنگ به گوش می‌رسید. صداها چنان بلند و مهیب بودند که گویی چیزی مثل کوه داشت فرو می‌ریخت. درست آن لحظه‌ای که سارا کنار پنجره رسید یک آن غرش سنگین انفجار و فروریختن سنگ‌ها چنان شدید و بلند و نزدیک شد که تمام فضای غم آلود صبحگاه کاروان‌سرا و محیط اطراف آن را پوشاند. سارا ترسیده و هراسان برگشت و پرسید:

-   این صداها از کجاست؟

تلی گفت:

-   بیا این طرف دخترم از هفت آسیاب است. دارند آسیاب‌ها را خراب می‌کنند.

یوسف زیر لب غرید:

-   آسیاب‌های سنگی بزرگ را دارند خراب می‌کنند. این مردم دیگر نباید نانی برای خوردن داشته باشند.

نسترن خاتون که روی صندلی چوبی شکسته‌ای نشسته و نگاه مات و اشک گرفته‌اش را به جایی نامعلوم دوخته بود و از آن همه رنج و ملال و کشت وکشتار و تاراج و ویرانی به خصوص از حمله و محاصره شب پیش به روستا و خآن‌ها ش و دستگیری سارا و زندانی شدنشان حال و وروز خوشی نداشت. روسری سفید گل‌دارش را روی صورتش کشید و در حالی که به آرامی می‌گریست نالید:

-   آسیاب‌ها می‌سوزند، آسیاب‌ها خراب می‌شوند و ما زیرسنگ آسیاب‌ها خرد خواهیم شد. چه فرق می‌کند. بگذار ملخ‌ها وکرکس‌ها در این سرزمین

اورمی‌زندگی کنند. بگذار دست‌ها و خنجرهایشان همیشه خونین بماند. این توفان به این زودی نخواهد خوابید. آخ سارا، آخ سارا، ای کاش هرگز به اینجا به این سرزمین نیامده بودی. ای کاش پدرت تو را از تفلیس نمی‌آورد. ای کاش این همه پاک و خوب نبودی، زیبایی و مهربانیت دشمن تو شدند سارا.

سارا گیج شده بود برگشت رفت مقابل نسترن خاتون ایستاد و خم شد و پرسید:

– آن‌ها کی‌اند؟ چرا می‌خواهند مرا بکشند؟

نسترن خاتون روسریش را که پایین لغزیده و قسمتی از صورتش را پوشانده بود کنار زد. سرش را بلند کرد نگاه پر از سوالش را توی صورت سارا دوخت و متعجب و حیرت زده گفت:

– مگر نمی‌دانی؟

سارا گیج و مات گفت: نه

نسترن خاتون متفکرانه سرش را پائین‌انداخت و گفت:

– خواهی دانست خیلی زود. فکرکن پدرت کی بود، مادرت کی بود؟ اصلا تو کی هستی سارا؟

سارا قامت راست کرد و ایستاد. حرف‌ها وسوال‌های نسترن خاتون گیج وحیرانش کرده بودند. نمی‌دانست چه باید بگوید. انگار زایمان و حوادث چند روز اخیر تمام هوش و حواس و حافظه‌اش را از او گرفته بودند. نمی‌توانست خیلی از مسائل را به خاطر بیاورد. بعضی از مسائل مثل تصویرهای گنگی از یک خاطره و یاد دور، یک لحظه در ذهن و یادش روشن وآشکار و بعد ناپدید می‌شدند. ضعیف و ناتوان شده بود. برگشت

از ناتوانی در یافتن پاسخ ، نگاه غم گرفته و پر از تشویش و سوالش را در چشم و صورت یوسف و بعد تلی دوخت. پی پاسخ بود. چون همیشه می‌خواست پاسخش را از زبان آن‌ها بشنود. احساس خلاء می‌کرد مثل ساختمانی بود که از درون فرو می‌ریخت. دست بر دیوار نهاد که تعادلش را حفظ کند و نیفتد. آرام به طرف پنجره برگشت و در حالی که مثل دوران کودکیش همان دورانی که در دیر به سر می‌برد. خود را در پناه دیوار پنجره قرار می‌داد. چشم به بیرون دوخت و زیر لب با خود زمزمه کرد:

– من کی هستم؟ من کی هستم؟

یک آن همه چیز، تمام آرزوها و خواسته‌ها وتمام آدم‌ها و اجسام و اشیای محیط برایش محو و نابود شدند، حجم فشرده‌ای از تصاویر و اشکال و خاطرات گذشته چون سیل گل‌آلود بر مغز و خاطرش هجوم آوردند و او کنار پنجره تکیه داده بر دیوار با احساسی آمیخته از تنهایی و ترس همان‌طور خود را می‌کاوید. ذهنش را، بودنش را و مرتب زیر لب می‌گفت و تکرار می‌کرد:

– من کی هستم؟ من کی هستم؟

از مادرش (سارو) هیچ یاد و خاطره‌ای در ذهن نداشت. جز عکس کهنه و زرد شده سیاه و سفیدی که مادرش سارو را کنار پدرش امیرخان در پیراهن سفید عروسی باکلاه گل‌دار و توری سفید که قسمتی از صورتش را پوشانده بود، نشان می‌داد و صلیب زمرّدین و قدی‌می‌نشان تقدس وراثتی خانواده که اکنون بر گردن او بود. در عکس در گردن مادرش بود. مادرش سارو چند روز بعد از تولد او و در اثر تب زایمان درگذشته بود و صلیب زمردین قدی‌می‌به نشان تقدس بنا به رسم خانواده به او رسیده بود.

او را مادر و پدربزرگ مادریش (تره زا و ژواخیم) نزد خود برده و تا هشت سالگی مراقبت و تربیت او را برعهده گرفته بودند و بعد بنا به رسم دیرین خانواده، همان‌طور که مادرش سارو را به دیر سپرده بودند. او را نیز برای تحصیل و تربیت مذهبی به دیر سپردند. تمام لحظه‌های صبح روزی که پدر و مادر بزرگش او را با خود به دیر بردند. بسیارکم رنگ اما تلخ، هنوز در خاطرش بود. صبح بارانی سردی بودکه او را سوار کالسکه کردند و همراه خود به دیر بردند و بعد از صحبت با خواهر روحانی پیری که مسئول دیر خواهران بود و انجام بعضی تشریفات که کمی‌به درازا کشید. آمدند او را بغل کردند و بوسیدند و به خواهر روحانی مسئول دیر سپردند و رفتند. سارا یادش بود که وقتی آن‌ها مقابل در بزرگ دیر سوار کالسکه شدند و کالسکه حرکت کرد. غم ناشناخته‌ای که تا آن روز برای او غریبه بود. همراه با احساس تنهایی و غربت و ترس. تمام وجودش را در برگرفت. هراسان وگریان تا دم در پشت سر آن‌ها دوید. اما کالسکه آن‌ها از دیر خارج شد و در دیر را بستند و او پشت در چوبی دیر گریان روی زمین نشست و چشم بر دیوارهای سنگی بلند و در چوبی بزرگ و پهن دیر دوخت وهای‌های گریست. نمی‌دانست چه اتفاقی افتاده و چرا او را آن جا گذاشتند و رفتند. قلب کوچکش از ترس و تنهایی تند می‌زد و با چشمان اشک‌آلود و ترس گرفته اطراف را نگاه می‌کرد. نمی‌دانست که چه باید بکند. خواهر روحانی پیر به همراه دو خواهر روحانی جوان آمد و او را بلند کرد و گفت بیا برویم دخترم و او را همراه خود کشان کشان به درون دیر بردند. هنگام گذر از راهرو نیمه تاریک با دیوارهای سنگی و شمعدآن‌ها ی روشن نصب شده برروی دیوارها و مجسمه‌ها و صلیب‌های بزرگ که

گاه بلندی آن‌ها تا سقف دیر می‌رسید. ترس غریبی بر تمام وجودش نشست. به طوری که پشتش تیرکشید و تمام وجودش لرزید اما نتوانست جیغ بکشد. فقط هم چنان گریه کرد و توجهی هم به حرف‌های خواهر روحانی نکرد. بعد از بالا رفتن از پله‌های سنگی باریک، به طبقه دوم دیر که رسیدند. یکی از خواهران روحانی بنام سونیا که صورتی رنگ پریده و لاغر و استخوانی سرد و بی‌روحی داشت از او خواست کلاه حصیری و لباس‌های حریر و گلی رنگ زیبایش را در آورد. وقتی او از در آوردن کلاه وپیراهنش سرباز زد و مقاوت کرد به دستور خواهر روحانی پیر دو خواهر روحانی جوان به زور پیراهنش را از تنش در آوردند. سارا دیگر هرگز آن لباس‌های حریر گلی رنگ زیبا و کلاه حصیری سبز رنگش را ندید اما همیشه در فکر و در آرزوی دوباره داشتن آن‌ها بود. بعد از در آوردن لباس‌هایش، پیراهنی سیاه‌رنگ بلند با یقیه‌ای سفید به او پوشاندند و روسری سفیدی برسرش بستند و بعد صلیب زمردین را که از کودکی به همراه داشت دوباره با دعا برگردنش آویختند. خواهر روحانی پیر که قدی کوتاه و صورتی گرد و مهربان داشت گفت:

– سارا دخترم آرام باش، گریه نکن، دیر محل غم و گریه نیست. دیرمحل محبت وعبادت است. پدر و مادربزرگت اگر تو را برای تحصیل وآموزش به دیر آوردند. دلیل داشتند. تو انتخاب شده‌ای و از مادری مقدس هستی و روزی باید به وظیفه مقدر شده‌ات در راه مسیح و دین او انجام دهی. این صلیب مقدس مال مادرت بود، حالا مال توست و هیچ وقت نباید از خودت دور نگه‌داری. آرام باش دخترم، تو هرگز این جا تنها نیستی. در این جا به تو همه چیز را خواهند آموخت.

اگر چه خواهر روحانی پیر با محبت و اطمینان حرف زد. ولی او هم چنان ترسیده و غمگین بود و از آن به بعد همیشه در دیر با احساسی از غربت و تنهایی به سر برد. شب‌ها تا دیرقت در رخت‌خوابش از ترس تاریکی و تنهایی لحافش را روی سرش می‌کشید و گریه می‌کرد اما کسی چندان توجهی به گریه‌های کودکانه او نداشت. بهترین لحظه‌ها برای او زمانی بود که با آموزگارانی که از بیرون برای آموزش زبان لاتین و فرانسه و روسی و علوم جدید می‌آمدند. مشغول صحبت می‌شد. سارا به یادگیری علوم و زبان علاقه داشت و استعداد خارق العاده‌ای از خود در یادگیری آن‌ها نشان می‌داد. سنگ صبور و هم رازش پدر یاکوب روحانی پیر کلیسای دیر بود که سارا هر یکشنبه بعد از مراسم دعا به دیدن او و برای اعتراف به گناهان ناکرده، بیان غم وغصه و آرزوها و دلتنگیش می‌رفت و همیشه از آرزویش یعنی رفتن و خلاصی از دیر و دیدن پدرش صحبت می‌کرد. پدر روحانی یاکوب اورا به رحمت و محبت خداوند امیدوار می‌ساخت. اما تاکید می‌کرد که باید توجه داشته باشد که او انتخاب شده است و باید روزی به وظیفه‌اش در راه دین مسیح عمل کند. اما هرگز به او نمی‌گفت و توضیح نمی‌داد که منظور از انتخاب شده چیست؟ و او هرگز نفهمید و ندانست که وظیفه مقدر شدهٔ مذهبی او چیست و چه است!؟ فقط این را دانسته بود و بعدها از پدرش هم آموخت و یاد گرفت که همه را دوست بدارد و با همه مهربان باشد و او اکنون با وجود جنگ و ویرانی، کشته شدن پدرش امیرخان، عمه نرگس و مردم روستا و شهر و دیارش باز به مهربانی فکر می‌کرد و همه چیز را در بازگشت صلح وآرامش و مهربانی می‌دید. راستی اوکی بود؟

بیشترین و بهترین خاطراتش را ازپدرش داشت. اگرچه تا نه سالگی هرگز او را ندیده بود و هرگز کسی از پدرش با او صحبت نکرده بود. جز مادر بزرگش ترزا که هنگام مرگش او را از دیر نزد خود فراخواند و عکس پدر و مادرش همان عکس سیاه و سفید کهنه و زرد شده را که همیشه نزد خود داشت به او نشان داد وگفت که او فرزند مردی از اهالی اورمیه آذربایجان ایران است. مردی تحصیل کرده و باکمال و ازخانوادهی بسیار اصیل و خوب. مادر بزرگش با وجود گفتن واقعیت و دادن نشانههای پدرش و تعریف از شخصیت و زیبایی وکمال او، با تاسف گفت:

ـ پدرت اگر چه مرد با کمال و خوبیست اما مسیحی و گرجی نیست و برای همین حق نداشت عاشق مادرت سارو شود و حق ندارد تو را هم ببیند و تو نباید او را ببینی حتی اگر هم به دیدنت بیاید.

سارا آن روز از حرفهای مادر بزرگش چیزی نفهمید اما دو سال بعد یک روز پدر روحانی یاکوب او را به نمازخانه دیر خواست و مرد نسبتا جوان خوش رو و خوش لباسی را به او معرفی کرد وگفت:

ـ دخترم خداوند خواسته که تو پدرت را ببینی و بشناسی. این مرد جوان پدر توست و خداوند بهتر میداند که من تنها شاهد تولد تو و درد و اشک مادرت و رنجهای پدرت یعنی این مرد بودهام.

آن روز پدرش برای او یک جفت کفش با پیراهنی گلی رنگ و بستهای شکلات وکمیپول آورده بود که پدر روحانی پول را گرفت و در صندوق کلیسا گذاشت از آن روز به بعد هر چند گاه پدرش با کمک کشیش در نمازخانه دیر به دیدن او میآمد تا این که یک روز عصر پدر روحانی یاکوب در حالی که مراقب بود کسی متوجه نشود. به دیدنش آمد و از او

خواست که لباس و وسائلش را بردارد و همراه پدرش برود. سارا خاطرش آمد که فقط تعداد کمی از کتاب‌هایش را همراه با عروسکش برداشت. عروسکی که مادر بزرگش برایش خریده بود و از کودکی هر شب در تنهایی هنگام خواب آن را بغل می‌کرد و می‌خوابید اگر چه در دیر داشتن و بغل کردن عروسک قدغن بود ولی سارا آن را همیشه با خود داشت. هنگام خدا حافظی کشیش یاکوب پیر ضمن دعا گفت:

– برو فرزندم، بهتره که همراه پدرت بروی. شاید تو به این جا تعلق نداری و اگر هم انتخاب شده‌ای. هر جا باشی کاری را که باید انجام دهی، انجام خواهی داد. چه بهتر که در خارج از کلیسا باشی. مثل مسیح و مریم مقدس و شاید هم تقدیر تو همینه. برو خداوند نگه‌دار تو باد.

سارا خوب خاطرش بود که وقتی همراه پدرش بعد از گذشتن از پله‌های باریک و دالانی سرد از در کوچک پشتی نمازخانه که در گوشه سمت راست و قسمت بیرونی دیر قرار داشت، بیرون آمدند دو اسب سیاه زین شده در فاصله کمی از در منتظر آن‌ها بودند. اسب‌هایی بلند و تنومندی که آن‌ها را از تفلیس به اورمیه آوردند. همان اسب‌های سیاه و مهربان که با وجود جنگ در اثر حمله روس‌ها و جیلوها تا زمان دست‌گیری او همیشه در اصطبل و یا در حیاط کاروان‌سرا منتظر او و حبه‌های قندی بودند که او هنگام نوازش و تیمار قبل از سوارشدن در کف دستانش می‌نهاد و به آن‌ها می‌داد و همیشه هنگام سواری یکی از آن‌ها ، جفت دیگر را مراقبت می‌کرد و همراه آن‌ها می‌آمد. برای همین سارا در شهر به دختر اسب سوار، صاحب دو اسب سیاه معروف شده بود. بسیاری هم در شهر دیده بودند که سارا کودکان و زنانی را که علاقه به سواری داشتند. به خصوص کودکان

معلول و افلیج را که توان راه رفتن نداشتند. سواراسب‌ها می‌کرد و با خود بگردش می‌برد و همین مهربانی و دوستی با مردم و زیبایی خیال انگیز او بود که سارا را معروف و محبوب اهالی شهر کرده بود.

سارااندیشید که اکنون اسب‌ها کجا هستند؟ یاد اسب‌ها وسرنوشت آن‌ها و حوادث روزهای گذشته، کشته شدن پدرش، عمه نرگس و اهالی روستای ساران تمام ذهن و جانش را در برگرفت و او را از خود ربود. می‌خواست بداند چرا پدرش را کشتند؟ آن‌ها کی بودند؟ چه کسانی آن‌ها را فرستاده بودند؟ و اسب‌ها آن دو اسب سیاه چه شده‌اند؟ نگاهش را که پر از پرسش واندوه بود از پنجره برگرفت و در چشم و نگاه تلی، یوسف و نسترن خاتون دوخت، سرش گیج می‌رفت ضعیف و ناتوان شده بود. خواست به جایی که خوابیده بود برگردد. تعادلش را از دست داد. دست بر دیوار نهاد که نیفتد. تلی شتابان کنارش آمد و با نگرانی پرسید:

ـ حالت خوبه؟

و بعد گفت: بیا بهتره که استراحت بکنی.

و در حالی که دست بر پشت و بازوی او می‌نهاد کمک کرد که سارا به محل خوابش برگردد و در رخت‌خوابش دراز بکشد. تلی وقتی دست بر بازوی راست سارا نهاد. سارا از سر حس درد، دست و بازویش را جمع کرد و تلی جای زخمی‌را که هنوز به شکل بر جسته بر بازوی راست سارا مانده بود لمس کرد. بعد از خوابیدن سارا که مدام زیر لب می‌گفت و می‌پرسید:

ـ من کی هستم!؟ آن‌ها چه شدند؟

همان جا پایین بستر سارا رو به روی شوهرش یوسف روی زمین نشست و نگاهش را به صورت یوسف دوخت. خاطرش آمد که هفت سال پیش آن شب که سارا را به بغلش دادند بازوی راست سارا زخمی و خونین بود. تلی آهی کشید و چشمانش را بست و در مرور خاطرات گذشته غرق شد.

۲

آن شب هوا سرد و مه گرفته بود. همراه با غرش رعد و بارش باران، باد تند می‌وزید و توفان به پا می‌کرد. تلی چون شب‌های دیگر خسته از کار و دلتنگ از تنهایی کنار پنجره نزدیک آتش‌دان نشسته بود و دکمهٔ پیراهن شوهرش یوسف را می‌دوخت. پسرش، تنها فرزندش یعقوب سال‌ها بود که آن‌ها و شهر و دیارشان را ترک کرده و رفته بود. هر وقت از شوهرش یوسف می‌پرسید. جوابش فقط این بود:

– رفته ایروان از آن جا به تفلیس خواهد رفت.

تلی از تفلیس خاطره و یاد خوشی نداشت. مردم آن جا را مردمی خشن می‌دانست و می‌ترسید. برای همین وقتی از شوهرش می‌پرسید که چرا گذاشتی به تفلیس برود. صدای یوسف بلند می‌شد:

– در تفلیس آشنا هست زن، کمکش می‌کنند جا و مکانش می‌دهند. کار برایش جور می‌کنند. خدا را شکرکن که رفت. اگر مانده بود. معلوم نبود چه می‌شد؟ چه بر سرش می‌آمد؟

تلی از صدای رعد و برق اگر چه می‌ترسید اما از صدای باران خوشش می‌آمد. دوست داشت که هم چنان مدام ببارد. لااقل از صدای گلوله وآه و زاری مردمان،کشته و تاراج شدگان که بهتر بود. آن شب شوهرش یوسف خسته‌تر از شب‌های پیشین کنار آتش‌دان نشسته، سرش بر پشتی غلتیده و خوابش برده بود. همیشه دیر وقت می‌آمد کارش با آمدن سپاه روس‌ها وتصرف شهر توسط آن‌ها و در این چند ماه اخیر با آمدن جیلوهای آشوری آواره از ترکیه به شهرهای اورمیه و سلماس و شورش آن‌ها سخت و سنگین و دشوار و بی مزد شده بود. تنها درآمد مختصرش ازاندک مسافران به خصوص مسافران خارجی بود. تعداد آن‌ها هم زیاد نبود سه فرانسوی یک سوئدی و دو فنلاندی با چند تاجر گرجی و ترک که در عمارت شمالی داخل کاروان‌سرا در قسمت اعیان نشین اقامت داشتند. تلی در انجام کارهای آن جا به یوسف کمک می‌کرد. یعنی نظافت اطاق‌ها، شستن و تعویض ملافه‌ها و آماده نمودن صبحانه و ناهار و شام مسافرها را انجام می‌داد. تمام آن کارهایی که در گذشته شاگرد یوسف سرگیس و زنش سدا انجام می‌دادند. اما سرگیس به جیلوها پیوسته و صاحب منصب شده و ششلول بسته بود، سوار بر اسب در فرماندهی دسته‌های بزرگ جیلو در شهر گشت می‌زد و هر از چندگاه به کاروان‌سرا و یوسف سری می‌زد و چایی می‌نوشید و استراحتی می‌کرد و از یوسف می‌خواست که نگران نباشد اگر مشکلی پیش آمد او را خبر کند. یوسف هم که برای گذران زندگی

ناگزیر شده بود آهنگری وکاه فروشی بکند. خوشحال بودکه لااقل او را دارد اما جیلوها وسربازهای روس که برای تعمیر تسمهٔ تفنگ و تعویض نعل اسب‌هایشان می‌آمدند. نه تنها پول نمی‌دادند. بلکه بد رفتاری هم می‌کردند. تنها شکر یوسف این بود که زنده‌اند، کاری به کار او و خانواده و کسب و کار او ندارند. خانه وکاروانسرا را تاراج نمی‌کنند. البته می‌شد حدس زد که به خاطر قرار گرفتن کاروانسرا با میهمان‌خانهٔ نسبتا مناسبش در میدان نزدیک بازار شهر که اکنون تنها میهمان‌خانه شهر بود. خواستهٔ بزرگان جیلو و روس‌ها بر این است که میهمان‌خانه هم چنان فعال و در امنیت و آرامش باشد. همین در امان ماندن کاروانسرا محل خوبی برای فعالیت پنهانی و تماس با تعدادی از مبارزین ملی وآزادی‌خواه شده بود که در کاروانسرا قرار ملاقات می‌گذاشتند، اسلحه رد و بدل می‌کردند و اسیران فراری را جا و پناه می‌دادند. نقش و فعالیت اصلی یوسف و تلی در همکاری با مبارزین آزادی‌خواه همین مسائل بود. تلی بسیار دیده بود که یوسف به همراه چند نفر دیگر پنهانی اسیران فراری را به اصطبل کاروانسرا می‌آورند. با وسائل آهنگری دستبند و زنجیرهای پایشان را باز می‌کنند و بعد از تعویض لباس آن‌ها و پوشاندن لباس‌های مبدل صبح روز بعد به همراه مسافرین که عازم شهرهای دیگر و یا روستاها بودند و یا از طریق دیگر فراریشان می‌دادند. گاه تلی هم با آن‌ها همکار می‌کرد و در نقش یکی از بستگان اسیر در می‌آمد اسیر فراری را در پتویی می‌پیچدند که سخت مریض است و تلی را کنارش می‌نشاندند که همراه و مراقبش است و یا درون تابوتی در ارابه قرار می‌داند و تلی گریان و نالان کنار تابوت در

ارابه می‌نشست و برای دفن کردن به گورستان خارج شهر می‌بردند و در طول راه و یا در گورستان اسیر را فراری می‌دادند.

باران سرد می‌بارید و در آن هنگام شب جز صدای بارش باران و آواز ناودان‌ها هیچ صدای دیگری نبود نه غرش رعدی نه عوعوی سگی و نه صدای پای رهگذری، سکوتی سنگین با تیرگی عمیق شب بر همه جا نشسته بود. انگار همه در خواب بودند و همه جا خیس از باران بود. گاه گاهی اگر برقی می‌درخشید از دورها بود از آن سوی کوهستان مور شهیدان که آسمان را در سیاهی بی‌انتهایش خطی آتشین و پر نور می‌کشید و همه جا را برای یک آن پوشیده از نور می‌کرد. بعد صدای غرشی از دور دست همه جا را فرا می‌گرفت. تلی کنار آتش‌دان همان‌طور که مشغول دوخت و دوز بود. به صدای باران گوش سپرده و در رویای خود گم بود. ناگه صدایی شنید. احساس کرد که در را می‌زنند. دست از دوختن برداشت. حواسش را جمع کرد و نفسش را حبس، کمی‌ترسیده بود در آن وقت شب کی می‌توانست باشد و این صدای چی بود؟ دوباره صداها را شنید. صدای نفس‌ها و حرکت اسب و کوبیده شدن چیزی مثل پا بر در و صدای ضعیف و خستهٔ مردی که او و شوهرش را صدا می‌زد. بلند شد کنار پنجره رفت اما جز صدای باران و آواز ناودان‌ها صدای دیگری نبود. برگشت نشست. سعی کرد خود را مشغول دوخت دوز کند که باز صدای در را شنید. دوباره بلند شد. دم پنجره رفت. این بار صدای در را خوب و واضح شنید. کسی انگار با پا بر در می‌کوبید. بخار پنجره را پاک کرد و چشم به بیرون دوخت. اما جز سیاهی شب چیزی به نظرش نرسید. در کاروان‌سرا بلند بود و به زحمت می‌شد از بالای آن میدان‌گاه را دید. بار دیگر صدای ماغ و حرکت

اسب‌ها را شنید. بعد صدای خسته و ضعیف مردی که او و شوهرش را صدا می‌زد. صدا انگار از دور دست می‌آمد. برگشت با ترس گفت:

ـ یوسف ، یوسف صدای در، در را می‌زنند.

یوسف که کنار آتش‌دان خوابش برده بود. یکه خورد. هراسان چشم گشود و گفت چی!؟

تلی گفت: کسانی پشت درند با اسب آمده‌اند.

یوسف بلند شد کنار پنجره رفت، بخار خیس پنجره را پاک کرد و پیشانیش را به شیشه چسباند و چشم به سیاهی شب دوخت اما چیزی ندید. تنش می‌لرزید، آوازهای دردناک دوباره در وجودش جان گرفته بودند. کنار پنجره نشست سرش را میان دستانش گرفت. تلی کنارش آمد و پرسید: چه شده؟

یوسف زیر لب زمزمه کرد: می‌ترسم.

تلی به گریه گفت: من هم می‌ترسم.

یوسف سرش را به دیوار تکیه داد و چشمانش را بست و به خوابی که دیده بوداندیشید. فضا و تصاویر خوابش بر ذهن و جان و تنش رخنه کرده و هنوز با او بودند. خوابی که هر لحظه‌اش با او بود و تمام تصاویرش از برابر دیدگانش می‌گذشتند. چشمانش را بست تا از آن‌ها رها شود اما رویاهای مضطربش با تصاویر منقلب و مه آلود دوباره در وجودش در برابر دیدگانش جان گرفتند:

بادهای سرد در وزشی بی‌امان، گوزن‌ها و هجوم ملخ‌ها در مه سرد و مردی زخمی‌با بالاپوشی تیره با دو اسب سیاه که به همراه یوسف دنبال جایی، سرپناهی می‌گشت و آن‌گاه، گروه گروه سربازهای روس همراه با شورشیان

جنگجوی جیلو بودند با قیافه‌های خشن، در لباس‌های کثیف و تیره و قمه و تفنگ‌های آویخته از شانه و کمر، از میان بخار زرد و آبی بر می‌آمدند. پاشنه پوتین‌های بلند و گلی خود را بر سر و صورت او و آن مرد زخمی می‌نهادند و می‌گذشتند، در حالی‌که به خشم آواز می‌خواندند و می‌خندیدند در سمت دیگر میدان جمع می‌شدند و به طرف آن‌ها که به دیوار و در کاروانسر چسبیده و به دنبال جان پناهی می‌گشتند. شلیک می‌کردند از هر سو و از همه اطراف اورمیه صدای گلوله می‌آمد. از توپراق قلعه از دروازه عسگرخان، از دروازهٔ یورد شاه از وسط بازار، از کوه سیر، از شهر چای، از وسط دریا از همه جا گلوله‌های آتشینی که در هوا صفیر می‌کشیدند و بعد مبدل به قطرات باران سرخ می‌شدند و بر سر و روی او و آن مرد زخمی‌می‌ریختند. همه جای یوسف سرخ و خونین شده بود. دست به سروصورتش می‌کشید. تمام تنش می‌سوخت همه جایش زخم بود. دست‌هایش، شکمش، پاهایش و صورت و لب‌هایش، قادر نبود حرف بزند. صدا در گلویش گره خورده بود. نفسش در نمی‌آمد، داشت خفه می‌شد. می‌دید خانه‌اش را آتش زده‌اند. چند جیلو به همراه سربازهای روس از گیسوان زنش تلی گرفته کشان کشان او را به میان تل آتش فروزان وسط میدان می‌برند. از خشم و اضطراب می‌سوخت. اما ناتوان از انجام هرکاری بود. نمی‌توانست حرکت بکند. می‌خواست فریاد بکشد، نمی‌توانست. می‌خواست بگوید که او این جاست، زنده است. اما صدایش بر نمی‌آمد. فقط دو تا اسب، دو تا اسب سیاه رنگ با قامت بلند و استوار از مقابلش می‌گذشتند. اسب‌ها خیس بودند و از دهانشان کف خونین بر زمین

می‌ریخت. اسب‌ها ماغ می‌کشیدند و بخاری سرخ در هوا می‌لرزید. اسب‌ها زخمی‌بودند.

تلی وحشت زده از حال بی‌قرار یوسف چشم به صورت او دوخته بود. یوسف خیس عرق به دیوار تکیه داده بود و می‌لرزید بعد از چند لحظه یک آن گویی چیزی در درونش فرو ریخت. چشمانش را گشود و نگاه ترس خورده‌اش را به تلی دوخت و گفت:

-   من در را باز می‌کنم.

بعد کمی‌تامل کرد و نگاهش را از نگاه تلی گرفت. در زندگی تمام کسش، رفیق و همدمش، عشق و مرادش تلی بود. نمی‌دانست چگونه ترس و وحشتش را از خواب تلخ و ناگوارش به او بگوید و تشریح کند. بلند شد، به طرف پستو رفت، درش را گشود و پرده را کنار زد. پوستین بلندش را به دوشش‌انداخت و تفنگش را در دست چپ زیر پوستین قایم نمود و در حالی که به طرف در اطاق می‌رفت، قمهٔ نسبتا بلندی را که دستهٔ استخوانی سیاه رنگی داشت از جعبهٔ چوبی رو طاقچه برداشت و به طرف تلی گرفت. تلی با نگاهی پر از ترس و التماس پرسید:

- حالا چه باید کرد؟

یوسف گفت:

- باید در را باز کرد. شاید مسافر و یا فرد وامانده و بی‌کس و بی‌پناهی باشد. اما اگر جیلوها و سالدات‌های روس بودند. من سعی می‌کنم مقابلشان بایستم و مقابله کنم و اگر نتوانستم نگذار دستشان به تو برسد. خودت را راحت کن. این قمه تیز و برنده است. تازه جلایش داده‌ام کافیست نوک قمه را در سینه ات فروکنی.

تلی در حالی که چشمان پر از اشکش را توی صورت لاغر واستخوانی شوهرش دوخته بود. قامتش مثل کتاب تا و وسط اتاق روی گلیم پهن شد. گفت:

- من نمی‌توانم.

یوسف بغض گرفته گفت:

- باید بتوانی شاید این چنین بهتر باشد. می‌دانم که خیلی سخت است اما مجبوریم. به ما یاد داده‌اند که بمیریم.

بغض نگذاشت دیگر چیزی بگوید. حرفش را برید. نگاهی غم‌آلود به تلی انداخت و بعد در را گشود و از پله‌ها پائین رفت. فانوس را از طاقچهٔ کنار در برداشت و در را گشود، وارد حیاط کاروانسرا شد. بیرون خاموشی غریبی همراه با سیاهی غلیظ و خیس شب بر همه جا نشسته بود. تنها صدای بارش باران بود و زوزهٔ خیف باد و صدای نفس‌های اسب که گاه گاهی به گوش می‌رسید. یوسف یقهٔ بالا پوشش را بالا زد و کلاهش را در سرش مرتب کرد و لبهٔ آن را پائین آورد که خیس نشود و در حالی که گام‌هایش را بلند و تند بر می‌داشت از حیاط گذشت. وارد دهلیز سرپوشیدهٔ کاروانسرا شد. پشت در چوبی و بلند و بزرگ کاروانسرا به گوش ایستاد. اینک دیگر صدای نفس‌ها و تکان و حرکت اسب‌ها را به خوبی می‌شنید. فکرکرد چه کسانی می‌توانند پشت در باشند و برای چه آمده‌اند؟ در این وقت شب، در این باران، مسافر! نه. نمی‌توانند مسافر باشند. یک لحظه فکر کرد که برود ابراهیم بیک و حکیم اسحاق را خبر کند.که صدای ضعیف و خستهٔ مردی را که او را می‌خواند همراه با صدای حرکت اسب‌ها شنید. صدای خستهٔ مرد، ترس و تردیدش را به هم زد. کلون را از پشت

در بلند کاروانسرا بر داشت. تنش را به لنگهٔ راست تکیه داد و لنگهٔ چپ در کاروانسر را گشود و بیرون رفت و فانوس را بالا گرفت. در سیاهی غلیظ محوطهٔ مقابل در کاروانسرا زیر باران فقط دوتا اسب ایستاده بودند. دو تا اسب سیاه. برگردهٔ یکیشان بار بود و برگردهٔ دیگری سواری با بالاپوش چرمی سیاه و خیس، با سر افتاده برسینه و خاموش. اسب‌ها خسته و خیس بودند و قطرات باران از صورت و یال‌هایشان می‌چکید. انگار مسافتی طولانی را یک سر به تاخت آمده بودند. همراه با بخار باران که از تنشان بر می‌خاست. بخاری سفید از منخرینشان بیرون می‌زد و بی‌تاب سرشان را به هر طرف می‌جنباندند و همراه با قطرات باران، قطرات خون از زیر بالاپوش سوار به زمین می‌چکید.

یوسف پیش رفت و فانوس را بالابرد و در برابر صورت مرد سوار گرفت. صورت مرد لاغر و تکیده بود و شیار زخمی کهنه بر گونهٔ راستش هویدا بود که حتی انبوه ریش مجعد سیاه تیره‌اش آن را نپوشانده بود. یوسف احساس کرد که سوار آشناست با کمی تردید بیشتر نزدیک شد و چشم توی صورت سوار دوخت و بعد با تعجب، بریده بریده گفت:

–   ا، امیر، امیرخان!؟

سوار سرش را بلند کرد و نگاه کم فروغش را به او دوخت و آرام و ضعیف زمزمه کرد:

– یوسف. یوسف

یوسف نتوانست تعجب و خوشحالیش را پنهان کند. برگشت به شتاب از حیاط گذشت، در را گشود و داد زد.

–   تلی، تلی، امیر خان، امیر خان آمده، بیا، بیا کمک کن.

تلی بلند شد ندانست که چگونه پله‌های باریک کم عرض خانه را شتابان طی کرد و خود را به دم در کاروانسرا رساند. سوار انگار روی زین اسب خشک شده بود. یوسف رفت که کمکش کند متوجه قطرات خونی شد که از زیر بالاپوش دست راست امیر خان به زمین می‌چکید. بالاپوش را کنار زد. امیرخان به زحمت دستش را بلند کرد و دختر بچۀ یازده و یا دوازده ساله‌ای را که در آغوشش خفته بود. پیش آورد. یوسف دخترک را بغل کرد و به تلی داد. موهای بور و طلایی تیره رنگ دخترک خیس شده بود و خون از زخم بازوی راستش بیرون می‌زد. تلی او را با شتاب به خانه برد. و یوسف دهنۀ اسب‌ها را گرفت و در حالی‌که سعی می‌کرد با آرامش و بدون صدا کارش را انجام دهد. اسب‌ها را به درون کاروانسرا برد و در را بست. امیرخان را که دست راست و قسمتی از پهلوی راست و شکمش در اثر اصابت گلوله زخمی‌شده بود از اسب پائین آورد و روی سکوی سنگی پیش در گاهی نشاند و اسب‌ها را به اصطبل برد و دهنه و زین و برگ آنها را گرفت و جلوشان علوفه وکاه و جو نهاد و دستی به تیمار برتنشان کشید و بعد از راحت نمودن آنها برگشت و در حالی‌که نمی‌توانست احساسش را پنهان کند و مرتب زیرلب می‌گفت:

– امیرخان، امیرخان، ارباب من امیر خان، عزیز من امیر خان.

امیر خان اما خیس و خسته روی سکوی سنگی نشسته سرش را به دیوار تکیه داده، پلک‌هایش بسته بود. یوسف به زحمت او را از جایش بلندکرد. تلی آمد وکمکش کرد و او را به خانه بردند. در رخت‌خوابی که تلی قبلا پهن کرده بود. خواباندند. تن امیر در اثر ساعت‌ها در یک حالت روی زین نشستن مثل چوبی خشک شده و به زحمت تا و راست می‌شد. صورتش

رنگ پریده و مهتابی بود و از زخم‌هایش قطره قطره خون بیرون می‌زد. ضعیف و ناتوان گه گاه چشمانش را می‌گشود و نگاه بی‌فروغش را به صورت آن‌ها می‌دوخت. تلی آب گرم آورد. لباس‌های امیرخان را در آوردند. زخم‌هایش را شسته و مرهم نهادند تا فردا حکیم پیره و یا حکیم اسرائیل بیاید و درمان اساسی بکند و بعد پیراهنی دیگر پوشاندند و امیر خان به خوابی عمیق فرو رفت. بعد از خواباندن امیر خان و بستن درهای کاروانسرا، یوسف خسته و نگران کنار آتشدان نشست و نگاهش را توی صورت زنش تلی دوخت. تلی هم مانند او نگران بود. ترسی عمیق همراه با سایه سنگین غمی‌ناآشنا بر چهره‌اش نشسته بود. هر دو می‌دانستند که نگرانی واضطراب‌شان از چیست؟ تن خسته و زخمی‌امیرخان و دخترش همه چیز را آشکار می‌کرد. پیدا بود که چندین روز بی‌وقفه راه آمده‌اند، شاید هم با جنگ و ستیز. چون وقتی ششلول امیر خان را از کمرش باز می‌کردند. بوی باروت سوخته می‌داد. تمام فشنگ‌هایش را شلیک کرده و فقط دو فشنگ برایش باقی مانده بود. یوسف فکرکرد به زودی سروکلهٔ مردان گرجی پیدا خواهد شد و شاید هم اکنون تعقیب‌کنندگان آمده‌اند و در اطراف کاروانسرا به کمین نشسته‌اند. یعنی این ممکن است؟ برای یک آن دچار ترس و وحشت شد. او خوب می‌دانست که سارو دختری که عشقش جان و هستی امیرخان را آتش زد متعلق به یک خانوادهٔ مذهبی و تقدیس شدهٔ قدی‌می‌است که از صدها سال پیش در تفلیس بوده‌اند و کلیسا و زیارتگاه داشته و دارند و هر چند گاه یکی از دختران و پسران طایفه برای دوام و بقا وگسترش کلیسا انتخاب و تقدیس می‌شد و می‌شود و زندگی و جان و هستیش را وقف کلیسا می‌کند. همین طایفه وکلیسای آن‌ها مردان

متعصب انتقام‌جوی خشن زیادی دارندکه می‌توانند همان زخمی‌کنندگان امیرخان و دخترش باشند. آیا آن‌ها امیرخان را با جنگ وگریز هم چنان تعقیب کرده‌اند؟ اگر تعقیب کرده‌اند. اکنون کجا هستند؟ او که هنگام گشودن در و آوردن امیرخان و اسب‌ها به درون کاروانسرا در اطراف میدان مقابل کاروانسرا کسی را ندیده بود. با خود فکر کرد اگر گرجی‌ها فردا آمدند چه باید بکند؟ و یا در روزهای بعد اصلا امیرخان را چگونه وکجا پنهان کند؟ امیرخان برایش عزیز بود.

۳

امیر خان بعد از تلی عزیزترین کس و دوست یوسف و همبازی دوران کودکی و هم مدرسه‌اش بود. اگر چه آن‌ها به خاطر رفتن امیرخان به تفلیس برای تحصیل در دیار غربت و مسائل دیگر هرگز نتوانسته بودند کنار هم باشند. کار و فعالیت کنند اما همیشه دوست و پناه هم بودند. امیر خان برعکس دل روشن و مهربانش زندگی پر رنج و تلخی داشت. برای او انگار زندگی لبخند نداشت و در هیچ سال و زمانی آرامش نیافت. شاید هم این سرنوشت و تقدیر او بود در کودکی مادرش را از دست داده بود. پدرش پاشاخان که با زن دیگری ازدواج کرده بود تربیت و نگهداری او را از همان کودکی به خواهرش نرگس خاتون سپرده بود. نرگس خاتون عمهٔ امیرخان در عمارت خانه باغی خود در باغ شخصیش در ده ساران به سر می‌برد.

زنی بود جسور و شجاع و زیبا در جوانی دل‌باختگان و خواستگاران بسیار داشت اما او دل در گرو عشق یک افسر جوان از خانواده نه چندان مطرح و ثروتمند سپرده بود ولی به خاطر مخالفت پدرش نتوانسته بود به عشق و دلداده‌اش برسد و با مرد دلخواهش ازدواج کند و ناگزیر و به اصرار و تصمیم و اجبار پدرش تن به ازدواج با پسر عموی مسنش داده بود که هرگز به او علاقه نداشت و از آن رو هرگز نتوانسته بود او را به عنوان شوهرش را قبول کند و بپذیرد و بعد از دو سال در اولین فرصت یعنی یک ماه بعد از فوت پدرش از او جدا شده بود و همراه دو خواهر بزرگش نسترن خاتون و گلاب خاتون که ازدواج نکرده و پیردختران مجرد و تنها بودند به ملک شخصیش در نزدیکی شهر در دهکده ساران که مالکش بود برگشته و در کوشکی که در وسط باغ بزرگی در ضلع شرقی ده احداث کرده بود و به کوشک ساران معروف شده بود. ساکن شده و به کار کشاورزی و دامداری مشغول بود. به آبادی ده ساران و رفاه و راحتی مردم آن جا می‌رسید. علاوه بر پل و آب بند و آسیاب بسیار بزرگی با چند انبار ساخته و راه‌انداخته بود.

نرگس خاتون همیشه سوار بر اسب در لباسی تیره در حالی که چارقد گلدار زری دوزی شده‌ای را به سر می‌نهاد. همراه با دو پیشکار و خدمتکارش حیدر و الیاس به همه جا و همهٔ کشتزارها و مزارع و اصطبل و دامهایش سر می‌زد و سرکشی می‌کرد و از روزی که امیرخان را برادرش به او سپرده بود قسمتی از کار و زندگیش مراقبت و تربیت امیرخان شده بود. یوسف خوب بخاطر داشت که اولین بار امیرخان را در همان باغ دید و با او آشنا شد. خاطرش بود در دوران کودکی در روزهایی که مادرش برای کار به

کوشک اربابی نرگس خاتون در آن باغ بزرگ می‌رفت. گه گاه او را هم که هفت و هشت سال بیشتر نداشت با خود می‌برد در یکی از همین روزها بود که یوسف با امیرخان آشنا و همبازی شد. بعد از گذشت چندی که انگار اواخر تابستان بود یک روز نرگس خاتون از مادر یوسف پرسید:

- سوره این پسر تو چند سالشه؟

- هشت سالشه خانوم

- دوست داری درس بخونه

- تا شما چه فرمائید

- اسمت چی پسر؟

- یوسف

مادرش بر شانه‌اش زد و با شرمندگی وپوزش حرفش را قطع کرد و گفت:

- نوکر شما یوسف، خانوم

- خوب یوسف از هفته آینده با امیرخان به مدرسه می‌روی

و در خدمت او خواهی بود.

چند روز بعد بنا به تصمیم نرگس خاتون او همراه امیرخان به مدرسه شبانه روزی مسیونرهای امریکایی که در شهر و درکوی یورد شاه قرار داشت رفتند. یوسف خوب بخاطر داشت که مدت شش سال همراه با امیرخان در مدرسه درکنار او بود. ظهر پنجشنبهٔ هر هفته حیدر مباشرجوان نرگس خاتون با درشکه تک اسبش می‌آمد و آن‌ها را با خود به ده می‌برد و در ده در عمارت اربابی بعد از گرفتن حمام و پوشیدن لباس‌های تمیز و اتو شده وگاه تازه، امیرخان می‌رفت مقابل اجاق دیواری می‌نشست و چشم برشعله‌های آتش می‌دوخت و در رویاهای خود غرق می‌شد. نرگس خاتون

که شیفتهٔ امیر خان بود و او را چون فرزندی دوست می‌داشت. لحظه‌ها نگران چشم بر چهرهٔ گرفته و متفکر او می‌دوخت و بعد بی آن که چیزی بگوید و یا بپرسد بلند می‌شد کنار پنجره مشرف بر ایوان می‌رفت و چشم به بیرون می‌نهاد و غم امیرخان را از بی‌مادری و تنهایی می‌دانست و برای همین مرتب به همه و به خصوص به او (یوسف) سفارش می‌کرد که امیرخان را تنها نگذارند. با پایان یافتن تعطیلات آخر هفته یعنی بعد از سه روز استراحت صبح روز دوشنبه حیدر می‌آمد و آن‌ها را با درشکه به مدرسه باز می‌گرداند. روزها و سال‌های دوران مدرسه پرشتاب گذشت و وقتی دورهٔ مدرسهٔ میسیون امریکایی را تمام کردند. به توصیه خانم میلر معلم مدرسه نرگس خاتون امیر خان را برای ادامه تحصیل به تفلیس گرجستان فرستاد.

یوسف نمی‌دانست که برای امیرخان در تفلیس چه گذشت. فقط شنیده و می‌دانست که او در تفلیس وارد دانشگاه شده و حقوق خوانده و در اثر آشنایی با فلسفه، فکر واندیشهٔ، فیلسوفان وآزدی‌خواهان اروپا، فکر و عقیده‌اش عوض شده و به جرگهٔ دانشجویان ترقی‌خواه پیوسته بوده و درسال آخر تحصیلش در دانشگاه بایک دختر زیبای گرجی به نام سارو آشنا و دوست و عاشق هم شده و پنهانی با هم ازدواج کرده‌اند. اما همین ازدواج باعث سرگردانی آن‌ها شده بود. سارو از یک خانواده بزرگ مسیحی ارتدوکس سنتی قدیمی و معروف تفلیس بود. نمی‌توانست و هرگز خانواده و قوم و طایفه او اجازه چنان کاری را نمی‌دادند. برای همین پدر و مادر سارو اجازه خواستگاری و ازدواج آن‌ها را نپذیرفته و امیرخان را مورد تهدید و آزار و اذیت قرار داده بودند. امیرخان برای یوسف تعریف کرده

بود که وقتی به تمام خواست‌های او پاسخ منفی دادند وتمام تلاش‌های او بی نتیجه ماند. سارو از او خواست که با هم بگریزند و پنهانی ازدواج کنند. پس ناگزیر با قرار قبلی از تفلیس به یک دهکده دور گریخته و در کلیسای کوچک آن جا ازدواج کردند و کلبه کوچکی را برای زندگی اجاره نمودند به این امید که بعد از چند ماه خانواده سارو موافقت کنند و آن‌ها را میان خودشان بپذیرند. اما چنان نشد. بعد از بیست روز فامیل و افراد خانوادهٔ سارو محل زندگی آن‌ها را یافتند. به آن دهکده آمده سارو را برگردانده و امیر خان را به ادعای خودشان تنبیه با تازیانه مجبورکرده بودند که تفلیس را ترک کند. یوسف خاطرش بود او و تلی تازه عروسی کرده بودند که امیر خان به اورمیه برگشت اما دیگر آن امیر خان گذشته نبود. عوض شده بود. هم قیافه‌اش هم رفتار و طرز لباس پوشیدنش و هم فکر واندیشه‌اش مردی شده بود بلند قد، خوش سیما با چشمانی نافذ و شخصیتی فروتن که همه را تحت تاثیرصحبت و رفتارش قرار می‌داد.

نرگس خاتون شاد و مغرور از بازگشت امیرخان هر چند شب در عمارت بزرگ خود در ده ساران جشن و ضیافتی به مناسبت بازگشت و فراغت از تحصیل او برگزار می‌کرد. بسیاری از ضیافت‌های شبانه با حضور بزرگان و اعیان و اشراف شهر برگزار می‌شد. نرگس خاتون دوست داشت امیرخان دختری را از میان دختران اعیان شهر انتخاب کند. اما امیرخان اعتنایی به آن‌ها نداشت. نه به آن‌ها و نه به مهمانان و بزرگان و اشراف شهرکه برای تبریک و آشنایی می‌آمدند. در برخوردی کوتاه بسیار رسمی با کلماتی سنجیده و مودبانه پاسخ تبریک و محبت آن‌ها را می‌داد و بعد کنار می‌ایستاد و ساکت می‌ماند. حتی با پدر خود نیز چندان نزدیک و صمیمی نبود،

صحبت نمی‌کرد.گویی تنها کسش نرگس خاتون بود وبس. بعد از گذشت دو ماه در یک شامگاه امیرخان مثل دوران کودکیش در ایوان کنار نرگس خاتون نشست و دردرد و دلش را برای اوگشود و با او از همه چیز گفت از دوران تحصیلش در دانشگاه، غم عشق و دلدادگیش با سارو دختر زیبای گرجی و از جریان ازدواجش با سارو و خیلی چیزهای دیگر. نرگس خاتون که شادمان از تحصیل و باز گشت امیر خان بود لحظه‌ها ساکت اما متفکر او را پائید و بعد پرسید:

- حالا چه تصمیمی داری، می‌خواهی چه کنی؟

امیر خان گفت:

- نمی‌دانم ولی باید به تفلیس برگردم. سارو منتظرمه

نرگس خاتون که غم واندوه او را درک می‌کرد. دستش را رو شانه امیرخان نهاد وآن را از سر محبت و حمایت و همدلی فشرد وگفت:

- باشد برگرد ، برگرد برو و سارو را بردار و بیار، اما حالا نه منتظر باش تا اوضاع کمی‌درست شود

امیرخان حدود سه ماه دیگر در انتظار بازگشت ماند تا تابستان بگذرد و اوضاع خوب شود. در طول این مدت اغلب اوقاتش را در عمارت اربابی ساران کنار نرگس خاتون به مطالعه می‌گذارند. کمتر به دیدار کسی و یا دوستی می‌رفت و یا برای خرید و گردش به شهر می‌آمد و یا در مهمانی و یا ضیافتی دیده می‌شد. بیشتر علاقه به دیدار با مردم عادی و به خصوص گفتگو با جوآن‌ها داشت. در اطاق یکی از خانه باغی‌های کوچک که در حاشیه یکی از باغ‌های نرگس خاتون قرار داشت برای کودکان و جو آن‌ها که بسیاری از آن‌ها از شهر و روستاهای اطراف می‌آمدند. کلاس درس

تشکیل داده بود. و زبان فارسی و فرانسه و ریاضی یاد می‌داد و هر چند وقت جلسه دیدار وگفتگو با مردان و زنان روستا را تشکیل می‌داد و گاه در شهر برحسب اتفاق در مجلسی و جلسه‌ای حضور می‌یافت و در دیدار و صحبت‌های خود با مردم از ترقی و پیشرفت کشورهای غربی می‌گفت و از تغییر فکر واندیشه در اثر تاثیر نوع مدارس و سازمان‌های اجتماعی در سایه علم واتحاد صحبت می‌کرد و مردم به خصوص جو آن‌ها را به یادگیری علوم و فنون و فکر واندیشه‌های تازه و دوستی وپیوستگی و ایجاد تشکیلاتی بمانند حزب دعوت می‌کرد و می‌گفت:

– بدانید هیچ کس به فکر شما نیست اگر اتفاقی بیفتد هیچ کس از شما دفاع نخواهد کرد. باید به فکر خودتان باشید. اگر با هم متحد شوید و تشکیلاتی درست کنید، علم وآگاهیتان را بالا ببرید با عقل و تدبیر و قدرت می‌توانید مملکت، شهر و خانه و مال و ناموستان را حفظ کنید وگرنه همیشه محتاج این و آن خواهید بود. دیگران بخصوص کشورهای بیگانه در امور شما دخالت خواهندکرد. بلوا و شورش خواهد بود. باید به مدرسه بروید. علم و دانش مدرن را یاد بگیرید وآگاه باشید و بدانید بشرآزاد خلق شده و حق آزادی و آگاهی از همه چیز را دارد.

همین حرف‌ها وکارها باعث شدند که دیگر نه حکومت و نه روس‌ها و نه گروه‌های مذهبی و قومی و سیاسی تحملش نکنند و روس‌ها درصدد دستگیریش برآیند و یمین الدوله حاکم شهر امنیه‌ها را مامور دستگیریش کرد. امیرخان دیگر مجبور به ترک اورمیه بود . البته خودش نیز به خاطر سارو قصد رفتن داشت.یوسف خوب به خاطر داشت که چند روز مانده به پائیز نزدیک شامگاه بود که امیرخان همراه نرگس خاتون و حیدر و

الیاس   محافظ و مباشر نرگس خاتون به کاروانسرا آمدند. کاروانسرا از املاک و مستغلات نرگس خاتون بود که اداره آن را با مهمان‌خانه ودکان‌های آهنگری و چوب و چرم و ذغال و ادویه و داروفروشی اطرافش به یوسف سپرده بود تا برگردش کار و درآمد آن‌ها نظارت داشته باشد. نرگس خاتون به یوسف اعتماد کامل داشت از روزی که یوسف همراه با امیرخان به مدرسه می‌رفت او را از معتمدین و مباشران خود می‌دانست و روزی که یوسف با تلی دختر حاج علی کداخدای ده ازدواج کرد. نرگس خاتون عمارت دو طبقه پیش درگاهی کاروانسرا را که پنجره‌های بالاخانه‌ی آن مشرف به در کاوانسرا و میدان مقابل آن بود در اختیار آن‌ها قرار داد وبه حقوق و در آمد یوسف افزود تا آن‌ها زندگی راحتی داشته باشند و یوسف مدیون از این همه محبت اودر انجام کارها دقت زیادی می‌کرد. به تمام امور کاروانسرا با دقت می‌رسید. در اثر تلاش یوسف کاروانسرا آبادتر و مشتری آن افزون‌تر و درآمدش بیشتر شده بود. وقتی شامگاه نرگس خاتون با امیرخان و دیگر همراهنش رسیدند. یوسف و تلی شادمان به استقبالشان رفتند در اطاق بزرگ بالاخانهٔ آسایش و استراحت آن‌ها را فراهم ساختند. همان شب بعد از صرف شام، نرگس خاتون از او و تلی خواست که به همراه امیرخان برای آوردن سارو به تفلیس بروند و گفت:

- حیدر تمام لوازم سفر از اسب و درشکه و تفنگ، پول و خوراک مورد احتیاج چند هفته سفر شما را فراهم کرده.

یوسف پرسید:

- مگر سارو کجاست!؟ که این همه تدارک واحتیاط لازم است

امیرخان گفت:

– درکلیساست یعنی در کلیسا نگه‌اش داشته‌اند. بارداره و ماه‌های آخرشه. خانواده‌اش خواسته‌اند که درکلیسا تحت نظر باشد. با این که او و زن من است اما من حق دیدن و صحبت با او را ندارم. خانواده و طایفه آن‌ها اعتقادات و سنت‌های عجیبی دارند. من خیلی نگرانشم. باید هر طور شده او را نجات بدهم و به ارومیه بیاورم. برای همین به تنهایی نمی‌توانم. به کمک تو و تلی احتیاج دارم.

بعد از گفتن این حرف‌ها به پشتی تکیه داد و رویش را به طرف پنجره برگرداند و نگاهش را از پنجره به بیرون دوخت. غم سیاه وکهنه و سنگینی در نگاهش موج می‌خورد و درونش را می‌کاوید. یوسف فهمید که گرفتاری او سخت وغم او دل‌گزاست.

همان شب وسایل سفرشان را آماده کردند و فردای آن روز صبح زود به همراه امیرخان به طرف جلفا حرکت کردند. نرگس خاتون تا دروازۀ شهر آن‌ها را بدرقه کرد و بعد برگشت و رفت. سفر به تفلیس هفده روز طول کشید. آن‌ها نخست به جلفا رفتند و بعد از گذشتن از مرز راهی ایروان شدند. در ایروان چند روزی میهمان پیادور ارمنی اهل ارومیه که امیرخان را می‌شناخت و به خانوادۀ امیرخان ارادت داشت، بودند و بعد راهی تفلیس شدند و در تفلیس به منزل هوهانس دوست صمیمی و هم‌کلاسی امیرخان رفتند. هوهانس وقتی آن‌ها را دید از بازگشت و تصمیم امیرخان بسیار خوشحال شد. چند روز که گذشت نامه امیرخان را در کلیسا به دست سارو رساند و با بردن امیرخان در لباس و قیافه مبدل به کلیسا ترتیب ملاقات مخفیانۀ آن‌ها را داد و بعد از آن دیدار و ملاقات بعدی بود که نقشه فرار سارو کشیده شد.

❋ ❋ ❋

سیلی از خاطرات گذشته به ذهن و خاطر یوسف هجوم آورده بودند و او کنار در انبار نشسته یک یک آن‌ها را مرور می‌کرد. نگاهش را به تلی دوخته بود که روبرویش کنار تخت‌خواب نه چندان مناسب سارا روی حصیر نشسته بود. تلی فقط زنش نبود، رفیق و همدم و همراه تمام لحظه‌های زندگیش بود. همانطورکه چشمش به تلی بود، سرش را به دیوار تکیه داد و در جهان مه آلود یادها و خاطره‌های گذشته غوطه ور شد.

۴

شامگاه هوا تازه رو به تاریکی گذاشته بود که هوهانس بر در کوبید. از صبح که سارو با قرار قبلی، مخفیانه از کلیسا خارج شده و با درشکه‌ای که او (یوسف) در خیابان خلوت و باریک جنوبی نزدیک دیر خواهران نگه داشته بود، همراه با امیرخان به خانهٔ هوهانس آمده بود. هوهانس ترسیده و نگران و مضطرب بود. او اهل تفلیس بود و مردم آنجا بخصوص خانوادهٔ سارو را خوب می‌شناخت و می‌دانست که از طایفه مذهبی قدیمی بسیار بزرگ و گسترده‌ای هستند وکمی و شاید بیش از نیمی از اهالی تفلیس از اعضای آن طایفه و قرابت نزدیک با آن‌ها دارند و کلیسای ارتدوکس شمالی تفلیس متعلق به آن‌ها ست. پس فرار و ازدواج دختری از این خانواده که نوعی تقدس وراثتی دارد با مردی غریب غیر گرجی از دین وآئین و

سرزمین دیگر، یک نوع توهین به حرمت و شرافت و تقدس ارثی خانواده و قوانین کلیسای آنهاست. برای همین بسیار نگران بود. نمی‌دانست که چه باید بکند. عشق و محبت بی حد و پاک امیرخان و سارو به یکدیگر چنان بود که ناخودآگاه مثل یک نیرو و حس ناشناخته‌ای همه را وادار به کمک و خدمت به آنها می‌کرد. اما باردار بودن سارو و نامشخص بودن زمان زایمان او که روزهای آخر بارداریش را می‌گذراند بر نگرانی امیرخان و همه افزوده بود. هوهانس بعد از آگاهی از باردار بودن سارو، بیرو رفت مدتی قدم زد و فکر کرد و بعد متفکر اما مصمم بی‌آن که چیزی بگوید کیف پولش را برداشت و رفت. ساعتی نگذشته بود که برگشت. شتاب‌زده و هراسان بود به امیرخان گفت تا کسی متوجه شما نشده. باید از این جا بروید

امیر خان پرسید: کجا؟

گفت:

- تا من وسائل سفر شما را فراهم کنم شما بهتره از این جا بروید واز شهر خارج شوید. ماندن شما در این جا خطرناکه، این جا برای شما امن نیست. امیرخان ناراحت و نگران گفت:

- ولی با وضعی که سارو دارد امکان رفتن و سفردراز و طولانی ممکن نیست. من خیلی نگرانم، او درد دارد. فکر می‌کنم بهتر است که برگردد. من با او خیلی صحبت کرده‌ام اما قبول نکرده. تو هم با او صحبت کن و بگو تا وقت هست و می‌تواند برگردد و اگر مسئله و مشکل و یا خطری هم هست من حاضرم همراه او بروم و حقیقت را به آنها بگویم و همه چیز را به عهده بگیرم.

هوهانس که چشم در چشم امیرخان دوخته بود. غم و نگرانی عمیقی را
که اورا بی‌طاقت کرده بود دریافت. آرام برای دلگرمی دست بر شانه او زد
و گفت:

- نگران نباش دوست من، سارو وضع حال و مسائلش را بهتر از من و تو
می‌داند. شاید او بیشتر از هر چیز نگران آینده فرزندش است و برای همین
می‌خواهد با تو بیاید و پیش تو بماند. حالا که او تصمیمش را گرفته چارهٔ
دیگری نیست. بایدکاری را که شروع کرده‌اید، تمام کنیم. اما باید هوشیار
باشید. چون هر جا بروید. آن‌ها دنبال شما خواهند آمد. مطمئنم همین حالا
هم دنبال شما می‌گردند. برای همین من از بودن شما در این جا نگرانم
چون آن‌ها می‌دانند که تو با من در دانشگاه دوست و هم‌کلاس بوده‌ای.
حتما سراغ من خواهند آمد. پس بهتر است هر چه زودتر از این جا بروید.
- کجا؟

- می‌روید به خانه عمهٔ من، نزدیک دروازهٔ شرقی در محلهٔ
لزگی‌هاست با پسرعمه‌ام صحبت کرده‌ام آن‌ها منتظر شما
هستند

و بعد در حالی که در را می‌گشود که از خانه خارج شودگفت:
- کمی عجله کنید

درشکه را دم در نگه داشته بود. تلی و سارو کنار هم نشستند و امیرخان
رو به روی آن‌ها و من (یوسف) که کلاه گبی هوهانس را گذاشته بودم.
کنار هوهانس نشستم. هوهانس درشکه را از میان کوچه‌های خلوت و
باریک به سمت دروازهٔ شرقی راند. کوچه‌های پوشیده از سنگ‌فرش بودند
با ساختم آن‌های سنگی و گاه آجری بلند که بهم پیوسته از هر طرف بر

عرصهٔ باریک کوچه سایه‌انداخته بودند. لباس‌های شسته و آویخته بر ریسمان کشیده شده میان پنجره و یا بالکن ساختم آنها در عرض کوچه‌ها با باد تاب می‌خوردند. درشکه از میان کوچه‌ها که می‌گذشت. صدای چرخ‌ها همراه با صدای نعل اسب‌ها بر سنگ‌فرش کوچه‌ها با صدای زنگ‌های آویخته برگردن اسب‌ها در سکوت وخاموشی کوچه‌ها می‌پیچید و انعکاس می‌یافت و میان دیوارها و پنجره‌ها و بالکن خانه‌ها پژواک می‌گرفت. می‌رفت و می‌آمد گویی همه را صدا می‌زد. به همه خبر می‌داد و می‌گفت:

– بیائید، بیائید ببینید. همه را خبر کنید. اینها دارند می‌روند، اینها دختر شما سارو را می‌برند.

بعد از گذشتن از چند کوچه به خیابان نسبتا وسیعی رسیدند و به سمت شرق تفلیس پیچیدند. نزدیک ظهر به محلهٔ لزگی‌ها نزدیک دروازهٔ شرقی رسیدند. خانهٔ عمهٔ هوهانس در انتهای کوچه بن بست کوتاهی قرار داشت ساختمان خانه از آجر بود با ایوان نسبتا بزرگ با دو ستون بلند و در چوبی سبز رنگ که به داخل ساختمان باز می‌شد.

هاسیک پسر عمهٔ هوهانس آنها را به داخل خانه راهنمایی کرد و در اطاقی گرم و از پیش آماده شده جا داد.کمی بعد عمهٔ هوهانس در ظرفی بزرگ سوپ آورد با نان جو و ظرفی مربای آلبالو. همه گرسنه بودند. بعد از خوردن کاسه‌ای سوپ با نان جو هوهانس فنجانی چای نوشید و رفت. تلی و سارو دراز کشیدند و خوابیدند. اما او و امیرخان نگران کنار هم نشستند و بی‌هیچ صحبتی نگاهشان را به تابلوی نقاشی روی دیوار مقابل دوختند. تابلویی از شکارگاه با تصویر گوزنی زخمی افتاده پائین صخره

سنگی در شیب ملایم منتهی به دره و دورتر قله‌های برفی بلند بود در سایه سار غروب. تابلو تفسیر دیگری از جریان زندگی واندوه هستی بود اما نگرانی آن‌ها از چیزی دیگربود. هیچ یک حوصله حرف زدن را نداشتند. می‌خواستند با خود تنها باشند و در تنهایی خود، خود را و مسائل خود را مرور کنند. لحظه‌ها همانطور به کندی می‌گذشت و هر چندگاه عمهٔ پیر هوهانس می‌آمد و حال سارو را می‌پرسید اما با امیرخان و تلی و او کاری نداشت. پیر زن حتی نیم نگاهی هم به آن‌ها نمی‌کرد. یک راست نزد سارو می‌رفت، دستی به موها و پیشانی او می‌کشید.چند کلمه به گرجی با او صحبت می‌کرد و بعد در حالی که با دستمال سفید گل‌دارش اشک‌هایش را پاک می‌کرد. بلند می‌شد و می‌رفت. بعد از رفتن او سارو می‌گفت که پیر زن نگران اوست. نگران او و بچه اش و دلش برای مادر او می‌سوزد که حالا چه می‌کند و او را نصیحت می‌کند که پیش خانواده‌اش برگردد. امیرخان که اضطراب و نگرانی در چهره و لحن صدا و صحبتش روشن و آشکار بود گفت:

– من هم فکر می‌کنم تا اتفاقی نیفتاده بهتره است برگردی من نگران سلامتی تو هستم.

سارو گفت:

– نه هر اتفاقی هم بیفتد من دیگر بر نمی‌گردم. اگر برگردم آن‌ها علاوه بر من تو را هم می‌کشند.

– ولی تو

سارو با تندی حرف امیرخان را قطع کرد وگفت:

– بس کن دیگر

امیرخان وقتی جواب تند سارو را شنید دیگر چیزی نگفت و سکوت کرد و در خود فرو رفت. آشکار بود که او نگران وضع سلامتی ساروست. شامگاه هوا تازه تاریک شده بود که هوهانس باهاسیک آمد. گفت:

- بلند شوید باید عجله کنید.

همه بلند شده و بیرون آمدند، هوهانس فانوس روشنی را بر دست گرفته بود و در حالی‌که جلوتر از همه راه می‌رفت گفت:

- متاسفم نتوانستم درشگه را داخل کوچه بیاورم. ترسیدم همه متوجه شوند.آن را نزدیک دروازه سرکوچه نگه داشته‌ایم ادوارد دوست هاسیک کنار آن مانده تا ما شما را به آن جا ببریم.

باران ریز می‌بارید و سنگ‌فرش کوچه را خیس و براق کرده بود. سر کوچه که رسیدند ادوارد دوست هاسیک کنار درشکه با اسب زین شده دیگری منتظر بود. هوهانس گفت:

- یوسف تو اسب را سوار شو

و بعد رو به امیرخان کرد و گفت:

- امیر تو هم درشکه را بران

و بعد فانوس را بالای درشکه نهاد و گفت:

- فانوس هم را همراه خود داشته باشید

اشکش گرفته بود. نمی‌دانست چه باید بگوید. امیرخان او را بغل کرد و شانه‌اش را بوسید وگفت:

- ای کاش بتوانم روزی جبران کنم

هوهانس گفت:

- نیاز به جبران نیست وظیفه‌ام بود و باید انجام می‌دادم

بعد همراه با هاسیک و ادوارد با همه خداحافظی کرد وگفت:

- سوار شوید و راه بیفتید. ماهم تا بیرون دروازه همراه شما می‌آییم. سعی کنید. تا ایروان نایستید اگر اسب‌ها خسته شدند جای آن‌ها را عوض کنید.

بعد رو کرد به امیرخان و گفت:

-این سکه اشرفی‌های طلا که داده بودی خرج نشدند پیش تو باشند بهتره، به کارت می‌آیند.

امیرخان یک آن گیج و مات مثل برق گرفته‌ها ایستاد. نمی‌دانست چه باید بکند. بغضش گرفته بود. لبش می‌جنبید اما صدایش بر نمی‌آمد. انگار نمی‌توانست حرف بزند به زحمت دستش را پیش آورد و اشرفی‌ها را گرفت و در جیبش گذاشت و چند لحظه‌ای سرش را با حال دگرگون به زیر افکند و بعد سرش را بلند کرد و نگاه شرمگین مملو از محبت و تشکر و ستایشش را در نگاه هوهانس دوخت و گفت:

- تو که روزی به اورمیه خواهی آمد؟

هوهانس گفت:

- بله وقتی آرامش شد، حتما خواهم آمد

امیر خان گفت:

- حتما خواهی آمد حتما. برای همه چیز متشکرم دوست من هوهانس که احساساتی شده و بغضش گرفته بود با دست بر شانه امیرخان زد و گفت:

- بهتره دیگر راه بیفتید.

تا بیرون دروازه شرقی هوهانس همراه هاسیک و ادوارد پیاده کنار درشکه آمدند و بعد دست تکان داده و خداحافظی کردند و رفتند. راه ایروان ناهمواره پر سنگ و لاخ بود و باران سرد شبانه بر گل ولای و ناهمواری و دشواری آن افزوده بود. شب تا سحر راه رفتند سحرگاه هنگام طلوع آفتاب کنار چشمه ساری که درختان سنجد و بید اطرافش را فرا گرفته بودند نزدیک آسیابی برای استراحت و صرف صبحانه توقف کردند. یوسف اسب‌ها را تیمار داد و در قسمت پائین چشمه که پوشیده از علف و یونجه بود و درخت‌ها مانع دید بودند به درختان بست. همه خسته بودند به خصوص سارو که درد داشت و ناهمواری راه به همراه نگرانی و ترس بر ناراحتیش افزوده بود و مرتب می‌گفت:

- ای کاش تعقیبمان نکنند.

انگار از این که آن‌ها را تعقیب کنند و او را برگردانند وحشت داشت برای صبحانه کمی چای با عسل نوشید و زیر درخت سنجد همان جایی که امیرخان با کمک تلی زیرانداز و پتویش را پهن کرده بودند دراز کشید و پتو را در خود پیچید و خوابش برد. امیرخان دراز نکشید همان جا نزدیک سارو پای درخت سنجد نشست و به تنهٔ درخت تکیه داد و چشمانش را بست. او هم نگران بود. نگرانی او بیشتر از وضع سارو و ناهمواری راه و مشکلات سفر بود. با وجود سرمای هوا، گرمای آفتاب تازه دمیدهٔ صبحگاهی لذت بخش بود. نفهمیدند کی خوابشان برد. ساعت کمی از ظهر گذشته بود که امیرخان همه را بیدار کرد وگفت:

- سارو خون ریزی دارد ودردش شدیدتر شده انگار وقت زایمانش است.

سارو رنگ پریده و نزار چشمان آبی زیبا اما کم فروغش را به چهرهٔ نگران امیرخان دوخته بود و حرف نمی‌زد. تلی بلند شد نزد او رفت. یوسف گفت:

- شاید بتوانیم از آسیابان و یا زنش کمک بگیریم

امیرخان رفت کمی بعد با زن آسیابان برگشت. زن آسیابان که پیرزن خوشرو و مهربان و بسیار دنیا دیده به نظر می‌رسید همراه خود شیشهٔ عرق گیاهی را که برای کم کردن درد زائو خوب بود آورده بود. پیرزن دستی به پیشانی سارو کشید و نگاهی دقیق به صلیب زمردین روی سینهٔ ساروانداخت و بعد در حالیکه از سارو می‌خواست کمی از عرق گیاه دارویی برای کم کردن درد و خون ریزی بنوشد از امیرخان پرسید:

- گفتید عازم ایروان هستید

- بله.

- این عروس زیبا باید از خانوادهٔ بسیاری مقدسی باشد. تعجب می‌کنم نباید با این وضع و حال همراه شما می‌آمد.

و بعد در حالیکه سرش را به طرف کوهستان برمی‌گرداند و با دست برج ناقوس کلیسایی را که در دور دست در دامنه کوهستان بسیار کوچک دیده می‌شد، نشان می‌داد گفت:

-   کمی پائین‌تر نزدیک آبادی پای کوه کلیسا و دیر است.

بعد نگاهش را در نگاه امیرخان با معنی خاصی دوخت وگفت:

-   به دیر بروید وکمک بخواهید وگرنه باید به تفلیس برگردید. اما من مطمئنم آن‌ها به این عروس محترم کمک خواهند کرد.

امکان برگشتن به تفلیس نبود. سارو گفت:

- بهتر است که به دیر برویم

با احتیاط سارو را سوار درشکه کرده و راه افتادند. ولی دیر وآبادی کنار آن چندان نزدیک نبود. راهش دراز، ناهموار و پر پیچ و خم بود. ساعتی به غروب مانده بود که به دیر رسیدند. از چند روستایی که از وضع آبادی و دیر پرسیدند فهمیدند که آبادی همان چند خانه و مزرعه کوچک اطراف کلیسا و دیر است و تمام مردم آبادی برای دیر کار می‌کنند.

باد شروع به وزیدن کرده بود و ابرهای سیاه از دور پیدا می‌شدند. می‌شد حدس زد که شب سرد و بارانی در پیش است. امیرخان گفت:

- یوسف در دیر را بزن اگر راهمان دهند وکمکمان کنند شانس

آورده ایم وگرنه باید به تفلیس برگردیم.

یوسف چند بار بر در دیر کوفت. منتظر شدند کمی با تاخیر خدمتکار پیری که یک پایش می‌لنگید. در چوبی دیر را گشود وقتی آن‌ها را دید و از وضع و حالشان با خبر شد رفت کشیش لاغر و نحیف و میانسالی را که می‌شد حدس زد سرپرست و مسئول دیر است خبر کرد. کشیش آمد بعد از پرس و جو و گفتگوی کوتاهی با امیرخان نگاهی به اطراف و چهرهٔ تک تک آن‌هاانداخت و وقتی به کنارسارو که درون درشکه خوابیده بود رفت و چشمش به صلیب زمردین او افتاد، قامت راست کرد و ایستاد و در حالی که زیر لب دعا می‌خواند با دست بر سینه صلیب کشید و بعد برگشت و به مستخدم پیری که در را گشوده بود گفت:

- زود برو خواهران روحانی را خبر کن.

و بعد رو به امیرخان کرد وگفت:

- خداوند خواسته که این بانوی محترم در دیر فارغ شوند. ما از

این لطف خدا و مسیح شکرگذاریم. لطفا ایشان را از درشکه پایین بیاورید.

کمی بعد خواهران روحانی آمدند و سارو را که درد و خونریزیش شدید شده بود به درون دیر بردند. کشیش هم به امیرخان گفت که تا زایمان و بهبود حال سارو می‌توانید در دیر بمانید.

و آن‌ها خوشحال از این همه کمک کشیش و این که می‌توانستند در دیر بمانند با کمک و راهنمایی مستخدم پیر به درون دیر رفتند و در راهرو عریض و طویلی که طاق بلند و پر از نقش و نگار داشت و به دیر خواهران منتهی می‌شد منتظر شدند. هوای راهرو تاریک و نمور بود و در هر دو طرف بر دیوارهای آن میان پنجره‌های باریک و بلندش شمعدان‌هایی باشمع‌های روشن نصب شده بود.کف راهرو ازسنگ‌های ناهمگون اما مربع و مستطیل شکل بود که در طول زمان صیقل یافته و براق شده بودند. نزدیک یکی از پنجره زیر روشنایی شمعدان به اشاره امیرخان روی نیمکت دراز چوبی نشستند. امیرخان بی قرار بود. بعد از کمی بلند شد و ایستاد و بعد بی‌قرار در طول راهرو شروع به قدم زدن کرد. صدای ناله‌های سارو از درد در راهرو می‌پیچید و قلب و روح او را زخم می‌زد و هر لحظه که ناله‌های سارو اوج می‌گرفتند. امیر خان می‌ایستاد به دیوار تکیه می‌داد. چشمانش را می‌بست و در خود فرو می‌رفت.

هنوز ساعتی از ورود آن‌ها به دیر نگذشته بود که صدای کوبیده شدن در دیر به طور ممتد و با ضرب آهنگ محکم به گوش رسید. انگار کسانی بخاطر انجام کاری مهم شتاب داشتند و یا حامل پیام بسیار مهمی بودند. در را که گشودند صدای بلند و محکم چند مرد به گوش رسید و بعد

صدای محکم قدم‌ها بود که نزدیک می‌شدند. یوسف که نگاه کرد دید دو خواهر روحانی با یک کشیش و سه نظامی‌تنومند درحالی‌که هوهانس و زن آسیابان را به همراه خود دارند از پیش درگاهی گذشتند و وارد راهرو شدند. هوهانس نمی‌توانست خوب راه برود سرو صورتش زخمی و پیراهنش پاره وخونین بود. تعادل نداشت و معلوم بود که به زحمت خودش را روی پا نگه داشته است. دست‌هایش را از پشت بسته بودند و ماموری بازویش را گرفته بود و به زور او را پیش می‌راند.کشیش دیر هراسان از وضع به وجود آمده به ورود ناگهانی و خصمانه آن‌ها مرتب اعتراض می‌کرد. اما آن‌ها توجهی به اعتراض‌های او نداشتند. یوسف برگشت تا امیرخان را خبر کند. دید امیرخان نگران اما با قامتی استوار وسط راهرو ایستاده با خشم نزدیک شدن آن‌ها را می‌پاید. وارد راهرو که شدند. کشیشی که از تفلیس همراه با مردان مسلح نظامی و دو خواهر روحانی آمده بود. خشمگین با دست امیر خان را نشان داد و به صدای بلند گفت:

– این همان دزد است

و بعد درحالی‌که چند قدم به طرف امیرخان برمی‌داشت و با اشاره دست مردان مسلح را برای دست‌گیری امیرخان فرا می‌خواند ادامه داد:

– من حکم دست‌گیری این مرد را دارم. او اغوا گرست او دختر خانواده مقدس بنی کریستوا و کلیسای تفلیس را اغوا کرده و ربوده است. شما آقا باید مجازات شوید.

امیرخان که معلوم بود. انتظار چنین اتفاق و برخوردی را داشت نگاهی به صورت همه آن‌ها انداخت. زن آسیابان ترسیده مرتب می‌گفت:
– بله خودشانند. این‌ها هستند.

هوهانس اما با نگاه حاکی از تاسف به امیرخان می‌فهماند که او چیزی نگفته است و خواست که حرف بزند ماموری که بازویش را گرفته بود با مشت محکم بر دهانش کوبید. امیرخان خشمگین و معترض خواست که مانع شود. ماموران مسلح بر سرش ریختند. دو نفر از آن‌ها دستانش را گرفته و سومی با قنداق تفنگ بر سر و صورتش کوبید. خون از پیشانی امیرخان جاری و قسمتی ازصورتش را پوشاند. بی اعتنا به اعتراض‌های کشیش دیر که مرتب پشت سرهم می‌گفت:

– این درست نیست، این جا کلیساست او و دیگران به این جا پناه آورده‌اند. شما حق ندارید او را دستگیر کنید.

دستان امیرخان را از پشت بستند و کشان کشان بطرف در بردند. یوسف دندان‌هایش را در هم فشرده و از ناتوانیش در کمک به امیرخان در خود می‌شکست و مات و متحیر کنار تلی ایستاده و تماشا می‌کرد. یک لحظه که نگاهش به نگاه امیرخان خورد. امیرخان گفت:

– این جا نمانید برگردید به اورمیه.

دیگر نتوانست چیز دیگری بگوید. مردان مسلح کشان کشان بردنش و بعد دو خواهر روحانی که از تفلیس آمده بودند برای اطلاع از وضع سارو به قسمت دیر خواهران رفتند.کشیش دیر که از وضع پیش آمده بسیار ناراحت بود. نزد یوسف و تلی آمد وآرام گفت:

– تا فرصت است و آن‌ها متوجه شما نشده‌اند. از اینجا بروید. (با اشاره به مستخدم پیر دیر ادامه داد) این مرد خوب خدا شما را کمک می‌کند.

یوسف درمانده و پریشان دست تلی را گرفت و با کمک نگهبان پیر از در دیر بیرون آمدند. نمی‌دانستند چه باید بکنند. آیا بمانند و یا برگردند به

اورمیه. سوار درشکه شدند و راه افتادند و در حالیکه می‌دانستند امیرخان تنها و اسیر است. اما آن‌ها چه می‌توانستند بکنند از تلی پرسید:

- حالا چه باید بکنیم؟

تلی گفت:

- بهتراست همان کاری را بکنیم که امیر خان خواست

- برگردیم؟

- بله

کشتار در باغ ساران

۱

آفتاب تازه دمیده بود، که نرگس خاتون آمد. حیدر کالسکه رانش همراه با
یک تفنگچی بنام الیاس که در پشت کالسکه نشسته بود. کالسکه را وارد
کاروانسرا کردند و در مقابل پله‌های ساختمان خانهٔ یوسف نگه داشتند.
بسیار با احتیاط عمل می‌کردند و سعی داشتند زیاد سروصدا نکنند و حضور
آن‌ها در کاروانسرا زیاد به چشم نیاید. بعد از ورود و بستن در کاروانسرا،
نرگس خاتون از کالسکه پیاده شد. روسری بلند و سیاهی به سر داشت و
پیراهنی خاکستری تیره با گل‌های ریز سرخ و جلیقه وکت مشکی با حاشیهٔ
ملیله دوزی شده به تن، ده تیرکوچکی که به کمر بسته بود از زیر جلیقه‌اش
پیدا بود. بعد از پیاده شدن تور سیاه مقابل صورتش را کنار زد و به یوسف

که تا کنار در کالسکه به استقبال آمده و دست بر سینه به احترام ایستاده بود. آمرانه و با تاکید گفت:

- فرستاده‌ات خبر را آورد. بهتر بود که خودت می‌آمدی کجا هستند؟ اول می‌خواهم دختر بچه را ببینم.

یوسف در حالی‌که با دست در و پله‌های طبقه بالای منزلش را نشان می‌داد گفت:

- بفرمایید، بفرمایید بالا هستند، خوابیده‌اند خانم. بنده نوازی فرموده‌اید. دست بوس و غلام شما هستم. باید ببخشید. شرمنده‌ام که نتوانستم خدمت برسم. دیشب دیروقت بود که آمدند هردو زخمی بودند. تمام شب مشغول پرستاری بودیم. در حال حاضر خوابیده‌اند.

تلی بالای پله‌ها به پیشوازش آمد. نرگس خاتون که علاوه بر اشتیاق دیدار نوعی ترس و نگرانی در حرکات وگفتارش دیده می‌شد پرسید:

- کجاست دختر بچه؟ تلی تو دیده‌ای بگو چگونه است، چطوره؟ چه شکلیه؟

یوسف از پشت سر گفت:

- خانم امیر خان در همین اطاق هستند. خوابیده‌اند.

نرگس خاتون باز با تاکید و آمرانه گفت:

- نه، گفتم که اول دختره. اول می‌خواهم دختر بچه را ببینم. تلی او کجاست؟

تلی در اطاقی را باز کرد که پنجره کوچکش به میدان مقابل کاروانسرا باز می‌شد. دختر بچه را در تخت‌خوابی بزرگ خوابانده بودند. تلی زخم بازوی راستش را که در اثر برخورد گلوله خراشی سطحی برداشته بود تمیزکرده

و با پارچه‌ای سفیدی بسته بود. دخترک که خواب بود از سرو صدای آن‌ها چشم گشود و بیدار شد و نگاه ترس گرفته و غریب و نگرانش را در نگاه و صورت آن‌ها دوخت از جایش نیمه خیز شد و در رخت‌خوابش نشست. گنگ و ترسیده، غریبانه آن‌ها را نگاه می‌کرد. نرگس خاتون آغوشش را گشود و به طرفش رفت و خم شد وگفت:

ـ اوه عزیزم من عمه نرگس هستم، عمه نرگس، عمهٔ بابات کوچولویم، چقدر خوشحالم که تو را می‌بینم.

بعد کنارش در تخت‌خواب نشست و او را در آغوش کشید و در حالی‌که موهای قهوه‌ای روشن مایل به طلایی او را نوازش می‌کرد و می‌بوسید زیر لب نزدیک گوش دخترک زمزمه می‌کرد:

ـ عزیزم، دلبندم تو همان‌طور هستی که فکر می‌کردم، دیگر نمی‌گذارم تنها بمانی دیگر نمی‌گذارم.

بعد از لحظه‌ها نوازش، دختر بچه را که همان‌طور ساکت و گنگ و مات آن‌ها را نگاه می‌کرد و حرف نمی‌زد در رخت‌خواب نشاند و رو به تلی کرد و گفت:

ـ صبحانه این بچه را آماده کن. اگر امیرخان بیدار شده می‌خواهم ببینمش.

بعد رو به یوسف کرد و پرسید:

ـ حکیم پیره را خبر کرده‌اید که بیاید امیر خان را ببیند؟ گفتی زخم‌هایش خیلی عمیقند؟

یوسف گفت:

- زخم شانه و بازویشان چندان مهم نیستند. خراشی سطحی هستند. اما زخم گلوله‌ای که به پهلویشان خورده عمیق است. خوشبختانه خونریزیش قطع شده اما فکر می‌کنم گلوله هنوز در پهلویشان مانده باشد.

نرگس خاتون با چهره‌ای نگران و در هم گفت:

- پس چرا این جا هستی؟ معطل نکن مرد. حیدر با کالسکه‌اش آن پائین منتظره، با او برو حکیم پیره و اسراییل را بیاور، زودباش مرد، به حیدر بگو خانم می‌گوید شتاب کند. این‌جا برای امیرخان چندان امن نیست. باید هر چه زودتر از این‌جا ببریمش، الیاس و یک نفر دیگر را بگمار که مراقب اطراف باشند. مبادا گرجی‌ها و روس‌ها آمده و متوجه شوند. مبادا به وجود امیرخان در این جا پی ببرند. شتاب کن مرد.

امیرخان همچنان بی حال ، ضعیف با رخساری پریده رنگ در رختخواب خوابیده بود. نرگس خاتون وقتی بالای سرش آمد پلکهای سیاه بر جسته اش روی هم افتاده ونفسش آرام اما دردناک برمی‌آمد.دهانش نسبتا باز بود و رجی از دندآن‌ها ی سفیدش از زیر سبیلش دیده می‌شد.نرگس خاتون وقتی دستش رادرمیان دستانش گرفت و صدایش کرد. پلک‌هایش را گشود، زغال مردمک‌هایش را بر دیدگان نرگس خاتون دوخت و لبخندی کم رنگ از رضایت بر لبانش نقش بست و بعد پلک‌ها را بر هم نهاد. نرگس خاتون از تلی پرسید:

- چیزی بهش داده‌اید، چیزی خورده؟

تلی گفت: نه خانم

نرگس خاتون با نگرانی گفت:

- اما باید یه چیزی بخورد که نیرو بگیرد

تلی شیر گرم آماده کرد وآورد و نرگس خاتون با عسل قاطی و چند قاشق در گلوی خشکیدهٔ امیر خان ریخت تا کمی توان از دست رفته‌اش را بیابد. ساعتی بعد حکیم پیره به همراه حکیم اسراییل آمد. بعد از معاینه مشخص شدکه گلوله در پهلوی امیرخان گیرکرده و مانده و امکان عفونت و بخصوص خونریزی مجدد هست. طبیبان ناگزیر جای زخم را بایدکمی می‌شکافتند وگلوله را در می‌آوردند. کار جراحی کمی طول کشید. ساعتی از ظهر گذشته بود که تمام شد. نرگس خاتون خوشحال و امیدوار به دلیل نبود پول رایج با سکه‌ای طلا از هریک از آن‌ها قدردانی کرد. بعد از رفتن طبیبان، امیرخان را که به هوش آمده بود همراه با دخترش سارا با احتیاط در کالسکه نشاندند و در حالیکه مراقب بودند کسی متوجه آن‌ها نشود و زیاد جلب نظر و توجه دیگران را نکنند بطرف کوشک و املاک شخصی نرگس خاتون در دهکده ساران راه افتادند.

امیرخان مدت یک ماه در ساران در کوشک با شکوه عمه نرگس بستری بود. بعد از یک ماه کم کم زخم‌هایش بهبود یافت و حالش بهتر شد و از بستر برخاست اما یاد و خاطره سارو و غم مرگ و از دست دادن او و دردی ناگفته بود که همیشه بر هستی امیرخان سایه‌انداخته و جان و دلش را در هم می‌فشرد و او همیشه ساکت و خاموش در خود فرو می‌رفت و از درون فرو می‌ریخت. تنها امید و شادی دلش دخترش سارا بود. کمتر از خانه و باغ بیرون می‌آمد و کمتر در میان جمع دیده می‌شد و بیشترین وقت روزش را با دخترش می‌گذراند. تمام دانسته‌هایش را به او یاد می‌داد. برای او علاوه بر پدر معلم هم بود و با کمک عمه‌اش نسترن خاتون که زنی درس خوانده و اهل کتاب بود برای سارا کلاس درس گذاشته بود. در دو روز

هفته ساعتی ادبیات فارسی و در جوار آن ساعاتی زبان‌های ترکی، روسی، فرانسه و انگلیسی به او یاد می‌دادند. عمه‌اش نسترن خاتون بیشتر از او به زبان فارسی و فرانسه مسلط بود و آن زبان‌ها را او درس می‌داد و در سه روز آخر هفته ساعاتی به درس‌های ریاضی، جغرافیا و علم زیست شناسی و فلسفه اختصاص داشت. امیرخان به سارا درس می‌داد با او تمرین می‌کرد و خود نیز با او می‌آموخت. نرگس خاتون هم که شاهد غم وعشق و علاقه و انزوای امیرخان بود. چیزی نمی‌گفت و همه چیز را موکول به گذشت زمان کرده بود و با توجه به اوضاع نه چندان امن و بد شهر. بسیار خوشحال و راضی بود که امیر خان هم چنان در ساران در کنار او بماند و از آسیب دور باشد و هر چندگاه سارا را سوار بر اسب می‌کرد و همراه خود به گردش در ده و میان باغ‌ها و مزارع می‌برد و به گونه‌ای کار سرکشی به روستا و املاک و باغ وکشت و برخورد با روستائیان وکارگران را به او یاد می‌داد. با گذشت ماه‌ها سارا قد کشیده، بزرگتر و زیباتر و عزیز و محبوب همه، تمام اهل خانواده و روستا شده بود. اما با بدتر شدن اوضاع شهر و منطقه بسیاری از مردم در فکرکوچ و مهاجرت و ترک اورمیه و دیگر شهرهای منطقه بودند. نرگس خاتون هم که شاهد و ناظر وقایع و اتفافات بود از حضور و آینده سارا و امیرخان نگران بود و در فکر این بود که برای حفظ جان و سلامتی و امنیت امیرخان و سارا آن‌ها را روانه استانبول ترکیه کند. اما امیرخان راضی نبود. می‌گفت امنیت او در آن جا در کنار نرگس خاتون و دیگران بیشتر از هر جای دیگر است و حاضر نبود جای دیگری برود.

۲

دم دمه‌های صبح روز شنبه هفته آخر شهریور ماه بود که کدخدا همراه با حیدر و الیاس نرگس خاتون را از خواب بیدار کردند و خبر آمدن جیلوها و محاصره ساران را دادند. نرگس خاتون وقتی خبر را شنید، دانست که روز سخت و دشوار و خونینی را در پیش دارند و شاید هم جنگی طولانی در پیش داشته باشند. نشست کمی فکر کرد و بعد پرسید:

ـ کی و از کدام طرف آمده‌اند و اکنون کجا هستند؟

کدخدا گفت:

ـ نمی‌دانیم، نورس عروس میرزا محمد که خانه‌شان در انتهای ده نزدیک کوه است. نیمه شب که برای آوردن کوزه آب به ایوان می‌رود. صداهایی می‌شنود. نگاه که می‌کند می‌بیند عده زیادی از جیلوها در دامنه کوه و پائین

کنار نهر کمین کرده‌اند. برمی‌گردد و میرزا محمد را خبر می‌کند و میرزا محمد هم آمد به من گفت، من هم چند نفری را به اطراف فرستادم. رفتند و پنهانی به هرسو سرک کشیدند و آمدند و گفتند که جیلوها با تعدادی ارمنی و گرجی هستند. تمام ده را به غیر از طرف رودخانه محاصره کرده‌اند. فکر می‌کنم منتظر طلوع آفتاب هستند.

نرگس خاتون نگران پرسید:

ـ همه را آگاه و آماده کرده‌اید.

ـ بله هر چه تفنگ و فشنگ داشتیم بین مردان تقسیم کردیم و همه را پای دیوارها و پشت بام‌ها و کنار دروازه روستا گذاشته‌ایم. گفته‌ایم آماده و بسیار مراقب باشند.

باغ و عمارت اربابی نرگس خاتون در میان دیگر باغ‌ها در ضلع شرقی روستا نزدیک رودخانه و دور از دسترس مهاجمان   قرار داشت و می‌شد گفت امن‌ترین مکان دهکده ساران بود و برای همین نرگس خاتون از کداخدا خواست که نخست تمام زنان وکودکان روستا را به باغ منتقل و در چادرها و آلاچیق‌هایی که میان درختان با شاخه و برگ می‌شد ساخت جای دهند و پل روی نهر نزدیک باغ را که تنها راه ارتباطی باغ بود خراب کنند و تعدادی از مردان روستا را برای نگهبانی و مراقبت از باغ بگذارد و به فکر نان و غذای اهالی هم باشد و تا می‌توانند از انبار آسیاب روستا مراقبت کنند و اگر هم میسر شد کسی را به شهر بفرستد و به یوسف اوضاع پیش آمده را خبر دهند و بگویند که با حکومت و بزرگان شهر و سران جیلوها تماس بگیرد و برای نجات اهالی ساران بکوشد که همه در خطر هستند و از حیدر و الیاس خواست که به زیرزمین عمارت بروند و هر چه

تفنگ و فشنگ و باروت است از صندوق‌ها در بیاورند و آماده سازند و راه‌های مخفی روستا و عمارت را باز کنند و در جاهای حساس بمب و تله انفجاری بگذارند بعد از رهسپار کردن آن‌ها متفکر نشست و منتظر ماند.

خواهرش نسترن خاتون که سحرخیز بود و زودتر از او از موضوع مطلع شده بود کنارش آمد و پرسید:

– می‌خواهی چه کنی، نمی‌خواهی امیرخان را بیدار و خبر کنی؟

نرگس خاتون گفت:

– منتظرم تا بیدار شود

– من فکر می‌کنم بیدارش کنید بهتر است.

– خوب شما بیدارش کنید.

نسترن خاتون رفت و امیرخان را بیدار و او را از اوضاع پیش آمده باخبر کرد. امیرخان با همان سکون و آرامش همیشگیش آمد و نشست پرسید:

– کی آمده‌اند؟

نرگس خاتون گفت:

– نیمه شب نورس عروس میرزا محمد دیده و کدخدا و دیگران را خبر کرده‌اند. کدخدا هم آمد به ما خبر داد.

– چه کار کرده‌اید؟

– مردان ده را آماده و مسلح کرده‌ایم. در و دروازه‌ها را بسته‌ایم گفته‌ام زن و بچه‌ها را بیاورند توی باغ بعد ببینیم که چه می‌شود؟

– ای کاش یکی را می‌فرستادید تا ببینیم برای چه آمده‌اند و چه می‌خواهند؟ شاید این جا موقتا اطراق کرده‌اند، قصد جای دیگری را دارند؟

– کجا را؟

- چه می‌دانم من فکر می‌کنم باید با آن‌ها صحبت کنیم اگر قصدشان این جا بود شاید بتوانیم با صحبت و پرداخت غرامت. چه می‌دانم پیشکش و یا هر چه که اسمش است راضیشان کنیم. من تعدادی از سران آن‌ها را از گذشته از دوره مدرسه شبانه روزی مسیونرها می‌شناسم. شاید بتوانیم با آن‌ها صحبت بکنیم و اگر خواستند هر چه پول داشته باشیم می‌دهیم.

نرگس خاتون گفت:

- من هم به این عقیده‌ام اما نمی‌توانم بگذارم که تو خطر کنی و برای صحبت نزد آن‌ها بروی. میان آن‌ها حتما چند گرجی هم هست. سلامتی تو و سارا برایم از همه مهم‌تر است. سعی می‌کنم کدخدا را با یکی نزد آن‌ها بفرستم. اگر راضی شدند که غرامت می‌دهیم و اگر نشدند دیگر چاره نداریم با آن‌ها می‌جنگیم. راه مخفی که به پشت آسیاب می‌رسد را می‌شناسی. صبح که خبر آمدن جیلوها را شنیدم. نخست به حیدر گفتم با چند نفر دیگر درش را که به پائین سرداب زیرزمین بود گشودند و تا انتهای آن رفتند. اگر درگیری شد می‌توانیم از پشت به آن‌ها حمله کنیم.

- با کدام نیرو عمه. این روستاییان که نظامی نیستند.

- آن‌ها هم نیستند. من همه آن‌ها را می‌شناسم چه جیلوهایی که از چند سال پیش ازآن ور مرز به این جا پناه آوردند و ما مردم احساساتی بدبخت قبولشان کردیم و جا و مکان و کار دادیم و نگذاشتیم درکوچه‌ها بگردند وگدایی بکنند و از گرسنگی بمیرند و چه فدائیان آشوری این جا، آن‌هایی که از قدیم این جا بوده‌اند و اهل این شهر و روستاها هستند و تا دیروز به آشنایی و احوال پرسی با ما افتخار می‌کردند. نه هیچ یک از آن‌ها نه نظامی هستند و نه نظامی‌گری بلدند. نه عزیزم اینها فقط تحریک شده و

شورشی‌اند همین. زمانش برسد همه شان فرار می‌کنند. من می‌دانم آدم‌های روستا من از آن‌ها دلیرترند.

– ولی تعداد تفنگچیان روستای شما خیلی کمند.

– برای همین دنبال راه حل و باج و خراج هستم.

– باج وخراج بله، باج و خراج منظور من هم همین بود. فکر می‌کنم برای نجات همه و جلوگیری از جنگ و خونریزی تنها راه حل مناسب باشد . پس اگر اجازه بفرمایید من می‌روم شاید توانستم با آن‌ها تماس بگیرم و صحبت کنم.

– نه تو نه، اول بگذار. کداخدا با چند نفر دیگر با پرچم سفید برود با آن‌ها صحبت کند اگر راضی شدند آن وقت تو و من و حیدر با هم می‌رویم. البته اگر مطمئن شدیم.

– ولی

– ولی بی ولی. تو اگر می‌خواهی کمک کنی به وضع مردمی که به باغ پناه آورده‌اند برس. ضمنا بگو در غربی باغ را کلا ببندند و گل بگیرند. اگر چه آن جا امن است گوشه دور باغ است و فکر نمی‌کنم از آن طرف بیایند. با این همه باید احتیاط کرد.

– بله باید احتیاط کرد.

– حالا تو بهتره به آن جا برسی. پاشو عزیزم پاشو چند نفر را بردار، هم به وضع مردم برس هم آن در را ببند.

امیرخان بلند شد و در حالی‌که کتش را می‌پوشید پرسید:

– سارا بیدارشده؟

– نه هنوز!

راه افتاد و هنگام خروج از در برگشت وگفت:

- بیدار که شده نگذارید بیاید بیرون. مراقبش باشید.

نرگس خاتون گفت:

- تو هم مراقب خود باش

و با نگاهش تا میان درختان خیابان غربی تعقیبش کرد. بعد برگشت رو به نسترن خاتون کرد و پرسید:

- چرا سارا هنوز بیدار نشده؟

نسترن خاتون گفت: نمی‌دانم

- سری به او بزن اگر بیدار شده بود. کنارش باش.

خواستید بیارید پائین و صبحانه‌اش را بدهید و مراقبش باشید.گمان می‌کنم ما روز سختی در پیش داریم. خیلی نگرانم خواهر. خیلی

بعد رو کرد به یکی از خدمتکارانش و پرسید:

- کدخدا هنوز نیامده

- نه خانم هنوز نیامده‌اند.

نشست و آرنج دستانش را بر روی میز نهاد و صورتش را میان دستانش گرفت و نگاه متفکر و نگرانش را از پشت پنجره ایوان به باغ دوخت. ساعتی به ظهر مانده بود که صدای شلیک چند گلوله از انتهای سمت در غربی باغ برخاست. نرگس خاتون هراسان به ایوان دوید و نگاهش را به سمت خیابان غربی باغ و صدای شلیک گلوله‌ها دوخت. در پی شلیک چند گلوله از سمت ضلع غربی باغ، شلیک و انفجار گلوله‌های توپ و ناله و فریاد و فغان مردم ده از سطح روستا برخاست. نرگس خاتون همانطور که

نگران چشم بر ضلع غربی باغ و گوش به صدای گلوله و ناله و فغان مردم سپرده بود. از پله‌های ایوان شروع به پائین رفتن کرد حیدر مباشرش که در کنارش بود. نگران گفت:

ـ برگردید. نروید خانم.

که ناگهان صدای سه گلوله‌ی پی درپی که در نزدیکی و از ناحیه درون باغ شلیک شدند برخاست و در پی آن‌ها شلیک گلوله‌های دیگر. با انفجار گلوله‌ها از ضلع غربی باغ تعداد زیادی از کبوترها وکلاغ‌هایی که بر درختان بلند باغ لانه داشتند هراسیده برخاستند. نرگس خاتون دید که امیرخان در حالی که دست بر سینهٔ زخمی و خونینش نهاده افتان و خیزان از انتهای خیابان غربی باغ به طرف آن‌ها می‌آید. جیغ درد آلودی کشید و به طرف امیرخان دوید. امیر خان که توان و تعادلش را از دست داد بود و به زحمت راه می‌رفت کمی مانده به عمارت وسط راه افتاد. نرگس خاتون تا رسید زار وگریان سرش را بلند کرد و در سینه فشرد و بعد بر زانو نهاد نگاه کرد. سه گلوله‌ای که از پشت شلیک شده بودند از کتف چپ امیرخان گذشته و سینه‌اش را شکافته بودند و خون از میان انگشتان دست امیرخان که بر روی زخم سینه‌اش نهاده بود بیرون می‌زد. نرگس خاتون نمی‌دانست که چه باید بکند فقط فریاد می‌زد وکمک می‌خواست. خواهرانش نسترن خاتون و گلاب خاتون همراه حیدر دوان خود را به آن‌ها رساندند. اما کار از کار گذشته بود. امیرخان با رخساری زرد که خون از کنار لبش جاری بود. چشمان خیس و نگران و مملو از غمش را توی صورت نرگس خاتون دوخته بود و در حالی‌که به زحمت حرف می زد گفت:

- آن‌ها گرجی بودند. همراه جیلوها آمده‌اند. نگذار سارا را ببرند. نگذار سارا را ببرند، آ، آخ نگذار.

دیگر نتوانست چیزی بگوید نگاهش مات و دهانش باز ماند. نرگس خاتون سرش را در آغوش فشرد و ناله‌های بلند از دل کشید و زار زار گریست. در این هنگام حیدر که به ته باغ رفته و برگشته بود و بسیار هراسان بود. گفت:

- باید بروید، توی عمارت خانم. جیلوها حمله‌شان را شروع کرده‌اند. تعدادشان خیلی زیاده، می‌گویند سردسته‌شان ظریفه خانم زن آقا پطرسه. اهالی ده دارند دفاع می‌کنند. شما باید بروید تو.

نرگس خاتون سرش را بلند کرد خواهرانش را گریان با حیدر بالای سرش دید. چشمش که به خواهرش نسترن خاتون افتاد یاد سارا افتاد. سر امیرخان را آرام زمین گذاشت و بلند شد و به خواهرش نسترن خاتون گفت:

- با من بیا

تمام وجودش مملو از خشم بود. با پشت دست اشک گونه‌هایش را پاک کرد. کسی دیگر شده بود. وجودی سرشار از انتقام. نگاهش را به حیدر و چند نفر دیگر دوخت و در حالی که با دست اشاره به تن بی جان امیرخان می‌کرد گفت:

- اول این را بیارید به ایوان و بعد برگردید و به آن‌هایی که در باغ پناه گرفته‌اند به خصوص به زن‌ها و بچه‌ها و پیرها بگویید هر چه شاخه و برگ تر است پای سرتاسر دیوارهای باغ جمع کنند و آتش بزنند آتش اگر دود بکند چه بهتر، دید آن کثافت‌ها را کور می‌کند. بعد عجله کنید. هر چند نفر که می‌توانید از راه مخفی که گشوده‌اید بروید وآن تله‌ها را مفنجر کنید و

برگردید. حالا که آنها جنگ می‌خواهند ما جنگ را نشانشان می‌دهیم. بروید و زود برگردید.

بعد شتابان برگشت و به عمارت آمد و دست سارا را که پشت پنجره مشرف بر ایوان ایستاده و هراسیده و غمگین چشم به بیرون به جنازه پدرش دوخته بود گرفت و گفت:

- بیا برویم عجله کن عزیزم.

و بعد او را همراه خودش پائین عمارت برد و در انتهای زیرزمین پشت انبار هیزم. چند آجر از دیوار پشتی را برداشت جای مخفی کوچکی در آن پشت میان دیوار بود که سبد گرد بزرگی با تشکچه و بالش در آن قرار داشت. سارا را بلند کرد و کمک کرد که داخل سبد بنشیند و بعد رفت بالا پوش و کلاه سارا را با صندوقچه‌ای کوچک وآهنین همراه با کیسه‌ای کشمش و گردو و کوزه آبی نه چندان کوچک آورد. صندوقچه را که پر از جواهرات و سکه‌های اشرفی بزرگ طلا بود با برگه‌ی سندهای مختلف کنار سارا قرار داد و با تاکید گفت:

- تو این جا می‌مانی. این طلا و جواهرات مال تو هستند و این سندها قباله‌های املاک ماست که از این به بعد مال توست تا وقتی که کسی از ما وآشنایان نیامده و مطمئن نشدی نباید از اینجا بیرون بیایی. این کیسه کشمش و گردو و این کوزه آب برای چند روز کافیست خدا حفظت کند عزیزم.

بعد در حالی‌که می‌گریست سارا در سینه فشرد و بوسید و گفت:

- نترس من و عمه نسترن همین نزدیک‌ها هستیم. نمی‌گذاریم کسی دستش به تو برسد.

سارا میان سبد نشست و نگاه پر از اشک و ترسش را تو صورت نرگس خاتون دوخت. تنش می‌لرزید و زبانش بند آمده بود و قادر به حرف زدن نبود. نرگس خاتون که متوجه حال و وضع روحی سارا شده بود. برای نوازش دست بر صورت سارا کشید و بعد شانه‌های او را در میان دستانش محکم گرفت و نگاهش را در نگاه او دوخت و در حالی که او را آرام تکان می‌داد با صدای محکم گفت:

- سعی کن شجاع باشی، تو نباید بترسی. تو وارث خانواده ما هستی تو باید زنده بمانی. اگر در این جا بمانی هیچکس دستش به تو نمی‌رسد. گفتم من و عمه نسترن همین جا در این نزدیک‌ها هستیم. حالا آرام بنشین و اگر توانستی چشمانت را ببند و بخواب.

بعد باز او را بوسید و دوباره آجرهای دیوار را مرتب و منظم چید. به طوریکه هیچ درز و سوراخی نگذاشت که نور و هوا وارد شود تنها از سوراخ کوچکی در انتهای گوشه سمت راست نزدیک سقف مخفیگاه نور ضعیفی همراه هوا وارد می‌شد. نرگس خاتون بعد از چیدن هیزم‌ها مقابل دیوار دوباره با صدای بلند سارا را خطاب قرار داد و گفت:

- سارا عزیزم نترس، من همین جا در این نزدیک‌ها هستم. بازم می‌آیم و به تو سر می‌زنم. سعی کن بخوابی. خدا حفظت کند دخترم.

بعد به نسترن خاتون که پیرتر از آن بود که بتواند از سارا محافظت کند. گفت:

- شما هم همین جا بمانید.

بعد نگاهی به اطراف انداخت و رفت. سارا صدای قدم‌های نرگس خاتون را که در زیر طاق زیر زمین انعکاس می‌یافت شنید که داشت دور می‌شد.

با دور شدن عمه نرگس اشک سارا دوباره جاری شد. دیدن تن خونین پدرش و صدای گلوله و ترس و ناله عمه نرگس و نشستن و مخفی شدن در میان دیوار در جایی تنگ و تاریک برای دختر نوجوانی به سن و سال او بسیار سخت و سنگین و طاقت فرسا بود. سارا خاطرش آمد در گذشته در آن زمان که در دیر به سر می‌برد. وقتی خواهر روحانی مسئول دیر خواهران می‌خواست او را تنبیه کند. با خود به طبقه پائین زیرزمین دیر می‌برد و در طبقه پائین نزدیک انبار و سرداب کلیسا در یک اطاق تاریک و نمور کوچک با سقف کوتاه که پوشیده از سنگ قبر بود زندانیش می‌کرد و توصیه و تکلیف می‌کرد که برای نجات خودش از عذاب خدا دعا بخواند و سارا از آن زمان یاد گرفته بود که برای این که نترسد بهتر است که دعا بخواند و حال باز همان احساس را یافته بود. احساس ترس و تنهایی. چشمانش را بست و شروع به دعا خواندن به درگاه خداوند کرد. نمی‌توانست تصویر صورت و تن خونین پدرش را از ذهن و حافظه‌اش دور کند. فهمیده بود که پدرش گلوله خورده اما نمی‌دانست که مرده است. از صدای گلوله و وحشت مردم ده و مسلح شدن آن‌ها فهمیده بود که اتفاق دیگری افتاده. پس همانطور که دعا می‌خواند چشمانش را بست و گوش به صدای انفجار توپ و گلوله سپرد. صدای انفجارها گاه نزدیک وگاه دور بود تا نیمه‌های شب صدای گلوله و انفجارها همچنان ادامه داشت. در طول آن مدت نرگس خاتون چندین بار آمده و او را صدا زده و امید داده بود. آخرین بار اواخر شب کمی مانده به بامداد بود که آمد و او را صدا زد و گفت که همان جاست و او را تشویق کرد که بخوابد. ساعتی بعد از آمدن و رفتن آخرین بار نرگس خاتون بود که صدای مهیب شلیک توپ‌ها و

تفنگ‌ها شدت بیشتری گرفت صداها هر لحظه نزدیک و نزدیک‌تر می‌شدند جنگ بشدت ادامه داشت. جیلوها از هر سو حمله کرده و دست به کشتار و تاراج و ویرانی زده بودند و مردم ده که در باغ و اطراف عمارت اربابی نرگس خاتون جمع شده بودند و با وجود کاهش و کمبود اسلحه و بخصوص فشنگ هم چنان دلیرانه می‌جنگیدند و دفاع می‌کردند اما با گذشت زمان کم کم باروت و فشنگ و مهمات آن‌ها کم و رو به تمام شدن بود. اما در عوض نیروی کمکی تازه‌ای به جیلوها رسیده بود و برای همین آن‌ها روحیه گرفته با آوردن یک غلاده توپ دیگر توانستند حصار باغ اربابی نرگس خاتون را بشکافند و عمارت او را و مدافعان را به توپ بندند اما با وجود ریختن قسمتی از عمارت اهالی ده همراه نرگس خاتون همچنان به مقاوت و جنگ ادامه دادند و کار در نهایت به جنگ تن به تن با چوب و دشنه و بیل و تبر و شلیک از نزدیک و روبرو رسیده بود. وقتی ظریفه خانم زن آقا پطرس فرمانده جیلوها که فرماندهی حمله به ده و عمارت نرگس خاتون را به عهده داشت. هنگام جنگ توسط گلوله طپانچه نرگس خاتون زخمی شد و او را به زحمت از میدان بدر بردند. جیلوها که کشته بسیار داده و با زخمی شدن ظریفه خانم روحیه‌شان ضعیف شده و امکان پیروزی را محال می‌دیدند. برای این که بتوانند نیروهایشان را جمع کرده و عقب نشینی بکنند و در هنگام عقب نشینی از حمله و تعقیب مردم ده و دیگر دهات نزدیک در امان بمانند با تمام توان از هرسو عمارت را به توپ بستند. سارا که از صدای انفجار گلو و فریاد مردم بیدار مانده و گوش به صداها سپرده بود. وقتی صدای انفجارهای پیاپی توپ‌ها و فروریختن ساختمان را شنید. شروع به گریه و جیغ و فریاد کرد و پشت سر هم نرگس

خاتون را صدا زد. اما از نرگس خاتون هیچ خبری نشد وقتی گلوله توپ دیوار بالای سر او را در قسمت طبقه دوم عمارت فروریخت و سارا صدای مهیب ریختن آن را در بالای سرش شنید. از شدت ترس چشمانش را بست و دیگر چیزی نفهمید.

ظهر روز بعد وقتی صدای نفس‌ها و بگوشش رسید و شنید که کسی هیزم‌های مقابل پناهگاه را برداشته و در حال برداشتن آجرهای دیوار است سارا چشمانش را گشود. اما در تاریک محض فضای جان پناه و تابش نور بیرون که توان دید او را گرفته بود نتوانست خوب ببیند ولی از لحن صدا او را شناخت. تلی بود که با صدای گرفته و غم آلودی او را صدا می‌زد و مرتب می‌گفت:

– سارا عزیزم بیدار شو. نترس عزیزم. خانمم نترس منم تلی

سارا گریان از جایش بلند شد صندوقچه کوچک جواهرات و کیسه اسناد و مدارک را همانطور که نرگس خاتون سپرده بود میان دستانش در آغوش داشت و نتوانست دستانش را بطرف تلی بگشاید. تلی ناگزیر از بازوانش گرفت و او را از مخفیگاه میان دیوار بیرون آورد و در آغوشش فشرد و در حالی‌که همراه با سارا می‌گریست گفت:

– نترس عزیزم، دیگر تنها نیستی. بیا برویم

نور ضعیف و کم رنگی که از دریچه نزدیک سقف و سوراخ شکاف مانندی که در اثر اصابت گلوله توپ در دیوار روبرویی ایجاد شده بود، می‌تابید فضای تیره و تاریک انباری را کمی روشن کرده بود. تمام لوازم و وسائل بهم ریخته و تکه‌های سنگ وآجر و چوب کف انباری را پوشانده بودند. به زحمت خود را به پله‌ها رساندند وقتی به طبقه بالا رسیدند. سارا نسترن

را دید که با دست شکسته و بسته و پیشانی خونین با حال نزار وگیج و غم زده درگوشه‌ای میان اشیای شکسته و داغون نشسته است. نسترن خاتون او راکه دید با چشم اشکبار دست سالمش را به طرف او برای آغوش گشود. سارا گریان

رفت و خود را در آغوش او انداخت و گریست و بعد برگشت نگاهی به اطراف انداخت دید که قسمتی از سقف خانه فروریخته و تمام در و پنجره‌ها شکسته و سوخته و وسائل و اشیا خانه شکسته و همه جا پراکنده است. عکس بزرگ عمه نرگس به همراه پدرش با قاب شکسته کف تالار افتاده بود. رفت، عکس را با قاب شکسته‌اش برداشت و روی طاقچه‌ای که سالم مانده بود گذاشت از وضع ویران خانه و وسائل حیرت زده شده بود.گیج و منگ اطراف را نگاه کرد نمی‌توانست باورکند. هیاهو وگریه و زاری را که از بیرون می‌آمد نمی‌شنید و یا اگر می‌شنید اما توجه نداشت. تلی که پشت سرش بود و دو دستش را بر شانه‌های او نهاده و از او محافظت می‌کرد. خواست از رفتن او به بیرون و ایوان جلوگیری کند اما سارا بی توجه به فشار آرام دستان و حرف‌های تلی که مرتب می‌گفت نه عزیزم نرو آن جا امن نیست. در را گشود و به ایوان رفت. نسترن خاتون با همه ضعف و پیری و احوال زارش آمد و گفت:

– سارا دخترم برگرد

بیرون هوا گرفته و دود آلود بود. دود هنوز از بعضی خانه‌های روستا که آتش گرفته بودند بالا می‌رفت. بسیاری از درختان باغ شکسته و سوخته بودند و دیوارهای باغ از چند قسمت ریخته و خراب شده بود. پائین در محوطه مقابل ایوان کنار حوض گرد برزگ مقابل پله‌ها جنازه تعدادی از

کشته شدگان را کنار هم چیده بودند. تعدادی از روستاییان در چمن زار بیرون از باغ مشغول کندن زمین بودند. سارا نگاهش را از اطراف گرفت دوباره چشم بر خیابان باریک غربی باغ که از کنار حوض و از میان درختان شکسته و افتاده به در غربی باغ منتهی می‌شد دوخت. بعد چشم به اطراف گرداند ناگهان چشمش به جنازه پدرش و عمه نرگس و گلاب خاتون خورد که در سمت راست محوطه کنار پرچین‌های باغچه گل سرخ زیر درخت سیب قرارداشتند. دست نسترن خاتون را گرفت و آرام از کنار نرده‌های شکسته ایوان گذشت و از پله‌ها پائین رفت. یوسف که آستین‌های پیراهنش را بالا زده همراه کدخدا و چند مرد دیگر مشغول کار جابه‌جایی و رسیدگی به وضع کشته‌ها و وضع آشفته باغ و حمل جنازه‌ها بود. چشمش که به سارا افتاد. برای این که مانع از پائین آمدن او شود در حالیکه با حرکت دست و به صدای بلند به تلی فریاد می‌زد که:

– چرا گذاشتی بیاد بیرون؟

چند قدم به طرف سارا برداشت بعد نگاهش که به نسترن خاتون افتاد. ایستاد وکلاهش را از سر برداشت و مات خیره چشم بر سارا دوخت. کدخدا و مردان و زنانی که مشغول کار بودند. دست از کار کشیدند وآمدند کنار هم کمی دورتر از یوسف ایستادند حیدر که دست و سرزخمیش را با پارچه‌ای سفید بسته و در حاشیه کناری حوض نشسته بود بلند شد و نزدیک آمد. سارا از پله‌ها پائین آمد بالای سر جنازه امیرخان و نرگس خاتون که رسید. لحظه‌ها همانطور ساکت ایستاد و نگاهش را بر آن‌ها دوخت اشک آرام ازگونه‌هایش جاری بود. بعد نشست و صندوقچه کوچک و کیسه سند و قباله‌ها را که در دست داشت زمین گذاشت و در حالی‌که

آرام می‌گریست دست بر صورت نرگس خاتون کشید و لکه خون گونه
او را پاک کرد و بعد خم شد و صورت او را بوسید و بعد دست بر سر
پدرش امیرخان کشید و صورت او را هم بوسید. تمام جماعت روستا مردان
و زنانی که از جنگ جان سالم به در برده بودند و آن جا ایستاده بودند. زار،
زار می‌گریستند. سارا بعد از لحظه‌ها بلند شد و چشم به اطراف گرداندند
و نگاه بر عمارت و خرابی‌های آن دوخت یادش آمد که نرگس خاتون به
تاکید گفته بود که این جا، تمام روستا و دیگر ملک‌هایی که قباله‌شان در
این کیسه است. مال توست اگر خراب شدند بسازش و نگهش دار.
کلید کوچک صندوقچه را که نرگس خاتون بر گردنش آویخته بود از
گردنش در آورد و به طرف تلی که آمده وکنار آن‌ها ایستاده گرفت و
گفت: بازش کن.
تلی متعجب گفت: حالا ! برای چه می‌خواهی باز کنی؟
سارا نگاهی به یوسف که نزدیک‌تر آمده بود و بعد به نسترن خاتون
انداخت. باز به تلی گفت: بازش کن
یوسف با اشاره به تلی گفت که بازش کند.
تلی کلید صندوقچه را گرفت و در آن را گشود. صندوقچه پر از سکه‌های
اشرفی بزرگ طلا بود. سارا کدخدا را با اشاره دست نزدیک خواند و دو
مشت از اشرفی‌ها را برداشت و در کف دستان کدخدا ریخت و با اشاره به
عمارت و باغ و ده و گفت: بسازش
کدخدا خم شد و دست سارا را بوسید و درحالی‌که اشرفیها را در جیب
کتش می‌ریخت چند قدم عقب رفت. گفت:

- خدا شما را حفظ کند. حالا دیگر شما ارباب و صاحب ما هستید. هر چه بفرمایید در خدمتیم. غلام شما هستیم به روی چشم می‌سازمیش. از اولش هم بهتر.

دیگر روستایی‌ها هم دست به سینه مرتب می‌گفتند. خدا شما را حفظ کند.

یوسف در حالی‌که به طرف عمارت اشاره می‌کرد گفت:

- حالا بهتره که شما و نسترن خاتون با تلی بروید توی عمارت و استراحت کنید. ما کارها را انجام می‌دهیم

بعد رو کرد به حیدر وگفت:

- برو کالسکه را آماده کن به اسب‌ها برس. ظهر نشده باید به شهر برگردیم.

کدخدا هم که کنار یوسف ایستاده بود با تحکم به حیدر گفت:

- می‌دانی که از این به بعد در خدمت سارا خانم خواهی بود

حیدر گفت:

- هر چه بفرمایند. من غلام خانم بودم و غلام سارا خانم هم هستم.

سارا با چشمان خیس در حالی‌که نمی‌توانست از نرگس خاتون و پدرش چشم برگیرد نگاهش را به عمارت دوخت. غوغای غمی سیاه تمام وجودش را در برگرفته بود. با وجود این که یوسف، کدخدا و تمام روستاییان همه به احترامش ایستاده و در سکوت چشم بر او دوخته بودند. احساس تنهایی و بی‌کسی تمام وجودش را در هم می‌فشرد. خواست به طرف پله‌ها برود اما نتوانست قدم‌هایش سنگین و ناتوان بودند. نمی‌توانست و دلش نمی‌خواست برود. می‌خواست لحظه‌ها کنار پیکر نرگس خاتون و پدرش امیرخان بنشیند و نگاهشان کند. کنار آن‌ها احساس تنهایی نمی‌کرد. برگشت دوباره آن‌ها را نگاه کرد. تن بی جان و خونین آن‌ها کنار هم به

درازا افتاده بود و باد بی‌رمق از رویشان می‌گذشت. لحظه‌ها همانطور آن‌ها را نگاه کرد و بعد در حالیکه زار زار می‌گریست دست عمه پیرش نسترن خاتون را گرفت و همراه تلی به طرف عمارت راه افتاد.

سارا و تنهایی اورمیه

۱

آیدین حکیم خان پزشک جوان خوش فکر وخوش سیمایی بود از اهالی اورمیه. قامتی نازک و قدی متوسط و صورتی گرد استخوانی و چشمانی سیاه وگیرا داشت. موی سرش بلند بود و به طرز فرنگی‌ها لباس می‌پوشید اما هرگز چون دیگر مردان و مد آن روزگار کلاه بر سر نمی‌گذاشت. بسیار موقر و آداب دادن و در عین حال فردی خجالتی بود. مادرش ترکان خاتون از نوادگان ناصرالدین شاه و پدرش نصیرالدوله از صاحب منصبان دیوانی دربار ناصری بود که بعد از سال‌ها خدمت دیوانی به دلیل کهولت به زادگاهش برگشته و به املاک خود می‌رسید. آیدین تحصیلاتش را در مدرسه طب استانبول به پایان رسانده و با شروع جنگ جهانی چندی بودکه به زادگاهش اورمیه برگشته و مطب و شفاخانه‌ای در نزدیکی بازار اورمیه

در سرای پدرش نصیرالدوله تاسیس و به طبابت و تیمار بیماران مشغول بود. با حکیم افشلیم خان و حکیم یوناتان از فارغ التحصیلان مدرسه طب میسیونرهای امریکایی و از سران مسیحیان شورشی و دکتر پاکارد امریکایی به مناسبت شغل و حرفه‌اش دوستی و مراوت داشت و گاه عمل جراحی بیمارانش را در بیمارستان وست منیستر میسیون امریکایی که تنها بیمارستان مجهز شهر بود انجام می‌داد اما از ته دل ناراحت و دلتنگ از اوضاع آشفته شهر و دیار و بی‌توجهی حکومت مرکزی بود. آیدین که مدت زیادی در استانبول بسر برده بود و اطلاعات زیادی از دلایل شروع جنگ جهانی و انقلاب سوسیالیستی روسیه و اوضاع جهانی و منطقه داشت و وضع منطقه و مسائل پیش آمده را حاصل رقابت دولت‌ها و جنگ جهانی می‌دانست و همیشه تلاش داشت در کنار ارتباط دائم با مسیحیان جیلو و کردها به خصوص اسماعیل آقا سیمتگو که یک بار هم برای معالجه مادر او به دهکده چهریق محل اقامت اصلی سیمتگو رفته بود نسبت به حفظ آرامش شهر کمک کند و مدام از دوستان و اهالی شهر هم می‌خواست و توصیه می‌کرد که تشکیلاتی فراهم کنند و نیروی متمرکزی برای حفظ جان و اموال خود بوجود آورند و این فکر و توصیه‌ها همانند توصیه و عقیده و فکر امیرخان پدر سارا بود.

سارا، آیدین حکیم خان را عصر روزی دید و با او آشنا شد که سربازان روس با همکاری جیلوها بازار ارومیه را آتش زده و به تاراج برده بودند و آیدین حکیم که شفاخانه‌اش نزدیک بازار بود و برای مداوای زخمی‌ها امن نبود. ناگزیر با موافقت و تشویق یوسف تعدادی از زخمی‌های بی پناه و فراری را برای مداوا به کاروانسرا آورده بود و قرار بود که یوسف با

کمک گروهی از اهالی ترتیب پناه و جابه‌جایی بیماران فراری را بدهد. تلی اما نگران بود و می‌ترسید خبر درز کند و کاروانسرا هم مورد تهدید و حمله قرار بگیرد. وقتی موضوع را با سارا که بالا پوشش را پوشیده و آماده برگشتن به منزلشان در ساران نزد نسترن خاتون بود در میان گذاشت. سارا لحظه‌ها بالا پله‌ها به دیوار تکیه داد و در فکر فرو رفت. عادتش این بود همیشه وقتی با مسئله تازه‌ای روبرو می‌شد نخست لحظه‌ها در مورد آن فکر می‌کرد این را از پدرش آموخته و یاد گرفته بود و همیشه از کمک و پناه دادن به درماندگان و نیازمندان استقبال می‌کرد اما این بار قضیه فرق می‌کرد و برای همین بعد از کمی فکر رو به تلی کرد و پرسید:

-گفتی چند سرباز ترک آذری روسیه با دو نفر از افراد کاظم خان؟

– بله

– سربازان روسیه را چرا؟

– نمی‌دانم انگار به مردم پیوسته بوده‌اند و در زد و خورد زخمی شده‌اند.

– اگر کنسولگری و فرماندهی روسیه بفهمد؟

– من هم از این نگرانم!

سارا از پله‌ها پائین رفت و در را گشود و بیرون آمد و به حیدر که کالسکه را آماده کرده و همراه دو محافظ دیگرش مراد و یونس مقابل در منتظر او بود. گفت که کمی دیگر صبر کنند.

عصر بود، هوا گرفته و سرد، چند سالی از واقعه حمله به روستا و کشته شدن عمه نرگس و پدرش امیر خان می‌گذشت. سارا در این مدت قد کشیده و بالغ شده و تن و رخساری زیبا و وجودی پریوار یافته بود و با عمه پیر پدرش نسترن خاتون درکوشک اربابی عمه نرگس که ساختمان آن

را بازسازی و به طرز مناسب و با شکوهی آراسته بود به سر می‌برد و به کار بازسازی روستا و رفاه روستاییان و کمک و تشویق روستاییان به کشت و زرع بخصوص کشت گندم و جو و راه‌اندازی دوباره آسیاب‌ها مشغول بود و هر چندگاه نزد تلی و یوسف می‌آمد و روز و شبی را کنار آن‌ها می‌ماند و با همه ناآرامی و بدی اوضاع شهر، گاه همراه تلی سوار برکالسکه گشتی در شهر می‌زد و خریدی می‌کرد. تلی و یوسف مثل تخم چشمشان مراقبش بودند و حیدر با دو تفنگ‌چی جوان از روستائیان که کدخدا مامور کرده بود. همیشه محافظ او بودند. اما این مانع از ارتباط نزدیک او با مردم نبود. زیبایی و رفتار و ارتباط پر از محبت و کمک‌های بی‌دریغانه او به مردم بخصوص به آوارگان و آسیب دیدگان زبانزد شده و به دل مردم نشسته و تبدیل به وجودی پاک و مقدس و مظهر زیبایی شده بود. این محبوبیت او از یک سو مورد توجه نمایندگان دولت‌های خارجی و از سوی دیگر موجب نگرانی سرکردگان جیلوهای شورشی بود. به همین جهت در چند ماه گذشته چندین بار آقا پطرس سرکرده نظامی جیلوها توسط یکی از کشیشان که سابقه تحصیل در تفلیس را داشت. برای دلجویی و این که آن اتفاق یک اشتباه جنگی بوده نزد سارا فرستاده و گفته بود که او و تمام افراد و فامیل و اموال و روستا و روستائیانش بشرط عدم انجام هر کاری در امان هستند. اما سارا هیچ اعتمادی به آن‌ها نداشت و نمی‌توانست کشته شدن پدر و عمه نرگس و مردم روستا و شهر را به دست جیلوهای آشوری نادیده بگیرد و فراموش کند. عصر روزهایی که در کاروانسرا نزد تلی و یوسف به سر می‌برد با مهمان‌های خارجی که برای دیدار با دیگر خارجیان مقیم اورمیه و نوشیدن چای و قهوه به قهوه خانه کاروانسرا می‌آمدند و

بخصوص با مسیوکاژل سرپرست آمبولانس (بیمارستان سیار) فرانسوی و معاون او مسیو زریس که به تازگی به اورمیه آمده و در ساختمان کنار مسجد مناره نزدیک کنسولگری امریکا مستقر شده بودند و تعداد افراد آن به هفتاد نفر می‌رسید به گفتگو می‌نشست. مسیو کاژل و دیگران از این که در اورمیه دختر جوانی با آن شکل و شمایل و دانش آشنا به زبان فرانسه است بسیار خوشحال بودند و مسرت آن‌ها بیشتر از دیدن صلیب زمردین بر سینه سارا بودکه فکر می‌کردند. او نیز مسیحی و از آن‌هاست اما بعد از کمی صحبت و بحث در می‌یافتند که با فرد و وجود دیگر روبرو هستند و در این میان یاکمن افسر فنلاندی اصل سوئدی که به همراه چند نظامی دیگر سوئدی مدتی بود که در اورمیه و در کاروانسرا به سر می‌برد. بیشترین ارتباط و گفتگو و دوستی را با سارا داشت و خبرها و تصمیم‌های سران جیلو و نظامیان و نمایندگان دولت‌های خارجی درگیر در اورمیه را او به سارا می‌داد. یاکمن هر وقت سارا را می‌دید. بیاد دخترش می‌افتاد و اشک بر چشم می‌راند. یاکمن نقاشی چیره دست بود و در طول اقامت خود در اورمیه هر زمان که وقت می‌کرد از شهر و بازار و کوچه، ساختمان‌های شهر و هم چنین از مردان و بخصوص زنان در لباس‌های محلی دامن‌های بلند زری و پولک دوز از مناظر طبیعت بکر و زیبای دریاچه ارومیه طرح‌هایی برمی‌داشت و نقاشی می‌کرد اما مهمترین کار و اثر او زمانی طرح و شکل گرفت که یک روز عصر سارا بر حسب اتفاق پشته‌ای گندم بر شانه به کاروانسرا آمد. این درست زمانی بود که گروه کثیری از مردم روستاها و اطراف شهر در اثر حمله و کشتار و تاراج جیلوهای آشوری با حمایت سربازان روسیه به شهر هجوم و پناه آورده بودند. سارا که از ماجرا

با خبر شده و به کاروانسرا آمده بود از یوسف خواست که تعدادی از خانواده‌های پناهنده را تا آن جا که می‌تواند در محوطه پشتی کاروانسرا که دارای زمینی برزگ با چند ساختمان کاه گلی بود جا و مکان دهد. وقتی یوسف به مشکل تامین غذای پناهنده‌ها وآواره‌ها اشاره و سوال کرده بودکه غذایشان را چگونه تامین کند. سارا گفته بود که هرچه آرد در بازار است. خریداری کند. اما در بازار آرد پیدا نمی‌شد و برنج و گوشت و سایر مواد هم نایاب بود. پس ناگزیر از یوسف خواسته بود که گروه کثیری از همان روستائیان پناهنده را تحت مراقبت چند تفنگ‌چی روانه دشت و روستاها بکند و هر جا گندم کشته درونشده‌ای مانده باشد خریداری و درو و به کاروانسرا و آسیاب‌ها حمل کنند و یوسف با کمک شاگرد سابقش سرکیس که از فرماندهان جیلو بود به همان کار اقدام کرده و گندم‌های درو شده را به محوطه پشتی کاروانسرا حمل و با کمک تعدادی از روستائی‌های پناهنده خرمنی فراهم کرده بود و بعد از برداشت گندم، کاه حاصل از خرمن را برای تامین قسمتی از هزینه پناهنده‌ها می‌فروخت. این درست همزمان با عصر روزی بود که سارا برای سرکشی به کاروانسر آمد و هم زمان با آمدن او ارابه‌های بزرگ پشته‌های گندم‌های درو شده به کاروانسر رسیدند و سارا هم مطابق همان خوی و خصلت مردمی و همیاری که داشت خواست پشته‌ای گندم را بردارد که مورد اعتراض تلی و یوسف و دیگران واقع شد و فورا از دستش گرفتند. یاکمن که ناظر بر رفتار و کار سارا بود. از سارا خواست که به جای پشته چند دسته خوشه گندم را با رشته طنابی که بسته بود بر شانه بگیرد تا طرحی از او بکشد و سارا این کار را کرد و ساعتی بیحرک کنار دیوار نزدیک پشته‌های گندم ایستاد و یاکمن با شوق و ذوق

فراوانی که یافته بود شروع به طراحی و نقاشی سارا در ابعادی به بزرگی یک متر در هفتاد سانتی‌متر کرد. مردم محل، کلیه پناهنده‌ها و کسانی که در آن جا بودند به تماشای کار یاکمن ایستادند و چون تعداد بیشتری ازآن‌ها سارا را نمی‌شناختند و از طرز رفتار و مراقبت تلی و یوسف فکر می‌کردند سارا دختر آن‌هاست و یوسف را در آن چند روز به سبب فروش کاه،کاه فروش می‌نامیدند. به همان جهت سارا را سامانچی قیزی (دختر کاه فروش) صدا زده و نامیدند و از آن به بعد بسیاری از مردم شهر و اطراف و دیگر شهرها که سارا را نمی‌شناختند اما حسن رفتار و زیبایی بی مثال او را شنیده بودند هنگام صحبت از او و ذکر حسن او، از او بنام دخترکاه فروش اسم می‌بردند و همین اسم با سارا ماند و بعدها تبدیل به سمبل زیبا و پاکی شد. یاکمن بعد آن روز، مدت دوماه روی تابلوی نقاشی سیما و تن سارا کار کرد و روزی که برای اهدای تابلو در ساران در کوشک اربابی به دیدار سارا رفت و تابلو نقاشی را هم با خود برد و تقدیم کرد بقدری ماهرانه کشیده بود که موجب حیرت و تحسین سارا و نسترن خاتون شد و سارا بعدها شنید یاکمن در طول مدت دو ماهی که در کاروانسرا مشغول طرح و رنگ تابلو و نقش چهره سارا بود گروه گروه مردم شهر به دیدن تابلو و کار او می‌آمدند و از مهارت او دچار شگفتی می‌شدند و تابلو را هم تابلو دخترکاه فروش نامیده بودند. نسترن خاتون بعد از لحظه‌ها تماشای تابلو به تحسین آن پرداخت و ضمن سپاسگزاری و ستایش کار یاکمن و پذیرایی شایان از او سه سکه اشرفی طلا برای قدردانی به یاکمن اهدا کرد که موجب شادی یاکمن شد و به سارا و نسترن خاتون و دیگران گفت که آن ارزشمندترین

پول و هدیه‌ای‌ست که در عمرش دریافت کرده و همیشه آن‌ها را تا آخر عمر حفظ خواهد کرد.

و آن روز سارا بعد از این که از حیدر خواست که منتظر بماند. همراه تلی به انبار کاه کاروانسرا که در محوطه پشتی یعنی حیاط اندرونی کنار اصطبل اسب‌ها و گاو و گوسفندها قرار داشت رفت. در اصلی و ورودی قسمت پشتی کاروانسرا ازکوچه پشتی بود. معولا گاو و گوسفندها را از آن جامی آوردند و می‌بردند. طوری ساخته و تعبیه شده بود که برای ورود و خروج چهار پایان راحت باشد. البته در مخفی خوبی برای آوردن پنهانی زخمی‌ها و پناهنده‌ها هم بود. سارا و تلی وقتی به محوطه پشتی نزدیک   انبار کاه رسید. یوسف با کمک ابراهیم پسر کدخدا مشغول جوشاندن آب در دیگ مسی نسبتا بزرگی روی اجاق بود. نزدیکش یاکمن با یک مرد جوان نازک اندام خوش لباس که کتش را در آورده و با جلیقه و آستین‌های تا کرده ایستاده و مشغول صحبت بودند. وقتی سارا را همراه تلی دیدند صحبتشان را قطع کردند. یاکمن سلام و احوال پرسی کرد و مرد جوان نیز سلام داد و نگاهی به صورت و چشمان سارا انداخت و بعد ساکت و شرمگین کنار یاکمن ایستاد. بی‌شباهت به امیرخان نبود و مثل او مردی آرام و تودار و فهیم به نظر می‌رسید. سارا وقتی نگاهش به نگاه و چشمان او افتاد یک آن پشتش تیر کشید. لرزه‌ای خفیف در دل و تن و جانش احساس کرد و قلبش به طپش افتاد. این اولین بار بود که در زندگیش چنان حالت و احساسی به او دست می‌داد با گونه‌های برافروخته سلام آن‌ها را گرفت و نگاهش را به یوسف دوخت. یوسف که از دیدن او و در محوطه‌ی پشتی کروانسرا دست و پاچه شده بود گفت:

– شما نباید به این جا می‌آمدید. این جا مناسب شما نیست

سارا گفت:

– تلی نگران بود. به من گفت که چه اتفاقی افتاده. گفت که شما زخمی‌ها و پناهنده‌ها را به این جا آورده‌اید. او نگران است که مبادا خبر درز کند و به کاروانسرا هم حمله کنند. من آمدم که کمک کنم و ببینم که چه باید کرد. یوسف که احساس می‌شد از آمدن سارا به محوطه‌ی پشتی چندان راضی و خوشحال نیست کمی این پا وآن پا کرد و بعد در حالی‌که با دست به آیدین حکیم خان اشاره می‌کرد گفت:

–ای کاش می‌فرمودید من می‌آمدم. حقیقتش اوضاع شهر و بازار اصلا خوب نیست. صبح که سربازان شورشی روس همراه تعدادی از جیلوها به بازار هجوم بردند و تاراج و آتشش زدند. مطب و شفاخانه جناب آیدین حکیم خان هم کمی آسیب دید و دیگر امن نبود. نمی‌شد زخمی‌ها را آن جا مداوا کرد. چاره‌ای جز این نبود که بیاوریمشان این جا تا جناب حکیم خان این جا درمانشان کنند. جناب یاکمن هم خیلی کمک کردند. فکر همه چیز را کرده‌ایم جای نگرانی نیست. البته به جناب حکیم خان عرض کرده‌ام که تا فردا صبح می‌توانیم مریض‌ها را این جا نگه‌داریم. فردا باید از این جا ببریم.

سارا پرسید:

– جناب حکیم خان!؟

آیدین حکیم خان یک قدم به طرف آن‌ها برداشت و با شرمگینی گفت:

- بله من هستم. ببخشید دوشیزه سارا نباید شما را معذب می‌کردیم حقیقت ماجرا همان است که میرزا یوسف گفتند. قصد نداشتیم زخمی‌ها را به این جا بیاوریم ولی چاره نبود

بعد رو به یوسف کرد وگفت:

- بله حتما، زخمی‌ها را از این جا می‌بریم ولی کجا؟

یاکمن گفت: روستای شما

آیدین حکیم خان گفت:

- در روستای ما دیگر جا نیست مگر یک عده‌ای را بیرون کنیم

یاکمن گفت:

- خوب بیرونشان کنید. بگویید بروند به شهر و روستای خودشان نزد خانواده و فامیلشان!

یوسف معترضانه گفت:

- نزد کدام خانواده و فامیل، سربازهای فراری روسیه که این جا خانواده و فامیل ندارند. آن‌هایی هم که اهل این نواحی هستند. خانه‌شان تاراج و ویران و افراد خانواده و فامیلشان یا کشته شده‌اند و یا دربه‌در و سرگردان و آواره و پناهنده‌اند. دیگر جایی ندارند که بروند. مگر آن چند نفر از افراد کاظم خان قوشچی را بیرون کنند. بله به آن‌ها می‌توانیم بگوییم که برگردند و بروند به دهشان نزد کاظم خان.

آیدین حکیم خان گفت:

-آن‌ها خودشان خواهند رفت. فقط منتظرند تا زخمشان خوب و حالشان مساعد شود.

یاکمن گفت:

- پس مثل دو روز پیش ببریم به روستا یوسف یعنی ساران

آیدین حکیم خان هم حرف او را تایید کرد وگفت:

- بله ببریم به ساران

سارا متعجبانه گفت:

- ساران

یوسف و ابراهیم پسر کدخدا و مراد آسیابان که انتظار فاش شدن رازشان یعنی بردن فراریان و پناهندگان به ساران و پنهان کردن آنها را نداشتند. هاج و واج و وارفته نگاهی به سارا کردند و سرشان را پائین‌انداختند. سارا فهمید که تعدادی از فراریان را به ده او برده‌اند پرسید:

- چند نفرند، کجا پنهانشان کرده‌اید. چرا به من نگفته بودید؟

آیدین حکیم خان گفت:

- ببخشید اجازه بدهید من توضیح دهم چون

سارا با عصبانیت حرف او را قطع کرد و گفت:

- شما نه

این اولین بار بود که سارا با عصبانیت حرف کسی را قطع می‌کرد. آیدین لبخندی زد و ساکت شد و یک قدم که نزدیک آمده بود دوباره عقب رفت. سارا که متوجه رفتار و عصبانت خود شده بود و نمی‌دانست که چرا این کار کرد. لبخندی زد و گفت:

- ببخشید اجازه بدهید عمو یوسف بگویند

همین لبخند و رفتار نشان از احساس متفاوتی بود که سارا نسبت به آیدین حکیم خان یافته بود. یوسف گفت:

- پنج نفرند در انباری پشت آسیاب جا داده‌ایم

سارا کمی فکر کرد و بعد گفت:

- کار درستی کرده‌اید عمو

یوسف که جمله آخر سارا شنید گفت:

- پس می‌فرمائید این‌ها را هم ببریم آن جا

- بله اگر صلاح می‌دانید

آیدین حکیم خان پرسید:

- اما کی و چطوری؟

یوسف گفت:

- مثل دفعه پیش صبح زود. اما می‌ترسم شب بریزند این جا

آیدین حکیم خان گفت:

- اگر قرار شود که فردا صبح ببریم. آن وقت یکی از سربازهای روس را که زخمش عمیقه و گلوله در شکمش مانده و خون‌ریزی دارد باید هرچه زودتر جراحی کنیم و اگر هم جراحی کنیم تا چند روز نمی‌توانیم او را از جایش تکان بدهیم مگر ببریم مطب من و آن جا جراحی و بستریش کنیم و بعد هم تحویل کنسولگری بدهیم.

یوسف گفت:

- اگر تحویل کنسولگری بدهیم به جرم فرار اعدامش می‌کنند

- پس همین الان ببریمشان به ده آن جا جراحی و درمانشان کنیم

یاکمن گفت:

- بله من هم موافقم و همراه شما می‌آیم

- یوسف درمانده گفت:

- این وقت عصر

یاکمن گفت:

- نگران نباشید من همراه شما می‌آیم

- ولی وسیله کم داریم

- کالسکه سارا خانم هم هست

تلی ناراحت به اعتراض گفت:

- لطفا سارا خانم را قاطی این مسائل نکنید

یوسف که با تلی هم رای و موافق بود گفت:

- نه نمی‌توانیم از کالسکه سارا خانم استفاده کنیم

آیدین حکیم گفت:

- یا من باید بروم کالسکه‌ام را بیاورم و یا از اسب‌ها استفاده کنیم

سارا رو به آیدین حکیم کرد گفت:

- من باید زود برگردم به ده، تا حالا هم دیر کرده‌ام. شما و عمو یوسف اگر مایلید می‌توانید همراه من و تلی بیایید.آن‌ها هم آن افراد را با درشکه کاروانسرا با کمک جناب یاکمن می‌آورند البته کمی بعد از حرکت و رفتن ما باید حرکت کنند

این را گفت و برگشت و به یوسف گفت:

- عمو یوسف دیره باید راه بیفتیم.

تلی پرسید:

-کاروانسرا را چه کنیم؟

- عمو یوسف خودشان بهتر می‌دانند درهاش را می‌بندند و به حسن و سودابه و دیگر کارگرها می‌سپارند.

شامگاه بودکه حرکت کردند. حیدر شتاب داشت که قبل از تاریکی هوا زودتر به ده برسند. همراه با حرکت کالسکه که به سمت شمال غرب می‌رفتند. آفتاب در حال غروب در پشت کوه‌های مور شهیدان، قازان باش و قله بهادر بود. کالسکه پیچ و خم جاده را می‌پیمود و یوسف و تلی خاموش در خود فرو رفته و آیدین و سارا در حال گفتگو بودند. آیدین از استانبول و دانشگاه خود می‌گفت و از سفر خود به پاریس و از فرهنگ آن مناطق و مسائل و مشکلاتی که موجب شروع جنگ جهانی شده و انقلاب کمونیستی روسیه را زمینه شروع و خاتمه شعله‌های جنگ و همینطور روی کار آمدن مصطفی کمال پاشا در ترکیه می‌دانست. اما با وجود امید به پایان جنگ نگران از آینده و وضع منطقه بود و هم چنین نگران از بیماری قلبی مادرش ترکان خاتون و وقتی از بیماری و ناراحتی مادرش گفت سارا با او هم دردی وآرزوی سلامتی برای مادر او کرد و بعد گفت که باز شما با مادرتان بوده و محبت او را دیده‌اید ولی من هرگز مادرم را ندیده‌ام. با نزدیک شدن کالسکه به ده صحبت و صمیمیت آن‌ها هم که از لحاظ فکری و احساسی به هم خیلی نزدیک بودند بیشتر و نزدیک‌تر می‌شد و آن‌ها از همه چیز و همه مسائل با هم صحبت کردند و این صحبت آشنایی آن دو را به هم نزدیک و دوست و صمیمی‌کرد. وقتی به ساران رسیدند. یوسف از حیدر خواست که او و آیدین حکیم را نزدیک آسیاب ده پیاده کند. هنگام پیاده شدن. سارا از آیدین حکیم خان و یوسف خواست که بعد از تمام شدن کارشان همراه یاکمن برای صرف شام و استراحت به منزل آن‌ها بیایند.

در ایوان کوشک نسترن خانون نگران اخم کرده کنار نرده‌های ایستاده و نگران منتظر بود. وقتی کالسکه وارد باغ شد و دم پله‌ها ایستاد و سارا و تلی از آن پیاده شدند و حیدر کیف و وسائل و خرید آن‌ها را بالا آورد. نسترن خاتون با اشاره دست خواست که تلی و حیدر بایستند و با تلخی و ناراحتی گفت:

- تا این وقت کجا بودید؟ مگر نگفتم‌ام پیش از تاریک شدن هوا باید این جا باشید. این جوان است شما که دنیا دیده‌اید. می‌دانید اوضاع و احوال چطور است.

بعد با تحکم به حیدر گفت:

- برو اسب‌ها را از کالسکه را باز کن و استراحت بده. دیگر کسی به شهر نخواهد رفت.

این را گفت و با تلخی برگشت و در را گشود و تو رفت، سارا و تلی که متوجه ناراحتی و عصبانیت نسترن خاتون بودند. پشت سر او تو رفتند. نسترن خاتون از مستخدمه‌اش فرنگیس آب خواست و رو به سارا کرد و با اخم گفت:

- برو لباس‌هایت را عوض کن و به کارهایت برس

سارا گفت:

- چشم

و بعد دست در گردن نسترن خاتون آویخت و او را بوسید و گفت:

- ببخشید می‌دانم دیر کردیم اما عمو یوسف و آیدین حکیم خان می‌خواستند همراه ما بیایند برای همین تاخیر کردیم

- آیدین حکیم خان!؟ تلی تو می‌شناسی؟

- بله خانوم آیدین حکیم خان پسر نصیرالدوله هستند

سارا با ذوق و حرارت خاصی پرسید:

- عمه می‌شناسیدشان؟

- بله جناب نصیرالدوله دوست پدرم و خانواده ما هستند. با خانمشان ترکان خاتون هم آشنا هستم. خانواده بسیار خوب و اصل و نسب داری‌اند

نسترن خاتون بعد پرسید:

- گفتی برای شام و استراحت می‌آیند.

- بله

- پس تلی برو با فرنگیس تدارک شام را ببین. تو هم سارا برو به کارهایت برس.

کمی دیر وقت بود که آیدین حکیم خان همراه یوسف و یاکمن برای صرف شام آمدند و از این که دیرکرده بودند. بسیار پوزش خواستند. شب سر شام از اوضاع بد شهرو شورش جیلوها و کمک روس‌ها و دولت‌های دیگر به مسیحیان بسیار صحبت و بحث شد. نسترن خاتون تیپ و قیافه و رفتار و صحبت و شخصیت آیدین حکیم خان را بسیار برازنده دیده و پسندیده بود و صبح روز بعد هنگام بدرقه آن‌ها از آیدین حکیم خان خواست که سلام مخصوص او را خدمت مادرشان ترکان خاتون و پدرشان نصیرالدوله برساند و باز هم به دیدن آن‌ها بیاید. از آن روز به بعد هرچند گاه آیدین حکیم و سارا هم دیگر را در کاروانسرا و یا در کوشک ساران در حضور نسترن خاتون می‌دیدند و چند بار هم آیدین حکیم خان همراه با پدر و مادرش به دیدار آن‌ها آمدند و ترکان خاتون مادر آیدین آن‌ها را برای صرف نهار به منزلشان دعوت کرد. کم کم در اثر دیدار و صحبت بین

آیدین و سارا محبت و عشق جاری شد و نسترن خاتون که شاهد صحبت و طرز رفتار و نگاه آن‌ها به هم بود. با توجه به اوضاع و سن بالای خود بسیار علاقمند بود که سارا که حالا هفده سالش شده بود ازدواج کند و در صورت فوت او تنها و بی‌کس نماند از این رو از دوستی و روابط عاشقانه آن دو بسیار خرسند بود. بیشتر وقت‌ها بخصوص در روزهای ابری و بارانی که با سارا کنار هم در اطاق نشیمن به صحبت و گلدوزی می‌نشستند از آیدین تجلیل و تعریف می‌کرد و او را مرد جوان تحصیل کرده از خانواده خوب و اصیل و مناسب برای ازدواج می‌دانست و بطور غیر مستقیم موافقت خود را با ازدواج سارا با آیدین حکیم ابراز می‌کرد. اما اوضاع خوب نبود و روزگار، روزگار تیره.

۲

عصر روز شنبه اولین روز آبانماه بود، که بازیل نیکتین سر کنسول دولت روسیه در اورمیه همراه خانمش به دیدار سارا آمد. آمدن خانمش همراه او شاید شکل و جنبه غیر رسمی و دوستانه‌ی این دیدار بود. اما علاوه بر خانمش یک کشیش ارتدوکس بنام پیمن و آلکسی منشی کنسولگری همراه آن‌ها بودند. بر بالای سمت راست کالسکه‌اش پرچم بزرگ روسیه را با نشان دولتی نصب کرده بودند و علاوه بر کالسکه ران یک افسر و پنج سرباز مسلح سوار بر اسب در اطراف و پشت سر کالسکه به عنوان محافظ در حرکت بودند و یک سرجوخه مسلح هم کنار کالسکه ران نشسته بود. این اولین بار بود که بعد از سه بار اظهار تمایل و در خواست نیکتین، سارا پذیرفته بود که با او دیدار کند. نزدیک به چهار سال از آمدن و پناهنده

شدن جیلوهای آشوری در حوالی سلماس و ارومیه و دو سال از شورش وخودسری آن‌ها و همین طور حمله به روستا و کشته شدن پدرش امیرخان و عمه نرگس و جمعی از اهالی روستا می‌گذشت و در این مدت نه تنها اوضاع آرام نشده بود بلکه بر شورش و خودسری و کشتار و تاراج جیلوهای شورشی و کردها به سرکردگی اسمعیل آقا سمتگو افزوده شده بود. سارا اوضاع را درک کرده و اطلاع داشت که جیلوهای آشوری با حمایت سربازان روس و نمایندگان دولت‌های انگلیس و امریکا و فرانسه به یک توافق ضمنی در خصوص حاکمیت جیلوها بر شهر و منطقه رسیده‌اند. فقط مبارزین ملی و محلی و مردم غیر آشوری و نیروی‌های ترکیه عثمانی عامل و مورد اصلی ناراحتی و ترس و نگرانی آن‌ها هستند. حکومت محلی بی‌اختیار و بدون توان و قدرت بود و از حکومت مرکزی هم اقدامی صورت نمی‌گرفت. فقط تحرکاتی از جانب تبریز و گروه‌های دمکرات محلی در کار بود که باعث ترس سران شورشی و دولت‌های حامیشان شده بود و برای همین چندی بود که اقدام به نوعی حکومت نظامی و شهربندان کرده بودند از بعد از ظهر هر روز یک ساعت مانده به غروب آفتاب از مردم وامانده فلاکت زده شهرکسی حق نداشت که در کوچه و خیابان دیده شود. تنها در خانه‌ها و محل‌های خاصی با اجازه پست‌های بازرسی که آن‌ها هم جیلو بودند می‌توانستند حضور داشته باشند و در این میان کاروانسرای یوسف بهترین محل برای دیدار گروه‌های خارجی و عده‌ای از مستشاران نظامی سوئدی و فرانسوی و چند تاجر گرجی و لهستانی بود.

وقتی کالسکه نیکتین در خیابان شنی باریک که ازهر دو طرف با ردیف درختان سنجد و اقاقیا و چنار و سپیدار پوشیده شده بود آرام به در اصلی کوشک ساران نزدیک می‌شد.گروهی از اهالی به خصوص مردان جوان روستا که از حضور کالسکه و سواران نظامی روس بدگمان و نگران شده بودند با تفنگ و تپانچه و قمه و تبر و هر چه که یافته بودند به دم در باغ و اطراف آن ریختند. کدخدا که از آمدن کنسول روس خبر داشت. آن‌ها را آرام کرد اما نخواست که پراکنده شوند. چون خودش هم از دیدن چند سوار مسلح همراه کالسکه نگران شده بود. برای همین از آن‌ها خواست و گفت که در بیرون و درون و اطراف باغ آرام اما آماده بمانند و چنانچه اتفاقی بیفتد فورا اقدام کنند.کالسکه نیکتین بعد از ورود به باغ که دو مرد کاملا مسلح در بزرگ باغ را به روی کالسکه و همراهانش گشوده بودند در کنار حوض بزرگ مقابل پله‌های عمارت ایستاد. چند تفنگچی در ایوان کنار ستون‌ها ایستاده بودند. نیکتن در حال پیاده شدن نگاه که کرد دید که بر پشت بام ساختمان کوشک هم چند تفنگچی کمین کرده‌اند. دچار هراس شد اما نخواست بروز دهد. تعللی کرد و کنار کالسکه ران و سربازی که برایش در کالسکه را گشوده و به احترام ایستاده بود درحالی‌که کلاهش را مرتب و دستی به لباس‌هایش می‌کشید نگاهی دقیق به اطراف انداخت و بعد از کسب اطمینان از خانمش و دیگران خواست که پیاده شوند. سارا در لباسی رسمی‌که کت و دامن بلند مشکی با پیراهنی سفید که یقه آن را با نوار نازک اطلس سیاه گره پروانه‌ای کوچک زده بود و در حالی که حیدر به شدت مراقب او بود در بالای پله‌های ایوان به پیشوازشان آمد. نیکتین بر خلاف انتظار در چشم سارا چندان مرد پرصلابت و قوی نیامد در قیافه و

صورتش دغدغه و نگرانی و ترس به آشکارا پیدا بود و می‌شد حدس زد که مرد تحصیل‌کرده و آگاه از مسائل و اوضاع و احوال جهان و سیاست‌ورزی زیرک است. اما شجاع و پرشهامت نیست. نیکتین با نگاهی به اطراف و ضمن پاسخ به خوش آمد گویی سارا گفت:

- دوشیزه سارا می‌بینم که خیلی احتیاط می‌کنید. و شاید هم مردم، بله درسته، شنیده‌ام مردم به خصوص مردم روستایتان شما را خیلی دوست دارند

سارا لبخندی زد و در پاسخ گفت:

- چاره نیست جناب کنسول با وضعی که هست باید هم احتیاط کنیم. البته مردم و اهالی ساران لطف دارند. بفرمایید خیلی خوش آمدید.

- می‌بینم همانطور که گفته‌اند هستید

- چطور هستم؟

- زیبا، تیز هوش و زیرک و حاضر جواب

- شما لطف دارید

سارا این را گفت و به طرف خانم نیکتین و دیگر مهمانان رفت و ضمن احوال‌پرسی و خوش‌آمدگویی تعارف و دعوت کرد که داخل عمارت بروند. در تالار پذیرایی نسترن خاتون پیر در پیراهنی تیره خاکستری با شال سیاهی انداخته به شانه که نشان از عزاداری و دلتنگی او از مرگ خواهر و برادزاده و مردم روستایش را داشت. روی مبل گردویی با روکش سبز زیتونی تیره نشسته بود. نیکتین بعد از احوال پرسی با او و معرفی همرانش نگاهی دقیق به اطراف به وسائل و مبلمان، چلچراغ و گچبریها ونقش و نگارهای تالار انداخت، چشمش در دیوار روبرویش بالای اجاق دیواری

به تابلو بزرگ نیم تنه سارا همان تابلویی که یاکمن کشیده بود افتاد. نزدیک رفت لحظه‌ها آن را تماشا کرد و بعد در حالی که کار یاکمن را تحسین می‌کرد برگشت رو به سارا کرد و گفت:

ـ پس تابلو معروف سامانچی قیزی (دختر کاه فروش) اینه کار فوق العاده ایست. اما شما سامانچی قیزی هستید!؟

سارا با تبسمی‌کوتاه در حالی که کنار عمه‌اش نسترن خاتون ایستاده و منتظر نشستن نیکتین بود گفت:

ـ مردم خواستند که تابلوی مرا سامانچی قیزی بنامند. اگر به اسم دیگری هم صدایم بزنند اعتراضی نمی‌کنم

ـ اوه بله. شنیده بودم اما نمی‌دانستم که این همه به مسائل و عقاید مردم علاقمند و احترام قائلید

این جملات را با نگاهی حاکی از تحسین گفت، رفت، کنار خانمش نزدیک کشیش پیمن نشست. خدمتکارها شروع به پذیرایی کردند چای و شرینی آوردند و بعد از صرف چای و شیرینی و تعارف‌های معمولی و صحبت از مسائل جاری و روزانه، نیکتین رو به سارا کرد و به جای روسی به زبان فرانسه گفت:

ـ می‌دانید آمدن من به این جا به خاطر مسائل مهم مربوط به شما و اوضاع شهر است. اگر شما مایلید و دوست دارید که دیگران متوجه مسائل شما نشوند. می‌توانیم به زبان فرانسه و در گوشه دیگر تالار به طور خصوصی با هم صحبت کنیم.

سارا به نسترن خاتون که کنارش نشسته بود نگاه کرد و بعد گفت:

ـ نه من نگرانی و مشکلی ندارم و مایلم که شما هر طور که راحتید صحبت بفرمایید. البته عمه من درس خوانده و اهل کتاب هستند و به زبان فرانسه آشنایی کامل دارند و اگر موافق باشید من مایلم خانم شما و جناب اسقف و آقای منشی سفارت هم در جریان صحبت ما قرار بگیرند.

نیکتین خنده کوتاهی کرد و در حالی‌که در صندلیش جابه‌جا می‌شد. دستی به سبیل‌هایش کشید. چهره‌ای سفید، موهایی بور و چشمانی روشن داشت و در لباس بهاری کت و شلوار کرم و پیراهن سفید و پاپیون قهوه‌ای بسیار برازنده دیده می‌شد. نگاهی به خانمش کرد و بعد سرش را پائین انداخت و چشم بر گل‌های قالی دوخت و بعد از فکر و تاملی عمیق رو به سارا کرد و با قیافه وکلامی بسیار جدی و سرد و سخت گفت:

ـ دوشیز سارا مایلم بدانید که آمدن من به این جا به منزل شما با همراهانم بخاطر حفظ حرمت شما بوده و باز مایلم بدانید که من به خاطر سه موضوع و امر بسیار مهم برای این مذاکره غیر رسمی آمده‌ام.

صحبتش را قطع کرد و سرش را بلند کرد و چشم در صورت و چشم‌های سارا دوخت تا نشان تاثیر و انعکاس صحبتش را ببیند. سارا کمی مضطرب و عصبی و نگران به نظر می‌رسید. نیکتین با همان حالت در حالی که چشم در چشم سارا دوخته بود ادامه داد:

ـ قصد ما در این مهمانی و دیدار خصوصی و خانوادگی و مذاکره غیرر رسمی اعلام خواست و تصمیم دولت روسیه، مقامات شهر بخصوص انجمن موقت اداره و تامین امنیت شهر و خواست و تصمیم عالی جناب سرژ نماینده تام الاختیار سراسقف اعظم کلیسای ارتدوکس روسیه است. اما من شخصا مایلم این مسائل در این دیدار و گفتگوی دوستانه در جمع

مهمانان حل شود. عالی جناب پیمن نماینده و فرستاده ویژه جناب سرژ سراسقف اعظم و نماینده کلیسای ارتدوکس روسیه هستند. شکایت اهالی شهر تفلیس و خانواده مادری شما، موجب نگرانی کلیسای روسیه شده. عالی جناب آمده‌اند تا از نزدیک با شما صحبت کنند. من هم صحبت‌هایی دارم البته جناب منشی کنسولگری یادداشت برنمی‌دارند ولی شاهد و ناظر این گفتگو و اعلام و هشدار ما به شما خواهند بود.

سارا که سایه نگرانی بر چهره‌اش نشسته بود. نگاهی به صورت نسترن خاتون انداخت. سایه نگرانی را در چهره عمه پیرش نیز را دید. کمی تامل کرد و بعد پرسید:

- موضوع چیست، چه شکایتی، چه مسائلی؟

- شما، موضوع شما هستید دوشیزه سارا

نیکتین این را گفت و نگاهش را با رنگ و حالت خاصی در صورت سارا دوخت و بعد ادامه داد:

- شما به دلیل تولد در تفلیس از مادری گرجی تبعه و شهروند روسیه هستید و در خصوص شکایت اهالی و خانواده شما و خواست سر اسقفی، کنسولگری موظف به حمایت و حفظ جان شما و بازگرداندنتان به تفلیس است و در خصوص هئیت وکمسیون موقت اداره شهر که من هم به عنوان نماینده دولت روسیه در آن حضور و شرکت دارم به دلیل آشنایی شما به چند زبان و محبویتی که در میان اهالی غیر مسیحی منطقه دارید. بسیار مایل و اصرار به همکاری داریم. دوشیز سارا من و کنسولگری تاحدودی از عقاید و طرز فکر و خواست شما با خبریم و می‌دانیم که با گروه‌هایی از دمکرات‌ها و ملی گرایان و مخالفین حضور خارجیان در اورمیه وایران

تماس و تمایلاتی دارید و از همکاری وکمکتان در پناه دادن پناهندگان و زخمی‌ها، بخصوص سربازان فراری روس و دیگرکارهای پنهانتان باخبریم و از روابط خانواده شما با خانواده نصیرالدوله و جریان دوستی و عشق و صحبت و شایعه امکان نامزدی و ازدواج شما با جناب آیدین حکیم خان پسر نصیرالدوله هم مطلعیم. البته یقین داریم که این اخبار شایعه‌ای بیش نیستند و به دلیل تعلق شما به یک خانواده مسیحی و مقام و شان تقدیس شده شما به عنوان یک دوشیز مسیحی کلیسای ارتدوکس تفلیس هرگز چنین ازدواجی صورت نخواهد گرفت و ما شدیدا با آن بنا بخواست کلیسای روسیه مخالف و در صورت نیاز از آن ممانعت خواهیم کرد. البته خود شما به تعصب و شدت اعتقاد مردان گرجی طایفه خودتان واقفید و بی شک همیشه هم مواظب و مراقب خودتان هستید. شوخی نمی‌کنم با مردان مسلحی که همیشه و هر جا مراقب شما هستند و از باغ و خانه‌تان مراقبت می‌کنند. چنین برداشت کردم اما شما باید بدانید و مطمئن باشید بعنوان دوشیزه تقدیس شده کلیسای تفلیس تا زمانی که حدود تقدسی خودتان را نشکسته‌اید برای همه عزیز و مقدسید و کسی حتی فکر تعدی به شما را نمی‌کند و به عنوان تذکر در خصوص موضوعی دیگر، مایلم بدانید که کنسولگری روسیه در اورمیه چیزی کمتر از کنسولگری روسیه در بیت المقدس ندارد و ما قصد داریم. همانطورکه اراده‌مان را در جنگ هم نشان داده‌ایم از مردم نسطوری مسیحی کلدانی و آشوری حمایت کنیم و در این موضوع و تصمیم، دولت‌های فرانسه و انگلیس و امریکا با روسیه هم رای هستند و نمایندگانش در اورمیه که در هیئت حضور دارند از این تصمیم حمایت کرده‌اند و می‌کنند.

سارا با لبخندی که بیشتر برای پنهان کردن نگرانی و عصبانیتش بود در پاسخ گفت:

- جناب کنسول خانواده نصیرالدوله از قدیم از گذشته بسیار دور دوست خانواده‌ی ما بوده‌اند. دیدار و صحبت من با جناب آیدین حکیم خان با توجه به دوستی و روابط هر دو خانواده در حضور والدین و بزرگان و جمع اعضای خانواده و با موافقت عمه‌ام بوده. گرچه روابط عاطفی جز مسائل شخصی و خصوصی هر فرد است با این همه مایلم بدانیدکه من در این مورد مطابق سنت و رسم خانواده‌ام عمل کرده‌ام و تصمیم گیرنده اصلی در خصوص دوستی و روابط و ازدواج من، عمه‌ام که بزرگ طایفه و سرپرست من هستند می‌باشد و من مطابق خواست و اجازه ایشان عمل می‌کنم. اما ازپاکی و وقار وکرامت انسانی واخلاقی خودم هرگز عدول نمی‌کنم و به آن چیزی که مقدر شده و موظفم پایبندم و در خصوص مسئله‌ی حمایت کنسولگری روسیه از مردم نسطوری، فکر می‌کنم شما بهتر و بیشتر از همه اطلاع داریدکه در روسیه انقلاب شده و لنین و بلشویک‌های کمونیست بی خدا اکنون حاکمند و سپاه روسیه از جنگ عقب نشسته و در این جا هم در حال پراکندگی و ترک اورمیه هستند

- بله درست می‌گویید، انقلاب شده و دولت تازه روی کار آمده ولی هنوز دستور و سیاستی غیر از این صادر نشده و به ما نرسیده. من از سنت و رسم و رعایت اخلاق در خانواده شما مطلع هستم و احترام نسترن خاتون را واجب می‌دانم و مایلم در آینده در مورد این مسائل با ایشان و شما بسیار صحبت و مشورت کنم و از شما می‌خواهم و دعوت می‌کنم که برای

آشنایی بیشتر با مسائل و صحبت‌ها و اظهار نظرها به جلسه هیئت موقت بیایید و در آن شرکت کنید.

سارا با تعجب پرسید:

-به جلسه هیئت بیایم

-بله.

-چه هیئتی!؟

– هیئت دولت موقت مسحیان آشوری

– هوم، هیات دولت موقت. چه اسمی. آقای کنسول شما بهتر می‌دانید که آن هئیت و دولت غیر قانونیست.

– ولی تمام دولت‌های خارجی تایید وحمایت کرده‌اند

– بله فقط دولت‌های مسیحی اروپایی. جناب نیکتین من در آن زمان به دنیا نیامده و نبوده و ندیده‌ام اما از مرحوم پدرم و همین طور از عمه‌ام و دیگران که اهل این شهر و منطقه هستند و این جا زندگی کرده‌اند، شاهد و ناظر بوده‌اند. پرسیده و شنیده‌ام که قبل از شروع جنگ جهانی و آمدن و هجوم سپاهیان روسیه و دخالت انگلیس و فرانسه و عثمانی و دیگر کشورهای خارجی، این شهر و این منطقه، منطقه آرامی بوده و همه اهالی آن چه کرد چه آشوری و ارمنی مسیحی و چه کلیمی و چه ترک مسلمان و دیگران همه درکنار هم مثل اعضای یک خانواده و یا برادر و قوم خویش در صلح و صفا زندگی می‌کرده‌اند. اما شماها آمدید و اختلاف انداختید. جنگ به پا کردید و اکنون هم از من می‌خواهید که به هیئت بیایم. به هیئت بیایم یعنی از دولت و حاکمیت یک مشت شورشی که به شهر و دیار ما پناه آورده بودند. مردم این ناحیه آن‌ها را پناه و جا و مکان داده بودند و اکنون با

اسلحه شماها شوریده و ادعای حکومت دارند تایید کنم. این جیلوها از کجا آمده‌اند؟ لطفا به من بفرمایید اینها کی هستند؟ به چه حقی در این ناحیه سر به شورش گذاشته‌اند؟   نه من نمی‌توانم بپذیرم. شما از من می‌خواهید که به آن جا بیایم یعنی کار و حاکمیت شورشیان را تایید کنم. یعنی علیه مملکتم، شهر و دیارم، عمه و مردم روستایم اقدام کنم نه آقا نه نکتین که از خشم و طرز فکر و منطق سارا درمانده و مستاصل به نظر می‌رسید و احساس می‌شد که در درون با سارا هم رای و هم فکر است. بعد از شنیدن حرف‌های سارا لحن صحبتش را تغییر داد و با صدای آرام گفت:

– باید در نظر بگیری که جماعت مسیحی این ناحیه حق تاریخی و قانونی خود را می‌خواهند. البته من احساسات شما را درک می‌کنم. می‌دانم که شما از ناامنی و کشته شدن مردم شهر و حمله به روستا و کشته شدن عمه و پدرتان ناراحتید. اما آن حمله به روستای شما و روستا صفرکندی یک اتفاق جنگی اشتباه و یک خود سری بوده. من در مورد آن اعلامیه به تمام زبان‌ها دادم و ناراحتی و تاسف خودم را اعلام کردم و حفظ آرامش و امنیت همه، تمامی‌اهالی را خواستار شدم. من می‌دانم که جناب مارشیمون و آقا پطرس ایللو هم از آن واقعه بسیار ناراحت بودند و هستند و شنیده‌ام که جناب مارشیمون و آقا پطرس چند نوبت فرستاده‌ای را نزد شما فرستاده و عذر خواهی کرده‌اند با این همه اگر شما و عمه‌تان راضی باشید، جناب پطرس حاضرند که به دیدار شما بیایند و از نزدیک و حضورا عذر خواهی کنند. من فکر می‌کنم کمی باید منطقی باشید. از این گذشته، شما اهل تفلیس و از مادری گرجی هستید و شهروند روسیه محسوب می‌شوید.

حفظ سلامتی شما و خانواده‌تان به عهده ماست. شما می‌توانید و باید هم پرچم روسیه را بر بام خانه‌تان بزنید. اگر این کار را بکنید احدی به شما و روستایتان تعدی و تعرض نخواهد کرد. من با خودم پرچمی را به این منظور آورده‌ام.

-نه نیازی نیست، ما نمی‌توانیم پرچم روسیه را بر بام خانه‌هایمان بزنیم. چنین کاری خلاف هویت ماست.

-گوش کنید دوشیزه سارا همان طور که قبلا هم گفتم، من از کارها و فعالیت شما هم با خبرم. از کمک و پناه دادن به فراریان و پناهندگان، از پناه دادن و کمک به سربازان فراری روسیه، از همه چیز. شما خوب می‌دانید که این کارها همه جرم هستند و می‌توانیم علیه شما اقدام کنیم در راه هم که می‌آمدم دیدم با این اوضاع و احوال و آن حمله اتفاقی که افتاده باز شما قصر و باغ و روستایتان را ساخته و آباد کرده‌اید و مزارعتان خوب و سبزند. دیدم کلی گندم و غیره کاشته‌اید. شما برای امنیت و حفظ آن‌ها و مسائلی که قبلا گفتم به کمک و حمایت ما احتیاج دارید

-یعنی پرچم روسیه امنیت می‌آورد !؟

-بله

سارا لبخندی زد وسرش را به تاسف تکان داد. نیکتین که دیگر عصبی وکاملا کلافه به نظر می‌رسید نگاهی به خانمش انداخت خانمش لبخند زنان گفت:

- سارا عزیزم چرا در مهمانی‌هایی که دعوت می‌کنند شرکت نمی‌کنی، باورکن خیلی خوب است که بیایی و با خانم‌ها و آقایان محترم شهر آشنا شوی . ما پنجشنبه عصر مهمانی و ضیافت کوچکی در کنسولگری داریم.

خیلی خوش حال می‌شوم که تو و نسترن خانم را در مهمانی ببینم. من از تو و نسترن خانم دعوت می‌کنم که پنجشنبه به خانه ما در کنسولگر بیایید و در مهمانی ما شرکت کنید.

نیکتین در تایید حرف خانمش گفت:

- بله بیایید من از شما انتظار دارم که فعال باشید مثل قیصر خانم شنیده‌ام که قیصر خانم که یکی از خانم‌های بسیار محترم این شهر هستند چندین بار شما را دعوت کرده‌اند ولی قبول نکرده‌اید. به جلسات رسمی و دولتی هم نمی‌آیید. این درست نیست. من همین الان از شما رسما دعوت می‌کنم. اگر نیایید واقعا متاسف می‌شوم.

سارا با فشار دست نسترن خاتون به طرف او برگشت و نگاهش را بر او دوخت. نسترن خاتون که بسیار ناراحت و نگران به نظر می‌رسید آرام گفت:

- قبول کن

سارا رو به خانم نیکتین کرد و گفت:

- از دعوت شما ممنونم. عمه‌ام می‌فرمایند که اگر دعوتی برای مهمانی باشد حتما شرکت خواهیم کرد.

خانم نیکتین خوشحال گفت:

- متشکرم خوشحال می‌شوم که شما را در مهمانی ببینم یادتان باشد پنجشنبه عصر. البته فردا آقای الکسی دعوت نامه رسمی را خدمت شما می‌آورند.

نیکتین خوشحال از جواب و قبول سارا رویش را به طرف کشیش پیمن که ساکت و متفکر نشسته بود برگرداند و منتظر صحبت او شد. کشیش پیمن که مردی لاغر اندام با صورت استخوانی و ریش سیاه بلند و بسیار

مهربان می‌نمود از جایش بلند شد و با ادب و رفتاری خاصی که معمولا در برابر مقدسین انجام می‌دهند رو به سارا کرد و گفت:

-دوشیزه سارا اجاز می‌خواهم که بگویم که از لحظه‌ای که شما را دیده‌ام دعای مریم باکره مقدس را مرتب زیر لب خوانده‌ام و احساس می‌کنم آن نور خداوند را که در چهره مریم مقدس بوده در چهره شما می‌بینم. من بسیار مفتخرم و مامورم که به شما اطلاع دهم و بخواهم در اولین فرصت، هروقت که تصمیم گرفتید به زادگاهتان برگردید خانواده شما و کلیسای تفلیس خواهان بازگشت شما هستند. شما فرزند و دختر باکره تقدیس شده آن‌ها هستید. عالیجناب سرژ و عالی جناب ایلیا رئیس میسیون ارتدوکس کلیسای روسیه هر دو از من خواسته‌اند که ضمن ابلاغ دعا و احترام آن‌ها به شما بگویم که میسیون و نمایندگی کلیسای ارتدوکس روسیه آماده است تا وسائل بازگشت آرام و امن و راحت شما را فراهم کند.

سارا لبخند تلخی زد و گفت:

- متشکرم پدر. من قصد بازگشت و رفتن به تفلیس را ندارم. من هنوز عزادارهستم. احساس می‌کنم که این جا به من نیاز دارد. این جا کسانی را دارم که گذشته و تبار و امید من هستند و من به آن‌ها متعلقم.

-ولی شما به کلیسا تعلق دارید

-کلیسا هم به مردم تعلق دارد و برای مردم است

-بله برای هدایت مردم است

-من هم یکی از همین مردم هستم

-دخترم خداوند و مسیح نظر لطف برتو دارند در پناه کلیسا قرار بگیر

-من در پناه خداوند هستم ولی نمی‌توانم به کلیسا برگردم

-کلیسا مامن و خانه توست

-نه مامن و خانه من از این جا میان همین مردم است. و نمی‌توانم کشته شدن مردم بی گناه را ببینم و نادیده بگیرم

-شما کافرها را بی گناه می‌گویید

- من آن‌ها را هم وطن، هم خون، برادر و خواهر و ملت خودم می‌دانم، همه آن‌ها که کشته شده‌اند.

- دوشیز سارا امیدوارم متوجه موقعیت و صلیبی که به گردن دارید باشید.آن صلیب صدها سال است که فقط به مقدسین تعلق دارد و شما هم تقدیس و انتخاب شده و از مادری مقدس هستید.

- پس اجازه بدهید مثل آن‌ها عمل کنم.

سارا این را گفت و برافروخته درحالیکه چشمانش پر از اشک شده بود از جایش بلند شد و رو به کشیش پیمن کرد و با کلماتی شمرده و لحنی جدی گفت:

- جناب پیمن به عالی جناب سرژ و عالی جناب ایلیا بفرمایید که سارا و یا به گفته شما دوشیزه (باکره) سارا گفت: کلیسای من میان مردم است. من این جا می‌مانم و به آن چه خداوند خواسته و مقدر شده و من باید عمل کنم، عمل می‌کنم. بفرمایید.

بعد برگشت و چشم بر آتش اجاق دیواری دوخت کشیش پیمن سری به احترام خم کرد و صلیب بر سینه کشید. مسیو نیکتین که نمی‌توانست تحسین خودش را از رفتار و شجاعت و صحبت و عقاید سارا پنهان سازد با شنیدن آخرین جمله و کلمات سارا بخصوص جمله (مقدر شده) که انعکاس و معنای دیگری از بعد مذهبی داشت و می‌دانست که برای کشیش

پیمن مفهومی بسیار گسترده دارد و بسیار مهم و تعیین کننده است. فهمید که مذاکره به آخر رسیده و تمام است و باید بروند. نگاهی به خانمش و دیگران انداخت و همگی از جایشان بلند شدند. کشیش پیمن که بسیار تحت تاثیر سارا قرار گرفته بود مرتب بر سینه صلیب می‌کشید و سر خم می‌کرد. بانگاه و اشاره نیکتین او هم آماده رفتن شد. نسترن خاتون که حال دگرگون و روی برگرداندن سارا دید بلند شد و دستی به نوازش به شانه سارا کشید و همراه با سارا از مسیو نیکتین و خانمش و دیگران به خاطر تشریف آوردنشان تشکر وآنها را تا پای پله‌های ایوان بدرقه کرد.

٭٭٭

فردای آن روز در فاصله دو ساعت از هم، دو فرستاده، یکی الکسی منشی کنسولگری روسیه که دعوت نامه رسمی وکتبی کنسولگری برای شرکت در ضیافت عصر پنجشنبه را آورد و تحویل داد و رفت و بعداز او نزدیک ظهر فرستاده اعتماد الدوله فرماندار که حاج امیر تومان افشار نیز همراه او بود با کالسکه فرمانداری آمد. حاج امیر تومان که از افراد سر شناس و از خانواده‌های خوش نام شهر بود و با اعتماد الدوله فرماندار و نیکتین کنسول روس دوستی و روابط حسنه داشت. گویا به توصیه نیکتین و مشورت و صلاح دید فرماندار برای دیدار و راضی نمودن سارا برای شرکت در مجلس خاصی که قرار بود روز چهارشنبه آینده در ساختمان حکومتی تشکیل شود، آمده بود. سارا نمی‌دانست که اصرار آنها برای شرکت او در آن مجلس برای چیست؟ آیا به خاطرگذشته او و خانواده مادری او و حساسیت کلیسای ارتدوکس روسیه نسبت به سرنوشت و حرمت اوست و یا بخاطر مصائب پیش آمده، بخصوص حمله به دهکده ساران و کشته شدن عمه و

پدر اوست که موجب سرافکندگی و ناراحتی سران گروه‌های مسیحی و دولت‌های حامی آن‌ها شده بود و آن‌ها در صدد رفع کدرت و دلجویی از او هستند و یا نیرنگی در کار است می‌خواهند او را جزیی از خود معرفی کنند و از نفوذ و محبوبیت او و خانواده او میان برزگان و روحانیون و عامه مردم مسلمان ترک محل و اعتماد آن‌ها به او و خانواده او استفاده کنند. چرا که هنوز یاد کمک و خدمت و محبت عمه نرگس و پدرش امیرخان که از لحاظ فکری میان جوانان و نواندیشان شهر بخصوص میان گروه‌های ملی گرا و دمکرات نفوذ زیادی داشت در خاطر مردم شهر بود. وقتی حاج امیر تومان که در گذشته از کمک و حمایت پدر نسترن خاتون بسیار بهرمند شده بود همراه منشی دیوانی فرمانداركه حامل نامه ودعوتنامه بود وارد شد. نسترن خاتون نتوانست تعجب خودش را پنهان کند با لحنی سرشار از تعجب گفت:

-جناب امیر تومان قدم رنجه فرموده‌اید. آفتاب از کدام سمت طلوع کرده و چه شده که یاد ما افتاده‌اید؟

حاج امیر تومان مردی بود تقریبا چهل ساله با قدی متوسط صورتی گرد و چشمانی سیاه با دماغ بزرگ که لباس خاکستری به تن و کلاهی فینه به سر داشت و بسیار آدم آداب دان و شرمگین به نظر می‌رسید با تبسمی حاکی از شرمندگی گفت:

- شرمنده‌ام نسترن خاتون، کم و پیش از مسائل و اتفاقات و مصائبی که برای شما و خانواده محترم و روستائیان شما پیش آمده با خبرم و از روزی که شنیده‌ام باورکنید بسیار غمگین و ناراحتم، خداوند روح بهرام خان و روح نرگس خاتون و امیرخان را شاد و قرین رحمت کند. می‌دانم پیش از

این باید خدمت می‌رسیدم. برادرم حاج امیر منظم هم قصد داشت برای هم دردی و تسلیت خدمت برسد. اما اوضاع را که می‌بینید و خودتان در جریان مسائل هستید. والا ارادت و دین ما را به شما و خانواده محترم مخصوصا خدا بیامرز بهرام خان پدرتان خوب می‌دانید. اما اوضاع اصلا خوب نیست. این جیلوها با حمایتی که روس و انگلیس و دیگران از آن‌ها دارند دیگر خدا را بنده نیستند. امروز صبح جلسه‌ای در فرمانداری در حضور جناب اعتمادواله با جناب نیکتین کنسول روس که گویا دیروز این جا مهمان شما بوده و با جناب مستر شید نماینده امریکا و آقا پطروس ایللو داشتم. بسیار در مورد شما و خانواده شما و دوشیزه سارا و سواد و شخصیت و چیز دانی ایشان که موجب حیرت و تحسین همگان است صحبت شد و همه از حوادث و مصائب پیش آمده به خانواده شما بسیار متاسف بودند. جناب اعتمادواله و جناب نیکتین رسما در حضور همه بر حفظ امنیت و جان و مال شما و بخصوص دوشیزه سارا تاکید داشتند و به آقا پطروس چند بار تاکید وتذکر دادند. من هم معتقدم شما از موقعیت پیش آمده استقبال و استفاده کنید. اگر خودتان نمی‌توانید حتما سارا خانم در مجلسی که روز چهارشنبه تشکیل خواهد شد و بعدها هم در صورت امکان در جلسه‌های دیگر شرکت کنند. باور کنید کمتر خانواده‌ای از موقعیت شما برخورداراست.

نسترن خاتون پرسید:

-چه موقعیتی جناب امیر تومان؟

-توجه همه، توجه حکومت، کلیسا و مهمتر از همه کنسولگری روسیه. من جای شما بودم پرچم روسیه را بر سر باغ و خانه و دروازه ده می‌زدم و در امنیت و آرامش به سر می‌بردم.

سارا که کنار نسترن خاتون ساکت نشسته و گوش می‌داد پرسید:

-کدام پرچم را جناب امیرتومان، پرچم سرخ را و یا آبی سفید و سرخ را؟ مطلع هستید که در روسیه انقلاب شده و بلشویک‌ها روی کار آمده‌اند. پرچم سرخ بر افراشته‌اند و سپاهیان روس هم در حال ترک منطقه هستند.

-ولی هنوز هستند.

-دارند می‌روند.

-تا کی بروند. دوشیزه خانم، انقلاب هم شده باشد آن‌ها هنوز هستند و نفوذ دارند بهتره توصیه مرا بپذیرید.

نسترن خاتون گفت:

-از توصیه و توجه شما ممنونم جناب امیر تومان بی شک شما با نیت خیر این توصیه را می‌فرمایید ولی من نمی‌توانم این کار را بکنم و به سارا و دیگران هم اجازه‌ی این کار را نمی‌دهم. من و شما از مسائل دنیا وگردش زمانه با خبریم، امروز آن‌ها هستند. فردا و یا سال دیگر که رفتند آن وقت چه؟ نه جناب امیر تومان بهتر است همین طور که هستیم باشیم.

-من هم همین منظور را دارم و امروز که همراه جناب رحمت الله خان معتمد الوزرا منشی دیوانی خدمت رسیده‌ام به همین منظور است، که از موقعیت استفاده کنید

-بر بام خانه‌مان پرچم روسیه را بزنیم

-نه

-پس چی؟

-با حکومت، با هیئت امنیت شهر و غیره مرتبط شوید. مثل همه در مهمانی و جلسات شرکت کنید.

-جناب امیر تومان من دیگر خیلی پیرم توان کار زیاد را ندارم. البته تا نرگس خاتون خدا بیامرز زنده بود. همه کارها بعهده او بود. به همه چیز می‌رسید در مهمانی و جلسات شرکت می‌کرد، مهمانی می‌داد خود شما هم باید بیاد داشته باشید. دعوت می‌شدید اما حالا نه من توان دارم و نه اوضاع اجازه چنین کارهایی را می‌دهد. مردم این همه گرسنه و آواره و درمانده آن وقت ما بیاییم در مهمانی یا جلسه شرکت کنیم و یا سور و مهمانی دهیم. من که شرمم می‌آید.

-ولی تشکیل یک مجلس مهم برای رسیدگی به همین چیزها، یعنی برقراری امنیت و آرامش و کمک به مردم است. حالا کسانی به منظوری دیگر مهمانی می‌دهند آن بماند. من هم با شما موافقم. در این اوضاع احوال مجلس سور به منظورهایی و بده بستان سیاسی برگزار کردن خوب نیست.

-چرا این مسائل را به فامیلتان قیصر خانم نمی‌فرمایید. شنیده‌ام. هم با کنسولگری‌ها در ارتباط است هم با جیلوهای مسیحی و هم با کردها. هفته پیش گویا اسمعیل آقا سیمتگو مهمان خاص ایشان بوده‌اند

-بله من هم بودم. مجلس خوبی بود

-هم طرب بود و هم سیاست

-بله شما که قیصرخانم را می‌شناسید. زن سیاستمداریست. پیش از هر چیز به فکر مسائل و منافع خودش است. این روزها در این اوضاع و احوال بیشتر نگران پسرانش است مخصوصا پسر کوچکش حسین خان، تلاش دارد که با کمک آبولانس لژیون فرانسوی او را به سویس و یا فرانسه بفرستد.گفتم که همه بفکر منافع خودشانند. شما هم باید بفکر منافع

خودتان باشید و از موقعیتی که با وجود دوشیزه سارا دارید استفاده کنید. باور کنید من صلاح خانواده شما را می‌خواهم.

-چه بکنیم؟

-ببینید به عقیده من کمی‌باید هوشیار بود. چند روزیست که کاپیتان کراسی وآقای کاریو فرستادگان جنرال دیسترویل نماینده تام الاختیار قشون انگلیس به اورمیه آمده‌اند و روز چهارشنبه جلسه و یا مجلس بسیار مهمی با نمایندگان گروه‌ها و معتمدین شهر و نمایندگان دولت‌های خارجی در اورمیه در ساختمان حکومتی با حضور جناب اعتمادالدوله حاکم برگزار خواهد شد. لابد می‌دانید وگرنه باید به اطلاع برسانم که بنا به تصمیم دول اروپایی تمام مسائل منطقه از گرجستان تا عراق و ایران و هند درید قدرت و تصمیم جنرال دیسترویل است و تصمیم گیرنده و همه کاره اوست. این را جناب نیکتین هم تاکید کردند.

-مگر سیاست روسیه و اوضاع جنگ در دنیا تغییر نکرده

-بله ولی هنوز سیاست همان است و همه کارها دست جنرال انگلیسیست. جناب معتمدالوزرا هم خوب می‌دانند که حتی انقلاب در اروپا هم اتفاق بیفتد باز سیاست همان است و انگلیسی‌ها در راس آن قرار دارند. من پیشنهاد می‌کنم اگر خود شما نمی‌توانید دوشیزه سارا که بیشتر منظور نظر هستند. شرکت کنند.

معتمدالوزرا که نسبت به امیر تومان جوانتر بودند و تا آن لحظه ساکت نشسته و گوش می‌داد. وارد صحبت شد و در حالی که نامه اعتمادالدوله حاکم را به نسترن خاتون می‌داد گفت:

-همانطور که جناب امیرتومان فرمودند. قرار است مجلس بسیار مهم و بزرگی با شرکت نمایندگان کلیه گروه‌ها و اقشار و بزرگان و معتمدین و نمایندگان دولت خارجی تشکیل شود. جناب اعتمادالدوله شخصا از من خواستند که در معیت جناب امیر تومان خدمت برسم و دعوتنامه را تقدیم کنم.

نسترن خاتون پاکت نامه را گشود و نامه را به دست سارا داد. نامه با مرکب بنفش سیاه به خط خوش نوشته شده بود و از آن‌ها برای شرکت در مجلس روز چهارشنبه دعوت کرده بود. سارا نامه را خواند و بعد گفت: متاسفانه عمه‌ام نمی‌توانند شرکت کنند اما اگر اجازه دادند و موافقت کردند. من حتما شرکت خواهم کرد. حاج امیرتومان خوشنود گفت حتما بیایید و بعد به صرف چای و شیرینی و صحبت در خصوص سایر مسائل، اوضاع و احوال جنگ جهانی، انقلاب روسیه، کمبود آذوقه، نبود امنیت و غیره پرداختند.

۳

چهارشنبه از نیمه‌های شب باران می‌بارید. بارانی ریز و تند. بهار به نیمه رسیده و همه جا سبز و تر و پر طروات شده بود اما هنوز هوا کمی خنک و سرد بود. سارا بالا پوشی گشاد به رنگ کرم روشن که بیشتر به سفیدی می‌زد پوشیده و روسری سفید با حاشیه‌ی زرد نخودی به سرکرده بود و بیشتر به راهبه‌ای سفید پوش می‌ماند اما با وجود آن همه دقت و رعایت باز قامت ظریف و زیبایش در آن لباس گشاد و بلند و سفید هم چنان طناز و چشم نواز و زیبا بود. وقتی وارد مجلس شد. تمام نگاه‌ها به طرف او

برگشت. به توصیه و تاکید نسترن خاتون حیدر با دو جوان مسلح دیگر هم چنان همراه و مراقب او بودند. اگر چه هنگام ورود به تالار ساختمان حکومت. سربازان روس و افراد مسلح جیلو در بیرون از در ورودی و ماموران حکومتی که در داخل ساختمان نزدیک در ورودی مستقر بودند از ورود و همراهی حیدر ممانعت می‌کردند ولی وقتی با اعتراض‌های سارا روبرو شدند موافقت کردند که حیدر او را تا صندلیش همراهی کند و بعد برگردد و سارا از حیدر خواست که بیرون کنار کالسکه منتظر بماند. حضور دختر جوانی به آن سن و سال در آن مجلس کمی که نه بلکه بسیار زیاد مورد تعجب اکثر حضار و اشخاص حاضر در جلسه بود. تعداد خانم‌ها در مجلس اندک بود یعنی بغیر از خانم نیکتین، دکترس میلر از مسیونرهای امریکایی و دو خواهر روحانی لازاریست فرانسوی و ظریفه خانم زن آقا پطروس سردسته نظامی و سیاسی جیلوها و قیصر خانم مالک معروف زن دیگری در آن مجلس حضور نداشت. خانم نیکتین به استقبالش آمد و ضمن احوال پرسی و خوش آمد گویی دست او را گرفت و خواست که نزدیک و کنار او بنشیند. اگر چه سارا از نزدیکی و صمیمیت با او پرهیز داشت و عمل و رفتار او و شوهرش را نوعی سیاست بازی مذموم بر نشان دادن تعلق و وابستگی و نزدیکی سارا به آن‌ها می‌دانست اما در آن جو و فضا و در میان آن همه مرد و جماعت جلسه تنها با خانم نیکتین آشنا بود و چاره‌ای نداشت که کنار او بنشیند. اما هنگام نشستن برخلاف خواست خانم نیکتین در سمت چپ او و در بین او و خواهر الیزا از لازاریست‌های فرانسوی نشست. فضای تالار چندان پر نور نبود و صندلی‌ها به موازات طول و عرض تالار بشکل مستطیل در دو ردیف چیده شده بودند و هریک

از جهت و ضلع‌ها را به یک و یا دو گروه از دین و اقوام شهر و منطقه و شخصیت‌های وابسته به آن‌ها اختصاص داده بودند. ضلع شمالی مخصوص نمایندگان گروه‌های خارجی بود. سارا از این که در آن قسمت نزدیک خانم نیکتین می‌نشست چندان خوشنود نبود. بعد از نشستن و صحبتی کوتاه با خانم نیکتین و معرفی خود و آشنایی با خواهر الیزا نگاه که کرد دید مجلس پرشده و تمام افراد و نمایندگان دعوت شده همه آمده و حضور دارند و در جای خود نشسته‌اند در بالا مجلس اعتمادالدوله حاکم نشسته بود و پشت سرش معتمد الوزرای منشی و رحمت الله خان بیات مسئول دیوانی حکومت کنارش نشسته بود و نزدیک به اعتمادالدوله یعنی بین او و نیکتین کنسول روس یک افسر و یک فرد غیر نظامی در لباس فراک رسمی که گمان می‌شد نمایندگان دولت و ارتش انگلیس باشند، نشسته بودند و در حال نگاه کردن و مطالعه نقشه و نوشته و یا گزارشی بودند که انگار تازه به دستشان رسیده بود. در فاصله کمی از آن‌ها نیکتین کنسول روس همراه چند نظامی و بعد آن‌ها مسیو کاژل و هیئت نظامی آمبولانس لژیون فرانسه و بعد از آن‌ها یاکمن با دیگر نظامیان خارجی نشسته بودند که یاکمن تا چشمش به سارا افتاد نیمه خیز شد و با سر سلامی‌داد. در سمت مقابل درست روبروی آن‌ها نمایندگان گروه‌ها و هیئت‌های مذهبی از جمله چند کشیش کاتولیک کلدانی به عنوان نمایندگان کلیسای شرق و بعد نمایندگان کلیسای پروتستان و پرسبیترین و مسیونرهای مدرسه یکشنبه‌های امریکا به همراه دکتر پاکارد پزشک مسیونر و رئیس بیمارستان امریکایی وست منیستر و آقای شید نماینده دولت امریکا و بعد از آن‌ها نمایندگان کلیسای ارتدوکس روسیه نشسته

بودند که سارا کشیش پیمن را در پشت سر عالیجناب سرژ سر اسقف و نماینده تام احتیار کلیسای روسیه و پدر ایلیا نماینده کلیسای تفلیس دید و تا چشم کشیش پیمن به او خورد نیم خیز شد و ادای احترامی‌کرد و پشت سرهم شروع به صلیب کشیدن و دعا خواندن کرد. سارا خنده‌اش گرفت. دست بر روی صلیب زمردین روی سینه اش نهاد و آن را که یادگار مادرش بود و بسیار دوست داشت در میان مشت خود آرام فشرد و بعد روی که برگرداند در سمت چپ در دو ردیف بزرگ و دراز نمایندگان گرجی‌ها و گروه‌های ارمنی و آشوریان فدائی و آشوریها جیلو با ردیف قطار فشنگها بسته بر کمر و سینه نشسته بودند. هیچ کدام اسلحه‌شان همراهشان نبود. پشت سرشان درهای ورودی تالار قرار داشت و در وسط آن‌ها و درراسشان آقا پطرس ایللو و زنش ظریفه خانم با یک مرد غیر نظامی و یک مار و یاروحانی کوتاه قد که می‌شد حدس زد مارشیمون است نشسته بود. سارا تا چشمش به آقا پطرس وزنش افتاد آن‌ها با لبخند و خم کردن سر و بیان جمله‌ای به زبان آشوری به او سلام کردند. سارا با سردی و بیان کوتاه و بریده سلام آن‌ها را گرفت و به سرعت سرش را به سمت و طرف دیگر گرداند در طرف دیگر به درازا در دو ردیف نمایندگان مسلمان گروه‌های ترک آذری وکردها قرار داشتند که در میان کردها کاکاطه را شناخت این مرد چندین بار یدیدن پدرش امیرخان آمده بود و بسیار مرد مهربانی بود و در میان ترک‌های آذری آقای بابا اوف و میرهاشم آقازاده حاجی شیخ الاسلام سید محمد پیشنماز و حاجی فقیه و علامه ارموی و ملاهادی کربندی با جمعی از اعیان و معتمدین شهر نشسته بودند.کمی پائین‌تر از آن‌ها میرزا محمد تمدن و رحمت الله خان توفیق که از دوستان

پدرش امیرخان بودند و دیگر شخصیت‌های محلی و نمایندگان گروهای ملی‌گرا و دمکرات و سایر اقشار از جمله مالکین و تجار و بازاریان و چند کلیمی اهل اورمیه با نماینده کنیسه اورمیه نشسته بودند. اکثر نمایندگان ترک وکردسر به زیر داشتند و با حالتی غریب چون شکست خورده‌ها طوری با روحیه‌ی ضعیف نشسته بودند که سارا از این حالت نشستن و وضع روحی آن‌ها دلتنگ شد و احساس غم کرد. خیلی دلش می‌خواست که میان آن‌ها می‌نشست. سارا همانطور که نگاه می‌کرد نزدیک میرزا تمدن آیدین حکیم خان را دید که به او لبخند می‌زد و سر خم می‌کرد با دیدن او احساس گرمای خاصی در وجودش دوید و با لبخند پاسخ او را داد. خانم نیکتین که کنار او نشسته و ناظر بر نگاه و رفتار او و در آن چند لحظه کوتاه بود. وقتی سلام و لبخند آشنای آیدین حکیم و سارا را دید گفت:

-با جناب حکیم خیلی دوست وآشنا هستید؟

-بله. دوستی و رفت آمد خانوادگی داریم

-چقدر خوب، مرد جوان تحصیل‌کرده وخوبی است

-بله

-گویا خیلی روشنفکر و میهن پرست است

-بله

-به عقیده من اهالی ترک وآذری اورمیه به این چنین نماینده‌ها احتیاج دارند. اما افسوس که تعدادشان کم است و شانس زیادی هم برای حال وآینده ندارند

-ولی خوب فعالیت می‌کنند خیلی دلم می‌خواست من هم میان نمایندگان اهالی ترک وآذری شهر می‌نشستم

سارا وقتی این جمله را گفت. خانم نیکتین متعجب پرسید:

-چرا می‌خواهی میان آن‌ها باشی نه سارا تو ترک مسلمان و اهل اورمیه نیستی بهتره به موقعیتی که داری توجه کنی. حیف توست که جز آن‌ها باشی.

سارا با رنجش خاصی آهی کشید وگفت:

-نه، حیف که میان آن‌ها نیستم. نگاه کنید ببینید این مردم چقدر مردمی‌آرام و صلح دوستند. طوری شرمگین و خجل نشسته‌اند که انگار آن‌ها خارجی و یا شورشی و غریبه‌اند و این خارجی‌ها و دیگران همین جیلوها که از جاهای دیگر آمده‌اند و به این جا پناهنده شده‌اند. اهل و صاحب این جا، این شهر و منطقه هستند.

-سارا جان کمی خوب فکر کن دنیا دارد عوض می‌شود در کشور ما حکومت انقلابی که روی کار آمده، فکر و عقیده و مرام تازه دارد. دنیا را مال همه و مردم دنیا را به پیوستگی می‌خواند و همه را تشویق به انترناسیونال یا چطور بگویم جهان وطنی می‌کند. خوب در اورمیه هم از گذشته ارمنی‌ها و آشوری‌ها و دیگر مسیحی‌ها بوده‌اند آن‌ها هم حق دارند.

-بله همه حق دارند اما نه با شورش و جنگ و تاراج و کشتار، ای کاش می‌شد به همه شما خارجی‌ها گفت از این جا بروید. بگذارید مردم این منطقه خودشان تصمیم بگیرند

-همین کار را می‌کنند. امروز این جلسه برای همین است اما تو نیاید ماها را مقصر بدانی.

-ولی تا خارجی‌ها دخالت نداشتند. اوضاع این چنین نبود. نیروهای خارجی آمدند و با خود جنگ و تاراج و ناامنی آوردند.

-یعنی آن‌ها بروند اوضاع درست می‌شود

-نمی‌دانم ولی من دخالت خارجی‌ها را خوب نمی‌دانم. نگاه کنید ببینید این انگلیس‌ها، فرانسوی‌ها و روس‌ها این جا چه می‌کنند. خوب شما خانم کنسول هستید و باید باشید اما بقیه چی؟ نه من تردید دارم.

-ولی سارا دنیا در جنگ است، اگر کشور ما به رهبری صدر لنین ترک جنگ نمی‌کرد. شاید جنگ تا سال‌ها ادامه می‌یافت. حالا جنگ در دنیا و در این ناحیه هم در حال تمام شدن است و این جلسه برای همین است. خارجی‌ها همه بزودی می‌روند و تو هم باید بروی.

-نه من اهل این جا هستم می‌مانم

-نمی‌توانی سارا. حرف مرا گوش کن کمی هوشیار باش نمی‌توانی یعنی نمی‌گذارند این جا بمانی. تو باید برگردی به تفلیس. من جای تو بودم هر چه زودتر حتی برای مدت کوتاهی هم شده از این جا می‌رفتم و بعد از آرام شدن اوضاع در وقت مناسب برمی‌گشتم.

سارا مات و متحیر از حرف‌های خانم نیکتین که احساس کرد نوعی هشدار دوستانه و خیر خواهانه برای اوست گفت:

-ولی من نمی‌توانم، آخه چرا باید من از این جا بروم؟

-فکر کن تو کی هستی سارا؟

خانم نیکتین این جمله را گفت و چون جلسه شروع می‌شد لبخند زد و صورتش را برگرداند و سارا متغییر از حرف‌های او در فکر فرو رفت. جلسه با سخنان کوتاه اعتمادالدوله حاکم که تاکید بر حاکمیت دولت و یک پارچگی کشور و نگرانی از ناامنی و اغتشاش و خودسری گروه‌ها و دخالت خارجی‌ها و قتل و غارت بود شروع شد او به کمبود آذوقه و نبود امنیت

برای کشت بخصوص کشت دیم بهاری بدلیل ناآرامی چند سال اخیر اشاره کرد و نگرانیش را از بروز فاجعه و مشکلات دیگر در منطقه اظهار داشت و همه را به چاره‌اندیشی و پرهیز از کینه جویی و برخورد و به دوستی و همزیستی دعوت کرد. وقتی صحبتهای اعتمادالدوله حاکم با کف زدن و ابراز احساسات حاضرین تمام شد. سارا امیر تومان وبرادرش امیر منظم را دید که در سمت دیگر اعتمادالدوله در ردیف دوم نشسته بودند. سخنران بعدی کاپیتان کراسی افسر انگلیسی و نماینده ارتش بریتانیا بود که جلسه هم به همین منظور تشکیل شده بود یعنی آشنایی با او و شنیدن سخنان و سیاست تازه ارتش و دولت انگلیس.

کاپیتان کراسی که چشمانی سبز و زرد برجسته تیله مانند و قامتی درازو تن لاغر داشت. فردی بسیار سرد و بی روح می‌نمود و به چهره‌اش هم که خیره می‌شدی نمی‌توانستی حالت و احساس او را بفهمی و دریابی. او با همان چهره و تیپ سرد و بی روح خود برخاست و با کلماتی سرد و بی روح شروع به صحبت کرد. میرزا یوسف خان لسان الحضور معلم مدرسه امریکایی معرفت مترجم سخنان او بود. کاپیتان کراسی با شرحی از اوضاع جهانی شروع به صحبت کرد و از جنگ در عرصه جهان و اوضاع و آینده جهان بخصوص کشورهای اروپایی و دیگر کشورها جهان و از تصمیم و سیاست کشورهای اروپایی بخصوص انگلیس صحبت کرد. اما هیچ اشاره‌ای به اوضاع شهر اورمیه و منطقه بطور روشن نکرد و هیچ پاسخ روشنی به سوالات و خواسته مردم وگروه‌های مسیحی و مسلمان نداد. گویا هنوز تصمیم وسیاست روشنی در خصوص مسائل منطقه گرفته نشده بود و یا او بی خبر بود و یا این که نمی‌خواست آن را بگوید و برملا کند. فقط

تنها مسئله و موضوعی که به آن تاکید داشت. حمایت از مردم مسیحی منطقه و حفظ وضع موجود و انتظار بود و برای همین نه کسی و گروهی را تائید کرد و نه رد. بعد از سخنرانی او آقای کاریو مستشار مالی ارتش بریتانیا که مردی کوتاه قد با صورت گرد و سر طاس و نسبتا خوش رو بود و کاپیتان کراسی را در این ماموریت همراهی می‌کرد شروع به صحبت کرد و بطور غیر مستقیم از تصمیم دولت و ارتش بریتانیا در کمک به نیروهای مسیحی گفت و تاکید کرد که با توجه به اوضاع جنگ و منطقه. ستاد ارتش بریتانیا مستقر در منطقه تدارکات لازم را برای انتقال و استقرار آشوریان و جیلوهای آواره و فراری چه در ایران و چه در ترکیه در نزدیکی‌های همدان و کرکوک و موصل و بغداد را فراهم کرده و درصورت نیاز و برهم خوردن تعادل و نظم فعلی منطقه آن‌ها را کوچ داده و در اردوگاهای مناطقی که تعیین شده است مستقر خواهد کرد وگفت تنها و بزرگترین مشکل در حال حاضرکمبود آذوقه است و ما در حال حاضر مشغول جمع کردن گندم و جو و سایر مواد غذایی و انتقال آن‌ها به کرکوک و موصل هستیم. همین جملات آخر آقای کاریو علت مسافرت و تصمیم آن‌ها را فاش ساخت و همه فهمیدند که علت آمدن آن‌ها علاوه بر بررسی اوضاع و تهیه آذوقه امکان انتقال مسحیان آشوری و جیلو به کرکوک و دیگر مناطق در آینده است و این سیاست در حقیقت اینده‌ی نامعلوم مردم آشوری و ارمنی و جیلو منطقه را نشان می‌داد و می‌شد حدس زد که باید در انتظار و خامت اوضاع در آینده نزدیک بود. بعد از پایان سخنرانی آقای کاریو از پیچ پیچ و گفتگویی که میان حضار در جریان بود می‌شد شنید که هیچ یک از گروه‌ها چه گروه‌های مسلمان و ملی شهرو منطقه که حضور آن‌ها را نوعی

فریبکاری و سیاست بازی حدس می‌زدند و تاکید بر هوشیار بودن داشتند و چه گروه‌های مسیحی آشوری و رهبرانشان مارشمیون و آقا پطروس هم که پی به تصمیم آن‌ها برده بودند اخم کرده و نگران با افراد کناریش صحبت می‌کردند. بعد از کمی‌تنفس به ترتیب نخست نیکتین کنسول روسیه شروع به صحبت کرد و در صحبت‌هایش با توجه به اوضاع منطقه سیاستمدارانه تاکید بر بی‌طرفی روسیه در مسائل منطقه نمود اما تاکید کرد که روسیه ناگزیر به حمایت از اتباع کشور روسیه و دولتهای متحدش است. بعد از او آقای بیات مسئول دیوانی و نماینده وزارت خارجه و امور مرزی وکمرکات دولت ایران در منطقه شروع به صحبت کرد که وی از مشکلات مردم شهر و منطقه و مشاهدات خود گفت و به معاهده‌های بین المللی در بی‌طرفی دولت ایران و مشکلات اقوام و گروه‌های مذهبی منطقه اشاره کرد. بعد از او آقا پطرس ایللو به سخنرانی پرداخت و بر حق قانونی و تاریخی ملت آشوری در منطقه اشاره کرد وگفت:

– ما حق حداقل یک دولت خودمختار در منطقه را با توجه به اسناد تاریخی داریم اما حال که اوضاع و سیاست چنین است و ما سال‌هاست با مردم ترک آذری وکرد هموطن و هم ولایت هستیم و کنار هم با همزیستی و مدارا زندگی کرده‌ایم. باید آن‌ها بخصوص مردم ترک آذری کتبا این را بخواهند و بنویسند که مایل به مدارا و همزیستی با مردم آشوری هستند و در این مدت از طرف آشوری‌ها زیانی به آن‌ها وارد نشده و ما ملت پیوسته آشوری کلدانی و جیلو مسئولیت عمل کرد گروه‌های خود سر را بعهده نمی‌گیریم.

این سخنان آقا پطرس موج همهمه و اعتراض را میان حضار جلسه بخصوص نمایندگان ترک آذری و اعضای دولت و حکومت محلی ایجاد کرد. وقتی همهمه‌ها فروکش کرد. سارا دید که هیچ عکس العمل و اعتراضی نشد و کسی به اعتراض و پاسخگویی برنخواست. ناراحت و دگرگون در حالیکه با نوک انگشتان بر روی میز می‌زد تا توجه همه را جلب و اجازه صحبت و سوال را بگیرد رو به آقا پطرس کرد وگفت:

-مردم ترک آذری مسلمان حتما می‌نویسند که با شما همشهری و همزیستی و دوستی داشته‌اند و شما هم امنیت آنها را فراهم کرده‌اید. اما آیا شما هم می‌نویسید که تمام این جنگ و خونریزی و تاراج‌ها توسط چه کسانی انجام شده؟

آقا پطروس سرخ شده و ناراحت از سوال سارا گفت:

-گفتم که گروه‌های خودسر

-این گروه‌های خودسر کی هستند. چه کسانی آنها را مسلح کرده و مسئولیت آنها با کیست؟ اگر با شما نیست و شما نمی‌شناسید لابد سپاه روسیه و یا انگلس آنها را مسلح کرده و مسئولیت آنها هم بعهده آنهاست.

-نمی‌دانم

-پس این مردان مسلح آشوری که در شهر می‌گردند و راه‌ها را بسته‌اند. این گروه‌هایی که به خانه‌ها و به روستاها هجوم می‌برند و قتل و غارت می‌کنند. گروه‌های خود سرند و شما نمی‌دانید و نمی‌شناسید و ظریفه خانم را هم که با چندگروه مسلح آشوری جیلو به روستاها حمله می‌کند خودسر است و شما نمی‌شناسید

آقا پطرس که انتظار این نوع برخورد و سوال‌ها را نداشت نگاهی به زنش ظریفه خانم کرد و سرخ شده و خشمگین وگفت:
-دوشیزه سارا من از اتفاقی که به روستای شما و مرحوم پدر و عمه و مردم روستای شما افتاد متاسفم آن واقعه یک اشتباه بود.
-ولی مسئولیت آن باکیست؟ اگر با شما نیست لابد با روسیه و انگلیس است وگرنه او (اشاره به ظریفه خانم) یک خودسر است
-نه او خودسر نیست. ایشان عضو کمیته ملی خودمختاری ملت آشور است.
-پس کمیته مسئول است و چون اسلحه گرفته و به کشتار دست زده و از طرف نیروهای روسیه وانگلیس حمایت شده غیر قانونی وشورشیست و بعنوان یک فرد خودسر شورشی گناهکارو مسئول کشتارهاست وباید محاکمه شود
وقتی سارا این جمله راگفت نیکتین کنسول روس با اعتراض گفت:
-دوشیزه سارا لطفا
آقا پطروس درمانده و عصبی نگاهش را به زنش ظریفه خانم دوخت و ظریفه خانم خشمگین در حالی که از جای خود بر خاسته و با صدا بلند شبیه به فریاد سارا راخطاب قرار می‌داد و گفت:
-تو به چه جراتی این حرف‌ها را می‌زنی، تو کی هستی؟
سارا در حالی‌که روسریش را روی سرش مرتب می‌کرد. نگاه سرشار از انزجار خود را به او دوخت و بعد رویش را برگرداند و آرام اما با صدای رسا و موثر که در گوش تمام حاضران جلسه طنین انداخت گفت:

-من آن فرد انتخاب شده‌ام که مقدر بود و باید به این جا به این جلسه می‌آمدم و به شما و دیگران این حرف‌ها را می‌گفتم و هشدار می‌دادم. بدانید همه را روز دادرسی است و خداوند بهترین دادرس است.

این جملات را گفت و لحظه‌ای ایستاد و چشمانش را بست. کف دستانش را بر هم نهاد و مقابل صورتش یعنی چانه و دهانش گرفت و سرش را خم کرد و زیر لب دعا خواند کلماتش چنان انعکاس تاثیرگذاری داشت که تمام حضار را به سکوت و تائید کشاند و در حالیکه روحانیون و جمعیت ترک مسلمان حاضر در جلسه صلوات می‌فرستادند اسقف سرژ که متوجه ابراز احساسات و حمایت گروه‌های ترک مسلمان شده بود با پدر ایلیا متاثر از حرف‌های سارا همراه هیئت مذهبی کلیسای ارتدوکسی بلند شده و بر سینه صلیب کشیدند و این عمل آن‌ها تاثیری بسیار عمیقی بر مجلس نهاد و نشان از حمایت آشکار و پی چون و چرای کلیسای روسیه وتفلیس از سارا بود. سارا نگاهی تشکر آمیز به آن‌ها کردو نشست و سر به زیر افکند. نمی‌دانست چطور و چگونه بدون فکر و نیت قبلی دست به اعتراض زد و آن حرف‌ها را گفت. اما از عمل خود راضی بود و احساس می‌کرد که آن تنها کاری بود که در دفاع از مردم شهر و بیان حقیقت و خون‌های ریخته شده می‌شد کرد. آقاپطرس که احساس می‌شد در یک محاکمه غیر مستقیم اما علنی محکوم شده آرام رفت و کنار زنش ظریفه خانم نشست. سکوتی بهت‌آور وسنگین بر جلسه حاکم شده بود انگار آن چه که باید انجام می‌شد، شد و دیگر موضوعی در کار نیست. اکثر حضار حتی گروه‌های آشوری جیلو نگاهشان به سارا بود. نیکتین کنسول روسیه و هیئت

انگلیسی نگران از جو جلسه نگاهی به اعتمادالدوله کردند و اعتمادالدوله چند تک سرفه کرد و بعدختم و پایان جلسه را اعلام داشت وگفت:

-جلسه خوبی بود و امید که دوستی و همکاری میان همه همشهریان عزیز را بیشتر بکند . خوب جلسه تمام است و وقت صرف چای وشیرینی و بحث و گفتگو و آشنایی است. بفرمایید خانمها وآقایان. انشالله که روزهای خوبی درپیش است

با پایان یافتن جلسه سارا بلند شد و از خانم نیکتین و خواهر الیزا خداحافظی کرد و به خانم نیکتین قول داد که فردا در مهمانی کنسولگری خواهد بود. برگشت که برود امیر تومان را دید که کنارش ایستاده. امیر تومان گفت:

-دخترم جناب اعتمادالدوله می‌خواهند شما را ببینند.

سارا همراه امیر تومان نزد اعتمادالدوله رفت. اعتمالدوله که مشغول صحبت با نیکتین و کاپیتان کراسی وآقای کاریو بود. ضمن احوال پرسی و اظهار خوش‌وقتی از دیدن سارا و معرفی او به کاپیتان کراسی و دیگران گفت:

-دوشیزه سارا بسیار ممنونم که دعوت ما را قبول کرده و به جلسه آمدید. شنیده بودم که دختر فهمیده و شجاعی هستی فکر می‌کنم آن چه که می‌خواستی بگویی، گفتی.

-نه عالی جناب آن چه راکه باید گفته می‌شد گفتم

اعتمادالدوله حاکم خندید و بعد پرسید:

-خوب شما که با زبان این‌ها آشنا هستید. مجلس را چطور دیدید و از صحبت‌های این انگلیسی‌ها و دیگران چه نتیجه‌ای گرفتی؟

-فکر می‌کنم آن‌ها سیاست‌مدار و دروغگوهای خوبی نبودند عالی جناب!

اعتمادالدوله خندید و گفت: چطور؟

-هیچ کدام نمی‌خواستند بگویند که برای چه آمده‌اند و هدف و سیاستشان چیست. اما گفتند، گفتند که برای بررسی اوضاع و خرید و تهیه آذوقه و انتقال مسیحیان جیلو وآشوری آمده‌اند. من فکر می‌کنم سیاست قبلی آن‌ها عوض شده و نگرانند بخصوص با انقلاب روسیه از خلایی که در منطقه بوجود آمده نگرانند.

اعتمادالدوله سری تکان داد وگفت: آفرین، آفرین

بعد پرسید:

-فکر می‌کنی چه می‌شود و چه باید کرد؟

-نمی‌دانم حضرت والا اما فکر می‌کنم اوضاع بدتر بشود و باید مراقب همه چیز بود.

-مراقب همه چیز؟

-بله مراقب خانه‌ها و زندگی به خصوص آذوقه منظورم آرد وگندم و خودمان

-خودمان!؟

-بله خودمان منظورم سرمان

اعتمادالدوله خندید و گفت: بله فهمیدم سرمان

سارا احترامی کرد و گفت:

-اگر اجازه بفرمایید من باید برگردم. عمه‌ام تنهاست و فکر می‌کنم الان بسیار نگران باشند.

اعتمالدوله گفت:

-بله البته استدعا دارم که سلام مخصوص مرا خدمت عمه فخیمه محترمتان نسترن خانم برسانید امیدوارم باز شما را در مجلسی دیگر ملاقات کنیم

سارا گفت: امیدوارم

برگشت از نیکتین وکاپیتان کراسی و دیگران خداحافظی کرد و دید که عالیجناب اسقف سرژ ودیگران در آن نزدیکی منتظر او هستند سارا در حالیکه صلیب گردنش را در میان دست خود گرفته بود نزد آنها رفت و چند قدم مانده ایستاد و با خم کردن سر و خواندن دعا به اسقف و همرانش سلام و احترام کرد. عالی جناب اسقف سرژ با لبخند و محبت جواب سلام و احترام سارا را داد وگفت:

-دخترم سارا چقدر خوشحالم که تو را می‌بینم. خداوند محبت و برکتش را به تو داده. تو همانطور هستی که می‌گفتند و من حدس می‌زدم. عیسی مسیح حامی‌تو باشد.

سارا صلیبی برسینه کشید و تشکر کرد. اسقف سرژ یک قدم نزدیکتر آمد و با صمیمیت گفت:

-دخترم شنیدی که وضع چیست؟ ما به زودی از این جا خواهیم رفت. تو هم بهتره تصمیمت را بگیری وآماده شوی. کلیسا منتظر توست. فکر می‌کنم آن چه که مقدر بود و تو باید انجام می‌دادی، انجام داده‌ای و آن چه را که باید با زندگی در میان مردم می‌آموختی، آموخته‌ای حالا زمان برگشتن به تفلیس به کلیسا و نزد خانواده‌ات است.

سارا دوباره سر خم نمود و احترام کرد وگفت:

-بله پدر

بعد اجازه خواست که برود. اسقف سرژ با دست صلیبی در هوا کشید و دعایی خواند و به کشیش پیمن اشاره کرد که سارا را تا دم در همراهی کند و گفت:

-برو دخترم بدان که خداوند و مسیح همیشه حامی منتخبین خودش است و آن‌ها را تنها نمی‌گذارد و کلیسا هم همیشه حامی و پشتیبان توست اما یادت باشد باید به خانه‌ات کلیسا برگردی برو.

سارا دوباره تعظیم کرد و برگشت و در حالیکه پدر پیمن همراهیش می‌کرد به طرف در راه افتاد از مقابل گروه گرجی‌ها که می‌گذشت آن‌ها همه به احترام ایستاده و با شوق و ذوق نگاهشان را بر صورت او دوخته زیر لب آرام دعا می‌خواندند و بر سینه صلیب می‌کشیدند و از مقابل آشوری‌ها و جیلوها که می‌گذشت آن‌ها هم با احترام به او می‌نگریستند چشمش به آقا پطرس که افتاد با خم کردن سر خداحافظی کرد. آقا پطرس هم که از حضور و وجود و شخصیت و رفتار او وامانده بود. سری به احترام خم کرد. نزدیک در خروجی گروه‌های ترک آذری مسلمان شهر در حال خروج بودند سارا ملاهادی و حاجی شیخ الاسلام و سید محمد پیشنماز را که دید روسریش را روی صورتش پائین کشید و سلام داد. شیخ الاسلام همراه ملاهادی ایستاد و دست بر سینه نهادند و جواب سلام سارا را هر دو با محبت و احترام دادند و به همراهان خود اشاره کردند که به ایستند. تمام افراد و شخصیت‌ها و نمایندگان ترک و مسلمان شهر در حالی که با محبت و احترام به سارا می‌نگریستند ایستادند و منتظر ماندند که سارا خارج شود. سارا با خم کردن سر و تشکر از آن‌ها از تالار بیرون آمد. بیرون در محوطه

سبز حیاط فرمانداری نزدیک در آیدین حکیم خان که منتظر او بود. وقتی او را دید پیش آمد و گفت:

-سارا من می‌خواستم تو را ببینم. باید با تو صحبت کنم

سارا که از دیدن او شاد اما شرمگین و سرخ شده بود گفت:

-آیدین خان الان نه. الان باید زود برگردم، عمه‌ام نگران‌ه

-فردا چطور؟

-فردا به کنسولگری دعوت شده‌ایم

-به کنسولگری روسیه؟

-بله، شما هم اگر بودید، خیلی خوب می‌شد

-سعی می‌کنم باشم.

آیدین حکیم این را گفت و با سارا خداحافظی کرد و به تالار برگشت. حیدر با محافظین کنار کالسکه بیرون نزدیک در فرمانداری منتظر او بودند. سارا از پدر پیمن که تا کنار کالسکه او را همراهی کرده بود تشکر و خداحافظی کرد و سوار شد و به باغ ساران برگشت.

۴

روز پنجشنبه از ظهر سارا برای مهمانی کنسولگری روسیه آماده می‌شد. تلی و فرنگیس کمکش می‌کردند. نسترن خاتون نشسته بود و تماشا و انتخاب می‌کرد. سارا هر لباسی را که می‌پوشید نسترن خاتون که مراقب بود تا ظرافت و زیبایی او زیاد جلوه نکند، به بهانه‌ای نمی‌پسندید. یکی را خیلی بلند و دیگر را خیلی کهنه و از مد افتاده و یکی را بخاطر رنگ و بعضی را بخاطر کوتاهی دامن و یا آستین و یقه باز و مناسب نبودن برای

مهمانی شب نمی‌پسندید و رد می‌کرد و می‌گفت نه در بیار زیبا و یا مناسب نیست. تقریبا سارا تمام لباس‌های رسمی و مخصوص مهمانیش را پوشیده بود و نسترن خاتون با وجود تحسین و لبخندی حاکی از برازندگی و زیبایی آن‌ها در تن سارا. نپسندیده و به بهانه‌ای رد کرده بود. سارا آخر سر وامانده و خسته میان لباس‌ها که دور برش ریخته بود نشست و گفت:

پس چه بپوشم؟

تلی و فرنگیس هر دو خندیدند. سارا ناگهان یاد کمد و لباس‌های عمه نرگس افتاد. می‌دانست که تعدادی از آن‌ها را به سفارش عمه نرگس از سن پطرزبورک آورده‌اند. رو به فرنگیس کرد وگفت:

- برو کمد لباس‌های عمه نرگس را باز کن.

تلی متعجب گفت:

-می‌خواهی لباس‌های نرگس خاتون را بپوشی. نه، نمی‌گذارم آن‌ها را بپوشی

نسترن خاتون گفت:

-چرا نه تلی، بگذار بپوشه، آن‌ها مال اوست، او اگر نپوشه پس به چه دردی می‌خورند

-ولی خانم

-تلی، اگر نرگس خاتون الان زنده بود و آن‌ها را در تن سارا می‌دید خیلی خوشحال می‌شد. برو فرنگیس برو کلید را بردار و در کمد نرگس خاتون را باز کن.

سارا شاد دوان دوان با فرنگیس بالارفت. تلی نتوانست دوام بیاورد او هم پشت سرآن‌ها آمد. وقتی درکمد نرگس خاتون را باز کردند. بوی عطر او

همراه با یاد او در فضا پیچید. سارا یک لحظه ایستاد، از یاد و خاطره عمه نرگس ومهربانی او اشکش گرفت. آهی کشید و نشست و اشک‌هایش را که به گونه‌هایش غلتیده بود پاک کرد. تلی که او را در آن حالت دید نهیب زد:

-بلند شو این جا که برای گریه نیامده‌ای؟ در این بعد از ظهر روح و خاطره نرگس خاتون را کدر نکن. بلند شو، بلندشو لباس‌ها را ببین.

سارا اشک‌هایش را پاک کرد و بلند شد و لباس‌های کمد را بدقت نگاه کرد وگشت و از میان آن‌ها کت و دامنی به رنگ ارغوانی تیره که بیشتر به سیاهی می‌زد با پیراهنی به همان رنگ و کلاهی از همان پارچه را انتخاب کرد و به فرنگیس گفت:

- این‌ها را می‌خواهم

تلی گفت:

-این کت دامن با پیراهن و کفش و کلاه را سال‌ها پیش تاجر باشی آقای یف به سفارش نرگس خاتون از سن پطربورک آورد. اما کوچک بود و به تن نرگس خاتون نشد . لباس گران قیمتی است.

بعد کمک کرد و سارا کت دامن را که مطابق مد آن زمان دامنی بلند و کتی با یقه پهن و دکمه‌های گرد و درشت داشت پوشید و کفش‌ها را جیر سیاه پاشنه بلند را به پا کرد و کلاه را به سرنهاد و تور آن را روی صورت و چشم‌ها منظم کرد و همراه تلی و فرنگیس پائین آمد. نسترن خاتون و تلی و فرنگیس همانطور زل زده و مات و حیران با لذت نگاهش می‌کردند و هیچ کدام نمی‌توانستند تحسین خود را پنهان کنند.آخر سر نسترن خاتون که از لذت و تحسین زیبایی او اشکش گرفته بود. گفت:

-من هر چه تلاش می‌کنم نمی‌توانم زیبایی تو را پنهان کنم. خداوند تو را چطور آفریده؟ تو چه هستی؟ فرشته‌ای و یا پری هستی و یا چه؟ آخ ای کاش امیرخان و نرگس خاتون بودند و تو را می‌دیدند. این لباس واقعا مناسب و برازنده توست

بعد روکرد به تلی و گفت:

-برو، برو گردنبند مروارید سه رج مرا بیار و تو هم فرنگیس برو اسپند وکندر دود کن. خدا حفطت کند دخترم

بعد از ظهر وقتی در کالسکه نشستند و روانه مهمانی کنسولگری روسیه شدند کمی تاخیر کرده بودند و برای همین دیرتر از همه مهمانان به مهمانی رسیدند. درسر راهشان تلی را مقابل کاروانسرا پیاده کرده بودند و قرار بود شامگاه هنگام بازگشت از مهمانی به کاروانسرا بروند و شب را آن جا نزد تلی و یوسف بگذرانند. در ورودی کنسولگری آراسته و چند سرباز با یونیفرم تشریفاتی شلوار آبی و کت سرخ با یراق‌ها و سردوشی‌های و واکسل‌های برجسته‌ئ سفید کنار در ایستاده بودند وقتی حیدر کالسکه را نگه‌داشت یکی از سربازها نزدیک آمد و در کالسکه را برای نسترن خاتون و سارا گشود و به احترام ایستاد. بعد از پیاده شدن آن‌ها حیدر را راهنمایی کردند که به محل کالسکه‌ها براند و منتظر بماند. مهمانی در تالار پذیرایی کنسولگری در طبقه اول برگزار بود وقتی وارد شدند. خانم و آقای نیکتین به استقبالشان آمدند. سارا بسته هدیه را که گلدانی نقره ای بود به خانم نیکتین داد . خانم نیکتین تشکر کرد و بعد از روبوسی وخوش آمد گویی گفت:

-خیلی متشکرم این جشن علاوه برروز ملی روسیه برای قدردانی از جناب اعتمادالدوله وخدمات ایشان هم است

نسترن خاتون پرسید: برای قدردانی؟

آقای نیکتین گفت:

-بله برای قدرانی. چون ایشان عوض شده‌اند یعنی ماموریتشان تمام شده و دارند می‌روند و ما دیگر ایشان را که دوست خوبی برای ما بودند نخواهیم دید. البته ما هم به زودی خواهیم رفت

سارا پرسید:

-دارند می‌روند. کجا؟

-تبریز و شاید هم تهران. به جای ایشان جناب اجلاالمک آمده‌اند. بله بفرمایید

وقتی وارد تالار شدند همه سرها به طرفشان برگشت و نگاه‌ها به آن‌ها دوخته شد. سارا نگاه کرد دید تقریبا همه افراد سرشناسی که در مجلس دیروز بودند در آن جا حضور دارند. آیدین حکیم با دکتر پاکارد امریکایی و حکیم داود و حکیم افشیلیم خان در گوشه‌ای مشغول صحبت بود. اعتماد الدوله حاکم مستعفی با کاپیتان کراسی و چند تن دیگر نشسته سرگرم صحبت و خوردن و نوشیدن بود. گروه موزیک سپاه روس در یونیفرم سفید در حال نواختن آهنگ آرامی بود و چند زن و مرد روسی و فرانسوی و ارمنی در حال رقص بودند و گروه‌های دیگری از مهم‌آن‌ها در اطراف مشغول صحبت و شادی بودند. سارا احساس کرد در آن اوضاع احوال برگزاری چنین مهمانی و جشنی چندان مساعد نیست و باید علت دیگری داشته باشد. شاید همانطور که آقای نیکتین گفت نوعی جشن خداحافظی

آن‌هاست. چون از مجلس دیروز احساس می‌شد که یک جابجایی در حال شکل گرفتن است و به جای روسیه انگلیس و امریکا قرار می‌گیرند یعنی روسیه کنار می‌رود و آن‌ها به جای او می‌نشینند و برای همین اعتمادالدوله هم عوض شده است در این فکر بود که خانم نیکتین آن‌ها را دعوت به نشستن کرد. قیصر خانم افشار که با گروهی از زنان و مردان در گوشه‌ای نشسته و مشغول صحبت بود تا آن‌ها را دید بلندشد همراه امیر تومان نزد آن‌ها آمد. قیصر خانم زنی لاغر وکوتاه قد وسیه چرده و بسیار مجلس آرا و حراف بود. لباس سفید گلدار وگشاد با کت ماهوت قهوه‌ای به تن داشت و روسری سفید حریر بلندش را زیر چانه گره زده و گردنبند طلای بلندش که تا پائین سینه آویزان بود، فشرده از اشرفی‌های طلای ناب بود. نزد آن‌ها که رسید دستانش را گشود و در حالیکه نسترن خاتون را بغل کرده و می‌بوسید و گفت:

-به به نسترن خاتون، بالاخره چشممان به جمال شما روشن شد. شما کجا و مهمانی کنسولگری روسیه کجا؟ دعوت می‌کنیم به مهمانی ما نمی‌آیید اما این جا!؟

نسترن خاتون گفت:

-باورکنید قیصر خانم این جا هم نمی‌خواستیم بیاییم جناب امیر تومان خبر دارند. آن قدر اصرار کردند که ناگزیر شدیم والا توی این اوضاع احوال چه مهمانی؟ دل و دماغی نیست

-می‌دانم از همه چیز خبر دارم

بعد به طرف سارا برگشت و درحالی که می‌گفت:

-به به این هم دختر زیبای گل سارا

سارا را بغل کرد و بوسید. بوسیدنش اما بوسیدن نبود بادکشی بود که بر صورت سارا چسبید بعد از بوسیدن ادامه داد:

-سارا جان تعریفت را خیلی شنیده‌ام. خیلی دلم می‌خواست ببینمت به به ماشاالله یک فرشته هستی. همه جا صحبت توست. زیبایی و مهربانی و فهم و سوادت زبان زده شده. مخصوصا صحبت‌هایت در مجلس دیروز همه را متاثر کرده در شهر همه اهالی از تو صحبت می‌کنند شدی پشت و پناه ملت. الان چند لحظه پیش از آمدن شما جناب اعتمالدواله با جناب امیر تومان و مستر شید و کاپیتان کراسی صحبت از تو می‌کردند. باید خیلی مراقب باشی دخترم. حیف شد که جناب اعتمالدواله عوض شدند. روس‌ها هم که دارند می‌روند.

نسترن خاتون با تعجب پرسید:

-دارند می‌روند

-بله. بیشتر ازچند ماه و شاید یک سالی این جا نیستند. قشون روس دارد همه جا را تخلیه می‌کند. از این به بعد باید امیدمان کنسولگری امریکا و این جناب شید و نماینده‌های انگلیس باشه. روزگار همینه، سیاست مادر و پدر نداره. یک روز روس‌ها و جناب نیکتین یک روز هم جناب مستر شید امریکایی. خوب بگذریم. نسترن جاتون بگو چطوری برای امیر خان و نرگس خاتون خیلی متاسف شدم. همهٔ ما را داغدار کرد. چه می‌شود کرد عزیزم اوضاع همینه، تو بهتره کمی هوشیار باشی بالاخره باید هوای همه را داشت. مخصوصا که این دختر گلت سارا را که داری باید خیلی فعال و هوشیار باشی

آیدین حکیم که از هم صحبت‌هایش جدا شده بود نزد آن‌ها آمد. قیصر خانم تا آیدین را دید گفت:

-این هم آیدین حکیم خان پسر جناب نصیرالدواله. ماشالله چشم و چراغ همه ماست.

آیدین با همه سلام و احوال پرسی کرد و نزد آن‌ها نشست. تا صرف شام سارا همراه با نسترن خاتون با بسیار از مهم‌آن‌ها هم صحبت شدند کاپیتان کراسی هنگام صرف شام نزد سارا آمد وگفت:

-دوشیزه سارا صحبت‌های دیروز شما بسیار جالب بود. شنیده‌ام مردم شما را خیلی دوست دارند.

سارا گفت:

-مردم محبت دارند

کاپیتان کراسی که چشمان بر آمده و بی‌حالتش بر سردی چهره‌اش افزوده بود گفت:

-بله برای همین ما روی شما خیلی حساب می‌کنیم و امیدواریم شما را زیاد ببینیم.

میسیو کوژل که به آن‌ها پیوسته بود گفت:

-بله دوشیز سارا باید بیشتر فعال باشند

سارا برای این که به حرف‌های آن‌ها پاسخی داده باشد گفت:

-بله سعی می‌کنم

بعد در مورد خیلی از مسائل صحبت کردند. بعد از صرف شام و گفتگو با آقای نیکتین و صرف چای نسترن خاتون به دلیل کهولت اجازه خواست که مرخص شوند.آن‌ها که دیریتر از همه مهم آن‌ها آمده بودند زودتر از

همه با بدرقه نیکتین و خانمش مجلس را ترک کردند. آیدین حکیم هم همراه آن‌ها آمد. و در پای کالسکه هنگام خداحافظی نسترن خاتون از او خواست که سلامش را خدمت مادر و پدرش برساند. آیدین در جواب گفت:

ـ آن‌ها هم خدمت شما سلام داشتند. مخصوصا مادرم و به من سپرده بودند که خدمت شما عرض کنم که اگر اجازه بفرمایید پنجشنبه هفته آینده بعد از ظهر خدمت برسند

نسترن خاتون با چهره گشاد گفت:

ـ منزل خودشان است لطف بفرمایند. شماهم هر وقت خواستید تشریف بیاورید منزل خودتان است. فکر می‌کنم سارا هم از دیدن شما خوشحال می‌شود

آیدین تشکر کرد و آن‌ها سوار شدند و حیدر کالسکه را به طرف کاروانسرا راند.

عروسی

۱

یاسمن‌های خیابان غربی باغ ساران گل‌هایشان افشان با سپیدارها و افراها تمام طول خیابان را پوشانده بودند. کالسکه مهم‌آن‌ها بعد از ورود به باغ و گذر از میان ردیف گل‌های یاسمن و سایه سار درختان، بعد از دور زدن میدان اطراف حوض بزرگ در پای پله‌های منتهی به ایوان عمارت می‌ایستادند و مهم آن‌ها پیاده شده و منتظر می‌ماندند. کالسکه آیدین حکیم خان آخرین کالسکه‌ای بود که با عود و اسپند و چراغ پیشواز و همراهی شد. صبح روز چهارشنبه اولین هفته تابستان بود و جشن ازدواج و عروسی سارا با آیدین حکیم خان با همه تردیدها و دلشوره‌های سارا در جمع کوچک خانواده و فامیل و آشنایان و مردم روستای ساران با احتیاط و به طور خصوصی برگزار می‌شد.

شامگاه جمعه هفته پیش که نسترن خاتون کدخدا، یوسف و تعدادی از ریش سفیدان فامیل را برای مشورت خواست و موضوع عروسی و دلایل ازدواج سارا با آیدین حکیم خان را با آن‌ها در میان گذاشت و از آن‌ها نظر خواست اگرچه همگی از آن خبر شاد و خرسند شدند بخصوص که آیدین حکیم خان را جوانی تحصیل‌کرده و با لیاقت و از خانواده اصیل و همسری مناسبی برای دوشیزه سارا می‌دانستند اما باتوجه به شرایط پیش آمده واوضاع و احوال شهر و منطقه، بیم از آن داشتند که خبر عروسی در آن اوضاع در اطراف شهر و روستا پخش گردد و باعث تحریک مسیحیان بخصوص گرجیها شود و برای همین همگی هم نظر و هم رای با نسترن خاتون صلاح در آن دانستند که عروسی بدون سروصدا و بسیار آرام و پوشیده برگزار شود و از این رو صبح روز چهارشنبه با طلوع آفتاب کدخدا به سفارش نسترن خاتون درهای دروازه ساران را بست و تمام مردان روستا را مسلح کرد و ورود و خروج را ممنوع و بر تعداد تفنگچی‌های افزود و به همه سپرد که شادی و سرور خود را بدون سروصدا درخانه‌ها و درون باغ برگزار کنند و از شعله‌ور نمودن هیمه آتش بر سر کوی و بر زن و پشت بام‌ها و تپه کنار روستا به رسم دیرین بپرهیزند و بخواست نسترن خاتون، کدخدا پسرش ابراهیم را با چند جوان دیگر مامور آماده نمودن هفده گوسفند به تعداد هفده سال سارا برای قربانی و تقسیم گوشت آن میان مردم و هم چنین تهیه و پخت غذا برای مهمانان کرده بود. مردم روستا زن و مرد و جوان و پیر آگاه از اوضاع هر چند که آرام بودند اما شاد و یک دل و یک جان خانه‌ها را رفته و کوچه‌ها را تمیز کرده و با لباس‌های نو در انتهای باغ کنار مطبخ خانه اربابی فرش گسترده بعد از سال‌ها مشغول رقص

و پایکوبی بودند. به غیر از خانواده نصیرالدوله و تعدادی از فامیل سارا یاکمن افسر سوئدی همراه یوسف و تلی آمده بود. یوسف، حیدر را با کالسکه برای آوردن شیخ الاسلام سید محمد پیشنماز برای خواندن خطبه و بستن عقد فرستاده بود.

اما سارا که از صبح لباس سفید عروسی پوشیده و تاج عروسی از مروارید و تور سفید برسر نهاده و خود را برای برای مراسم عقد و عروسیش آماده کرده بود دلش گرفته بود. نمی‌دانست از چه آن همه دلش تنگ و درونش مشوش است. در اطاقش در طبقه دوم عمارت، کنار پنجره ایستاده و چشم بر خیابان و آمدن کالسکه مهمانان دوخته بود. خیابانی که صبح‌ها و عصرهای بسیار، محل قدم زدن و فکر کردن او بود. یاد و خاطره کشته شدن پدرش بدست فرستاده‌های کلیسای تفلیس، حرف‌های نیکتین بخصوص خانمش، پیغام‌های مکرر عالیجناب سژر و کلیسای اسقفی تفلیس و روسیه برای بازگشتن و پیوستن به کلیسا از یک سو و از سویی دیگر دلبستگی و تعلقش به خانواده پدرش و مردم روستا و شهرش و عهدی که با خود و پدر و عمه نرگس و نسترن خاتون بسته بود و هم چنین عشق و علاقه و دلبستگی که به آیدین از همان اولین دیدار یافته بود مشکل و کلاف پیچیده عمرش شده بودند. ماه‌های بهار به آرامش گذشته بودند. در آن چند ماه ساعات بسیاری را در روزهای هفته با آیدین در آن خیابان در سایه سار درختان و در میان عطر دل انگیز شکوفه‌های یاسمن و یاس قدم زده و از عشق و دوست داشتن گفته بودند. اما اکنون دل و جان سارا برافروخته و در تریید و اندوه می‌سوخت. ناآرام وپر دغدغه و مشوش بود و از آینده و اتفاقات آن واهمه داشت و می‌ترسید. از روزی که خود را

یافته و شناخته بود زندگیش در میان حادثه و تهدید و ترس و فرار و گریز گذشته بود و اکنون که می‌خواست با مردی که دوست دارد و عاشقانه به او مهر می‌ورزید، ازدواج کند. باز تشویش و ترس به سراغش آمده بودند و او نگران از آینده و روزهای نیامده به این می‌اندیشید که آیا باز تهدیدها و ترس‌ها و پنهان شدن‌ها خواهد بود باز مجبور خواهد شد به مانند پدر و مادرش بگریزند. پدرش ناگزیر بود اما او چرا؟ هر چه فکر می‌کرد نمی‌توانست علتی برای پنهان شدن و فرار خود پیدا بکند. برای همین هم نمی‌خواست دیگر بگریزد. نمی‌خواست بخواست آیدین به استانبول برود. به پدرش می‌اندیشد و به سرگردانی و جریان اندوهگین زندگی و مرگ او. نمی‌خواست مثل پدرش سرگردان شود و با حسرت و اندوه عشق، عمر به سر برد. می‌خواست همان جا در همان عمارت و باغ که مال او و خانواده او بود میان مردمی‌که به او مهر می‌ورزیدند بماند و زندگی کند. چرا برود، کجا برود؟ اگر این جا برای او آرامش نبود در کجا می‌توانست امنیت و آرامش را پیدا کند. پس باید بماند و می‌ماند چون می‌داند در تفلیس برای او آینده‌ای نیست و اگر باز گردد ممکن است چون مادرش کشته شود، پدرش امیرخان هم به او گفته و سفارش کرده بود که هرگز به تفلیس برنگردد و او حاضر نبود به خاطر رسم و سنت و اعتقاد طایفه‌ای قربانی شود. در چند ماه گذشته اگرچه اوضاع آرام و آرامش و امیدواری میان مردم بیشتر شده بود اما دل و جان او در آن چند ماه اگرچه پر از شور وعشق آیدین حکیم خان بود اما در دغدغه و ترس و تردید گذشته بود. البته آیدین حکیم خان از ترس و تردید و دغدغه‌های اخبر داشت. همان‌طور که نسترن خاتون و دیگران باخبر بودند، اگر چه او هرگز تصمیم برفتن به تفلیس و

بازگشت به کلیسا را نداشت اما از پی‌گیری و تهدید گرجی‌ها هم واهمه داشت. او خوب می‌دانست که رفتن به تفلیس به همراه گروه ارتدوگسی کلیسای روسیه پذیرفتن خواست و آئین آن‌ها یعنی بازگشتن به کلیسا، سفر بی بازگشت است اما ماندن در اورمیه هم همیشه در خطر بودن است بخصوص که دلسپرده آیدین بود.آیدین عقیده داشت که برای مدت یکی دو سال تا آرام شدن اوضاع به استانبول بروند ولی اوضاع عثمانی هم به خاطر جنگ ناآرام و نابسامان بود و معلوم نبود که بتوانند به سلامت خود را به استانبول برسانند. یوسف وتلی هم با آیدین هم عقیده بودند. نسترن خاتون اما راه نجات او را فقط در ازدواج و همراه داشتن شوهر می‌دانست و معتقد بود با ازدواج موضوع تهدید و بازگشت به کلیسا حل و تمام می‌شود. اما با وجود چنان عقیده‌ای همچنان از اقدام گرجی‌ها نگران بود و می‌ترسید بخصوص از خوی انتقام‌گیری آن‌ها آن سان که امیرخان را هم کشته بودند وحشت داشت. سارا با وجود چنین مسائل و واهمه‌هایی بعد از روزها تصمیم به ازدواج با آیدین و ماندن نزد نسترن خاتون و مردم شهر دیارش را گرفته بود و حاضر نشد برای یک لحظه هم عمه‌اش نسترن خاتون و مردم روستا و شهرش را ترک کند و برای هر اتفاقی هم آماده شد. گاه فکر می‌کرد که اگر پدرش و عمه نرگس هم زنده بودند آن‌ها هم او را به این کار و تصمیم تشویق می‌کردند و او دوست داشت که نگهبان املاک و وصایای عمه نرگس و خون پدرش باشد. با این وجود از صبح که بیدار شده و خود را برای جشن عروسیش آماده کرده بود نمی‌دانست چرا آن همه مشوش و نگران بود. وقتی نسترن خاتون به اطاقش آمد و او

را گرفته کنار پنجره دید و فهمید که دلتنگی او چیست. سارا را در آغوش کشید و در حالی که نوازشش می‌کرد گفت:

-دخترم این دلشوره تو از عروسی و تغییر زندگی توست، همه‌ئ دختران وقت عروسی دچار چنین دلشوره و تشویش می‌شوند. شاد باش عزیزم امروز روز شادی و عروسی توست. تو باید از همه بیشتر شاد باشی.

نسترن خاتون اگر چه این حرف‌ها را می‌زد اما پیدا بود که پیرزن خودش هم دل نگران است. تلی که پشت سر نسترن خاتون آمده بود. وارد شد وگفت حاج آقا شیخ الاسلام آمده همه منتظر شما هستند. سارا بلند شد نگاهش را از پشت پنجره به خیابان باریک باغ انداخت و بعد برگشت در حالی که نسترن خاتون بازوی او را گرفته بود و تلی پیشاپیش جلوتر می‌رفت و خبر آمدن عروس را می‌داد از پله‌ها پائین رفتند. پائین کنار پله‌ها آیدن حکیم خان با تبسم و نگاهی سرشار از عشق منتظر اوبود. ساعتی به ظهر مانده بود که شیخ الاسلام مراسم عقد را در حضور تمام اعضا خانواده و ریش سفیدان برگزار کرد و خطبه عقد آن دو را خواند. بعد ازمراسم عقد و صرف نهار تا شامگاه پایکوبی وشادی بود. مردم روستا مراسم رقص و پایکوبی را به صحن مقابل ایوان عمارت آورده بودند و به ضرب و آهنگ طبل و سورنا می‌رقصیدند، سارا هم همراه با آیدین و تلی و یوسف و یاکمن به جمع آن‌ها پیوسته بود و با آن‌ها می‌رقصید و شادمانی می‌کرد. نسترن خاتون نمی‌توانست چشم از سارا برگیرد. اگرچه دلش می‌خواست اوضاع آرام بود و او می‌توانست جشن عروسی مفصلی با حضور بسیاری از آشنایان و فامیل و دوستان و بزرگان شهر و منطقه برگزار کند. اما با توجه به اوضاع منطقه و سن و سال خود، خوش حال بود که اکنون سارا کسی

را کنار خود دارد و اگر برای او اتفاقی بیفتد دیگر تنها نیست. اما چه کسی می‌توانست آینده و عمر ومرگ خود را تصور و پیش بینی کند. تنها چیزی که هست همان زمان و فرصت اندک بودن است و او از این فرصت اندک برای برگزاری عقد و عروسی سارا با شرکت دوستان و فامیل و روستائیان استفاده کرده بود. حقیقت این بود که بعد از سال‌ها غم و جنگ و ترس و ویرانی، آن روز و شب تنها شب و روزی بود که همه کنار هم گردآمده و به رقص و پایکوبی پرداختند و غم‌ها و نگرانی‌هایشان را فراموش کرده و به روزهای دیگر سپردند.

۲

سارا فرار کن، آن‌ها آمده‌اند بلند شو برو تو، خودت را پنهان کن، آن‌ها آمده‌اند، آن‌ها آمده‌اند، آن‌ها این جا هستند.

تلی هراسان، فریاد کشان به طرف ایوان می‌دوید که سارا را خبر کند. سارا که نزدیک نرده‌های ایوان کنار گل‌های شمعدانی روی صندلی نشسته و مشغول مطالعه بود از شنیدن صدای ترس‌آلود و هراسناک تلی نگران بلند شد و به طرف پله‌های ایوان که تلی بالا می‌آمد رفت و با نگرانی دست او را گرفت و پرسید:

-چه شده تلی آن‌ها کی‌اند، از کجا آمده‌اند؟

-همان‌هایی که پدرت را کشتند

-هم آن‌هایی که پدرم را کشتند؟

سارا این را گفت و دست بر نرده‌ها نهاد. چیزی در درونش فرو ریخت. غم و ترسی دیرین با خشمی ناآشنا بر جان و دلش نشست و تمام وجودش را لرزاندند. غم و ترسی که از کودکی می‌شناخت و با آن به سر برده بود. چه آن زمانی که در تفلیس در آن دیر قدیمی در اطاقی کوچک و تاریک شب‌های بسیاری را در تنهایی با غم و ترس به سر برد و چه آن زمانی که پدرش را کشتند و او نالان وگریان بر بالینش نشست. اکنون آن غم و ترس کهنه و آشنای دیرین دوباره باز آمده و بر دل و جانش نشسته و با خشمی ناآشنا تمام عرصه وجودش را در برگرفته بودند. کمی مکث کرد و بعد آرام در حالی که از پله‌ها پائین می‌رفت با صدایی گرفته پرسید:

-کجا هستند؟

-آن جا، پشت پرچین‌های باغچه نزدیک حوض کمین کرده‌اند.

سارا نگاهش را به طرف پرچین‌ها انداخت، قامت خمیده دو مرد تفنگ بدست را پشت پرچین‌های نزدیک باغچه گل‌های کنار خیابان حوض دید که خم شده و خود را پشت پرچین‌های شمشادهای کنار باغچه گل‌ها پنهان کرده و او را نگاه می‌کردند.

اوایل پائیز بود و برگ‌ها تازه شروع به زرد شدن و ریختن کرده بودند. پیش از سه ماه از عروسی سارا می‌گذشت. سارا باردار شده بود و شکمش کمی بالا آمده بود. در طول آن سه ماه با وجود این که بیشتر در عمارت باغی پیش نسترن خاتون و یا در شهر نزد خانواده آیدین به سر برده و سرگرم و گرفتار کارهای شخصی و خانواده بود و کمتر در شهر و روستا رفت و آمد کرده و با افراد و شخصیت‌های خاص محلی دیدار و در مجالس ومهمانی دیده شده بود اما با وجود این پیام‌های مکرر زیادی از طرف

کنسولگری، هیئت ارتدوکس روسیه و جمعیت گرجی‌ها وکلیسای تفلیس برای بازگشت به تفلیس و کلیسا دریافت کرده بود و از سه ماه پیش که ازدواجش با آیدین حکیم خان آشکار شده و سر زبان‌ها افتاده بود پیام‌ها هم تغییر کرده و رو به تهدید گذاشته بودند. آیدین حکیم خان را هم تهدید کرده بودند که خواهند کشت.

نسترن خاتون که صدای تلی را شنیده بود نگران به ایوان آمد و از سارا خواست که برگردد و زود به درون عمارت بیاید. اما سارا توجهی به نگرانی و حرف‌های او نکرد. تلی هم نتوانست جلو او را بگیرد. از پله‌های ایوان پائین رفت. از زیر درخت انار کنار ایوان گذشت و به طرف پرچین‌های کنار باغچه گل‌ها رفت. خسته و ملول بود. می‌خواست حقیقت را بداند و تکلیفش را برای همیشه روشن کند. اگر قرار است او را بکشند. بگذار بکشند. تا کی می‌توانست فرار کند و خود را مخفی سازد. نمی‌خواست دیگر با ترس و واهمه زندگی کند و نمی‌خواست هم چنان هر چند روز، نامه و پیغام و کاغذی دریافت کند و کسی را بپذیرد و پیغام‌های تهدیدآمیز را بشنود. می‌خواست حرفش را به عاملین و فرستادگان آن‌ها و دیگران و همه بزند و نشان دهد که دیگر ترسی از آن‌ها ندارد، تصمیمش را گرفته بود و همانطور که بارها به افراد و اشخاص مختلفی که بدیدنش می‌آمدند و پیغام می‌آوردند گفته بود. می‌خواست به آن دو مرد گرجی هم بزند و بگوید که او مال هیچ قوم و گروه و دین مذهب نیست و به هیچ یک از آن‌ها تعلق و بستگی ندارد. او یک فرد و یک زن آزاد است و می‌خواهد آزاد در ملک و مملکت خود کنار خانواده‌اش زندگی کند. نسترن خاتون با همه پیری سراسیمه نگران پشت سر سارا می‌آمد قصد داشت اگر بخواهند

سارا را بزنند خودش را سپر بلای او سازد و همانطور که پشت سارا می‌آمد ملتمسانه می‌گفت:

-سارا برگرد. نرو دخترم. خدا را آن‌ها برای کشتن تو آمده‌اند.

اما نمی‌توانست جلو او را بگیرد. سارا بی‌توجه به هشدار و خواست او به طرف پرچین‌ها رفت. نزدیک پرچین‌ها که رسید ایستاد و نگاهش را به صورت ونگاه آن دو مرد گرجی کمین کرده پشت پرچینها دوخت. دومرد گرجی بسیار شبیه و عین هم انگار یک نفر بودند. جفت، برادر، دوست و هم سان هم. هیکلی قوی و بلند داشتند، ریشی کم پشت کوتاه با صورتی پهن و گرد و چشمانی برآمده به رنگ سبز زرد بی‌حالت وکلاهی چرکین بر سر، وقتی متوجه نزدیک شدن سارا شدند. مات و متحیر و ترس گرفته هم چنان که او را می‌پائیدند از جایی که نشسته بودند برخاستند. یکی از مردان با صدای لرزان و ترس گرفته به دیگری گفت:

-وینکوری ساراست

دیگری گفت:

-ساکت باش می‌دانم

سارا همان جا مقابل آن‌ها کنار برچین‌ها ایستاد، نگاهش را توی صورت و چشم‌های آن‌ها دوخت و بعد دستانش را گشود و سینه‌اش را فراخ کرد و با صدای گرفته وگریه‌آلودی گفت:

-بله من سارا هستم. شماها اگر بکشتن من آمده‌اید. بیاید مرا بکشید. مردان گرجی شرم زده با گام‌های نامتعادل در حالی که بر سینه صلیب می‌کشیدند چند قدم عقب رفته و گفتند:

-سارای مقدس تو باید برگردی، تو گرجی هستی، تو دختر کلیسای ما هستی، نباید خلاف بکنی و این جا بمانی، اگر برنگردی ما مجبوریم، به ما گفته‌اند که تو را بکشیم اما ما نمی‌توانیم.

سارا گفت:

-ولی من نمی‌توانم برگردم، من دیگر دختر کلیسای شما نیستم

-نه تو سارا دختر مقدس کلیسای ما هستی

-ولی من نمی‌توانم

سارا این را گفت و از میان پرچین‌ها گذشت و به آن دو مرد نزدیکتر شد. مردان گرجی وقتی نزدیک شدن سارا را دیدند شرم زده و هراسان در حالی که با گام‌های کوتاه عقب عقب می‌رفتند بر سینه صلیب کشیدند، برگشتند، شروع بدویدن به طرف انتهای باغ که دیوارش کوتاه بود کردند و در حال دویدن به صدای بلند و فریاد زنان گفتند:

-سارا، سارای مقدس تو باید برگردی، تو دختر کلیسای مایی، رحم کن، کار را بد نکن و برگرد، ما نمی‌توانیم تو را بکشیم.

سارا گفت:

-ولی من نمی‌توانم، نمی‌توانم

در همان لحظه کدخدا و حیدر و دیگر مردان ده که توسط تلی و فرنگیس باخبر شده بودند. تفنگ بدست و دوان دوان سر رسیدند و شلیک کنان سر درپی آن‌ها نهادند. سارا دادکشید:

-تعقیبشان نکنید، بگذارید بروند.

بعد سرش را رو دستانشان گذاشت و به تنه درختی که کنارش ایستاده بود تکیه داد و شروع به گریستن کرد. نسترن خاتون که پشت سرش ایستاده بود. بغلش کرد و گفت:

-بیا برویم دخترم.

غمگین و ملول از سرنوشت و شخصیتی که داشت. برگشت سرش را بر شانه نسترن خاتون نهاد و در حالی که می‌گریست همراه با او به درون عمارت رفت.

ساعتی بعد نسترن خاتون کدخدا و حیدر و دیگر مردان دهکده را خواست و به آن‌ها توپید که چرا مراقب نبوده‌اند که آن دو مردگرجی براحتی وارد باغ شده و پشت پرچین‌ها برای کشتن سارا کمین کنند و اگر تلی نمی‌دید؟ خدا می‌دانست که چه اتفاقی می‌افتاد. بعد از گلایه و تذکر بسیار از کدخدا خواست که افراد بیشتری در همه جای ده و به خصوص اطراف باغ بگمارد. شامگاه آیدین حکیم خان و یوسف که از موضوع با خبر شده بودند به ساران آمدند، کدخدا و حیدر و چند تن از ریش سفیدان هم آمدند و بعد از صحبت و بحث و مشورت طولانی با نسترن خانم به این نتیجه رسیدند که بر ارتفاع دیوارهای ساران بی‌افزایند و مراقبت را بیشتر کنند و هم چنین مصلحت را در این دیدند که سارا دیگر نباید در یک محل و خانه و باغ مشخصی بماند. باید هر چند روز محل اقامتش را عوض کند در شهر گاه در کاروانسرا گاه در منزل نصیرالدوله خانواده آیدین و در دهکده ساران گاه در باغ نزد نسترن خاتون و یا در خانه یکی از اهال ساران به سر برد و همیشه در هرجا مثل گذشته چند تفنگ‌چی همراه با حیدر مراقب او باشند. از آن روز به بعد سارا ناگزیر هر چند روز در یکی ازمحل‌هایی که

فقط افراد خانواده‌اش می‌دانستد و خبر داشتند می‌ماند و روزهای بارداری را با پنهان شدن می‌گذراند.

روزهای بلوا

۱

تلی از صبح روی سکوی سنگی پشت در کاروانسرا نشسته بود و می‌گریست. آن روز، روز آخر زمستان بود. فردا سال عوض می‌شد و بهار می‌آمد. نوروز می‌شد اما کسی دیگر در فکر بهار و عید نوروز نبود. اصلا کسی نمانده بود. جز جنازه‌های پراکنده، درها و دیوارهای فروریخته و خانه‌های تاراج شده و اسیران خسته و شکسته که پای در زنجیر در انتظار اعدام بودند. دیوارهای کاروانسرا بلند بودند و در چوبی بزرگ کاروانسرا با درکوب و گل میخ‌های قهوه‌ای زنگ زده و سوخته‌اش میان دیوارها و پیش درگاهی مثل قابی کهنه می‌ماند و بوی کهنگی و استقامت می‌داد. تلی هم چنان که پشت در روی سکوی کوتاه سنگی دهلیز سرپوشیده نشسته

بود، گوش به فریاد و ناله و صدای گلوله‌ها و دشنام‌ها و گاه صدای پای اسیران و نعل اسب‌ها و ارابه‌ها سپرده بود و می‌گریست. از دو روز پیش که مارشیمون رهبر روحانی جیلوها و همراهانش در نزدیکی سلماس به دست اسمعیل آقا سمتگو و افرادش کشته شده بود. جیلوها خشمگین دست به کشتار و تاراج زده بودند و بعد از دو روز برای ترساندن مردم و قدرت نمایی عده‌ای را که از سلماس و روستاها اسیر گرفته و به اورمیه آورد بودند. بعد از گرداندن در خیابان‌ها به بیرون شهر برده و اعدام می‌کردند. هوا سرد بود و برفی بی‌رمق پراکند و آرام و کند می‌بارید، تلی که نشسته و منتظر بود. هر بار صدای پا و عبور گروهی را با آه و ناله می‌شنید، می‌فهمید که گروه دیگری از اسیران را برای اعدام می‌برند. همراه با صدای آه و ناله اسیران دشنام جیلوهای محافظ بود که معلق در هوا در هر گوش و جانی نفوذ می‌کرد و می‌نشست و می‌گزید. تلی گریان بلند می‌شد و از سوراخ کوچک درز کنار در چشم بر بیرون به خیابان و میدان مقابل کاروانسرا می‌دوخت. نخست چند فرمانده جیلو را می‌دید سوار بر اسب و بعد مردان و زنان وکودکان اسیر را می‌دید که در ردیف‌های دو الی سه و یا چهار نفری که پاهایشان با طناب و یا زنجیر به هم بسته شده بود در صفی طولانی در حالی که جیلوهای مسلح پیاده از هر طرف آن‌ها را کنترل و قروق کرده بودند، شکسته و خراب به سمت دروازه توپراق قلعه می‌رفتند و هنگام گذر بخصوص آن‌هایی که زخمی و یا پیر و بیمار بودند می‌افتادند و اسیران دیگر مجبور بودند آن‌ها را در میان سرما و گل و یخ بلند کنند و با خود بکشند و ببرند وگرنه همان جا با گلوله جیلوها کشته می‌شدند. تلی می‌دید اسیران خسته بودند، زن‌ها و کودکان می‌نالیدند و

مردان زخمی، شکسته و بسته در خود می‌مردند. آن‌ها را از طریق دروازه توپراق قلعه به خارج از شهر می‌بردند. یوسف که صبح برای نجات اسیران گریخته و جان بدر برده، رفته بود از چند نفر شنیده و برای اطمینان رفته و از دور دیده بود که جیلوها در بیرون شهر در گودالی میان باغ‌های نزدیک رودخانه و یا در شیب کنار مصب رودخانه‌های بکشلو و شهرچای اسیران را جمع کرده و به گلوله می‌بندند و بعد از به گلوله بستن اسب‌ها وگاوهای تاراج و ربوده شده را از روی جنازه‌ها و زخمی‌ها عبور می‌دهند. باد بی‌رمق و خسته می‌وزید. برف می‌بارید و تن اسیران زخمی زیر سم اسب‌ها وگاوها له و داغون و متلاشی می‌شد و خون جاری از تن کشته شدگان اسیر با یخ و برف و گل قاطی و جویی از خاک و یخ و خون و برف به طرف رودخانه روان می‌شد و گاه تعدادی از اسیران در اثر ضربه لگد و سم اسب‌ها وگاوها به رودخانه پرت می‌شدند وگاه اسب‌ها وگاوهایی که نمی‌خواستند از روی کشته‌ها و جنازه‌ها بگذرند، رم کرده و می‌گریختند. و چندی دور نرفته با تیر جیلوهای عاصی کشته می‌شدند و جنازه‌شان به روخانه می‌افتاد آن گاه از پشت مه و برف نگاه که می‌کردی می‌دیدی رودخانه سرخ است، رودخانه خون است، رودخانه گاو است و اسب است رودخانه تن متلاشی شده اسیران است، رودخانه رنگ عزای تمام شهر است. باد از روی رودخانه می‌گذشت و بی‌رمق و زخمی به سمت شهر می‌وزید و بوی مرگ می‌آورد. بعد از هر قتل و عام و کشتار و اعدام جیلوهای مسلح با هیاهو پیاده و سواره همراه با ارابه‌ها و اسب‌های تاراج شده به شهر باز می‌گشتند. بارش برف را نشان خیر و شکوفایی و تایید کارشان می‌دانستند و شروع به هیاهو

و شلیک‌های هوایی می‌کردند. یوسف از غم اسیران آن قدر گریسته بود که چشمانش سرخ شده بودند.

نزدیک ظهر که از صداها و رفت وآمدها وکشتارها کمی‌کاسته شد. تلی غمگین بلند شد و به طرف پله‌های خانه راه افتاد. نخست قصد داشت سری به سارا که روزهای آخر بارداریش را می‌گذراند و در بالاخانه منزل آن‌ها دراز کشیده و استراحت می‌کرد بزند و بعد در تدارک ناهار باشد. به فکر شوهرش یوسف هم بود. در حالی که به سمت پله‌های خانه‌شان می‌رفت، نگاه که کرد دید در آن سرما و برف که زمین یخ زده و سفت و سخت مثل سنگ است یوسف با کلنگ مشغول کندن پای کنده درخت خشکیده و ررفتن با آن است. فهمید که تمام کار و حال او از دلتنگی و غم است. در گذشته معمولا در کاروانسرا برای عبور و مرور و آمد و شد مسافران و مراجعه کنندگان باز بود. اما از چند روز پیش بخصوص از روز کشته شدن مارشیمون. یوسف در کاروانسرا را برای در امان ماندن کاروانسرا و مسافران از هجوم جیلوها بسته و صلاح در آن دیده بود که فقط در کوچک تعبیه شده در پائین لنگه چپ در بزرگ و اصلی کاروانسرا که مخصوص آمد و شد اشخاص پیاده بود در صورت نیاز باز و مورد استفاده باشد. البته در آن اوضاع و احوال فقط چهار و یا پنج مسافر در کاروانسرا بود یعنی به جز یاکمن و چند افسر فرانسوی و یک تاجر روس و یک تاجر لهستانی مسافر دیگری نبود. آن‌ها هم منتظر آرام شدن اوضاع برای ترک اورمیه بودند. آمبولانس هیئت نظامیان فرانسوی قصد ترک اورمیه را داشت و افراد زیادی می‌خواستند همراه آن‌ها راهی اروپا شوند. حتی شنیده شده بود که نیکتین کنسول روس که ماموریتش در اورمیه تمام

شده بود به همراه خانواده‌اش قصد دارد همراه هیئت فرانسوی که از راه ارمنستان و گرجستان راهی اروپا و فرانسه بودند. همراه آن‌ها به فرانسه برود و به سارا هم پیغام فرستاده بود که او هم بهتر است که همراه آن‌ها راهی فرانسه شود. یاکمن و یوسف هم صلاح در آن می‌دیدند. اما وضع جسمانی و سنگینی سارا از یک سو و از سوی دیگر گذر و عبور آن‌ها از گرجستان که می‌توانست برای سارا بسیار خطرناک باشد باعث مخالفت نسترن خاتون و آیدین و مانع از همراه شدن سارا با آن هیئت نظامی‌شده بود بخصوص که شنیده بود مسیو کوژل سرپرست آمبولانس فرد معتقد و مذهبی‌ست و رابطه بسیار نزدیک و صمیمانه‌ای با اسقف کلیسای روس و گرجستان دارد و برای همین از همراه شدن با آن‌ها سر بازده بود چون روزهای آخر بارداریش بود برای اطمینان بیشتر و دسترس بودن ماما و طبیبان دیگر علاوه بر آیدیم جکیم خان چند روزی بودکه آمده و در کاروانسرا نزد یوسف و تلی به سر می‌برد و یوسف هم و به دلیل اوضاع بد شهر و حضور او در کاروانسرا درهای اصلی را بسته و کلون پهن و بلند سنگین آن را انداخته و استوار کرده بود..

تلی تازه به پای پله‌های ساختمان منزلشان رسیده بود که صدای در را شنید. کسی بردر کاروان‌سرا می‌کوبید. حدس زد که ملک خوشابه است چون از صبح هربار که از درز کنار در چشم بر بیرون نهاده بود. چشمش به ملک خوشابه افتاده بود که در گوشه میدان مقابل در کاروانسرا کنار دیوار گز کرده و یقه بالاپوشش را بالا برده و لبه کلاهش را پائین کشیده و منتظر بود و هراسان اطراف را می‌پایید.گویی نگران بود نگران چیزی و یا اتفاقی از صبح دو بار آمده و بر در کاروانسرا کوبیده بود اما تلی در را نگشوده بود.

برگشت که به طرف در برود. یوسف را دید که به طرف در می‌رود و آرام به او گفت:

- من باز می‌کنم.

تلی نگران ایستاد. حدسش درست بود. یوسف که در را گشود ملک خوشابه بود، تو آمد و کلاهش را برداشت و پشت در بعد از صحبتی کوتاه به دیوار تکیه داد و منتظر ایستاد. یوسف برگشت وآمد و به تلی که نگران ایستاده بود گفت:

-سارا بیدار شده؟

-نمی‌دانم

-ملک خوشابه می‌خواهد او را ببیند، برو ببین بیدار شده و اگر خواب بود هم بیدارش کن بگو ملک خوشابه به دیدنش آمده، پیغام مهمی با او دارد. برو

-مگر به او گفتی که سارا این جاست؟

-خودش می‌دانست

-از کجا؟

-نمی‌دانم

-تو که این خوشابه را می‌شناسی، می‌دانی که از آن‌هاست

-می‌دانم اما دوست و نمک خورده امیرخان است برو

-ولی..

-ولی ندارد زن برو خیلی مهمه

-پس بگو بیاید تو

-گفتم، قبول نکرد. همان جا می‌خواهد سارا ببیند و حرفش را بزند و برود.

تلی بالا رفت و به سارا که بیدارشده و مشغول عوض کردن لباس‌هایش بود، خبرآمدن ملک خوشابه و قصد دیدار با او را داد. سارا ملک خوشابه را خوب می‌شناخت. او دوست دوران کودکی و مدرسه پدرش بود در گذشته در آن روزهایی که پدرش امیرخان زنده بود ملک خوشابه هر چندگاه به منزل آن‌ها می‌آمد و ناهار و یا شام مهمان آن‌ها می‌شد و ساعت‌های زیادی را با امیر خان به صحبت و ذکر خاطرات می‌گذراند. سارا بلند شد و کتش را پوشید و شال پشمیش را به سر کرد و از تلی پرسید:

-کجاست؟

-پائین پشت در کاروانسرا

-چرا نگفتید بیاید بالا

-گفتیم، نخواست، می‌خواهد تو را ببیند و برود. مثل این که پیغامی دارد

-چه پیغامی؟

-نمی‌دانم. می‌خواهد تو را ببیند و به خودت بگوید

سارا همراه تلی که مراقبش بود. در را گشود و پائین رفت، حیدر که پشت در ورودی کنار پله‌های نشسته و نگهبانی می‌داد. تا سارا دید. بلند شد و گفت:

-خانم نروید. یکی از سران مسیحی آن بیرون است.

سارا تبس می‌کرد و گفت:

-می‌شناسمش آقا حیدر، ملک خوشابه دوست پدرم است. او برای دیدن من آمده. نگران نباش

حیدر در را گشود و نخست خودش بیرون رفت و در حالی که بسیار مراقب بود. در را نگه داشت تا سارا همراه تلی بیرون آمدند. ملک خوشابه تا سارا را دید چند قدم نزدیک‌تر آمد. کمی‌نگران و مضطرب به نظر می‌رسید. انگار عجله داشت، می‌خواست حرفش را بزند و پیغامش را بدهد وبرود. نزدیک سارا که رسید نگاهی به سر و وضع سارا انداخت و بعد در حالی که از نگاه و صدایش نگرانی می‌بارید. با مهربانی و محبت با سارا احوال پرسی کرد وگفت:

-دخترم حالت چطور است؟ می‌بینم بارداری و خیلی سنگین شده‌ای.

-به لطف شما خوب هستم، بله روزهای آخره و خیلی سنگین شده‌ام، شما چطورید، خانواده خوب و سلامت هستند؟

-بله خوبند.

-سلام مرا خدمت خانم برسانید. چرا تشریف نیاوردید تو

-ممنونم دخترم. نمی‌توانم، عجله دارم باید برگردم، از صبح به دنبال تو بودم، به ساران رفتم گفتند آن جا نیستی در منزل جناب نصیرالدوله هم نبودی، فهمیدم باید این جا باشی. برای همین از صبح منتظر بودم، دوبار در را زدم کسی باز نکرد، بالاخره بار سوم یوسف آمد و در را گشود. خدا را شکر که سلامتی

-خوبم.

-دخترم می‌دانی که من دوست و نمک خورده و مدیون خانواده بخصوص مرحوم پدرت هستم و هرگز محبت‌های مرحوم نرگس خانم و مرحوم پدرت امیرخان را که دوست بسیار عزیز من بود فراموش نمی‌کنم و هر چه بتوانم و از دستم بیاید برای خدمت وحمایت از تو انجام می‌دهم.

خودت بهتر از من از وضع و اوضاع با خبری. دیروز عصر با خبر شدم که دستور دستگیری تو آمده و دارند دنبال تو می‌گردند.

–کی‌ها، جیلوها و یا گرجی‌ها وروس‌ها؟

–نمی‌دانم ولی فکر می‌کنم گرجی‌ها و روس‌ها باشند، دستور کلیسا را دارند، خودت بهتر می‌دانی که جیلوها و دیگر مسیحیان هم با آن‌ها همکاری دارند. من از لحظه‌ای که شنیدم در فکر تو بودم و امروز آمده بودم تا ترتیب خروج و فرار تو را همراه گروه فرانسوی‌ها بدهم با خواهر الیزا هم صحبت کرده بودم اما با این وضعی که تو داری فکر نمی‌کنم بتوانی. فکر می‌کنم بهتراست در جای امن دیگری به غیر از این جا پنهان شوی. یک جایی دور به غیر از این جا و باغ، البته بدون این‌ها چون این‌ها، این یوسف و زنش هرجا باشند آن‌ها فکر می‌کنند که تو آن جا هستی. سعی کن تا عصر از این جا بروی، عجله کن چون به این جا حمله خواهند کرد.

–حمله خواهند کرد؟

–بله

–کجا بروم؟

–هر جا که برایت امن باشد، خودت بهتر می‌دانی این شهر دیگر برای تو و شوهرت امن نیست.

–برای هیچ کس نیست.

–بله درست است برای هیچ کس نیست. اما تو مورد نظری و حکم کلیسا در خصوص دستگیریت صادر شده. سعی کن هر چه زودتر جایی پنهان شوی و اگر نتوانستی و اگر دنبالت آمدند و جایی نداشتی برو به کلیسای

انجیلی نزد پدر سونتاک، او نگهت می‌دارد و اگر آن جا هم نتوانستی و یا امن نبود بیا به خانه من پدر سونتاک و آقای یوسف می‌شناسند ولی هر چه می‌توانی زودتر اقدام کن، خدا حفظت کند دخترم، خدا روح امیرخان را از من شاد و راضی کند.

ملک خوشابه صلیبی بر سینه کشید و سری به احترام خم کرد و بعد کلاهش را بر سر نهاد و برگشت و خداحافظی کرد و رفت. سارا همانطور مات و حیرت زده مانده بود از آن چه شنیده بود و وضع نابسامانی که بر شهر حاکم بود دچار وحشت شده بود. یک آن به فکر شوهرش آیدین افتاد. ملک خوشابه گفته بود. شهر برای او هم امن نیست. نگران او شد و آرام به یوسف گفت:

-عمو می‌توانی کسی را نزد آیدین بفرستید. فکر می‌کنم من هر چه زودتر باید از این جا بروم.

یوسف ناراحت و بغض گرفته گفت:

-بله دخترم باید به فکر جای امنی برای تو باشیم. من فکر می‌کنم بهترین جا برای شما انبار پشت آسیاب است. البته اگر تا حال سالم مانده باشد.

-پس کسی را بفرستید و آیدین را خبر کنید

-خودم می‌روم، شما هم بفرمایید تو و در را ببندید و به هیچ کس هم باز نکنید.

یوسف کلاهش را بر سر نهاد و یقیه بالاپوشش را بالا کشید و راه افتاد و رفت. سارا همراه با تلی وحیدر رفتن یوسف را که از میان در کوچک تعبیه شده در پائین لنگ راست در کاروانسرا خارج شد و آن را پشت سرش بست نگاه کردند. با رفتن یوسف احساس تنهایی و ترس و ناامنی بر دل

سارا نشست، هوا سرد و گرفته و ابری بود و برف آرام ریز اما بی رمق می‌بارید. انگار در ابرها و هوا نیز توان و حوصله‌ای نمانده بود.

در زندگی گاه لحظه‌هایی است که همه چیز به نهایت خود می‌رسد. بن‌بست و بی‌چرایی محضی که دیگر فکر و پاسخی برای آن نیست جز پذیرفتن آن، وضعیتی که دیگر توان و حوصله مقابله با آن هم نیست. سارا احساس می‌کرد که در چنان وضعیتی گرفتار آمده. نگاهش را بر آسمان و برف و باد سردی که می‌وزید دوخت، بعد به اطراف ساختمان و محوطه کاروانسرا انداخت آیا دوباره باز آن جا را می‌دید و در آن جا بسر می‌برد. چشمش به درشکه‌اش و اسب‌هایش افتاد که کنار هم نزدیک درشکه ایستاده بودند و انگار او را نگاه می‌کردند. دو اسب سیاه، همان اسب‌هایی که او را همراه پدرش از تفلیس به اورمیه آورده بودند. فکر کرد اکنون اگر چه پیر شده‌اند اما شاید لازم باشد و مجبورشوند او را دوباره به تفلیس برگردانند. از آن فکر تمام تنش لرزید. غم تلخ آوارگی بر دلش نشست. تلی که کنارش ایستاده بود. وقتی رنگ پریدیگی و لرزش خفیف تن او را دید. دست برشانه‌اش نهاد و گفت:

-سردت شده خانوم بیا برویم تو.

بعد به حیدر گفت:

-تو هم برو کالسکه خانوم را آماده کن

آن نخستین بار بود که تلی او را خانوم صدا می‌کرد. سارا تا آن جا که به خاطر داشت. تلی همیشه او را دخترم خطاب و صدا کرده بود. لبخندی زد و از تلی پرسید:

-امروز چه روزیست؟

-امروز آخرین روز زمستان است خانومه من

-آخرین روز زمستان

-بله، فردا عید نوروز است، اما چه عیدی چه بهاری؟

سارا به طرف در ساختمان منزل یوسف و تلی راه افتاد و در حال رفتن به حیدر گفت:

-درشکه و اسب‌ها را بگذار همین جا بمانند عمو، اگر قرار باشد برویم، باید پیاده برویم

حیدر با تعجب گفت:

-پیاده مگر ممکنه خانوم، با این وضع شما نمی‌توانید پیاده به کوچه و خیابان بروید.

-می‌رویم، من برای جمع کردن و برداشتن تعدادی از وسائلم باید به منزلمان، منظورم به منزل نصیرالدوله بروم. با درشکه برویم همه متوجه می‌شوند. فکر می‌کنم به تنهایی با لباس مبدل بروم بهتر باشد، تلی گفت:

-بگذارید آیدین خان و یوسف بیایند، بعد ببینیم چه می‌کنیم

-بله تا آمدن آن‌ها صبر می‌کنیم اما باید آماده هم باشیم، آقا حیدر به اصغر بگو آن جا درآن پشت بام مراقب باشد.

-چشم خانوم.

کمی از ظهر گذشته بود که آیدین حکیم خان همراه یوسف آمد. هر دو ترسیده و نگران از وضع آشفته شهر بودند. دیگر همه می‌دانستند که به کاروانسرا هم حمله خواهد شد. یوسف و تلی اساسیه و وسائل مهمشان را جمع کرده و در درشکه نهاده و قصد داشتند. در صورت حمله و تخریب

و تاراج کاروانسرا به ده بروند. با این همه یوسف قصد داشت تا آخرین لحظه تا جایی که می‌توانست بماند و کاروانسرا را حفظ کند و اصرار داشت که تلی همراه سارا و آیدین حکیم تا شب نشده به ده بروند. اما آیدین حکیم خان با توجه به تزدیک بودن زمان زایمان سارا و هر لحظه امکان آن و نگران از وضع جسمی سارا که ممکن است زایمان با مشکل و دشواری روبرو شود و نیاز به جراحی و عمل سزارین باشد و آن هم جز در بیمارستان در جای دیگری امکان پذیر نبود. با وجود اوضاع آشفته شهر و خطر حمله وتهدید و دستگیری سارا می‌خواست تا آن جا که می‌توانند در شهر بمانند. بعد از صرف ناهار سارا و آیدین جداگانه با سر و وضع تغییر یافته راهی منزلشان در خانه نصیرالدوله پدر آیدین شدند و قرار گذاشتند که اگر میسر شد تا عصر و اگر نشد صبح روز بعد یوسف و تلی با کالسکه بیاند و آن‌ها را همراه خود به ده نزد نسترن خاتون ببرند.

سارا پیراهنی سرمه‌ای گشاد به تن کرده و روسری سرمه‌ای با حاشیه‌ای سفید که مخصوص خواهران کلیسای انجیلی بود به سر کرده بود و صلیب زمردین یادگار مادرش را از روی پیراهن برگردن آویخته بود تا کسی از جیلوها در راه مزاحمتی به او ایجاد نکنند. حیدر برای مراقبت پشت سر آن‌ها می‌آمد. هنگام رفتن تلی و یوسف که هر دو بسیار آشفته و ناراحت بودند و مرتب می‌گفتند:

-خیلی مراقب باشید، خانوم. خدایا اگر به شما اتفاقی بیفتد ما چه خواهیم کرد، جواب نسترن خاتون را چه خواهیم داد؟

سارا چون همیشه لبخندی زد و آن‌ها بغل نمود خداحافظی کرد و از کاروانسرا بیرون آمد. از سه راهی نسبتا پهن میدان مقابل کاروانسرا گذشتند

تمامی دکان‌ها بسته و در بسیاری از آن‌ها شکسته و تاراج و سوخته بود. تک توک عابر و گذرنده‌ای که بیشتر جیلوهای مسلح بودند دیده می‌شد. از محله ابوبکر که گذشتند تا باغ دلگشا که نزدیک گورستان قره صندوق بود، جنازه کشته شده‌ها در کوچه‌ها رها شده افتاده بود و از بالای چند خانه که تاراج شده و در آتش می‌سوخت دود برمی‌خواست. سارا حالش از آن همه پریشانی و ویرانی بهم خورده بود. به زحمت راه می‌رفت چشم بر مناره مسجد مناره دوخته بود که از دور دیده می‌شد و آن را نشان راه خانه نصیرالدوه کرده بود. باید بعد از گذشتن از کنار مسجد مناره و محله بابایوف و تیمچه نصیرالدوله به خانه باغ نصیرالدوله که در پشت تیمچه قرار داشت می‌رفتند. بعد از گذشتن از کنار مسجد مناره که کنسولگری و دفتر مسیونری امریکا در آن جا قرار داشت و آن روزها مستر شید کنسول ونماینده امریکا همه کاره بود و بسیاری از سران جیلو به آن جا رفت وآمد داشتند وگروه‌های جیلو در آن حوالی اجتماع می‌کردند. چشمش به گروهی از جیلوها افتاد که هیاهو کنان گویی از ماموریت کشتار و تاراج تازه باز می‌گشتند. عده‌ای سواره و تعدادی پیاده بودند. او را که دیدند چشم بر سر و وضع او و به حیدر که کنار او قدم برمی‌داشت و مراقب بود دوختند و تا چشمشان به صلیب روی سینه سارا افتاد نگاه برگرفته و رفتند. تا خانه نصیر الدوله سارا چندین بار ایستاد و نگاه به پشت سرانداخت تا از آمدن آیدین مطمئن شود. اما آیدین را ندید گویی او از راه و محله‌ی دیگری می‌آمد و یا خیلی از او فاصله داشت در سر تیمچه نصیرالدوله بود که آیدین را همراه یوسف ایستاده کنار در شفاخانه‌اش دید و همراه او راهی خانه شد. وقتی به در خانه نصیرالدوله رسیدند و در را گشوده می‌خواستند وارد

شوند سارا برگشت یوسف را دید که سرکوچه ایستاده و منتظر است که او
تو برود با تکان دست از او خداحافظی کرد و وارد حیاط خانه شد.

از سپیده صبح فردای آن روز سارا بیدار شده و همراه با ترکان خاتون مادر آیدین نزدیک پنجره نگران نشسته و چشم وگوش به در منتظر بودند از یوسف و تلی که قرار بود صبح زود بیایند و او و آیدین را همراه خود به ساران و جای امنی در آن جا ببرند خبری نشده بود. نمی‌دانستند که صدای گلوله و هیاهو که از اول شب برخاسته بود و تا نیمه‌های شب ادامه داشت از طرف کاروانسرا بوده و یا نه؟ آیا به کاروانسر حمله کرده و ویرانش کرده‌اند؟ اگر به آن جا حمله کرده باشند به سر یوسف و تلی و دیگران و کاروانسرا چه آمده؟ حیدر را فرستاده بودند که خبر بگیرد و آیدین رفته و در حیاط پشت در ایستاده و نگران منتظر بود. هیچ یک شب را خوب نخوابیده بودند و خواب‌هایشان همه سیاه بود. سارا هم چنان نگران از

پنجره چشم به بیرون دوخته بود که ناگهان هیاهو و صدای شلیک گلوله برخاست و در پی آن صدای فریاد و دشنام و ناله افراد از حیاط بگوش رسید. فهمیدند که به خانه آنها حمله کرده‌اند. سارا صدای حیدرا می‌شناخت و می‌شنید که پائین پله‌ها در حال جنگ و دفاع است اما بعد از چند لحظه با شلیک مداوم تفنگ‌ها و افتادن در خاموش شد و بعد صدای پاهایی را شنید که از پله‌ها بالا می‌آمدند. سارا برخاست که از پنجره بیرون را نگاه کند که چند گلوله به شیشه‌های پنجره خورد و از آن‌ها گذشتند و بر سقف اطاق نشستند و بعد گوی آتشینی به درون اطاق پرتاب شد. مادر پیر آیدین که بسیار ترسیده بود و می‌لرزید با رنگ و رخساره پریده به او گفت:

-دخترم من پیرم و همین جا می‌مانم تو برو پشت آن کمد نزدیک بخاری مخفی شد برو

سارا نگران آیدین بود و نمی‌دانست که بر سر او چه آمده. همانطور مات و حیران ایستاده بود که مادر آیدین از شانه‌اش گرفت و هلش داد و گفت:

-چرا ایستاده ای دارند می‌آیند برو توی کمد و یا پشت نیمکت کنار بخاری مخفی شو

سارا رفت توی کمد نشست اما در کمد را کامل نبست و از لای در چشم به بیرون دوخت. به هوای دود گرفته اطاق، به پرده‌های سرخ رنگ زری‌بافت عهد نیکلای، به پنجره‌های مشبک چوبی که می‌توانست هر روز از پشت آن کوهستان برفی مه گرفته سیر را تماشا کند، به کاشی‌های فیروزه‌ای رنگ و مبل و صندلی‌های چوبی با رو کش مخملی و به شعله‌های آتش که اکنون به جان پرده‌ها افتاده بودند. مادر آیدین شروع به سرفه کرده

بود که در اطاق با کوبیده شدن دو لگد گشوده شد و چند جیلو تو آمدند و تا وارد شدند یکی از جیلوها گلوی مادر آیدین را گرفت و بر زمین انداخت و با خشم و فریاد گفت:

-طلاها و جواهرت را بده

پیرزن که به زحمت می‌توانست حرف بزند بریده بریده با قسم و آیه در حالی که گردن بند و دستبندش را نشان می‌دادگفت:

-جواهرتم این‌ها هستند.

-بقیه کجا هستند، نقره‌ها چی؟

-نقره‌ها آن جا هستند

-بقیه طلا جواهراتت چی؟

-به خدا طلا و جواهر دیگر ندارم

مرد جیلوی که پا بر سینه پیرزن نهاده بود خم شد و گوشوارهای طلای پیرزن را از گوشش کشید و کند و لاله گوش پیرزن پاره و خون جاری شد و پیرزن پیچاره ناله‌ی ضعیفی کرد. مرد بعد از گوشواره‌ها گردنبند و دستبند و انگشتر طلای او را از گردن و دست و انگشتش در آورد و در حالی که از بدست آوردن آنها بسیار شادمان بود لگد محکمی بر پهلوی پیرزن کوبید و بعد گلوله‌ای را بر سینه‌اش شلیک کرد. تن پیرزن در خود پیچد و خون از سینه‌اش جاری شد. سارا وحشت زده و مبهوت از آن چه که دیده بود در حال گریستن بود که یکی از مردان در کمد را باز کرد و چشم بر او دوخت. مرد مسیحی لاغر اندام و بلند قدی بود. چشمانی درشت و سیاه داشت و ریشی کوتاه. سارا که صلیبش را در دست گرفته

بود.گریان چشم بر چشم مرد مسیحی دوخت. مرد چند لحظه‌ای به او نگاه کرد. تن و جان سارا از ترس می‌لرزید بعد آرام گفت:

-سارا خانم

سارا با تکان سر آرام گفت:

-بله

مرد لحظه‌ای متفکرانه ایستاد و بعد برگشت و در حالی که در کمد را دو باره می‌بست به همراهانش که مشغول تاراج وسایل اطاق ظرف‌های نقره روی میز و رفع بودند گفت:

-این کمد خالیست. چیزی در آن نیست

یکی از همرانش نزدیک آمد و پرسید:

-خوب نگاه کردی

مرد گفت: بله

دیگری گفت:

- بهتره زود از این جا برویم آتش الان همه جا را می‌گیرد و بعد راه افتادند و رفتند.

سارا همانطور توی کمد نشسته بود و دود داشت کم کم وارد کمد می‌شد که در کمد دوباره باز شد و آن مرد مسیحی دعایی خواند با دست صلیبی بر سینه کشید و بعد خم شد و دست دراز کرد و گفت:

-دست مرا بگیرید و بیایید بیرون خانم سارا. من اسحاق هستم. بیایید بیرون. الان آتش همه جا را می‌گیرد

سارا با کمک او از کمد بیرون آمد. تمام اطاق بهم ریخته و پنجره‌ها و پرده‌ها و میز و صندلی‌ها در حال سوختن بودند.گویی نفت روی همه چیز

ریخته بودند و شعله‌های آتش هر لحظه بیشتر می‌شد و بالا می‌رفت و دود شعله‌ها تمام فضای اطاق را گرفته بود و به زحمت می‌شد نفس کشید. سارا دستبند طلایش را در آورد به طرف مرد گرفت. مرد گفت:

- نه سارا خانم. گفتم که من اسحاق هستم اسحاق گوی تپه همان که سال پیش کمک کردید تا بیماری زنم را حکیم‌ها درمان کنند. کمک کردید تا لوازم خانه‌مان را جمع و جور کنیم و چند راس گاو و گوسفند بخریم. من هیچ وقت محبت و کمک شما را فراموش نمی‌کنم. شما سارا خانم پاک و مقدس هستید و این‌ها به بهانه پیدا کردن شما به دنبال تاراج هستند اما من از این‌ها نیستم بیایید من شما را باید از این جا خارج کنم. دود غلیظ بر خاسته از شعله‌های آتش امکان نفس کشیدن را گرفته بود سارا در حالی که سرفه می‌کرد تشکر کرد روسریش را روی صورتش کشید و با دست جلو دهانش را گرفت و همراه اسحاق از اطاق خارج شد و از پله پائین رفت. پائین پله‌ها به آستانه‌ی در ساختمان خانه که رسید تن زخمی نیم جان حیدر را دید که با نگاهی خسته و زخمی او را نگاه می‌کرد. بالای سر حیدر نشست و در حالی که می‌گریست دست بر شانه و صورت او کشید. حیدر که از جوانی در خدمت عمه نرگس و او بود و حال گویی با نگاه‌های بی‌رمقش خداحافظی می‌کرد. به زحمت نفس می‌کشید نمی‌توانست حرف بزند. خون راه دهان و گلویش را گرفته بود فقط به هر زحمتی بود با صدای گرفته و ناله مانندی گفت:

- مرا ببخشید خانم آن‌ها زیاد بودند، نتوانستم جلوشان را بگیرم مرا ببخشید.

سارا نمی‌دانست که چه باید بکند. نمی‌توانست حیدر را که آن همه وفادارانه به عمه نرگس و او خدمت کرده بود همان جا در آن وضع و حال بگذراد

و برود. اما با آن حال و روز و وضع و اوضاع چه می‌توانست بکند حیدر از چهره و نگاه سارا احساس او را فهمید و در حالی که با نگاه و تکان سر به سارا نشان می‌داد که احساس او را می‌فهمد با نگرانی و صدای گرفته گفت:

ـزود از این جا بروید خانم

سارا با چشم اشکبار برخاست و همراه اسحاق که سعی می‌کرد او را همراهی و بیشتر در پشت تنه خود پنهان سازد از حیاط گذشت به کنار در که رسید تن خونین شوهرش آیدین را دید که به پشت افتاده و سینه‌اش شکافته بود. چشمان آیدین باز بود انگار او را نگاه می‌کرد و از گوشه لبش هنوز خون می‌آمد. سارا نتوانست تاب بیاورد. نالان بر بالای سر آیدین نشست و درحالی که به شدت می‌گریست و می‌نالید سر او را در سینه فشرد. اما آیدین دیگر نفس نمی‌کشید. اسحاق که نگران بود با التماس و خواهش به زحمت سارا را بلند کرد وگفت:

ـسارا خانم خواهش می‌کنم. تا آن‌ها متوجه نشده‌اند شما باید از این جا بروید.

سارا گریان و درمانده به زحمت بلند شد و چشم بر صورت اسحاق دوخت. درمانده بود. نمی‌دانست چه بکند و کجا برود؟ دلش نمی‌خواست که از کنار آیدین دور شود. نمی‌توانست او و حیدر را همانطور آن جا رها کند و برود. اسحاق پرسید:

ـدر این نزدیکی‌ها کسی را می‌شناسید. جایی دارید که بروید؟

سارا گریان همان طور گیج و مات بدون توجه به حرف و سوال اسحاق چشم بر صورت و تن خونین آیدین دوخته بود و توجهی به حرف‌های اسحاق نداشت. اسحاق دوباره پرسید:

–سارا خانم لطفا بگویید در این حوالی جایی و منزل آشنایی دارید که بروید؟

سارا درمانده و ماتم زده گفت: نه

اسحاق که دید چند تن از جیلوها با اموال غارت کرده درحالی که او را صدا می‌زنند به طرف در می‌آیند. گفت:

–بهتره اول از این جا خارج شویم و بعد ببینیم که شما کجا   می‌توانید بروید؟

و از سارا خواست که همراه او از درحیاط خارج شود. سارا سنگین بود و درد داشت و به زحمت می‌توانست راه برود. بعد از خارج شدن از خانه و گذشتن از میان خیلی از جیلوها که همگی سرگرم غارت بودند به سمت کوچه پرپیچ و خمی پیچیدند که به تیمچه نصیرالدوله منتهی می‌شد و از کوچه گذشته به سر تیمچه که رسیدند ایستادند. سارا به دیوار تکیه داد. اسحاق دوباره پرسید:

–سارا خانم در این نزدیک‌ها فامیل و یا آشنایی دارید که به خانه آن‌ها بروید؟

سارا گفت:

–نه، اگر ممکنه می‌خواهم به کاروانسرا نزد یوسف بروم

اسحاق سری به تاسف تکان داد وگفت:

-فکر نمی‌کنم دیگر در کاروانسرا کسی باشد. چون شنیدم دیشب به آن جا حمله کرده و خرابش کرده‌اند.

سارا فهمید که کاروانسرا را هم خراب کرده‌اند. اما به سر تلی و یوسف چه آمده؟ خدا کند آن‌ها را نکشته باشند؟ با شنیدن خبر حمله به کاروانسرا و تاراج آن و دیدن خرابی و ویرانی شهر و جنازه‌های پراکنده در هر سو و آن چه که از صبح بر او گذشته بود به حقیقت وضع و اوضاع آشفته شهر و موقعیت خود پی برد و فهمید که دیگر کاملا تنهاست و دو راه و تصمیم بیشتر برای او نیست یا خود را تسلیم کند و یا برود و جایی پنهان شود و ببیند به سر عمه نسترن و مردم دهکده‌اش ساران و دیگران چه آمده و او چه باید بکند. درد و غم تمام وجودش را در برگرفته و بر دلش زخم می‌زدند فکر کرد حال که همه کس او را کشته و خانه و کاشانه اش را تاراج و ویران کرده‌اند و به دنبال دستگیری او هستند. دیگر از چه باید فرار کند؟ بهتر است که در همان جا بماند تا بیایند و او را دستگیر کنند و با خود ببرند. نه دیگر نباید فرار کند. حالت روحی دیگر یافته بود و همه چیز حتی بودن و ماندن برایش پوچ و هیچ شده بود. یک لحظه دست که به شکمش زد به فکر فرزندش، بچه‌ای که در شکم داشت افتاد. به یادگار آیدین فهمید که او ناگزیر به فرار است. حداقل تا زایمان فرزندش و سپردن او بدست عمه نسترن و یا یکی از نزدیکانش باید زنده بماند یک آن نیروی تازه ای پیدا کرد. باید مقاومت کند، باید فرزندش را نجات دهد. از دیواری که تکیه داده بود جدا شد و از اسحاق پرسید:

-می‌دانی محل کلیسای انجیلی کجاست؟ من باید نزد پدر سونتاک بروم.

-به کلیسا نزد پدر سونتاک!؟

-بله

-بله می‌دانم نزدیک برکه (گل) فتحعلی خان کمی بالاتر از کوی کلیسای حضرت مریم است من تا نزدیکی آنجا می‌برمت ولی نمی‌توانم تا در کلیسا بیایم. چون باید زود برگردم

-باشد تا نزدیک‌های آن ببر و از دور نشانم بده. بقیه‌اش را خودم می‌روم.

-باید خیلی مراقب باشید سارا خانم چون در همه جا به دنبال شما می‌گردند.

-بله می‌دانم

راه افتادند و بجای این که از تمیچه بگذرند و بعد از گذر از مقابل مسجد سردار از طریق محله‌ی بابایوف که نزدیکترین راه به کوچه کلیسای حضرت مریم و محل کلیسای انجیلی بود بروند. برای در امان ماندن سارا راه را کمی طولانی کرده و از سمت محله و دروازه یوردشاه روانه محله کلیسای حضرت مریم و برکه کرمعلی خان شدند. در راه که می‌رفتند. جنازه‌های کشته شدگان هر سو پراکنده افتاده بود و خانه‌های زیادی تاراج شده با در و پنجره‌های شکسته و در حال سوختن دیده می‌شد و هر چه به دروازه و باغ یوردشاه نزدیک می‌شدند بر تعداد جنازه‌های کشته شدگان افزوده می‌شد و گروه زیادی از مردم شهر در حال فرار بودند. نرسیده به دروازه از کنار نهری که در حاشیه باغ یوردشاه روان بود، به سمت برکه کرمعلی خان و محله کلیسای انجیلی که می‌پیچیدند جنازه زنی را دیدند با سه فرزندش که به طور فجیعی سلاخی شده و کنار نهر افتاده بود. یکی از بچه‌های زن که کوچکتر از همه و انگار شیرخواره بود، هنوز زنده بود. سارا تا آن صحنه را دید گریان در حالی که ناله‌های زوزه مانند از غم ودرد

از ته دل می‌کشید به طرف کودک دوید. اسحاق خواست جلوش را بگیرد نتوانست. سارا رفت و شال سرش را که پهن و بلند بود از گردنش باز کرد و خم شد و کودک را که بازو و شکمش زخمی بود و خون می‌رفت در شال سرش پیچید و خواست که بلند شود نتوانست تعادلش را از دست داد و داشت از رو به زمین می‌افتاد که دست و زانوی راستش را هایل کرد و بر زمین نهاد در اثر ضربه‌ای که با نهادن زانویش به زمین به پا و شکمش وارد شد. دردی شدید در شکم و دل و سینه‌اش پیچید و چیزی انگار پاره شد و گرمای آب و خون را در پاهایش حس کرد. همراه با درد، ضعف شدیدی در تمام تنش پیچید و چشمانش سیاهی رفت. کودک را که گریه می‌کرد همانطور در سینه فشرد و لحظه‌ها همانطور در همان جایی که به زانو نشسته بود ماند. اسحاق آمد و از بازویش گرفت و به زحمت بلندش کرد و پرسید:

−حالتان خوبه

و بعد که نگاهش به چهره رنگ پریده و عرق کرده و لرزان سارا و خونی که قطره قطره بر زمین می‌چکید افتاد، گفت:

−خون؟ خدایا. انگار شما دارید زایمان می‌کنید؟

سارا با همه ضعف و درد در حالی که کودک زخمی را در سینه فشرده بود با تکان سر و صدای گرفته گفت:

−الان نه ولی شروع شده

−پس باید هر چه زودتر به کلیسا بروید.

و بعد اسحاق در حالی که می‌گفت:

-این بچه را بگذارید همین جا. شما حالتان خوب نیست، خودتان درد دارید.

دستش را دراز کرد تا بچه را از سارا بگیرد. سارا گفت:

-نه

-ولی شما نمی‌توانید با این وضع او را هم همراه خودتان ببرید

-می‌توانم. خداوند کمکم می‌کند.

-کمی به فکر خودتان باشید خانم. این کودک را می‌خواهید کجا ببرید؟

-هرجایی که خودم بتوانم بروم

-برای چی؟

سارا با همه ضعف و دردی که داشت نگاهی پر معنی به صورت اسحاق انداخت و بعد گفت:

-فرض کن بچه من و یا بچه توست. چه فرق می‌کند. نمی‌توانم او را این جا رها کنم و بروم. باید با خودم ببرمش

اسحاق شرمگین سرش را از پاسخ سارا پائین انداخت و آرام گفت:

-خانم سارا بهتره راه بیفتیم

سارا با همه ضعف و دردش لنگان همراه اسحاق در حالی که بچه را در آغوش فشرده بود و قطره قطره خون از پایش به زمین می‌چکید راه افتاد بعد از طی مسافتی به نزدیکی برکه که رسیدند. اسحاق ایستاد و با دست ساختمان و طاق گرد و آجری بالای سر در چوبی بزرگ کلیسای انجیلی را نشان داد و گفت:

-کلیسای انجیلی پدر سونتاک همان جاست. من دیگر باید برگردم. چون مرا همراه شما ببینند برایم خطر دارد. مرا ببخشید سارا خانم. خداوند شما را حفظ کند. شما واقعا مثل مریم مقدس هستید.

سارا تشکر کرد و اسحاق برگشت و رفت. بعد از رفتن اسحاق سارا تنها به طرف کلیسا راه افتاد. نزدیک برکه کمی ایستاد نور برف‌هایی اطراف برکه چشمانش را اذیت می‌کرد. از باریکه راه کنار برکه و از مقابل مسجد لطفعلی خان گذشت و به محله آسوریان پیچید و بعد از گذشتن از چند پیچ به در کلیسای انجیلی که محوطه مقابل درش کمی پهن و عریض و سنگ‌فرش و جاروشده و تمیز بود رسید. کسی در آن حوالی نبود. کوچه خلوت و ساکت و خاموش بود. سارا که از شدت درد نمی‌توانست روی پا به ایستد سرش را بر در تکیه داد و کودک را که دیگر گریه نمی‌کرد با دست چپ بر شانه گرفت و با دست راست کوبه‌ی آهنین صلیب شکل در را بلند کرد و کوبید. و منتظر شد اما خبری نشد. دوباره اما این بار محکم کوبید. چند لحظه بعد پیر مردی که از تمام صورت او بیشتر دماغ بزرگ و پهن و دو دندان زرد و چرکین و از بقیه دندان‌های ریخته‌اش دیده می‌شد، در را باز کرد و می‌شد حدس زد که یکی از خدمه‌های کلیساست. سارا با همان حال نزار گفت:

-پدر سونتاک؟

پیرمرد انگار صدای سارا را نشنید و یا اگر شنید توجهی نکرد و پاسخی نداد فقط سراپای سارا را آرام و خونسرد وراانداز کرد و تا چشمش به صلیب روی سینه سارا افتاد برگشت و رفت و دقایقی بعد که برای سارا

بسیار طولانی بود. پدر سونتاک آمد و تا نگاهش به سارا افتاد با تعجب و حیرت گفت:

-سارا!!؟

سارا خسته و بی حال با رنگ و رخسار پریده گفت:

-پدر جایی نداشتم، حالم هم خوب نیست، همه جا هم دنبال من می‌گردند.

-بله دنبال شما می‌گردند

-اگر برای شما مزاحمتی نیست و خطری نداشته باشد می‌خواستم چند ساعتی در کلیسای شما پناه بگیرم.

کشیش سونتاک که مردی کوتاه قد و لاغر اندام با چهره‌ای مهتابی و مهربان بود با نگرانی نگاهی به اطراف انداخت و بعد نگاهش که به چهره رنگ پریده و قطره‌های خونی که از پای سارا می‌ریخت افتاد با مهربانی اما ترحم گفت:

-خدایا حال تو اصلا خوب نیست، پس درست می‌گفتند که تو بارداری، انگار وقت زایمانت رسیده؟

-بله پدر

-زود بیا تو دخترم

بعد پرسید:

-این بچه مال کیست؟

-نمی‌دانم لب نهر کنار جنازه مادرش بود، نمی‌توانستم او را همان جا بگذارم و بیایم

-با این وضع؟

سارا لبخند مهربانی زد و با همه ضعف و درد و بی‌حالیش گفت:

-به رحمت خداوند ایمان دارم پدر

کشیش سونتاک با حالی دگرگون از پاسخ سارا یک قدم عقب رفت و دعایی خواند و صلیبی بر سینه کشید و گفت:

-بله درست است، درست می‌گفتند. خداوند مرا ببخشد تو از برگزیدگان و مقدسینی

بعد با احترام از بازوی سارا گرفت و کمک کرد و او را در سکوی پیش درگاهی پشت در نشاند و رفت و خواهران دیر کلیسا را صدا زد. کمی بعد دو خواهر روحانی آمدند و سارا را همراه خود بردند و ساعتی بعد سارا نوزادی پسر بدنیا آورد. بعد از زایمان تن و پای سارا را تمیز و با حوله‌های گرم و خیس پاک کردند و لباس تازه و تمیزی پوشاندند و کنار نوزادش خواباندند. وقتی برایش کاچی با روغن افزوده داغ آورده بودند. پدر سونتاک به عیادتش آمد و گفت:

-دخترم خداوند خواسته بودکه تو بچه‌ات را درکلیسا بدنیا بیاوری. بالاخره باید همه بکر زایی مقدسین را بپذیرند

سارا با همه ی خستگی و ضعف در پاسخ گفت:

-ولی پدر، شوهر من آیدین حکیم خان بود.

پدر سونتاک توجهی به حرف‌های سارا نکرد و گفت:

-خسته‌ای و ضعیف شده‌ای دخترم، غذایت را بخور و استراحت کن و هیچ نگران نباش تا هر وقت که بخواهی می‌توانی این جا بمانی، تو مهمان مقدس مایی.

سارا که به یاد و در فکر آن بچه زخمی بود پرسید:

-آن بچه چه شد پدر؟

پدر سونتاک با لبخند گفت:

-حالش خوب است دخترم، خواهر روحانی ائما زخم‌هایش را بسته و خوابانده. تو نگران او نباش، غذایت را بخور و استراحت کن.

بعد از رفتن پدر سونتاک، سارا غذایش را خورد و از شدت خستگی به خواب عمیقی فرو رفت. ساعتی از غروب گذشته بود و سارا با کمک خواهر روحانی ائما مشغول شیر دادن به نوزادش بود که پدر سونتاک هراسان آمد و در حالی که بسیار نگران و برافروخته بود و گفت:

-بلند شو و عجله کن دخترم. گرجی‌های فرستاده کلیسای تفلیس همراه چند جیلو دم در هستند. آن‌ها برای بردن تو آمده‌اند. اگر قصد نداری با آن‌ها بروی و یا آن‌ها تو را ببرند. باید زود از این جا بروی.

خواهر ائما معترضانه گفت:

-ولی او تازه زایمان کرده، ضعیف و مریضه. در این وقت شب با این وضع و حال کجا برود؟

-ولی آن‌ها می‌دانند او این جاست.

-از کجا می‌دانند؟

-نمی‌دانم، اما یک مرد مسیحی بنام اسحاق را دست بسته همراه خود آورده‌اند؟

سارا وقتی نام اسحاق را شنید از دستگیری او متاسف و غمگین شد و احساس تقصیر کرد و فهمید که دیگر نمی‌تواند در کلیسا بماند و باید از آن جا برود. بلند شد کتش را پوشید و کفش‌هایش را بپا کرد و بچه‌اش را که خواهر ائما قنداق کرده و در پارچه‌ای پشمی پیچیده بود بغل کرد و گفت:

-برای همه چیز از شما متشکرم پدر، ببخشید که شما را به دردسر انداخته‌ام باید از کجا بروم؟

پدر سونتاک که از ناتوانی خود و بیرون کردن سارا در آن وقت شب از کلیسا بسیار ناراحت عصبی بود. خجل و شرمگین گفت:

-از در پشتی دخترم. من آن‌ها را کمی مشغول می‌کنم تا تو هر چه می‌توانی از این جا دور شوی. هر چه توان داری و می‌توانی هر چه تندتر از این محله برو و دور شو، برو به خانه‌ی ملک خوشابه. خانه‌اش چند محله پائین‌تر از این جایست.

خواهر روحانی ایما گفت:

-من همراهش می‌روم.

-نه نمی‌توانی چون من انکار کرده‌ام که او این جاست. اگر تو را همراه او ببینند و بگیرند. می‌فهمند دروغ گفته‌ایم آن‌ها حکم دارند تو را هم مثل آن مرد بیچاره اسحاق دستگیر می‌کنند.

کشیش سونتاک با چشمان پر، مقابل سارا ایستاد و با شرمندگی گفت:

-سارا دخترم مرا ببخش. خواهر ائما در پشتی را نشانت می‌دهد خداوند مسیح نگهبان و حامی تو باشد. خداحافظ

پدر سونتاک ناراحت و غمگین خداحافظی کرد و سارا با راهنمایی خواهر روحانی ائما که با شمعی افروخته جلوتر می‌رفت و راه را برای او نشان می‌داد پائین به زیر زمین کلیسا رفتند و بعد از گذشتن از راهرو تنگ و باریکی که دیوارهای سنگی نسبتا بلندی داشت در انتهای راهرو به در کوچک چوبی رسیدند که چند پله بالاتر از کف راهرو بود. خواهر ائما از

پله‌ها بالا رفت و کلید انداخت و در را باز کرد و نگاهی به اطراف انداخت و بعد برگشت سارا را بغل کرد و بوسید و گفت:

-خداحافظ دخترم. از کنار دیوارها برو و مراقب باش. از کوی ننه مریم که بگذری کمی پائین‌تر به محله گورستان قره صندوق می‌رسی. از آن جا به سمت چپ بپیچ چند کوچه بالاتر دروازه عسگر خان است. منزل ملک خوشابه در همان حوالیست. پیدا می‌کنی. خداحافظ

سارا از خواهر روحانی ائما خداحافظی کرد و بیرون آمد هوا سرد و یخ زده بود. نمی‌دانست در آن وقت شب و در آن سرما کجا باید برود. اسم قبرستان و محله قره صندوق برایش آشنا بود بعد از ظهر دیروز وقتی به خانه نصیرالدوله می‌رفت از مقابلش گذشته بود. محل منزل ملک خوشابه را نمی‌شناخت و نمی‌توانست در آن وقت شب که هیچ کس در اطراف نبود خانه او را از کی بپرسد و پیدا بکند. تصمیم گرفت به کاروانسرا برود. جایی جز آن جا نداشت. کاروانسرا برایش آشنا بود و آن جا احساسی ایمنی و آرامش می‌کرد. فکرکرد شاید یوسف و تلی و یا آشنایی در آن جا باشد و اگر ویران و تاراج هم شده باشد باز می‌تواند در گوشه‌ای از خرابه‌های آن شب را به صبح رساند و صبح راهی ده شود. با این فکر به طرف کاروانسرا راه افتاد کوچه‌ها خلوت و تاریک بودند و سارا با ترس و وحشت با همه ضعف و ناتوانی تند و تند قدم برمی‌داشت. چند بار نزدیک بود که بیفتد. از محله قره صندوق که می‌گذشت. سگ‌ها هو هو کنان دورش کردن و او در حالی که بسیار ترسیده بود و مرتّب دعا می‌خواند بچه‌اش را در بغل فشرده در پناه دیوارها به راهش ادامه داد. سگ‌ها مصافتی پارس کنان همراه و پشت سر او آمدند و بعد برگشته و رفتند و عجیب بود که به

او حمله نکردند. سارا که از ترس حمله سگ‌ها مسیر را تند و با شتاب آمده بود وقتی سگ‌ها رفتند. نگاهش را که به اطراف انداخت، دید در محله ابوبکر نزدیک میدان کاه و کاروانسراست. خسته شده بود قلبش تند می‌زد و ترسی غریب از تنهایی و تاریکی شب بر دلش نشسته بود با این همه می‌دانست که نباید بایستد باید برود او باید خود را و بچه‌اش را نجات دهد. از محله ابوبکر و یهودیان گذشت و وارد بازار سوخته و ویران شده کشمش و خشکبار شد. بعد از عبور از بازار نزدیک سه راه میدان کاه به کاروانسرا رسید نزدیک رفت. دید درهای چوبی بزرگ کاروانسرا شکسته و از جا کنده شده. پیش درگاهی و قسمتی از ساختمان کاروانسرا و بخصوص ساختمان منزل یوسف و تلی تخریب شده. در و پنجره‌هایش شکسته و اشیا و لوازم آن به غارت رفته اما ساختمان‌های انتهایی و بخصوص قسمتی از انبار و اصطبل حیوانات سالم هستند. با وجود ناراحتی از غارت و ویرانی کاروانسرا از سالم ماندن قسمتی از آن خوشحال شد. می‌توانست شب را در آن جا صبح کند. با این فکر از میان درهای شکسته و دیوار فروریخته کاروانسرا گذشت و وارد محوطه کاروانسرا شد. دیگر نمی‌ترسید. احساس آشنایی و امنیت می‌کرد. کمی‌که پیش رفت. صدای حرکت و نفس‌ها و ماغ اسب‌ها را شنید. نگاه که کرد اسب‌های سیاهش را بسته بر درشکه دید. همان اسب‌های سیاه پدرش هم‌آن‌هایی که در تمام این سال‌ها دوست و همدم او و در گردش‌هایش میان شهر و روستا بودند. اسب‌ها بسته به درشکه مقابل در یکی از انبارها که سقفش ریخته بود ایستاده بودند. نخست تعجب کرد و بعد خوش حال و امیدوار شد. فکر کرد شاید یوسف و تلی و یا آشنایی آن جاست. نزدیک رفت. اسب‌ها که

او را دیدند و بویش را شنیدند هورتی کشیدند و با نگاه‌های مضطرب اما آشنا نگاه بر او دوختند. از نگاه و حرکت مضطربانه اسب‌ها، پایی که مرتب بر زمین می‌کوبیدند. احساس بدی بر دل سارا نشست. ترسید. شاید درشکه و اسب‌ها را جیلوها و گرجی‌های مسلح تصاحب کرده باشند و اکنون آن‌ها در کاروانسرا هستند که برای دزدی و چپاول و بردن لوازم دیگر آمده‌اند اما هیچ کس در اطراف نبود. سارا با احتیاط نزدیک شد. تو و داخل درشکه را نگاه کرد. نور ماه در آن هوای سرد و رقیق همه جا را روشن و مهتابی کرده بود. می‌شد داخل درشکه را خوب دید. اما در داخل آن کسی و یا چیزی نبود. اسب‌ها برگشته هم چنان او را نگاه می‌کردند. باد سوز سرمای آزار دهنده‌ای داشت و اسب‌ها هم از سوز سرما آزرده بودند. سارا رفت دست بر دماغ و چشم و صورت آن‌ها کشید و بوسید. اشکش گرفته بود. نمی‌توانست باورکند در آن وقت شب در میان ویرانه‌های کاروانسرا در آن وضع و جو ترس و فرار و کشتار که برای او و هیچ کس جای امن و امیدی نبود. آن‌ها را بیابد. آن هم بسته بر درشکه گویی این خواسته خدا و تقدیر او بود و آن‌ها آماده بردن او بودند. در حال نوازش و درد دل و حرف زدن با اسب‌ها بود که صدای چند مرد را که به زبان آشوری با هم سر مسئله‌ای مجادله و بحث می‌کردند از انبار ته حیاط کاروانسرا شنید. انگار مردان جایی را می‌کندند. فهمید اشیا و چیزهای مثل طلا و جواهرات را که غارت و یا به زور تصاحب کرده‌اند. دارند دفن می‌کنند. ترسید اگر او را در آن جا می‌دیدند. کارش زار بود. دیگر نمی‌توانست در گوشه‌ای از کاروانسرای شب را به صبح رساند. راه دهکده‌اش ساران را که سال‌ها آمده و رفته بود، خوب می‌شناخت. تصمیم گرفت که برای نجات خود و

فرزندش به ساران برود. با همه ضعف و خستگی احساس حرکت و نیروی تازه‌ای یافته بود. پیشانی اسب‌ها را بوسید و بچه‌اش که را خوابیده بود تو درشکه گذاشت و بعد دهنه اسب‌ها را گرفت و آرام در حالی‌که سعی می‌کرد صدایی بلند نشود کشید و اسب‌ها همراه او حرکت کردند. از کاروانسرا که خارج شدند. سوار درشکه شد و عنان اسب‌ها را کشید و با سرعت به طرف ساران راه افتاد. به پشت سر و اطرافش نگاه نمی‌کرد نمی‌خواست بداند که آیا در اطراف او کسی و چیزی هست و یا متوجه شده و در تعقیب او هستند. نرسیده به دروازه تورپاق قلعه به طرف هفت آسیاب پیچید و از پل چوبی نهر گذشت و از جاده شنی مقابل آسیاب‌ها به طرف ساران راه افتاد. سکوتی محض و سرد در آن وقت شب بر جاده و مزارع و پیشه زارهای سوخته و شکسته و رها شده‌ی اطراف آسیاب‌ها و جاده حاکم بود. آسیاب‌ها کار نمی‌کردند و جز آسیاب بزرگ بقیه رها شده و خراب با پرو چرخ‌های شکسته متروک افتاده بودند و در زیر نور سفید ماه هیبت غم انگیزی داشتند. تنها صدایی که در فضا می‌پیچید صدای جاری آب نهر بود که با وجود سرما و یخ بندان هنوز جاری بود و هرچند گاه صدای پرنده‌ای غریب سکوت جاری و حاکم بر فضای شب را می‌شکست. جز آن‌ها چیزی وکسی و صدای پای وگذرنده‌ای نبود. جاده بود و صدای پای اسب‌ها و چرخ‌های درشکه. سارا احساس سرما و ضعف می‌کرد. اما امیدوار عنان را می‌تکاند و اسب‌ها را به حرکت و شتاب وا می‌داشت. اسب‌ها با وجود سرما وتاریکی شب آشنا بر راه بودند و احساس سارا را گویی فهمیده بودند و با شتاب به سوی ساران می‌تاختند. ساعتی بعد وقتی سارا ساختم‌آن‌های دهکده‌اش ساران و عمارت خود را از دور دید. امیدوار

عنان اسب‌ها را کشید و از سرعت آن‌ها کم کرد و به باریکه راه سبز و پوشیده از درخت در ساران که شیب ملایمی داشت پیچید از مقابل ساختمان آسیاب ده که سال پیش او آن را بازسازی کرده و راه انداخته بود گذشت به نزدیکی در باغ که نزدیک شد. در باغ را باز دید و آتشی شعله‌ور نزدیک آن می‌سوخت. سیاهی غلیظ شب و دود و نور متصاعد شده از هیمه آتش مانع از دیدن اطراف بود. سارا یک آن دچار وحشت و نگرانی شد. تصور کرد که به ده و باغ حمله کرده و در و عمارت را شکسته و ویران کرده‌اند. لابد به همراه مردم روستا عمه نسترن و دیگران هم کشته‌اند با همین تصور و فکر نگران به طرف در باغ پیش می‌رفت و با این امید که نسترن خاتون و دیگران زنده باشند و زیر لب می‌گفت:

-اگر هزار بار هم خراب بکنند باز از نو می‌سازمت.

به در باغ که رسید. دید تعداد زیادی از جیلوهای مسلح در آن جا هستند. و کنار آتش روشن نزدیک در بعضی ایستاده و بعضی چمباته زده‌اند. حالش خوب نبود. در اثر زایمان و خستگی و هیجان و ترس احساس ضعف می‌کرد. سرش گیج و چشمانش به سیاهی می‌رفت. با این همه تلاش داشت که خود را به عمارت و نزد نسترن خاتون برساند. باز دقیق که نگاه کرد کنار درکدخدا و یوسف را دید که با سرکیس شاگرد سابق یوسف که اکنون یکی از فرماندهان جیلوها بود و چند مرد گرجی مشغول صحبت هستند. دیگر به نزدیک در باغ رسیده بود. مردان مسلح جیلو و گرجی‌ها که درشکه او را دیدند برخاسته و ایستادند و چند نفر از آن‌ها به طرف درشکه آمده و از عنان اسب‌ها گرفته و درشکه را نگه داشتند. سرکیس نزدیک شد و تا چشمش به سارا افتاد با تعجب گفت:

-سارا!!؟

مردان مسلح جیلو وگرجی با شنیدن نام سارا همهمه کنان دور درشکه جمع شدند و با چشمان مشتاق اما متعجب او را زل زده و مرتب زیر لب می‌گفتند: سارا

سارا خسته و ناتوان درحالی‌که احساس بیماری و تب و لرز می‌کرد وقتی خود را در محاصره آن همه مرد مسلح دید. دچار وحشت بیشتر شد. سرکیس گفت:

-سارا خانم لطفا از درشکه بیایید پائین

سارا اما بی‌توجه به حرف سرکیس و هم چنین یوسف که آمده وکنار سرکیس ایستاده بود و از او می‌خواست که از درشکه پیاده شود همانطور ناراحت و مات آن‌ها را نگاه می‌کرد. قصد نداشت آن جا بایستد و پیاده شود. می‌خواست از میان آن‌ها بگذرد و به باغ نزد عمه نسترن برود. تب کرده بود، تنش می‌لرزید و هیچ توجهی به حرف و در خواست‌های مکرر سرکیس نداشت. عنان اسب‌ها را در دست فشرده بود و می‌کشید تا اسب‌ها را حرکت دهد و با حرکت و نیروی اسب‌ها محاصر مردان مسلح مسیحی را بشکافد. اسب‌ها هم می‌خواستند حرکت کنند و پیش بروند اما مردان مسلح اطراف را احاطه کرده و دو تن از آن‌ها از لگامشان گرفته و نمی‌گذشتند اسب‌ها پیش بروند و به همین جهت اسب‌ها یک گام پیش برمی‌داشتند و دو بار به عقب برمی‌گشتند و درشکه هی جلو و عقب می‌شد که ناگهان یکی از مردان گرجی دست دراز کرد و از بازوی سارا گرفت و کشید. سارا خواست مقاومت کند اما نتوانست و در اثرفشار دست مرد

گرجی از درشکه پائین افتاد و از حال رفت و دیگر نفهمید که چه شد و چه اتفاقی افتاد و چه بر او گذشت.

روز بعد نزدیک ظهر وقتی در انبار کاروانسرا به هوش آمد. خود را کنار نسترن خاتون و یوسف و تلی دید و بعد از پرسش‌های زیاد از یوسف و تلی و عمه نسترن و مرور افکار و خاطرات گذشته و عمیق ذهن خود. هوشیاریش را باز یافت و فهمید که در انبار کاروانسرا زندانیست

زندان و محاکمه در کلیسا

١

صبح ساعتی از برآمدن آفتاب گذشته بود که در چوبی انباری که آنها در آن زندانی بودند باز شد. دو سرباز گرجی سپاه روسیه وارد شده و کنار در ایستادند و بعد از ورود آنها خواهر روحانی سونیا همراه با دو خواهر روحانی دیگر وارد شدند. با ورود آنها نسترن خاتون، یوسف و تلی نگران از جایشان بلند شدند. سارا که تازه کودکش را شیر داده و خوابانده بود. پشت به در مشغول مرتب کردن لباسش بود. برگشت نگاهی به آنها کرد و آرام و خونسرد همانطور که نشسته بود منتظر ماند. فهمید که آنها بخاطر او آمده‌اند. چهره لاغر و کشیده و همیشه عصبی خواهر روحانی سونیا برایش آشنا بود. آن روزها که در تفلیس در دیر بسر می‌برد. یعنی دوره تزکیه و آموزش‌های دینی را در دیر می‌گذراند. خواهر سونیا همیشه با او

برخورد داشت و از رفتار و بی‌توجهی سارا به بعضی از مسائل دینی و درس‌ها و توجهش به مسائل دیگر ناراحت و نسبت به مسئله انتخاب و مقدس بودن سارا شک و اعتراض داشت و با او بسیار سخت گیر و گاه بعضی از روزها که سارا در اطاقش می‌ماند و یا نسبت به سن و سالش که در آن زمان دختر بچه‌ای بیش نبود و بازیگوشی می‌کرد و علاقه به مسائل و موضوع‌های دیگر غیر از مسائل دینی نشان می‌داد عصبی می‌شد و برای تنبیه او را مجبور می‌کرد که به زیر زمین تاریک و نمور دیر برود و سنگ‌های کف زیر زمین دیر را که چند گور اسقف با سنگ قبرهای بلند و بزرگ و نقوش برجسته هم در آن جا بود با دستمال خیس پاک کند و گرد خاکش را بروبد و سارا که دختر بچه بیش نبود. بسیار وقت‌ها در آن جا از ترس به گریه می‌افتاد و زاری می‌کرد تا این که خواهر مریا که جوان و مهربان بود می‌آمد و واسطه می‌شد و او را بیرون می‌آورد و سارا یادش بود که همیشه از ترس خواهر سونیا عروسک پارچه‌ایش را در زیر تختش مخفی می‌کرد. چون اگر خواهر سونیا می‌دید حتما پاره و سوزانده می‌شد. هر روز صبح بعد از نماز و دعا تمام وضع دست و سر و صورت او را وارسی می‌کرد و نسبت به صلیب و آویخته بودن آن از گردن بسیار حساس بود. اکنون او از تفلیس برای چی آمده بود؟ این سوالی بود که ذهن سارا را بخود مشغول و مشوش کرده بود. نکند می‌خواهند او را به تفلیس بازگردانند در این فکر بود که خواهر سونیا با همان چهره عصبی اما کمی برافروخته در برابرش ایستاد و در حالی که سعی می‌کرد خود را بی‌اعتنا نشان دهد به تاکید و با لحن و کلامی خشک گفت:

-بلند شوید، باید برویم

سارا همانطور که نشسته بود پرسید:

-کجا؟

-برای بازجویی و استنطاق. شما باید به خیلی از سوال‌ها پاسخ دهید
بعد از گفتن جمله آخرش به تمسخر نیش خندی زد نگاهش را به سارا
دوخت و منتظر ماند. سارا از جایش بلند شد و بی آن که توجهی به خواهر
سونیا بکند. روسریش را که به رنگ کم رنگ بنفش مایل به خاکستری
روشن بود. روی سرش انداخت و موهای خرمایی بلندش را مرتب و در
زیر آن پنهان کرد. چشمان آبی موربش غم آلود و گرفته بودند و چون
همیشه لبخند مهربانش را به لب داشت اما این بار تلخ بود، نسترن خاتون
وحشت زده بود و یوسف و تلی بهت زده و غمگین نگاهش می‌کردند.
سارا رفت دستی به سر و گونه بچه‌اش که در گهواره خوابیده بود کشید و
بعد خم شد دست و صورت نسترن خاتون را بوسید و برگشت مقابل
یوسف ایستاد با متانت وآرامش اما بغض گرفته گفت:

-مواظب عمه‌ام و بچه‌ام باشید، اگر برنگشتم که فکر نمی‌کنم برگردم این
جا نمانید برگردید به ساران

یوسف از شدت ناراحتی و بغض و عصبانیت دست و پایش سست شده
بود. به دیوار تکیه داده بود و مات و ناراحت اما با حسرت نگاه می‌کرد
این چندمین بار بود که او در چنین وضعیتی قرار می‌گرفت، یک بار وقتی
که امیرخان را در دیر نزدیک تفلیس زخمی و دستگیر کردند و بردند و بار
دیگر چند شب پیش سارا را که بیهوش شده بود می‌خواستند دست بسته
به زندان ببرند و او قادر به مقابله نبود و درآخر با کمک شاگردش سرکیس

توانست موافقت آنها را بگیرد و گذاشتند که او و تلی و نسترن خاتون همراه سارا بیایند و تا روشن شدن تکلیف سارا در انبار کاروانسرا کنار او باشند و اکنون که سارا را می‌بردند. تمام وجود یوسف مملو از بغض ناتوانی بود. توان حرف زدن را نداشت. فقط ساکت و ناتوان با حسرت و غم سارا را نگاه می‌کرد. نمی‌دانست که چه بگوید فقط با تکان دادن سر پاسخ سارا را داد. تلی پرسید:

-سارا اسمش چی، اسم پسرت را چه بگذاریم؟

خواهر سونیا که کنار سارا ایستاده بود، نگاه معنی داری به صلیب زمردین روی سینه سارا انداخت و آمرانه و با تاکید گفت:

-اسمش را انتخاب خواهیم کرد. باید برای غسل تعمید به کلیسا بیاورید.

سارا با شنیدن حرف‌های خواهر روحانی سونیا، صلیب زمردینش را در کف دستش گرفت و با حسرت آن را نگاه کرد و بعد میان مشتش فشرد، یاد مادرش و حسرت او در دلش شعله و رشد.کمی به صلیب نگاه کرد و بعد آن را از گردنش در آورد و جلو خواهر روحانی سونیا گرفت و گفت:

-بگیرید این مال کلیساست.

خواهر روحانی سونیا که غافلگیر شده بود وحشت زده یک قدم به عقب برداشت و در حالی که پشت سر هم صلیب می‌کشید و ورد و دعا می‌خواند ملتمسانه گفت:

-در مورد آن دادگاه شورای اسقفی باید تصمیم بگیرند. صلیب مقدس را بگردنتان بیاویزید، خواهش می‌کنم

سارا لبخندی زد و سرش را به تاسف تکان داد و نگاهی پر معنی به خواهر سونیا و دو خواهر روحانی دیگر انداخت و بعد صلیب را به گردنش آویخت و برگشت وگفت:

-امیر عیسی، به عمه نسترن هم قبلا گفته‌ام اسمش را بیاد و خاطره پدرم، امیر بگذارید، آیدین هم اسم امیر را دوست داشت و چون در کلیسا بدنیا آمد و پدر سونتاک عیسایش نامید. نامش را امیر عیسی بگذارید.

یوسف که از خشم قادر به حرف زدن نبود زیر لب به زحمت زمزمه کرد:

-باشد دخترم، اسمش را امیر عیسی می‌گذاریم

نسترن خاتون با صدای گرفته گفت:

-بله امیر عیسی پسر سارا، خوب شد که امیر خان نماند تا این همه مصیبت و رفتن تو را ببیند. آه ای خدا

خواهر روحانی سونیا بازوی سارا را فشرد و اشاره کرد که باید بروند و به نسترن خاتون و یوسف و تلی گفت:

-شماها می‌توانید برگردید و بروید به خانه‌هایتان

یکی از سربازان جلو آمد. طناب نازکی در دست داشت. شرم زده در حالی که سعی می‌کرد به صورت سارا نگاه نکند و نگاهش را از نگاه سارا می‌دزدید. اشاره کرد که باید دست‌هایش را ببندد

سارا پرسید: لازمه

خواهر سونیا پاسخ داد:

-بله دستور است که شما را دست بسته ببریم.

دو خواهر روحانی جلوتر حرکت کردند. مرد نگهبان در را باز کرد و آنها بیرون آمدند. هوا ابری و مه آلود بود، بوی سوختگی و دود فضا را انباشته بود و هنوز از میان بعضی از ساختمان‌های سوخته و ویران دود برمی‌خاست اما اوضاع نسبت به چند روز پیش آرام تر بود. سارا نگاه کرد میدان مقابل کاروانسرا که محل داد و ستد، رفت و آمد بود. خالی و غم زده و متروک شده بود. جیلوها و سربازان روس با تفنگ و قطار فشنگ آویخته بر شانه و سینه در همه جا ول می‌خوردند. تعدادی از آنها دور مرد ساز زنی که زیر درخت نشسته بود و ساز می‌زد جمع شده بودند. مرد ساز زن می‌خواند:

امان سارا ، جانم سارا آی سارا

گزل (زیبا) سارا، خانم سارا، پاک سارا

گلین (عروس) سارا ، بیگیم (بزرگم وسرورم) سارا، جان سارا

گل رحم ائیله (بیا رحم کن)

قویما بو ملته سن قانا (این مردم و یا این ملت را گرفتار خون و خون‌خواهی نساز)

خزان یلی قالخب هوا دوماندی (باد خزان برخاسته هوا توفانی ومه آلود است)

دشمن کلیب گونلریمیز یاماندی (دشمن آمده و روزهایمان پرفلاکت است)

هیش بیلمیرک صباحمیز نساندی(هیچ نمیدنیم فردایمان چگونه است)

امان سارا، جانم سارا، آی سارا

گل رحم ایله

قویما بو ملته سن قانا

مرد ساز زن که شور گرفته و می‌خواند با دیدن سارا که دست بسته همراه خواهران روحانی و سربازان از در ویران کاروانسرا بیرون آمد. آوازش را قطع کرد و بلندشد و همراه گروه زیادی از مردم که جمع شده و غمگین و ناراحت بردن سارا را با دست بسته می‌نگریستند. پیش آمد و چشم به سارا دوخت. مردم مرتب می‌گفتند:

‐سارا ست، آن ساراست. دارند می‌برندش، دارند سارا را می‌برند

شوری میان مردم برخاسته بود. همه از دستگیری و بردن سارا خشمگین و ناراحت بودند اما توان هیچ کاری را نداشتند. فقط ایستاده و چشم به سارا و کالسکه‌ای داشتند که مقابل در کاروانسرا ایستاده بود. در بزرگ کاروانسرا دیگر کاملا ویران شده بود و در و پنجره خانه یوسف و تلی و دیگر ساختمان‌ها هم همین طور، سارا از مقابل مردم جمع شده گذشت، حتی گرجی‌ها و جیلوها هم از شرم سرشان را پائین انداخته و مغموم بودند. کنار کالسکه که رسیدند ایستاد. نگاهی ازحسرت به در و دیوار ساختمان‌های ویران و حیاط بزرگ اما در هم ریخته کاروانسرا انداخت، هوا گرفته بود، دل او هم همین طور. یوسف از پشت پنجره دید که سارا گریه می‌کرد. خواهر سونیا که تمام توجه‌اش به حالت و رفتار و صحبت‌های سارا بود. بازوی او را فشرد و اشاره کرد که باید سوار شود. سارا کمی گیج بود، حالت دیگری داشت، احساس تنهایی و ترس می‌کرد. آرام اشک‌هایش را با دستمالش پاک کرد و سوار شد. خواهر سونیا و دیگران هم سوار شدند و سربازها بر بالا و پشت کالسکه رفته و جا گرفتند و کالسکه حرکت کرد. با حرکت کالسکه سارا احساس کرد که برای همیشه می‌رود. از پنجر پهلویی

کالسکه که نگاه کرد در انتهای حیاط کاروانسرا مقابل یکی از اصطبل‌ها که هنوز سالم بود اسب‌هایش را دید که کنار کالسکه‌اش ایستاده‌اند. همان دو اسب سیاه، اسب‌های پدرش امیرخان، همان اسب‌هایی که او را از تفلیس به اورمیه آورده بودند، همان اسب‌هایی که شبانه در آن سرما و تاریکی و ناامنی او را همراه بچه‌اش به ده بردند. اسب‌ها با نگاه غمزده رفتن او را نگاه می‌کردند. اسب‌ها خمیده بودند، اسب‌ها شکسته و خسته گویی می‌گریستند.

سارا فهمید که دیگر آن‌ها را نخواهد دید. چشمانش را بست و در دل بر سرنوشت خود و همه چیز گریست.

هوای اطاق سرد بود و سارا احساس سرما می‌کرد. آن روز، سومین روز فروردین ماه بود و چهار روز از زایمان و تولد فرزند او می‌گذشت. او را در اطاق کوچکی در زیر زمین کلیسا زندانی کرده بودند. اطاق فقط یک پنجره کوچک نزدیک سقف داشت که نور کم رنگی از آن به داخل آن می‌تابید و به دلیل ارتفاع و قرار گرفتن آن در بالا نزدیک سقف سارا بزحمت می‌توانست بیرون را ببیند و وقتی هم که روی انگشتان پایش می‌ایستاد و نگاه می‌کرد جز نرده‌های آهنین جلو پنجره و سنگ فرش مفروش حیاط پشتی کلیسا و تنه چند درخت چیز دیگری نمی‌دید. بر دیوار کنار پنجره عکسی از مسیح مصلوب و بر پائین آن تسبیحی کوتاه مزین به صلیبی فلزی نصب و آویخته بودند و بر طاقچه کوچک گود هرمی شکل

دیوار مقابل پنجره دو شمعدان کوچک سفالین با شمع‌های نیمه سوخته قرار داشت. کف اطاق با آجرهای مربع شکل مفروش شده بود و بر روی آن حصیری بزرگ انداخته بودند و در انتها در گوشه‌ی راست اطاق تخت چوبی باریکی قرار داشت و پارچه کهنه‌ای را که بی‌شباهت به روتختی نبود تا کرده و در انتهای تخت قرار داده بودند. چند ساعتی از آوردن سارا به کلیسا و زندانی کردنش در این اطاق می‌گذشت. او قبلا توصیف کلیسا و ساختمان دیر قدمی و تاریخی آن را شنیده بود اما هرگز تا صبح آن روز آن را ندیده بود. کلیسا در حاشیه شهر میان باغ‌ها و مزارع قرار داشت و ساختمان آن و دیر قدیمی‌کنار آن را هیات ارتدوکسی روسیه بعد از آمدن و مسلط شده سپاه روسیه به اورمیه مرمت کرده و در آن مستقر شده بودند. صبح وقتی او را با دست بسته مقابل در کلیسا از کالسکه پیاده می‌کردند. آقا پطروس سردسته اداری و نظامی جیلوها با آقای شید نماینده کنسولی امریکا و کاپیتان کراسی افسر انگلیسی و یک افسر روس و یک کشیش مشغول صحبت بودند. آقا پطروس وقتی سارا را دید با نگاه و لبخند معنی داری به سارا سلام داد اما دیگران رویشان را بطرف دیگری گرفتند و خود را به ندیدن زدند. سارا لحظه‌ای ایستاد. فهمید که باید وقار و توانمندی خود را حفظ کند. با وجود این که در اثر زایمان و حوادث چند روز گذشته بشدت لاغر وضعیف و ناتوان شده بود با این همه قامت راست کرد و با متانت و آرامش سلام آقا پطروس را گرفت و با گام‌های استوار همراه خواهران روحانی داخل کلیسا رفت. وقتی وارد کلیسا شد در راهرو کلیسا پدر سونتاک را دید که با حالت نزار و پژمرده و متفکر روی نیمکت نشسته و با کشیش جوانی مشغول گفتگو است. کشیش سونتاک او را که دید از

جایش برخاست و سلام کرد و دعایی خواند و صلیب کشید. سارا هم به تشکر و با خضوع جواب سلام او را داد. پدر سونتاک نگران خیره خیره به سارا نگریست اما نتوانست به سارا چیزی بگوید. چون خواهر روحانی سونیا که از بازوی سارا گرفته بود اشاره کرد که به انتهای راهرو و بعد به زیر زمین بروند. از راهرو گذشتند و از پله‌ها پائین که رفتند هوای سرد و نمور زیرزمین بر تن و جانشان نشست. نگهبانی که جلوتر از آن‌ها حرکت می‌کرد وقتی به مقابل در اطاق رسیدند نخست در اطاق را گشود و بعد بند دستان او را باز کرد و خواهر روحانی سونیا با اخم اما شرم گفت که، باید در اطاق منتظر بماند.

دو ساعتی از ظهر می‌گذشت و در این مدت هنوز کسی بدیدنش نیامده بود جز خواهر روحانی کریستیانا که دختر میان سال مهربانی بود و رفتار و برخوردی احترام آمیز با او داشت. ظهر وقتی در سینی کوچکی برای ناهار او سوپ با کمی نان آورد. سارا از او پرسید:

–مرا چرا به این جا آورده‌اند تا کی باید این جا منتظر بمانم؟

خواهر کریسیانا گفت:

–نمی‌دانم اما فکر می‌کنم تا پایان بازجویی و شاید محاکمه این جا خواهید بود و اگر بی گناهی و ایمانتان به کلیسا ثابت شود به تفلیس باز گردانده خواهید شد.

و بعد با دلسوزی و تمنا اضافه کرد:

–سارای مقدس لطفا بفکر جانتان باشید. از آن‌ها اطاعت کنید. بعدا می‌توانید به این جا باز گردید.

سارا متفکر و نگران سر به زیر افکند وگفت:

-دلم برای بچه‌ام تنگ شده فکر می‌کنم الان خیلی گرسنه باشد. همیشه همین موقع‌ها من به او شیر می‌دادم.

دوساعتی از ظهر می‌گذشت. سارا دلش بیشتر از قبل برای بچه‌اش و عمه نسترن و یوسف و تلی و خانه و مردم روستایش تنگ شده بود. چند بار بر در کوفته بود اما کسی جوابی نداده بود در همین فکر بود که در اطاق گشوده شد و خواهر سونیا به همراه خواهر کریستیانا که بچه سارا را در بغل داشت وارد شدند. سارا تا بچه‌اش را در آغوش کریستیانا دید با شوق و مهر از جایش بلند شد و آغوش گشوده بطرف او آمد. خواهر روحانی سونیا گفت:

-می‌توانی بچه‌ات را شیر بدهی. بعد از شیر دادن آماده شو باید به اطاق شور برویم. خواهر روحانی کریستیانا این جا خواهد ماند بعد از شیر دادن بچه‌ات را باید به او بسپاری.

سارا گفت:

-نه، می‌خواهم بچه‌ام پیشم باشد

-نمی‌توانی با بچه‌ات به اطاق شور بیایی. قدغنه

سارا بچه‌اش را آغوش گرفت و غرق بوسه نمود و در حالی که اشکش گرفته بود. رفت روی تخت چوبی نشست و مشغول شیر دادن به او شد. کمی بعد خواهر سونیا همراه نگهبان آمد و گفت:

-باید برویم.

سارا بلند شد بچه‌اش را به خواهر کریستیانا سپرد و بعد دستی به پیراهن و دامنش کشید و روسریش را روی سرش مرتب کرد و گفت:

-من آماده‌ام.

نگهبان با طناب پیش آمد. سارا ایستاد و با تعجب نگاه کرد، خواهر سونیا گفت:

-متاسفم دستور داده‌اند شما را با دستان بسته به اطاق شور ببریم.

دستان سارا را با طناب بستند و بعد از بالا رفتن از پله‌های زیر زمین و گذشتن از راهرو باریک از کلیسا خارج شدند. هنگام خروج سارا نسترن خاتون را به همراه یوسف و تلی دید که کنار سرکیس شاگرد یوسف ایستاده بودند. سارا فهمید که بچه‌اش را آن‌ها آورده‌اند. بعد از خروج از کلیسا به حیاط پشتی پیچیدند. حیاط پشتی کلیسا که دارای درختان تنومند و بلند و بسیار دنج و ساکت بود. ساختمان آجری کوچکی قرار داشت که بیشتر نمازخانه و یا محل اقامت و بحت و گفتگوی کشیشان بود. جلو در ساختمان توقفی کوتاه کردند و خواهر سونیا تو رفت و بعد بیرون آمد و به اشاره گفت که داخل شوند. سارا همراه خواهر سونیا و نگهبان تو رفت و بعد از گذشتن از راهروی کوتاه و چند در تو در تو وارد اطاق بیضی شکلی شدند که دور تا دورش کمدهای چوبی حاوی کتاب و میزهای مطالعه و عبادت با نیمکت‌های دراز بدون پشتی قرار داشت و در انتهای قسمت گرد اطاق که میزهایش نسبت به سایر میزها کمی بلند بود سه کشیش و دو مرد گرجی به عنوان اعضاء شور نشسته بودند و نیمکت کوچکی هم وسط اطاق بود که سارا بعد از ورود فهمید که آن را برای نشستن او گذاشته‌اند. سارا که همراه خواهر سونیا و نگهبان وارد شد. آن‌ها یعنی همان اعضا شور صحبتشان را قطع کرده و چشم به او دوختند. سارا

مقابل در همین طور ایستاد و منتظر ماند. کشیش نسبتا پیری که ماتیاس نام داشت و سردسته گروه بود و سارا تا آن موقع اورا هرگز ندیده بود با دست اشاره کرد و گفت:

-نزدیک‌تر بیایید.

خواهر سونیا به سارا اشاره کرد که نزدیک‌تر برود و او را تا کنار نیمکت کوچک وسط اطاق همراهی کرد و بعد رفت و کنار در پشت یکی از میزها نشست و به نگهبان هم اشاره کرد که کنار در هم چنان منتظر بماند. سارا کنار نیمکت ایستاد و چشم بر آن‌ها دوخت که خیره خیره وکنجکاو به او می‌نگریستند. سارا وقتی خوب دقیق شد. چهره کشیش پیمن را که در سمت چپ نشسته و سر به زیر افکنده بود شناخت. به اشاره کشیش ماتیاس پیر، کشیش جوانی که در سمت راست کنار آن دو مرد گرجی نشسته بود و معلوم بود که او هم از تفلیس آمده است بلند شد و بعد از دعا خطاب به سارا گفت:

-دوشیزه مریم بنی کریستوا مسختا ملقب به سارا شما متهم به کفر و ترک دین اجدادیتان مسیح و امتناع از بازگشت به کلیسا و رد مقام و منزلت کلیسا هستید. برای همین چون هیئت شور کلیسای تفلیس شما را جز مقدسان انتخاب شده می‌داند مایل است که بداند آیا آن چه که در مورد شما گفته شده بخصوص ترک دین مبین مسیح و رد مقام کلیسا درست است؟ آیا حقیقت دارد که شما حاضر به بازگشت به کلیسایی که به آن تعلق دارید نیستید؟ البته هیئت شور در مباحث خود به این اعتقاد رسیده که تمام این‌ها بخاطر زندگی و خدمت شما میان مردم بیگانه‌ی غیرمسیحی بوده و افترا و تهمت‌هایی بیش نیستند و شما با بازگشت به کلیسا پاسخ

روشن خودتان را به این تهمت‌ها خواهید داد. دوشیزه مریم بنی کریستوا ملقب به سارای مقدس آیا پاسخی دارید؟ چیزی هست که باید بگویید؟ و حاضرید به کلیسا برگردید؟

سارا سر به زیر افکنده بر حسب عادتی که از کودکی داشت در حالی که صلیب یادگاری مادرش را در میان دستانش فشرده بود. هم چنان خاموش ایستاده بود و زیر لب دعا می‌خواند و خداوند را در آن لحظه تنهایی به یاری وکمک می‌طلبید. برای اولین بار بود که در برابر هیئت شور مورد بازجویی و تفتیش عقیده قرار می‌گرفت. کشیش ماتیاس پیر که سکوت سارا را با آن حالت روحانی که صلیب را میان دستانش گرفته بود و زیر لب دعا می‌خواند دید گفت:

-چرا پاسخ نمی‌دهی دخترم. صلیب مقدس را برای چه میان دستانت گرفته‌ای. چه در زیر لب می‌خوانی؟

سارا سرش را بلند کرد وگفت:

-دعا می‌خوانم پدر

-دعا می‌خوانی؟

-بله

-دعا برای کی؟

-برای نجات خودم و برای نجات همه

-از چی؟

-از دروغ، از کینه و دشمنی پدر

کشیش پیر اندکی سکوت کرد و بعد گفت:

-گفته بودند که تو انتخاب شده‌ای. بسیار خوب چرا نمی‌نشینی دخترم، دستانت چرا بسته است

-موقع آمدن بستند

-می‌دانی برای چی؟

-نه

- چون تو متهم به ترک دین هستی اما من می‌بینم که صلیب مقدس را در دستانت گرفته‌ای آیا این درست است که ترک دین مسیح را کرده‌ای؟

-کی گفته پدر؟

-گزارش شده دخترم. اگر درست نیست آیا حاضری به کلیسا برگردی؟

-به کلیسا؟

-بله به کلیسای زادگاهت در تفلیس. جایی که که به آن تعلق داری؟

-نه

-نه!؟

کلمه نه را تمام اعضا شورای بازجویی با تعجت بیان و در حالی که نگاه پر از پرسش خود را در نگاه هم می‌نهادند تکرار کردند. کشیش الیاس همان کشیش جوانی که متن اتهام‌های سارا را خوانده بود به اشاره‌ی یکی از مردان گرجی حاضر در جلسه بلند شد خواست صحبت کند که کشیش ماتیاس پیر با اشاره دست او را به سکوت خواند و رو به سارا کرد و گفت:

-چرا نه دخترم، چرا نمی‌خواهی به کلیسایی که به آن تعلق داری برگردی. آیا تو از مسیح وکلیسا روی برگردانده‌ای؟

-نه عالی جناب

-پس مسئله چیست، چرا نمی‌خواهی در زادگاهت میان خانواده و مردمت باشی؟

-من می‌خواهم این جا نزد فامیل و قوم خویش و هم وطنانم مثل یک فرد معمولی و آزاد زندگی کنم عالی جناب برای همین حاضر نیستم به تفلیس برگردم.

-ولی آن طور که برای اعضای این شورا گفته و روشن شده مادر تو سارو از خانواده قدیمی وابسته به کلیسای تفلیس بوده و تو هم در تفلیس بدنیا آمده‌ای و در دیر بوده‌ای؟

-بله عالی جناب اما این جا بزرگ شده‌ام

کشیش الیاس دوباره بلند شد و از کشیش پیر اجازه خواست و رو به سارا کرد و پرسید:

-ممکن است به ما بگویید شما در تفلیس کجا بوده‌اید؟

-در دیر بودم

-در دیر بودید؟

-بله

-برای چی؟

-مرا برای تعلیم و تربیت به دیر سپرده بودند. خانواده‌ام، پدر و مادر بزرگم و شورای اسقفی کلیسای تفلیس معتقد بودند که انتخاب شده‌ام.

-پس چرا در دیر نماندی؟ آیا از دیر فرار کردی؟

-نه من فرار نکردم پدر خواست که با او بیایم

-ممکن است بما بگویی چطور، چگونه از تفلیس به این جا آمدی؟

-پدرم در دیر بدیدنم آمد.

-نوشته وگفته شده که پدرت حق و اجازه دیدن تو را نداشته ممکن است بگویی که پدرت چطور و چگونه بدیدن تو آمد. آیا با تو قبلا قرار داشت؟

-با کمک پدر یاکوب کشیش مهربان کلیسای دیر. من همیشه برای اعتراف و درد دل نزد پدر یاکوب می‌رفتم و از آرزوهایم با ایشان می‌گفتم. بخصوص که آرزو داشتم پدرم را ببینم. فکر می‌کنم به همان خاطر پدر یاکوب کمک کرد که پدرم را ببینم و با او به این جا بیایم.

-کی و چند بار پدرت را دیدی؟

-دو بار در کلیسا در حضور پدر یاکوب او را دیدم. من هرگز پدرم را قبلا ندیده و نمی‌شناختم. یک روز صبح پدر یاکوب مرا خواست و پدرم را به من معرفی کرد. بعد از آن یک بار دیگر هم بدیدنم آمد و در دفعه سوم که به دیدنم آمده بود پدر یاکوب گفت که بهتر است با پدرت بروی.

-و تو آمدی؟

-بله

-چطوری از دیر فرار کردی؟

-نمی‌دانم من بچه بودم. پدرم دستم را گرفت و از در پشتی کلیسا بیرون رفتیم و به اورمیه آمدیم

-پس تو کوچک بودی و ندانستی و پدرت تو را دزدید

-نه، ندزدید

-چرا پدرت تو را با راضی کردن کشیش یاکوب و جلب ترحم او دزدیده

-نه ندزدید، من خودم آمدم. چون می‌خواستم و آرزو داشتم که پیش پدرم باشم

-دوشیزه مریم بنی کریستوا آیا شما موقع آمدن تعقیب نشدید؟

-تعقیب!؟ نمی‌دانم

-گویا هنگام فرار شما همراه پدرتان بین ماموران کلیسا و جوانان خانواده بنی کریستوا که تعقیب کنندگان شما بوده‌اند و پدر شما جنگ و گریز و تیراندازی هم شده. چون چند تن از مردان تعقیب کننده که برای نجات شما تلاش می‌کرده‌اند توسط پدر شما زخمی و کشته شده‌اند.

-نمی‌دانم

-آیا شما زخمی‌نشدید؟ چون بما اطلاع داده‌اند که وقتی پدرتان به اورمیه می‌رسد. خودش از سینه و شکم و شما از ناحیه‌ی بازو زخمی بوده‌اید. حکیم ژوزف پیره و حکیم اسکندرخان که زخم‌های شما و پدرتان را بسته و درمان کرده‌اند این مسئله را تایید کرده‌اند. ممکن است جای زخم را روی بازویتان به هیئت شور نشان بدهید

-نمی‌توانم دستانم بسته است

کشیش الیاس به خواهر روحانی سونیا اشاره کرد که در نشان دادن جای زخم بازوی راست به سارا کمک کند و خواهر سونیا آمد و آستین دست راست سارا را بالا زد و جای زخم کهنه گلوله را نشان داد

-این همان جای زخم گلوله است و نشان می‌دهد که پدرتان شما را از دیر دزدیده و با خود به این جا آورد

-نه پدرم مرا ندزدید من خودم خواستم که با او بیایم

-چرا خواستی؟

-چون می‌خواستم نزد پدرم باشم

-نزد پدرتان باشید؟

سارا که از سوال‌های کشیش الیاس ناراحت و عصبی شده بود اشکش گرفت و در حالی که رویش را به طرف کشیش ماتیاس پیر کرده بود. بغض گرفته گفت:

-پدرم مهربانترین کسم و تنها امید زندگیم بود، من هرگز مادرم را ندیدم از او فقط یک عکس و همین صلیب مقدس را دارم. من می‌خواستم مثل هر کودک دیگری کنار خانواده‌ام، نزد پدر و مادرم باشم اما مادرم هنگام زایمان من مرده بود و من فقط پدرم را داشتم و با او آمدم.

کشیش الیاس صحبت سارا را قطع کرد وگفت:

-ولی پدر و مادر بزرگت که بودند.

-آنها مرا به دیر سپردند در دیر فقط رنج بود، کنترل و تنبیه.

سارا بعد از گفتن این جملات نگاهی به خواهر سونیا انداخت، کشیش پیر با تعجب پرسید:

-ولی تو انتخاب شده بودی آیا این را نمی‌دانستی؟

-نه عالی جناب، من کوچک بودم و توجهی به این مسئله نداشتم. می‌خواستم مثل هر دختر بچه‌ای آزاد باشم، بازی کنم، بگردم و روزی که با پدرم می‌خواستم بیایم پدر یاکوب موضوع انتخاب شدنم را برایم گفت، او گفت با پدرت برو دخترم، این شاید تقدیر و خواست خداوند است که تو از دیر بروی اگر انتخاب شده‌ای هر جا که باشی وظیفه‌ات را انجام خواهی داد.

-آیا به وظیفه و مسئولیتت انجام داده‌ای؟

-بله با کمک و خدمت به مردم، با از دست دادن عمه‌ام، کشته شدن مردم روستایم، شهرم و کشته شدن پدرم، شوهرم

اشک نگذاشت سارا به صحبتش ادامه دهد. کشیش ماتیاس پیر که حال دگرگون سارا دید بلند شد و گفت:

-برای امروز کافیست. دوشیزه مریم بنی کریستوا ملقب به سارا من در تو تمام نشانه‌های آن بشارت دهنده و خادم و مهربانی را می‌بینم و به تو نصحیت می‌کنم و می‌خواهم که تا فردا صبح خوب فکر کنی و تصمیمت را برای بازگشت به کلیسا بگیری و خودت را وکلیسا را نجات دهی.

بعد به خواهر روحانی سونیا اشاره کرد و گفت:

-او را به اطاقش برگردانید.

سارا بلند شد وگفت:

-عالی جناب ممکن است اجازه دهید بچه‌ام را نزد خودم داشته باشم.

-می‌توانی به او هر چند نوبت که لازم باشد شیر بدهی اما تو به ریاضت و دعا و بازگشت به اصل فطرت وجودت نیازمندی. بهتر است تنها بمانی و به خودت بازگردی

خواهر سونیا بازوی سارا را گرفت و او را همراه نگهبان به زندانش همان اطاقی که در زیر زمین کلیسا بود برگرداند. شامگاه هوا کاملا تاریک شده بود که خواهر روحانی کریستیانا که مامور نگهداری از بچه سارا بود. بچه‌اش برای شیر دادن نزد سارا آورد و به بهانه‌ای که باید به دعا و نماز شبش برسد، رفت و بسیار دیر برگشت و در حالی که لبخند مهربانی برلب داشت به سارا گفت:

-نگران بچه‌ات نباش. من مراقبش هستم. تو هم دعایت را بخوان و شامت را بخور و بخواب.

بعد بچه را که خواب بود گرفت و رفت. سارا نشست لحظه‌ها به زندگی وگذشته‌اش، کشته شدن عمه نرگس، پدرش امیرخان، شوهرش آیدین و مردم شهر و دیارش و دیگر مسائل فکر کرد در وجودش غوغایی از درد بود. نمی‌توانست دروغ بگوید و نمی‌خواست به کلیسا برگردد دیگر اعتقادی به آن نداشت. همانطور که روی تخت چوبی دراز کشیده بود خوابش برد و تا سحر که با صدای خواهر روحانی کریستیانا بیدار شد خواب پدرش را می‌دید و در خواب با او بود. در خواب پدرش امیر خان با چهره‌ای اندیشناک او را صدا زد و راه باریکی را به او نشان داد که تاریک بود و انتهایش دیده نمی‌شد و گفت مواظب باش سارا

سارا بلند شد و نشست، بعد از شیر دادن بچه‌اش منتظر ماند. ساعتی بعد خواهر روحانی سونیا همراه نگهبان آمد. دوباره دستانش را بستند و به اطاق شور بردند. وقتی روی نیمکت وسط اطاق مقابل اعضا شورای تفتیش نشست. کشیش ماتیاس پیر رو به سارا کرد و پرسید:

دخترم شب خوب فکر کردی تصمیمت را گرفتی. می‌خواهی به کلیسا برگردی

-بله عالی جناب فکر کردم. متاسفانه من نمی‌توانم به کلیسا برگردم. آن راه، برای من راه تاریکی است

-نه، نمی‌توانی به کلیسا برگردی، آن راه، راهی تاریک است؟

-بله عالیجناب

-این جواب بسیار خطرناکیست دخترم

کشیش الیاس که چون دیگر اعضا شورا متعجب و خشمگین از جواب سارا بود بلند شد و گفت:

-بله آن راه برای تو تاریک است. چون تو نه تنها نمی‌خواهی به کلیسا برگردی بلکه دینت را هم ترک کرده‌ای.

-نه چنین نیست.

-بله چنین است. تو از مدت‌ها پیش دینت را رها کرده‌ای و به راه تاریک رفته‌ای، برای نمونه تو به خواهر الیزا از خواهران لازاریست همراه آمبولانس هیات فرانسوی که بدیدنت آمده بوده و تو را برای کار در آمبولانس وکلیسا دعوت می‌کرده گفته‌ای که نمی‌خواهی با هیچ گروه مذهبی همکاری بکنی و در خدمت آن‌ها باشی و بعد در حین صحبت با او گفته‌ای که دین همه چیز ما را از ما گرفته، ما را استثمار و بیگانه با خود و دنیای خودمان کرده، گفته‌ای که ما باید در همه چیز و همه‌ی باورها و عادت‌ها و اعتقادهایمان تجدید نظر کنیم.

-این‌ها گفته‌های پدرم بود عالی جناب او یک روشنفکر بود. من فقط گفته‌های او را نقل کرده‌ام

-نظر و اعتقاد خود تو چیست؟

-من به خدمت و محبت وآرامش معتقدم عالی جناب و فکر می‌کنم برای آن خلق شده‌ام.

-برای خدمت و محبت؟

-بله و انجام فرایض خداوند

کشیش پیمن که تا آن لحظه ناراحت و نگران از جریان بازجویی ساکت نشسته بود. بلند شد و روبه کشیش ماتیاس پیر کرد و گفت:

-بله محبت، محبتی که عیسی مسیح توصیه و بشارت داده‌اند عالی جناب گفته بودم که او پاک و مقدس و انتخاب شده است.

کشیش ماتیاس پیر رو به سارا کرد و گفت:

-دوشیزه سارا اگر حرف‌های جناب پیمن را قبول کنیم شنیده‌ایم که ایشان وقتی پیام عالی جناب سزر و هیات ارتدوکسی را به شما بیان کرده و شما را در منزلتان در حضور جناب نکتین کنسول محترم روسیه و خانم ایشان و منشی کنسولگری دعوت به بازگشت به کلیسا کرده‌اند. شما قبول نکرده‌اید و گفته‌اید که کلیسای من میان مردم است.

-بله عالی جناب

-یعنی تو منکر شان کلیسا و مبشران الهی هستی؟

-نه عالی جناب من اعتقاد به فداکاری و خدمت به مردم دارم و معتقدم دین خداوند و کلیسا هم برای همین است

-اگر چنین اعتقادی داری پس چرا در صحبتی که با خانم نیکتین کنسول محترم روسیه و دوشیزه الیزا یکی از خواهران لازاریست فرانسوی داشته‌ای، گفته‌ای که این جنگ و خونریزی را شما دولت‌های مسیحی به بهانه دین مسیح برای کشتن غیر مسیحیان به پا کرده‌اید. می‌خواهید هم اختلاف بیندازید و هم مسلط شده و غارت کنید و کلیسا هم سکوت کرده و چشمش را در برابر این همه فجایع و جنایت بسته و نمی‌خواهد ببیند که دارد چه اتفاقی می‌افتد و نمی‌خواهد مردم هم ببینند. فقط می‌خواهد مردم

به مسیح و کلیسا فکر کنند و چشمشان را در برابر این همه جنایت ببندند. من برای همین از کلیسا بیزارم. منظورت از این سخنان چه بوده؟

-من بیاد ندارم که چنین حرف‌هایی گفته باشم. من با خانم نیکتین و دوشیزه الیزا در مجلسی که از طرف حکمران اورمیه تشکیل شده بود. صحبت و گفتگو داشتم و اگر چنین مسائلی هم مطرح شده و یا من گفته‌ام در حین صحبت و بحث در مسائل جاری و وقایع بوده. وقتی آن همه کشتار و تاراج و جنایت را آدم می‌بیند چگونه می‌تواند بی‌تفاوت باشد؟

سارا با یادآوری آن روزها گریه‌اش گرفت و دستان بسته‌اش را که صلیب یادگاری مادرش را که میان آن‌ها فشرده بود بالا برد و سرش را خم کرد و بر صلیب نهاد.

-چی می‌کنی داری دعا می‌خوانی؟

-دعا می‌کنم که خداوند مرا ببخشد. چون من نمی‌توانم بی‌تفاوت باشم

-بی تفاوت؟ منظورت از بی‌تفاوت چیست؟

-من می‌خواهم، یعنی سعی می‌کنم و در آن صحبت و گفتگو با آن‌ها هم سعی کرده‌ام عواطف و احساساتم را بیان کنم

-احساسات را بیان کنی با کفر گویی؟

-لطفا متوجه منظورم باشید عالی جناب من فقط واکنش و احساسات یک لحظه خودم را بیان کرده‌ام

-چرا از دین خداوند و مسیح نگفتی، چرا به کلیسا پناه نبردی؟

-چون اهل کلیسا با نام دین و کلیسا آن کشتارها را کردند

-چی!؟

کشیش الیاس با خشم بلند شد وگفت:

-بلی حقیقت همین است که گفت عالی جناب، او کلیسا و دین مسیح و مسحیان را متهم کرده

-من چنین کاری نکرده‌ام

-تو بدتر کرده‌ای، تو دین مسیح وکلیسا را مقصر و عامد قرار داده‌ای، تو دین وکلیسای ما را لکه دار کرده‌ای، تو کافر و مرتد شده‌ای.

-نه

-تو کفر گفته‌ای و زنا کرده‌ای

-نه

سارا در حالی که اشکش گرفته بود مرتب می‌گفت:

-نه من کفر نگفته‌ام من هرگز زنا نکرده‌ام آه خدای من، من همیشه پاک بوده‌ام.

کشیش ماتیاس پیر، کشیش الیاس جوان را که از جایش بلند شده و آمده و بالای سر سارا ایستاده بود و بر سر سارا داد می‌کشید دعوت به نشستن کرد و خطاب به سارا گفت:

-دوشیز سارا گرچه من و بسیاری دیگر و اکثر اعضا این شورا معتقدیم که حاملگی و کودک تو حاصل همان معجزه بکرزایی مقدسین و منتخبین است که از سلاله وکنیه مریم باکره مقدس هستند و هر چند گاه روی می‌دهد. با این همه معتقدیم بیان حقیقت از زبان تو و اعتراف به این بکرزایی بسیاری از شبهات و سوظن‌ها را نسبت به تو حل و رفع خواهد کرد البته در این خصوص شاهدانی هم داریم.

کشیش پیر اشاره کرد و نگهبان رفت و کمی بعد کشیش سونتاک همراه خواهر روحانی ائما که هر دو بسیار ترسیده و پریشان و نگران به نظر می‌رسیدند وارد اطاق شدند و کنار در ایستادند. کشیش ماتیاس پیر آن‌ها را نزدیکتر خواند و خطاب به کشیش سونتاک گفت:

-جناب سونتاک شما این خانم را می‌شناسید؟

-بله عالی جناب

-اسمشان چیست؟

-ایشان سارا هستند.

-از کجا ایشان را می‌شناسید؟

-اکثر مردم شهر ایشان را می‌شناسد. ایشان دختر مرحوم امیر خان از خانواده سرشناس و خوب شهر اورمیه هستند و بسیار خیر و با ایمان و نوع دوست می‌باشند. به چند زبان آشنایی دارند

-ایشان کی و چطور و در چه حال و وضعیتی به کلیسای شما پناه آوردند؟

-پنج روز پیش نزدیک ظهر بود که آمدند. حامله بودند و خونریزی داشتند

-شما شاهد زایمان ایشان بودید

-بله، البته من ایشان را به خواهر ائما سپردم و در دیر خواهران زایمان کردند

-شما ایشان را فقط به نام دوشیزه سارا می‌شناختید

-بله عالیجناب

-می‌دانستید و خبر داشتید و یا شنیده بودید که ایشان ازدواج کرده‌اند

-نه عالیجناب

-آیا شاهد بکرزایی ایشان بودید

-در این خصوص خواهر روحانی ائما می‌توانند نظر بدهند. ولی من می‌دانستم که ایشان دوشیزه هستند

- متشکرم جناب سونتاک

کشیش پیر بعد خطاب به خواهر روحانی ائما گفت:

- خواهر روحانی ائما آیا شما شاهد زایمان دوشیزه سارا بودید؟

-بله عالی جناب

-شما هنگام زایمان از او مراقبت و پرستاری و کمک کردید؟

-بله عالی جناب

-چه کسی قابله ایشان بود؟

-وقتی ایشان را جناب سونتاک به ما معرفی و تحویل دادند درد و خونریزی داشتند و وقت زایمانشان رسیده بود. نمی‌توانستیم قابله خبر کنیم یعنی وقت نداشتیم. اوضاع هم خوب نبود. ناگزیر من با کمک دیگر خواهران زایمان او را انجام دادیم

-هنگام زایمان متوجه بکرزایی ایشان شدید

-بله

-تایید وگواهی می‌کنید که ایشان دوشیزه بوده و بکرزایی کرده‌اند

-بله عالیجناب

-متشکرم خواهر ائما خداوند مسیح حامی‌شما باشد

کشیش سونتاک و خواهر ائما با حالت دگرگون و ترسیده از اطاق بیرون رفتند. بعد از رفتن آن‌ها کشیش ماتیاس پیر رو به سارا کرد وگفت:

-دوشیزه سارا گواهی شاهدان را شنیدی ممکن است خودت در این خصوص حقیقت را به ما بیان کنی؟

- من بکرزایی نکرده‌ام عالی جناب. من ازدواج کرده و شوهر داشتم شاید جناب کشیش سونتاک از مسئله ازدواج من بی‌خبر بوده‌اند.

-گواهی خواهر روحانی ائما چی؟

-گفتم که من ازدواج کرده و شوهر داشتم

کشیش الیاس با خشم خطاب به سارا گفت:

-شوهر داشتی؟

-بله آیدن حکیم خان شوهر من بود

-چنین اسمی ما نشنیده‌ایم.

رو به کشیش ماتیاس پیر کرد و پرسید:

-شما شنیده‌اید عالی جناب

-نه

-هیچ کس نشنیده اگر چنین فردی بوده و هست حالا کجاست؟

-او را کشتند. همان روزی که به منزلمان ریختند

-عجب گفتی با او ازدواج کرده بودی کی وکجا؟

-تابستان پیش در منزلمان در حضور خانواده‌هایمان جناب شیخ الاسلام پیشنماز عقدمان را خواند.

-شیخ الاسلام!؟ یک روحانی مسلمان عقد شما را خواند؟

-بله

-یعنی تو اعتراف می‌کنی که از دین مسیح و کلیسا روی برگردانده و خارج شده‌ای و به عقد یک فرد ترک آذری مسلمان در آمده‌ای و یک روحانی مسلمان عقد شما را خوانده؟

سارا که کم کم به حقیقت این بازجویی و تفتیش پی می‌برد دریافت که دیگر هیچ راه نجاتی برای او نیست، یا باید خواسته آن‌ها را بپذیرد و به آن چه که آن‌ها می‌گویند اعتراف کند و چشم به روی همه چیز ببندد و حتی کشته شدن پدر و شوهرش و همه و همه را فراموش کند و به کلیسا برگردد و یا برای مجازات آماده شود. هم چنان سکوت کرده بود و غرق در فکر و نگران از آینده خود بود که کشیش الیاس با صدای بلند گفت:

-جواب بدهید این شیخ الاسلام حالا کجاست؟

-نمی‌دانم اما شنیده‌ام او را در خانه‌اش با تمام خانواده‌اش خیلی فجیح کشته‌اند یعنی قتل عام کرده‌اند.

-پس شیخ الاسلام هم نیست. لابد او را هم کلیسا و مسیحیان کشته‌اند؟

-بله، نمایند کمیته مسیحیان آقای آلکساندر مناسریان هم تایید کرده. ایشان که بدیدن من آمده بود قتل فجیع شیخ الاسلام را نقل کرد می‌توانید از ایشان بپرسید

-بگذریم اگر حرف‌های تو را بپذیریم برای ما ثابت می‌شود که تو اقرار کردی و می‌کنی که پشت به کلیسا کرده و از دین مسیح خارج شده و با یک فرد مسلمان بطور غیر قانونی نزد یک روحانی مسلمان عقد کرده‌ای. اگر این‌ها را بپذیریم که غیر ممکن است. پس تو از دین خارج شده‌ای یعنی تو کافر شده‌ای و زنا کرده‌ای و مجازات زنی که مرتد شده و زنا کرده باشد مرگ با آتش است.

کشیش الیاس یک لحظه سکوت کرد و بعد با صدای بلندی گفت:

-دوشیزه سارا من تو را مرتد و گناهکار اعلام می‌کنم

سارا دریافت که همه چیز دیگر برای او تمام شده است. از روی نیمکتی که نشسته بود بلند شد و با نیشخندی تلخ و پر از درد نگاهش را بر کشیش الیاس دوخت. کشیش پیمن که ناراحت از مسائل و جریان باز جویی بود خطاب به کشیش ماتیاس پیر گفت، چند لحظه صبر کنید عالی جناب و بعد از جایش بلند شد و نزد سارا آمد و گفت:

-دخترم آیا حاضری حرف‌های جناب الیاس را رد کنی و به کلیسا برگردی. باورکن خدا و مسیح حامی تو هستند

سارا با تلخی و اشک غلتیده به گونه‌هاش گفت:

-خداوند و مسیح حامی شما و همه باشند پدر. من پاک بوده‌ام و پاک هستم و می‌خواهم میان مردم در زادگاهم زندگی کنم و به تفلیس و کلیسا و کلیسا بر نمی‌گردم

کشیش پیمن با رخساری رنگ پریده و ناراحت گفت:

-این تصمیم و جواب بسیار تلخ و خطرناکی است دخترم

کشیش ماتیاس پیر با شنیدن جواب سارا از جایش بلند شد و دیگر اعضای شورا هم با بلند شدن او بلند شدند کشیش ماتیاس پیر رو به سارا کرد و گفت:

-دوشیزه سارا گناهکاری تو بخاطر اعتراف و امتناع تو از بازگشت به کلیسا برای ما معلوم و آشکار است اما باز نیاز به بررسی و تحقیق است. تو به زندان برگردانده می‌شوی تا تشکیل دادگاه منتظر می‌مانی، دادگاه مجازات

تو را تعیین خواهد کرد. خداوند و مسیح شاهدند که من و اعضاء شور بسیار تلاش کردیم که تو را به دین و کلیسا برگردانیم .

بعد به خواهر روحانی سونیا اشاره و کرد و گفت:

-او را ببرید و تا تشکیل دادگاه برای هشدار و یادآوری عذاب خداوند هر شام پنج ضربه شلاق بر تن او باید نواخته شود. شاید که به ایمان خود بازگردد و خداوند بخاطر عذابی که می‌کشد از تقصیر او بگذرد و شاید هم او انتخاب شده‌ای است که برای جبران گناهان دیگران باید رنج بکشد و عذاب ببیند اگر این چنین باشد خداوند و مسیح مرا ببخشند.

۳

صبح روزی که بعد از چند ماه سارا را به دادگاه بردند ضعیف و ناتوان و بیمار بود. قامت بلندش شکسته، چهره‌اش رنگ پریده، گونه‌هایش زرد و چشمانش به گودی نشسته بودند در اثر ماه‌ها بر روی حصیری در کف زندان خفتن و شلاق‌هایی که هر شامگاه بر تنش نواخته بودند. لباس‌هایش چروکیده و کثیف و پاره و پاها و دست‌ها و قسمتی از پشت و شانه‌هایش زخم شده بودند و زانوی چپش در اثر ضربه لگد نگهبانی که مامور زدن شلاق بود. باد کرده بود. گیج و لنگان راه می‌رفت. وقتی لنگان وارد دادگاه که در اطاق بسیار بزرگی در قسمت شمالی کلیسا تشکیل شده بود شد.کشیش پیمن و پدر سونتاک را دید که با چهره‌ای گرفته پائین‌تر در قسمت شاهدان نشسته‌اند. هردو به احترام او بلند شدند. سارا که حالی دگرگون داشت سری به احترام برای آن‌ها خم کرد و سلام داد و با هدایت

خواهر روحانی سونیا رفت و در صندلی که در وسط اطاق روبروی قضات قرارداده بودند نشست و چشم بر اعضا دادگاه دوخت، اما این بار بر خلاف روزهای بازجویی و تفتیش بند دستانش را به اشاره رئیس دادگاه گشودند. اعضای دادگاه همان تیم و اعضا بازجویی او بودند با این تفاوت که کشیش پیمن که ایمان عمیقی به پاکی و مقدس بودن سارا داشت از گروه قضات کنار گذاشته شده و در جای شهود نشسته بود و به جای کشیش ماتیاس پیر که اکنون جز قضات بود اسقف الیا که چندی پیش به جای عالی جناب سزر به سرپرستی هیئت ارتدوکس انتخاب شده بود نشسته و رئیس دادگاه بود. سارا لحظاتی چشم بر اعضا دادگاه نهاد و بعد سرش را پائین انداخت و چشم بر آجرهای مربع شکل کف اطاق دوخت.

اسقف الیا بعد از نگاه به اعضای دادگاه سرفه کوتاهی کرد و شروع دادگاه و رسمیت آن را بر اساس موازین کلیسای ارتدوکسی اعلام کرد و از کشیش الیاس خواست که گزارشی از بازجویی و تفتیش سارا و شرح اتهامات او بخواند. کشیش الیاس که گویی ماهها در انتظار چنان روز و ساعتی بود و از ایفای چنان نقش و وظیفه‌ای لذت می‌برد. در سخنانی طولانی شرح کاملی از دو روز بازجویی و تفتش از سارا را ارائه داد و در آخر با جملات خشک و لحنی خشن اتهام‌های سارا را بر شمرد وگفت:

-عالی جناب. او منکر مقام و منزلت ربانی اسقف‌ها و مبشران دین خدا و مسیح و کلیساست و آنها را مقصر و مسئول جنگ‌ها و مصیبت‌ها می‌داند. او با وجود شهادت شاهدانی چون پدر سونتاک و خواهر روحانی ائما که شاهد زایمان و بکرزایی او بوده‌اند. منکر بکرزایی خود شد و اعتراف نمود

که از دین خود خارج شده و با فردی غیر مسیحی در حضور یک روحانی غیر مسیحی ازدواج کرده و فرزندش حاصل ازدواج با آن فرد است و نه بکرزایی و به جناب پیمن که او را دعوت به بازگشت به کلیسا نموده بودند، گفته بوده که کلیسای من میان مردم است. با این همه اعضاء شور باز به خواسته‌ی جناب پیمن او را دعوت به بازگشت به کلیسا کرد اما او که شیطان در وجودش رفته رافت ما وکلیسا را نپذیرفت و اعضا شور تصمیم گرفت که مدتی در زندان بماند و عذاب ببیند. تا شاید به فطرت خود بازگردد. حقیقت این است که او مرتد و کافر شده است و رای اعضا شور بر این است که باید به صلیب کشیده و در آتش سوزانده شود.

اسقف الیا بعد از شنیدن سخنان کشیش الیاس کمی تامل نمود و بعد از مشورت و صحبت کوتاه با کشیش ماتیاس پیر خطاب به قضات گفت:

- اعضاء محترم دادگاه سخنان جناب کشیش الیاس را شنیدید آیا گناهان و اتهام‌های دوشیزه مریم بنی کریستوا ملقب به سارا را تایید می‌کنید.

قضات دادگاه که همگی اعضائ هیات شور کلیسا بودند گفتند:

-بله

بعد اسقف الیا روی به کشیش پیمن و پدر سونتاک کرد و پرسید:

-جناب پیمن و جناب سونتاک آیا بر آن چه شاهد بوده‌اید و آن چه را که گفته‌اید و شهادت داده‌اید تایید می‌کنید.

کشیش پیمن و کشیش سونتاک هر دو بلند شدند و گفتند:

-بله تایید می‌کنیم اما تقاضای رافت و بخشش را بر او داریم

کشیش پیمن در ادامه صحبتش گفت:

-عالی جناب او جوان است و بی شک حوادث تلخ بر او اثر ناروا گذاشته‌اند. پیشنهاد می‌کنم که به دیر منتقل و مدتی مورد تعلیم و برخوردار از محبت شود. بی شک با گذشت زمان حقیقت بر او آشکار می‌شود و به فطرت خود باز می‌گردد

اسقف الیا از کشیش پیمن تشکر کرد و بعد رو به سارا کرد و گفت:

-دوشیزه مریم بنی کریستوا اتهام‌های خود را شنیدی آیا اعتراض داری؟

سارا که سر به زیر افکنده و نگاه بر آجرهای کف اطاق دوخته و در فکر و فضای دیگر بود. انگار سخنان اسقف الیا را نشنید و اگر هم شنید پاسخی نداد. اسقف الیا مجددا با صدای بلند سارا را خطاب قرارداد و گفت:

-دوشیزه مریم بنی کریستوا آیا نسبت به اتهاماتی که به تو وارد شده اعتراض و صحبتی داری؟

سارا سرش را بلند کرد و نگاهش را که مملو از اعتراض و رنج و درد بود بر اسقف الیا دوخت و گفت:

-اعتراض، اعتراض به چی عالی جناب؟

-اعتراض به گناهانی که متهم شده‌ای

-من گناهی مرتکب نشده‌ام و نمی‌دانم چرا با من این چنین برخورد می‌کنید. من را دستگیر کرده‌اید، ماه‌هاست که در زندانم و اجازه ندارم فرزندم را قوم خویش و فامیلم را ببینم از من از چه می‌خواهید؟

-از تو اعتراف و بازگشت به کلیسا را می‌خواهیم.

-اعتراف به چی؟

-اعتراف به حقانیت کلیسا،

-کلیسا؟

-بله کلیسا، بلند شوید و اعتراف کنید و از خداوند و مسیح طلب بخشایش کنید

سارا ناتوان وگیج و مریض حال همانطور که نشسته بود گفت:

-اگر گناهی کرده‌ام خداوند مسیح مرا ببخشد

اسقف الیا و اعضا دادگاه و دیگران که تقاضای بخشایش سارا شنیدند متعجب اما خوشحال نگاه بر هم کردند و بعد اسقف الیا گفت:

-بلند شوید و اعتراف کنید.

سارا هم چنان سرش بزیر بود ونگاهش بر آجرهای کف اطاق و مرتب می‌گفت:

-خداوند مرا ببخشد

اسقف الیا متعجب از بی‌توجهی سارا با صدای بلند و آمرانه و محکم گفت:

-دوشیزه مریم بنی کریستوا بلند شوید و اعتراف کنید. اعتراف کنید که گناهکار بوده‌اید و اکنون طلب عفو می‌کنید و به کلیسا برمی‌گردید.

با شنیدن جملات آخر اسقف الیا انگار پتکی را بر سر سارا کوبیدند و خنجری را در سینه‌اش فرو کردند. لرزش خفیفی در تمام وجودش پیچید. چشمانش را بست لحظه‌ای در خود فرو رفت و بعد تصمیمش را گرفت و با نیروی تازه یافته و در حالی که چشم بر صلیب زمردین یادگار مادرش دوخته بود به زحمت از جایش بلند شد و قامت راست کرد و نگاهش را در نگاه اسقف الیا و دیگر اعضا دادگاه دوخت و گفت:

-اسم من مریم بنی کریستوا نیست عالی جناب. نام من سارا بیگلربیگی افشار است. من دختر امیرخان و نوه سردار بهرام خان بیگلربیگی افشار

هستم. مادرم سارو دختر خانواده بنی کریستوا مسختا در تفلیس بود. من هرگز او را ندیدم، روزی که خودم را شناختم به من گفتند که مادرم دو روز بعد از تولد من فوت کرده از او فقط همین صلیب زمردین برایم بیادگار مانده و حسرتش که همیشه در سینه دارم. هشت ساله بودم که مرا به دیر سپردند. بی آن که خودم بخواهم.گفتندکه انتخاب شده‌ای. اما من معنی انتخاب شده را نمی‌دانستم و نمی‌خواستم به دیر بروم اما مادر و پدر بزرگم مرا به دیر تحویل دادند و رفتنند و من در دیر غریب و تنهاکه هنوز هم غم سنگین آن روزها را با خود دارم مثل یک زندانی ماندم و بسیار ناراحتی و زجر کشیدم. از همان روز اول آرزوی آزادی و ترک دیر را داشتم. برای همین وقتی پدرم برای بردنم آمد دیر را ترک کردم و همراه او به اورمیه آمدم اما کلیسای تفلیس و کسانی که می‌خواستند مرا برگردانند. نگذاشتند در آرامش زندگی کنم. آمدند پدرم را کشتند، عمه‌ام را کشتند. خانه و روستایم را ویران کردند. سال‌های سال در هر جایی تعقیبم کردند و از تابستان سال گذشته که ازدواج کرده بودم، تهدیدم کردندکه اگر به تفلیس و کلیسا برنگردم مرا و شوهرم را خواهند کشت و در آخرهم به تهدیدشان عمل کردند. شوهرم را کشتند و خودم را دستگیر و به کلیسا تحویل دادند و در کلیسا که برای من معنی مکان عبادت و نزدیک شدن به خدا و امنیت و آرامش را داشت. زندانی و هر روز شکنجه‌ام کردند و نگذاشتند فامیلم را ببینم، فرزندم را نزد خود داشته باشم. من نمی‌دانم کلیسا از من چه می‌خواهد؟ تنها گناه من این است که خواسته‌ام آزاد میان مردم و مثل همه زندگی کنم. گفته‌ام کلیسای من میان مردم است. این همان چیزی است که مسیح می‌گفت و من هم گفته و می‌گویم. کلیسای من همان محبتی است

که میان مردم است. ما باید آن را بشارت دهیم و حفظ کنیم. من نمی‌توانم این همه جنگ و خونریزی را که بنام کلیسا و دین مسیح و یا هر دین دیگری که به راه انداخته‌اند ببینم و ساکت بمانم. من به هیچ دین و آئینی که جنگ و کشتار را تایید کند تعلق ندارم

مکث کرد و برای چند لحظه‌ای چشمانش را بست تا نیرویی تازه بگیرد و بر ضعف جسمی و فکر و ذهن و احساسش مسلط شود و بعد ادامه داد: ‫-به من تهمت ناپاکی وکفر زده‌اند. آزارم داده‌اند. چون می‌خواستم و می‌خواهم آزاد کنار خانواده‌ام، مردم شهر و دیارم مثل هر فرد عادی زندگی کنم. من هیچ خطایی نکرده‌ام. همیشه پاک بوده و پاک زیسته‌ام و سعی کرده‌ام بنده پاک و خوب خدا باشم و آزاد زندگی کنم. من دیگر یک مسیحی ارتدوکس و دختر کلیسای شما نیستم و هرگز هم به کلیسای شما برنمی‌گردم. هر رایی که خواستید بدهید و مرا هر طور که می‌خواهید مجازات کنید. زندگی من دیگر تمام است.

سارا صحبتش را تمام کرد و نگاهش را توی صورت اعضا دادگاه دوخت. اشک آرام از گونه‌هایش روان شد. حالت دیگری داشت انگار به پایان خود رسیده بود و آن چه را که باید می‌گفت، گفته بود و آن چه راکه مقدر و خواست خدا بود و باید انجام می‌داد. انجام داده بود. چهره‌اش رنگ پریده و مهتابی شده و معصومیت دیگری یافته بود. با قامتی استوار و پرصلابت میان دادگاه در بهت و سکوت شرمگین اعضا دادگاه مصمم ایستاده و چشم بر آن‌ها دوخته بود.

هیچ یک از اعضاء دادگاه نمی‌دانستند که چه بگویند. لحظاتی به سکوت گذشت. بعد از لحظاتی، رئیس دادگاه اسقف الیا که انگار تحت فشار و ناخواسته صحبت می‌کرد و آن چه را که می‌گفت حرف و نظر و عقیده و خواست او نبود گفت:

-با این حرف‌ها و اعتراف‌ها تو دیگر یک مسیحی نیستی و باید مجازات شوی!

با دست به خواهر روحانی سونیا اشاره کرد وگفت:

-صلیب مقدس را از گردن او باز کنید

سارا معترضانه گفت:

-ولی این صلیب از مادرم به من رسیده یادگار اوست

اسقف الیا جواب داد:

-مادرتان یک مسیحی مقدس و معتقد بود، اما تو دیگر نه، صلیب مقدس را از او بگیرید. باید به تفلیس برگردانده و تحویل کلیسا شود

سارا صلیب زمردین را از گردنش باز کرد و بوسید و به خواهر سونیا داد و بعد در حالی که یقه پیراهنش را می‌گشود بغض آلود گفت:

-ولی جای آن را که همیشه بر سینه فشرده و دعا خوانده‌ام

بر سینه و در دل دارم آن را چطور از من خواهید گرفت؟

یقه پیراهنش راک ه گشود جای صلیب مثل جای زخم کهنه‌ای بر سینه‌اش نقش بسته بود. با مشاهده جای صلیب در سینه سارا تمام اعضا دادگاه با حیرت از جایشان بلند شدند. کشیش پیمن وکشیش سونتاک به زانو نشسته و صلیب کشیدند و همراه و هم صدا با کشیش ماتیاس پیر که مخالف مجازات سارا بود گفتند:

-عالی جناب دیگر نمی‌توان او را مجازات کرد، شما نباید اجازه بدهید.

اسقف الیا که بسیار دگرگون و آشفته شده بود و نمی‌دانست که چه باید بگوید و چه تصمیمی بگیرد. چند لحظه‌ای به فکر فرو رفت و بعد رو به نمایندگان کلیسای تفلیس و طایفه بنی کریستوا و اعضا دادگاه کرد و نظر خواست. اما آن‌ها هم با وجود این که خواهان مجازات سارا بودند دچار تردید شده بودند. اسقف الیا بعد از مشورت کوتاهی با اعضا دادگاه رو به سارا کرد و گفت:

-دوشیزه مریم بنی کریستوا ملقب به سارا تو متعلق به کلیسای تفلیس هستی در خصوص زندگی و گناهان تو باید شورای اسقفی کلیسای تفلیس تصمیم بگیرد. اما بخاطر خطاها و اعمال و مخالفتت با کلیسا و اعضا کلیسا در این جا و در این شهر برای آگاهی و عبرت عموم باید مجازات شوی.

بعد به خواهر روحانی سونیا اشاره کرد و گفت:

-اورا به زندان برگردانید. فردا نخست در شهر گردانده و بعد در برابر دیدگان مردم شهر به جرم مخالفت با کلیسا و دیگر اعمال خلافش با بیست ضربه تازیانه مجازات شود. بعد از مجازات به تفلیس برگردانده خواهد شد. خداوند و مسیح او را ببخشند.

سارا مصلوب دیگر

۱

صبح روز بعد وقتی کشیش الیاس همراه با خواهر روحانی کریستیانا و خواهر روحانی سونیا و دو نگهبان و یک مرد گرجی که هیکلی فربه و کوتاه و صورتی پهن و ریشی قرمز و چشمان برآمده زرد داشت برای بردن سارا آمد. ساعتی بود که سارا بیدار شده کنار تخت چوبی نشسته و چشم بر پنجره زندان دوخته بود که نور ضعیف و خاکستری از آن بدرون می‌تابید. بغیر از اندک زمان کوتاهی که نزدیک سپیده دم از خستگی خوابش برده بود شب را هیچ نخوابیده بود. تمام شب در تاریکی محض زندان زیرزمین کلیسا که از کودکی با چنان جا و مکانی آشنا و بسیار آن را تجربه کرده بود. روی تخت باریک و کوتاه چوبی نشست و به دیوار تکیه داد و چشم

بر زلال جاری تاریکی شب بیرون از پنجره دوخت که در آن حتی نور ماه و مهتاب هم دیده نمی‌شد. خاطراتش را در زندگی کوتاهش مرور کرد و به سرنوشت بدش اندیشید. سرنوشتی بدی که از روز تولد بر او انتخاب کرده بودند و او نتوانسته بود از آن بگریزد و رها شود و از روزی که از دیر گریخت و به همراه پدرش به ارومیه آمد. دنبالش آمدند و گفتند و خواستند که برگردد و اکنون او را به زور برمی‌گرداندند از مجازات شلاق نمی‌ترسید. می‌دانست که می‌خواهند او را جلو مردم شهر و دیارش که آن همه دوست داشت خوار و زبون کنند. برای همین تصمیم داشت غرور و متانتش را حفظ کند. چون به مردم شهر و دیارش اعتماد و اطمینان داشت. می‌دانست که او را می‌شناسد و می‌دانند که مسئله چیست؟ اما از رفتن و برده شدن به تفلیس وحشت داشت احساس ناامنی و تنهایی و مرگ می‌کرد. پدرش امیرخان در خواب به او گفته بود که آن راه، راه تاریک است. اکنون که می‌خواستند او را به تفلیس ببرند نمی‌دانست که با او چه خواهند کرد آیا او را خواهند کشت و یا چه؟ گریه‌اش گرفت. چرا نگذاشتند او کنار شوهرش خانواده و مردم روستایش، شهر و دیارش راحت زندگی کند؟ چرا نگذاشتند حتی چند روزی کنار بچه‌اش باشد و او را راحت در آغوش بگیرد و نمی‌دانست آیا بچه‌اش را به او خواهند داد و اجازه خواهند داد که بچه‌اش را ببیندونزد خود داشته باشد؟ بغضش گرفت. دلش می‌خواست در خانه‌شان در باغ ساران کنار نسترن خاتون بود و غم دلش را با او می‌گفت در شب‌ها و روزهای گذشته. یعنی تا روز پیش صلیب زمردین مادرش را همراه داشت و هرگاه دلتنگ و غمگین و ناامید می‌شد به آن پناه می‌برد،

در سینه‌اش می‌فشرد و غم تنهاییش را می‌شکست و احساس می‌کرد که تنها نیست. روح و سایه و یا حسی از مادرش در کنارش است. اکنون اما آن را نداشت. بغضش ترکید، گریه‌اش جاری شد از شدت غم و سرنوشت تلخ خود گریست، گریست تا سبک شد بعد از لحظه‌ها گریه و فکر به این نتیجه رسیدکه زندگی و سرنوشت او همین است دیگر چاره‌ای ندارد. باید حقیقت خود را و موقعیتش را قبول کند و بپذیرد که به مرحله دیگری از زندگی و بودنش رسیده است. همان مرحله‌ای که پدرش امیرخان آن را یگانگی عقل و احساس می‌گفت. مرحله‌ای که روحی تازه به او داده بود. بلند شد قدم زد به دیوارهای اطاق دست کشید. اطاقی که ماه‌ها در آن زندانی بود. بعد آمد و نشست و به دیوار تکیه داد و از خستگی خوابش برد. در خواب باز پدرش امیرخان را دید که با دو اسب سیاه همان اسب‌هایی که همیشه با او بودند آمده بود و می‌خواست او را ببرد و به او می‌گفت:

−سارا دخترم نترس، آرام باش تو به آن چه که می‌خواستی رسیده‌ای. بلند شو و بیا برویم

ساعتی بعد که چشم گشود آرام بود. با وجود این که می‌دانست که مجازات خواهد شد و روز آخر اقامت و حضور او در اورمیه است و شاید هم روز و لحظه‌های آخر عمر اوست و ممکن است در تفلیس او را به صلیب بکشند و بکشند اما غمگین و مشوش نبود، دیگر ترس و اضطراب هم نداشت پذیرفته بود که راه زندگی و رسالت او همین بوده است. آرام بود با روحی دیگر، روحی با آرامش عظیم. انگار همه چیز برای او به اوج و تکامل خود رسیده و تمام شده بود....

سپیده سر زده و هوا روشن شده بود و او با آن که شب را تمام نخوابیده بود اما هم چنان گشاده رو بود و با وجود خستگی صورتش رنگ و نور دیگر یافته بود و تبسم مهربانش را هم چنان بر لب داشت. وقتی کشیش الیاس و همراهانش در را گشودند از سفیدی و رنگ مهتابی صورت و چهره نورانی او در آن فضای تاریک و محقر و رنج‌آور اطاق یکه خورده و معطل ماندند و ناخودآگاه بر سینه صلیب کشیده و دعا خواندند و تا کشیش الیاس بخود بیاید و وارد شود. سارا برخاست و دستانش را برای بستن پیش آورد وگفت:

-من آماده‌ام.

کشیش الیاس شرمگین سر به زیر افکند و گفت:

-عجله‌ای نیست اول صبحانه‌تان بخورید بعد خانمی پیر که خود را عمه شما معرفی می‌کند با چند نفر آمده‌اند که شما را ببینند. صبحانه‌تان را بخورید و آن‌ها را ببینید. ما در همین نزدیکی منتظر می‌مانیم البته خواهر روحانی کریستیانا این جا نزد شما خواهد ماند.

کشیش الیاس با همراهانش رفت و خواهر کریستیانا مثل همیشه و هر روز صبح در سینی کوچکی چند قطعه شیرینی نازک کلیسا را با لیوانی آب آورده بود. سارا قطعه‌ای از شرینی را برداشت. خواهر کریستیانا که بسیار غمگین و ناراحت بود. سینی را کنار سارا رو تخت چوبی گذاشت و گفت:

-تا شما صبحانه‌تان می‌خورید من می‌روم پسرتان را می‌آورم

راه افتاد که برود برگشت و گفت:

-صبح امروز خانمی پیر که فکر می‌کنم عمه‌تان هستند. همراه با یک زن و چهار مرد آمد و چند سکه اشرفی طلا به صندوق کلیسا اهدا کرد و خواست که بچه‌ات را به او تحویل دهند. قبول نکردند اما اجازه دادند که تورا ببیند. سارا فهمید که عمه‌اش نسترن خاتون از تصمیم کلیسا و سرنوشت او با خبر شده و برای همین قصد داشته پسر او را تحویل بگیرد اشکش گرفت. او می‌دانست و همیشه احساس کرده بود و یک بار هم یکی از نگهبان‌ها به او گفته بود که نسترن خاتون هر روز برای دیدن او به در کلیسا می‌آید و ساعت‌ها منتظر می‌ماند اما نمی‌گذارند او را ببیند. در همین فکر بود که نگهبان در اطاق را گشود و نسترن خاتون و تلی و یوسف و سرکیس و یاکمن و کدخدا وارد شدند. نسترن خاتون پیر با این که بسیار سعی می‌کرد که خود را آرام نشان دهد. اما نتوانست پیر زن چنان در هم ریخته و ناراحت بود که توان حرف زدن را نداشت. وقتی روبروی سارا قرار گرفت اشک گونه‌هایش را پوشاند و در حالی که سارا را به آغوش می‌کشید مرتب گفت:

-آخ سارا عزیزم، دختر نازنیم با تو چه کرده‌اند؟ آه ای خدا

پیرزن از شدت ناراحتی می‌لرزید و قادر به صحبت نبود. سارا با این که اشکش گرفته بود سعی کرد خود را مقاوم نشان دهد و نسترن خاتون را دلداری داد و آرام کرد و گفت:

-مرا ببخشید من دختر خوبی برای شما نبودم

-تو از فرشته‌ها هم پاکتر و خوبتر بودی و هستی عزیزم

بعد با تلی و یوسف و یاکمن و سرکیس و کدخدا احوال پرسی کرد و از مردم دهکده‌اش ساران پرسید. آنها دورش کردند در همین حین خواهر

روحانی کریستیانا امیر عیسی را آورد همگی بطرف او برگشتند. سارا شوق زده دستانش را گشود و پسرش را در آغوش گرفت و در سینه فشرد و غرق بوسه کرد. پسرش در آن چند ماه بزرگ شده بود و با لبخند و نگاه‌های پرشور او را نگاه می‌کرد انگار خود او بود بسیار شباهت به خود او داشت. نسترن خاتون به التماس از سارا خواست که جانش را نجات دهد و گفت:

-دخترم حالا که می‌خواهند تو را به تفلیس ببرند هر چه می‌گویند قبول کن بگو توبه می‌کنی نگذار تو را شلاق بزنند. امید داشته باش همیشه اوضاع همین طور نخواهد ماند.

یوسف گفت:

-شما هر چه می‌گویند قبول کنید، نگران نباشید. هر طور شده نجاتتان می‌دهیم. حالا که تصمیم گرفته‌اند و شما را به تفلیس می‌برند. ما هم به تفلیس می‌آییم.

سارا گفت:

-مرا ببخشید، شماها را دوست دارم اما نمی‌توانم. اگر هر چه بگویند قبول کنم دیگر سارا نیستم آن وقت چگونه زنده بمانم. نه نمی‌توانم. از آن گذشته آن‌ها هم قبول نمی‌کنند. چون هر طور شده باید بهانه‌ای برای شلاق زدن و بردن من به تفلیس داشته باشند

سرکیس گفت:

-شما هر چه آن‌ها می‌گویند قبول کنید. بگویید تقاضای بخشش می‌کنید. می‌خواهید به کلیسا برگردید. نترسید نمی‌گذاریم شما را شلاق بزنند و دست بسته ببرند

یاکمن گفت:

-سارا ی عزیز لطفا

کدخدا گفت:

-خانم تمام مردان ده مسلح شده و آماده‌اند

نسترن خاتون گفت:

-کالسکه‌ات را آماده کرده وآورده‌ایم. اگر اجازه بدهند ما هم همراهت می‌آییم و اگر هم قبول نکردند پشت سرت خواهیم آمد نترس دخترم تنهایت نخواهیم گذاشت.

سارا دست‌های عمه‌اش را در میان دستانش گرفت و در حالی که می‌بوسید رو به کدخدا کرد و گفت:

-ممنونم اما نه، حق ندارید اقدامی بکنید. حاضر نیستم بخاطر من جنگ و دعوایی روی بدهد و کسی زخمی و صدمه ببیند. بگذارید این جنگ و خون ریزی تمام شود. شماها از اصل موضوع و مسئله خبر ندارید.آن‌ها یعنی یک عده‌ای نمی‌خواهند من این جا باشم. همانطور که نمی‌خواستند پدرم این جا باشد. برای همین با عنوان کردن حضور من در این جا خانواده و طایفه مادری مرا تحریک کرده‌اند. طایفه بنی کریستوا اگر مرا بنا به سنت و رسم و آئین کلیسایشان انتخاب شده و مقدس نامیده‌اند. برای این است که معتقدند هر چندگاه یک برگزیده‌ای پسر و یا دختری که پاک است و مقدس و انتخاب شده است. بدنیا می‌آید و برای جبران گناهان و نجات آن‌ها و دوام کلیسای آن‌ها فداکاری می‌کند، زجر می‌کشد و گاه کشته و مصلوب می‌شود. پدرم اگر مرا از دیر گرفت و به این جا آورد. بخاطر همین مسئله و برای نجات من بود و آن‌ها هم اگر در تمام این سال‌ها همیشه به

دنبال من بودند. بدلیل همین اعتقادشان برای نجات طایفه وکلیسایشان بود و امروز هم اگر می‌خواهند مرا به تفلیس ببرند بخاطر همین اعتقادشان است.

یوسف و کدخدا گفتند:

-نمی‌گذاریم

سارا گفت:

-نه، گفتم که نمی‌خواهم بخاطر من کسی صدمه ببیند و بمیرد

نسترن خاتون گفت:

-پس چه باید بکنیم؟

-باید منتظر بمانید. اگر زنده ماندم بالاخره روزی برمی‌گردم

-کی؟ من که عمرم به سر رسیده، ای کاش می‌مردم و تو را در این حال و این روز را نمی‌دیدم. ای کاش خدا مرا بکشد. ما بی تو چه خواهیم کرد؟

سارا با چشمان پر اشک و حال دگرگون نسترن خاتون را بغل کرد و بوسید و گفت:

-نه شما نباید بمیرید. شما باید بمانید. چون من روزی برخواهم گشت. شاید این خواست خداوند است. احساس می‌کنم که با مجازات من آرامش به سرزمین ما برخواهدگشت. بالاخره یکی باید تاوان گناهان همه بدهد، امروز، روز آخر من در این شهر و کنار شماست. من را از این جا خواهند برد ولی من تلاش خواهم کرد که برگردم و اگر نتوانستم می‌خواهم بدانید هر جا در هر شرایطی باشم. همیشه دلم پیش شما خواهد بود و شما را دعا

خواهم کرد. شما هم سعی کنید کنار هم خوب زندگی کنید و با هم مهربان باشید

همه‌شان می‌گریستند. نگهبان آمده بود و وقت خداحافظی بود. سارا پسرش را که درآغوش فشرده بود و مکرر می‌بوسید. با حسرت و غمی‌که توان گفتنش را نداشت به خواهر کریستیانا داد و با همه وداع کرد و گفت:

-مواظب هم باشید.

نسترن خاتون نمی‌توانست دل از سارا بکند. سارا را بغل کرده بود و می‌گریست و مرتب می‌گفت:

-خودت را نجات بده خواهش می‌کنم. هرچه می‌گویند قبول کن

نگهبان او را از سارا جدا کرد و او همراه با بقیه با حال زار رفت. خواهر روحانی کریستیانا که در تمام آن مدت گوشه‌ای ایستاده و ساکت منتظر بود. بعد از رفتن نسترن خاتون و دیگران کنار سارا که غمگین با اشک ریخته بر گونه‌ها نشسته بود. آمد وصلیب کوچک آویخته از تسبیح دعای خود را مقابل سارا گرفت گفت:

-بگیرید. لطفا این را با خودتان داشته باشید. کمکتان می‌کند

سارا نگاهی به صلیب و تسبیح انداخت و گفت:

-ممنونم دیگر نیازی به آن ندارم. مرا ببخش اگر زندانی خوبی نبودم. تو خیلی مهربان بودی از تو بسیار ممنونم.

خواهر کریستیانا شرمگین و ناراحت در حالی که اشکش گرفته بود گفت:

-شما باید مرا عفو کنید من نتوانستم به شما خدمت کنم اما مطمئن باشید که جبران خواهم کرد من همیشه نزد شما خواهم بود. نگران پسرتان هم نباشید من از او مراقبت می‌کنم

کشیش الیاس که آمده و دم در اطاق کنار نگهبان ایستاده و منتظر بود بر در زد. سارا برگشت او را که دید گفت:

-من حاضرم

کشیش الیاس گفت:

-بله ما هم آماده‌ایم وقت موعد ظهر است. برویم نزدیک ظهر می‌رسیم. دستان سارا را بستند و در حالی که خواهر روحانی سونیا بازویش را گرفته بود کشیش الیاس جلوتر دو نگهبان مسلح در دو طرفش و مردگرجی پشت سرش حرکت می‌کردند راه افتادند. خواهر کریستیانا که بسیار غمگین و متاثر بود همراه آن‌ها نرفت همان جا ماند بچه سارا را در آغوش گرفت و روی تخت چوبی همان جایی که سارا نشسته بود نشست و گریان رفتن سارا را تماشا کرد. حالت و حس عجیب و دیگری یافته بود. حالتی که برایش تازگی داشت. حس مطبوعی از بیداری و دگردیسی، احساس می‌کرد او هم زندانیست و باید مجازات شود.

سارا همراه کشیش الیاس و دیگران که بیرون آمد. تمام اطراف کلیسا پر از مردان گرجی و جیلو مسیحی مسلح بود. هوا برخلاف روزهای معمول تابستان گرفته و غبار آلود و ابری و خاکستری بود. تیرگی و غبار آلودگی هوا با بادی که می‌وزید برای مسیحیان و کشیشان و رهبران کلیسا نشان خوب و خوش‌آیندی نبود. اسب‌های سیاهش بسته به کالسکه‌اش کنار کوچه نزدیک در حیاط کلیسا ایستاده بودند. کشیش الیاس گفت:

-کالسکه‌تان را خانواده‌تان آوردند. خواستند که شما را با این کالسکه ببریم. گویا با این دو اسب سیاه از تفلیس آمده‌ای، اکنون آن‌ها تو را برمی‌گردانند.

اسب‌ها که سارا دیده و بویش را شنیده بودند بی قرار گردنشان کج کرد و به او نگاه می‌کردند. سارا گفت:

-اجازه می‌دهید نزدشان بروم و نوازششان کنم

کشیش الیاس گفت:

-برای چند لحظه مانعی ندارد

سارا رفت با دستان بسته پیشانی و صورت و گردن آن‌ها را نوازش کرد و سرش را بر پیشانی و گردن آن‌ها تکیه داد و آرام حرف‌هایش را بگوش آن‌ها زمزمه کرد. خوابش را که نزدیک سحر دیده بود به آن‌ها گفت اسب‌ها ناراحت گوش تیز کرده نگران نگاه می‌کردند و مدام هورت می‌کشیدند و سرشان را می‌جنباندند. بعد از دردل و نوازش آن‌ها برگشت که سوار کالسکه شود. کشیش الیاس گفت:

-شما نباید سوار شوید، دستور است که شما را پشت کالسکه ببندیم و در شهر بگردانیم

سارا لبخند تلخی زد و چیزی نگفت، دستان بسته‌اش را با طناب به پشت کالسکه بستند و کشیش الیاس و خواهر سونیا و مرد فربه گرجی سوار شدند و به نگهبان‌ها هم گفتند که پیاده همراه و اطراف سارا بیایند و مراقب باشند. اما هرچه عنان اسب‌ها را کشیدند و تلاش کردند. اسب‌ها حرکت نکردند. سارا که متوجه عناد اسب‌ها شده بود آن‌ها را صدا زد و خواست که راه بیفتند و اسب‌ها آرام حرکت کردند. یوسف و سرکیس و یاکمن و

کدخدا و چند مرد و زن دیگر از اهالی ساران که بیرون کنار کالسکه نسترن خاتون و همراه با او منتظر بودند وقتی سارا را دست بسته در پشت کالسکه پیاده دیدند آمدند در اطراف و پشت سر او راه افتادند. سارا را در حالی که مردان مسلح در اطراف درشکه سوار بر اسب و پیاده احاطه کرده بودند بسمت میدان نزدیک دروازه‌ی عسگرخان کمی بالاتر از محله مسیحیان و کوی مریم مقدس می‌بردند و در حال حرکت مردم پراکنده و رنج دیده کوچه و خیابان‌ها را به هو و سرزنش سارا فرا می‌خواندند اما مردم ناراحت و عصبی از کار آن‌ها و قصد کلیسا برای مجازات نمودن سارا اعتراض می‌کردند و پشت سرکالسکه و یا از راه دیگر رو به میدان نزدیک دروازه عسگرخان محل اجرای حکم نهاده بودند. سارا را از میان کوچه‌ها و خیابان‌ها که عبور می‌دادند با اندوه می‌دید که کوچه‌ها و خیابان‌های شهر هم چنان در هم ریخته. خانه‌ها تاراج و رها شده است و مردم غمگین و پریشان و بی‌سامان کنار خانه‌ها ایستاده‌اند و عده زیادی که خانه‌شان ویران شده و یا از روستاها و شهرهای دیگر به اورمیه پناه آورده‌اند کنار خیابان‌ها و یا میان باغ‌های بخصوص باغ‌های توت آلاچیق درسته کرده و چادر زده‌اند. سارا با اندوه نگاه می‌کرد و زیر لب آرام باخود می‌گفت:

-چرا چنین شد؟ چه کسی این دشمنی را میان مردم انداخت؟

چه کسی همه را بر هم شوراند؟

و بر تنهایی و ویرانی شهر و دیارش در دل می‌گریست.

بعد از گذشتن از کوچه‌ها و خیابان‌ها، هنگام گذر از کوی مسحیان تعداد اندکی از جیلوهای عاصی تحریک شده که در حال هیاهو بودند با تعدادی

از کودکان و جوانان مسیحی شروع به دشنام دادن به سارا و سنگ‌پرانی به طرف او کردند. اما اهالی مسیحی محله اعتراض کرده و مانع از کار آن‌ها شدند و در حالی که بشدت ناراحت بودند. هنگام گذر او از مقابلشان صلیب کشیده و دعا خواندند و پشت سرکالسکه گریان و اعتراض کنان راه افتادند. بعد از گذشتن از کوی مسیحیان و حاشیه برکه فتحعلی خان به میدان نزدیک دروازه‌ی عسگرخان محل اجرای حکم که رسیدند هیاهو و فریاد مردم جمع شده و ایستاده در اطراف میدان برخاست. کالسکه را در گوشه‌ای از میدان دور از خاک‌ریز کوتاهی نگه‌داشتند که روی آن صلیب چوبی با پایه کوتاه که می‌شد حدس زد با عجله از تیرهای چوبی سقف خانه و یا انبارهای فروریخته و ویران شده ساخته‌اند و چندان اعتمادی به برپایی و استواری او ندارند قرار داده بودند که بیشتر به صلیب بالا گورها می‌ماند و هدفشان نشاندن سارا به زانو به عنوان اطاعت در برابر آن و بستن او به آن برای اجرای مجازات شلاق بود. وقتی دستان بسته سارا را از پشت کالسکه باز کردند و در حالی که بخاطر خستگی و درد زانو می‌لنگید و نمی‌توانست خوب راه برود به وسط میدان آوردند هیاهو و اعتراض و اشک وآه جمعیت اوج گرفت. زنان و مردان، پیر و جوان حتی کودکان متعجب از این کار اسقف‌ها وکشیشان کلیسا بودند. مدام از هم می‌پرسیدند و می‌گفتند:

مگر او چه کرده؟ از او که این همه خوب و مهربان و نیکوکار بود و به درد و دل و داد همه می‌رسید چه خلافی سر زده؟

کم کم سوال‌ها و اعتراض‌ها بالا گرفت بخصوص وقتی سارا را کشان کشان به کنار صلیب چوبی قطور اما کوتاه بردند. مردم به صدای بلند فریاد می‌زدند:

–او را آزاد کنید. او بی گناه است، او نباید مجازات شود. مگر او چه کرده؟ غوغای عجیبی بود. همراه با عصیان و فریاد مردم باران شروع به باریدن کرده بود و باد غبار گرفته می‌توفید. سارا را که کشان به کنار صلیب روی خاک ریز برده بودند روسریش از سرش روی شانه‌هایش افتاده بود. با دستان بسته به زحمت روسریش را روی سرش کشید و مرتب کرد. روسریش همان روسری بنفش کم رنگ مایل به خاکستری بود که در طول مدت زندان چروک و کهنه شده بود. بعد از مرتب کردن روسریش با قامت بلند و استوار کنار صلیب روی خاک‌ریز ایستاد. تنش نازک، روی مهتابیش گشاد، نگاهش مهربان و چون همیشه و همه وقت لبخندی از محبت و مهر بر لبش بود. آرام رو به جمعیت ایستاد کف دستانش را بر هم نهاد و بی اعتنا به همه چیز زیر لب شروع به خواند دعا کرد. جمعیت وقتی آن حالت او را دیدند در حالی که بسیار منقلب شده و می‌گریستند همراه با او شروع بخواندن دعا کردند. اسقف الیا که همراه کشیش پیر ماتیاس و دیگر اعضا دادگاه و مردان گرجی نماینده طایفه کریستوا وکلیسای تفلیس با گروه زیادی از سران نیروهای جیلو مسیحی و دکتر پاکارد و آقا شید نماینده کنسولی امریکا و کاپیتان کراسی افسر انگلیسی و چند نظامی‌عالی رتبه روسیه کنار کالسکه‌هایشان در حاشیه میدان ایستاده و شاهد دعا خواندن سارا بود نگران از ناراحتی و اعتراض مردم قادر بخواندن حکم و شرح

رای دادگاه در محکوم نمودن سارا نشد. به کشیش الیاس اشاره کردکه او رای دادگاه را بخواند. چون سر وصدا و اعتراض مردم هر لحظه بیشتر می‌شد گفت که مختصر و سریع بخواند. کشیش الیاس جوان با قد کوتاه و تیپ و سیمای نه چندان روحانیش به میان میدان رفت و شروع بخواندن حکم دادگاه کرد:

-ای جماعت، ای مردم دین‌دار و غیور مسیحی که برای نجات دین و میهن مسیحی و بر پایی حکومت مسیحی جان‌فشانی‌هاکرده‌اید. آگاه و مطلع باشید که روحانیون و خدمت‌گذاران کلیسای شما برای حفظ دین و حرمت کلیسا از سال‌ها پیش یکی از فرزندان فریب خورده را که از مسیح و کلیسا روی برگردانده بود با رافت بسیار نصحیت و تشویق و دعوت به بازگشت به آغوش کلیسا نمود اما او نپذیرفت این ملحدکه شیطان در وجودش رخنه کرده نه تنها قبول نکرد بلکه اعتراف کرد که مرتد شده و کلیسا را قبول ندارد و با فردی غیر مسیحی ازدواج کرده است. هیئت شور کلیسا و دادگاه با رافت وگذشت به او مهلت داد اما در او موثر نشد و در آخر با توجه به اعتراف‌های خود او و شهادت شهود، دادگاه دینی و شورای اسقفی او را که از منتخبین کلیسای تفلیس است خطاکار دانست و محکوم به مجازات نمود. امروز این گناهکار ملحد معروف به سارا با بیست ضربه تازانه مجازات و بعد به تفلیس برده خواهد شد تا در خصوص گناهان و زندگی او شورای اسقفی کلیسای تفلیس تصمیم بگیرد. خداوند و مسیح از گناهان او بگذرد

بعد از اعلام شرح رای دادگاه اسقف الیا همراه اعضا دادگاه سر به زیر افکنده با قدم‌های لرزان به طرف سارا رفت. همه بخصوص گرجی‌ها از

این عمل اسقف الیا متعجب و شگفت زده شده بودند نزدیک سارا که رسید سر خم نمود و صلیب کشید و با صدای بغض آلود و لرزانی دعا خواند و گفت:

-تو پاک و بی‌گناهی اما مقرر شده بود که مجازات شوی. خداوند و مسیح از گناهان ما بگذرد.

بعد از خواندن دعا با حال دگرگون بازگشت. انگار اسقف الیا با این کار خود می‌خواست به بی‌گناهی سارا اعتراف و خود را بی تقصیر و از او طلب بخشش کند. بعد از بازگشت او به اشاره کشیش الیاس ماموران اجرای حکم که اکثرا مردان گرجی و جیلو بودند و برای شناخته نشدن روی خود را پوشانده بودند. نخست سارا را مجبور کردند که روی خاک ریز مقابل صلیب به زانو بنشیند آن گاه سرش را به صلیب تکیه دادند و دستانش را بر صلیب بستند و شروع به نواختن شلاق بر پشت و شانه‌های او کردند. با هر ضربه شلاق خون از پشت سارا جاری می‌شد و هیاهو و اعتراض مردم که عصیان زده فریاد می‌کشیدند:

-او بی گناه است. او را آزاد کنید. کافر و مرتد شماها هستید.

اوج می‌گرفت. سارا بی آن که آه و ناله و زاری کند زیر ضربات دردآور شلاق چشمانش را بسته بود و دعا می‌خواند. ضربات شلاق سنگین و دردآور بودند و تن و جان نازک و ضعیف و خسته او توان تحمل آن‌ها را نداشتند. زیر لب مرتب دعا می‌خواند و خدا را به کمک می‌طلبید که بتواند مقاومت کند. چهره پدرش در خوابی که بامداد نزدیک سحر دیده بود جلو چشمش بود و حرف‌هایش در گوشش انعکاس می‌یافت، سارا نترس، سارا

دیگر نمی‌ترسید ضربات شلاق از ده گذشته بود و حس درد را در پشت و شانه‌هایش از دست داده بود. دیگر شانه‌هایش را حس نمی‌کرد و دستانش توان حرکت را نداشتند. بیاد پسرش افتاد. تمام آرزویش دوباره در آغوش گرفتن او بود. اکنون اما چگونه می‌توانست با ضربه شلاقی که به بالای شانه‌اش خورد و شانه‌اش را شکافت و خون به صورتش پاشید او را در آغوش گیرد. با ضربات دیگر شلاق سارا دیگر توانش را از دست داد. دستانش شل و سست شدند. قامتش خمیده و سرش به پائین افتاد. چشمانش سیاهی رفت، دیگر صداها را گنگ تشخیص می‌داد و نفسش تنگ شده و ضربانش تند می‌زد. ناگهان یکی از ضربات شلاق به پشت گردنش خورد و ضربه دیگر از پشت دور قفسیه سینه‌اش با شدت تمام پیچید و پوست پهلو و پشتش را کند و درد جان گاهی با آن ضربه در تمام وجودش پیچید و او را از خود ربود و بیهوشش کرد. وقتی دستانش را از صلیب گشودند. بیهوش به زمین افتاد. با افتادن سارا با تن زخمی و خونین خشم و فریاد مردم برخاست. نسترن خاتون که با چشم اشکبار شاهد صحنه بود. تحملش را از دست داد. تلی نتوانست مانعش شود با همه پیری به طرف سارا دوید اما نگهبان‌ها جلوش را گرفتند و هلش دادند و به زمینش انداختند. تلی و یوسف رفتند و بلندش کردند. جماعت بخصوص عده‌ای از مردان و زنان دهکده ساران که آن صحنه را دیدند. خشمگین به طرف نگهبان‌ها حمله ور شدند. جنگ و ستیز و زد و خورد شدیدی بین مردم و نگهبانان درگرفت. نگهبان‌ها و نظامی‌ها و جیلوهای ایستاده در اطراف که مسلح بودند شروع به تیراندازی کردند و مردم را عقب راندند و چند نفری هم زخمی شدند. خواهر روحانی سونیا با کمک یک خواهر روحانی دیگر

پارچه سفید و دراز و پهن و بزرگی را آوردند و سارا را که بیهوش با تن نازک و ضعیفش زخمی و خونین افتاده بود در میان آن نهادند و برداشتند و بردند و در کالسکه‌اش گذاشتند. کالسکه را که اسب‌های سیاه آن را می‌کشیدند به طرف کلیسای ارتدوکسی راندند. تلی که پرسیده بود: او را کجا می‌برید؟

گفته بودند: به کلیسا به همان زندانش بر می‌گردانیم و فردا همراه با هیات ارتدوکسی به تفلیس خواهند برد.

هنگام عبور کالسکه تن بیهوش سارا از میان میدان و کوچه‌های شهر جماعت مسلمان و مسیحی ناراحت و غمگین کنار هم ایستاده دعا می‌خواندند و می‌گریستند. گویی همه چیز پایان یافته بود و عبور کالسکه سارا از میان مردم گرد آمده از هر قوم و گروه و دین و آئین منظره غم‌انگیزی از پایان یک فاجعه و سال‌ها جنگ و خونریزی و روزگار شکست بود. باد تند می‌وزید و باران تند می‌بارید و هوا سخت منقلب شده بود.

۲

صبح روز بعد، آفتاب تازه دمیده بود که یوسف و تلی به همراه یاکمن و سرکیس از نسترن خاتون خداحافظی کردند و در پی کاروان گروهی از سپاهیان روسیه که افراد هیات ارتدوکسی روسیه و بخصوص کلیسای تفلیس همراه آن‌ها بودند و سارا را نیز درکالسکه‌اش همراه خود می‌بردند راه افتادند. تلی با وجود این که دل خوشی از سفر بخصوص سفر به تفلیس نداشت اما خوشحال بود که در پی یافتن و برگرداندن سارا می‌رود و امیدوار بود بعد از سال‌ها پسرش یعقوب را در تفلیس خواهد دید و یوسف هم که به نسترن خاتون قول داده و با خود نیز عهد کرده بود که تا سارا را برنگرداند هرگز برنخواهد گشت. دل به کمک پسرش یعقوب و هوهانس دوست امیر خان بسته بود. با این همه فکر و نقشه سرکیس را هم بد نمی‌دانست که در صورت امکان در موقعیت مناسب سارا را بدزدند و با خود به اورمیه برگردانند. اما مشکل اصلی پسر سارا امیر عیسی بود که نمی‌دانستند که نزد سارا و در کالسکه اوست و یا نه و برای همین باید در یک فرصت مناسب به کالسکه سارا نزدیک می‌شدند و سارا را می‌دیدند و یا با کسی که به سارا نزدیک بود مثل خواهر روحانی کریستیانا که همیشه بچه سارا را نزد خود داشت و مراقب او بود تماس می‌گرفتند و از حال سارا با خبر و پیغامشان را به او می‌رساندند. یوسف امیدوار بود که قبل از رسیدن به مرز با نزدیک شدن به سربازان روسیه و دادن پول بتواند کمک و همکاری عده‌ای از آن‌ها

را برای فرار سارا جلب کند. سرکیس اما سر شوریده داشت او امیدوار بود که در طول راه در یک فرصت مناسب بتوانند از غفلت کاروان نیروهای روسی و هیات ارتدوکسی استفاده کنند و سارا را از بند آن‌ها فراری دهند یاکمن اما چندان امیدوار نبود. او اگرچه تا تفلیس همرا آن‌ها می‌آمد و بعد از رسیدن به تفلیس از آن‌ها جدا شده و به وطنش سوئد برمی‌گشت. اما بسیار علاقمند بود که در اولین فرصت سارا را از دست آن‌ها برهاند و در این راه برای هرگونه فداکاری و اقدام آماده بود. او معتقد بود که بهترین محل برای ارتباط با سارا در ایروان و یا تفلیس است و می‌گفت می‌توان از شلوغی و بزرگی شهر استفاده کرد اما نگران اوضاع بود. می‌گفت با انقلاب کمونیستی که شده معلوم نیست که اوضاع روسیه چطور است؟ و متعجب بود که چرا هیات ارتدوکس روسیه قصد و شتاب در بازگشت به روسیه را دارند. چون با تغییراتی که در جامعه روسیه با حاکم شدن کمونیست‌ها روی داده بود حتما کلیساها هم توان و نیرویشان کم و محدود و دیرها هم تعطیل می‌شدند.

با راه افتادن آن‌ها نسترن خاتون که به جهت پیری نتوانسته بود همراه آن‌ها برود اما هزینه سفر و ماه‌ها اقامت آن‌ها را فراهم کرده بود. همراه با کدخدا تا بیرون دروازه ساران آن‌ها را بدرقه و با چشم اشکبار از آن‌ها خداحافظی کرد و بسیار سفارش نمود که مراقب باشند و هر طور شده سارا را ببینند و از حال و روز او با خبر و او را برگردانند. با رفتن و دور شدن آن‌ها که غباری کوتاه از پی اسب‌ها و درشکه‌ها برجای ماند. نسترن خاتون احساس کرد که دیگر بسیار تنها شده است. همان جا ایستاد و لحظه‌های دور شدن

آن‌ها را تماشا کرد و در آن صبح تابستان که باد غبار گرفته می‌وزید و هوا ناخوش‌آیند بود بر تنهایی و سرنوشت خانواده و شهر خود و سارا گریست.

* * *

چند روز بعد از رفتن آن‌ها نزدیک عصر کدخدا نزد نسترن خاتون آمد و خبر دادکه تعداد زیادی از خانواده‌های مسیحی به در باغ و دروازه ساران آمده‌اند و می‌خواهند آن‌ها را در ده پناه دهیم. نسترن خاتون متعجب پرسید:

- برای چی، چرا پناه آورده‌اند؟

کدخدا گفت:

-مگر صدای توپ و گلوله عثمانی‌ها را نمی‌شنوید. از صبح شروع شده و تا حالا غریده‌اند. می‌گویند سربازان عثمانی وارد شهر شده و خیلی از مسیحیان را گرفته‌اند

-پس جیلوها و روس‌ها چه شده‌اند؟

-روس‌ها که رفته‌اند. آن‌ها به مملکتشان برگشته‌اند. جیلوها و دیگر مسحیان شورشی هم که جز آن‌ها بودند از روز پیش راه افتاده و رفته‌اند اما خبر رسیده که در چند جا راه را برآن‌ها بسته‌اند و وضع خوبی ندارند و آن‌هایی که مانده‌اند مخالف بوده و هیچ دخالتی در اتفاقات نداشته‌اند اما ترس از انتقام‌گیری دارند برای همین اکثر مسیحیان شهر و روستاهای اطراف به این جا آمده‌اند. نسترن خاتون تبسم تلخی کرد و بعد به کدخدا گفت :

-برو بگو آن‌ها را با حرمت در ده جا دهند

-نمی‌توانیم خانم به قدر کافی غذا نداریم

-قناعت می‌کنیم

-ولی معلوم نیست که همه‌شان بی‌گناه و هیچ‌کاره باشند

-آن‌ها به ما پناه آورده‌اند کدخدا ما کاری با گناه و عمل آن‌ها نداریم.

-ولی همین‌ها بودند که سارا خانم را زندانی و شکنجه کرده و با خود بردند.

نسترن خاتون وقتی جملات آخر کدخدا و اسم سارا را شنید لحظه‌ای مکث کرد و بعد گفت:

-کدخدا اگر سارا بود همین کار را می‌کرد. برو بگو آن‌ها را در ده جا دهند.

بعد برگشت رفت به اطاقش کنار پنجره رو به کوهستان نزدیک ده که در دامنه‌اش امیرخان و نرگس خاتون را به خاک سپرده بودند نشست و چشم به بیرون دوخت. دلش گرفته و ویران بود. ویران از آن چه بر آن‌ها رفته بود. سارا برای او و برای همه یک فرشته آرامش بخش بود. حال در این سال و روزگار تباهی بی او چه می‌توانست بکند. سارا گفته بود اگر وبران کردند دوباره بسازید و او اکنون باید همان کار را می‌کرد که سارا خواسته بود. خواسته و محبت او را نثار همه، حتی دشمنان او می‌کرد. از شدت غم و سرنوشت سارا دوباره اشکش گرفت. درحالی که بشدت می‌گریست، می‌گفت:

-آخ سارا، آخ سارا ای کاش بودی و می‌دیدی

ای کاش بودی و می‌دیدی!

۳

ماه‌ها از یوسف و تلی و سرنوشت سارا خبری نبود. بعدازگذشت نزدیک
به هفت ماه مسافری که از تفلیس آمده بود. نامه‌ای از یوسف و تلی آورد.
مسافر که یک مرد ارمنی بود وضع روسیه بخصوص شهرهای تفلیس و
ایروان را که در آن جاها بوده و زیسته بود. بسیار آشفته و بد می‌گفت و به
زحمت خود را به ایران و اورمیه رسانده بود. یوسف در نامه‌اش علاوه بر
سلام و اظهار ارادت با دلتنگی نوشته بود:

"تصدقتان گردم برابر فرموده و سفارش شما از همان روز حرکت پشت
سر و دنبال کاروان هیات ارتدوکسی که سپاهیان روسیه آن‌ها را همراهی و
حفاظت می‌کردند بودیم و از فاصله‌ای نزدیک آن‌ها را تعقیب و زیر نظر
داشتیم. ولی چون سربازان روسیه به شدت از هیات مراقبت می‌کردند
نتوانستیم به کالسکه سارا خانم نزدیک و او را ببینیم. تا به تفلیس برسیم

هفده روز طول کشید. البته سه روز در ایروان توقف و استراحت نمودیم و هم چنان کالسکه سارا خانم را زیر چشم داشتیم اما نتوانستیم او را ببینیم. بعد از رسیدن به تفلیس با کمک هوهانس دوست خدا بیامرز امیرخان برای یافتن و دیدن سارا خانم به دیر خواهران کلیسای شرقی تفلیس رفتیم و سارا خانم را پرسیدیم. آن‌ها نخست از وجود خانمی بنام سارا اظهار بی‌اطلاعی کردند اما چند روز بعد که دوباره مراجعه کردیم گفتند که او را به آن جا آورده بودند. مریض بوده و برای استراحت همراه گروهی از خواهران روحانی به یک دیر کوهستانی فرستاده‌اند. با راهنمایی هوهانس به همراه تلی، یاکمن و سرکیس به آن دیرکوهستانی دور رفتیم اما سارا خانم آن جا نبود و ساکنان دیر هم هیچ اطلاعی از او نداشتند. فقط یکی از خواهران روحانی گفت که شنیده است دختری به این نام که همراه کاروان بوده در راه بخاطر شدت بیماری فوت کرده و او را در نزدیکی ایروان بخاک سپرده‌اند. اما نمی‌دانست کجا و چگونه؟ دوباره باز به دیر کلیسای شرقی تفلیس مراجعه کردیم. این بارگفتند که مریض بوده و با کمک خانواده مادریش برای درمان به کیئف فرستاده شده. یاکمن که می‌بایست به کشورش برمی‌گشت. رهسپار کیئف شد و قول داد برای اطلاع از وضع سارا خانم و کسب خبر از وضع او همه جای کیئف را بگردد و اگر آن جا بود و او را پیدا کرد به او کمک کند و در صورت ممکن برای درمان با خود به سوئد ببرد اما اکنون که این کاغذ را می‌نویسم چهل روز از رفتنش گذشته، هنوز هیچ خبری از او نشده و ما هیچ نشان و خبری از سارا خانم نیافته‌ایم. جز این که هوهانس اخیرا از یک کشیش که با او دوست است شنیده که خواهر روحانی سونیا گفته که سارا بعد از آن مجازات سنگین

شلاق فوت کرده و او را شامگاه همان روز در بیرون از اورمیه نزدیک روستای چهار بخش بخاک سپرده‌اند و بچه‌اش را با کالسکه‌اش همراه آورده‌اند تا مردم آن نواحی متوجه نشوند. اما بعدا شنیده که به یکی گفته سارا خانم بعد از آن مجازات سخت مریض شده و در راه بازگشت به تفلیس درگذشته و او را در نزدیکی ایروان به خاک سپرده‌اند. اما خواهر روحانی سونیا نگفته که پسر سارا امیر عیسی چه شده و به سر آن بچه چه آمده؟ کنیزتان تلی می‌گوید که خواهر روحانی کریستیانا به سارا خانم قول داده بوده که از بچه‌اش مراقبت خواهد کرد و بی‌شک او می‌داند که بچه سارا کجاست و به سر سارا چه آمده؟ آیا فوت کرده و یا به یک جای دور فرستاده شده و یا نزد خانواده مادرش در تفلیس است؟ و معلوم نیست این گفته‌های و شنیده‌ها درست هستند و یا نه؟ اما شایعه است که سارا خانم مریض بوده و بعد از رسیدن به تفلیس او را از گروه خواهران روحانی جدا کرده و به جای دور و نامعلومی فرستاده‌اند. گویا سارا خانم خود را اهل ایران معرفی کرده و تقاضا کرده که به او اجازه دهند به ایران واورمیه برگردد. معلوم نیست که قبول کرده‌اند و گذاشته‌اند او به اورمیه برگردد، یا نه؟ سرکیس رفته و در ایروان مقیم شده و به دنبال یافتن خبر و نشانی از سارا خانم است و قصد دارد در اولین فرصت به اورمیه برگردد اما خروج از روسیه ممنوع است و به سختی موافقت می‌کنند و آنهایی که فرار می‌کنند کشته می‌شوند. من و تلی اکنون در تفلیس نزد پسرمان یعقوب هستیم اما تفلیس مثل گذشته نیست. اوضاع آن مثل دیگر شهرهای روسیه بهم ریخته است و هیچ نظمی در کار نیست، تنها نیروهای حاکم حزب

بلوشویک و ترس همه از آنها وارتشیان سرخ وکمیته‌هاست. کلیساها دیگر مثل گذشته حرمت ندارند و فعال نیستند. بسیاری از آنها بسته شده‌اند. ما هم چنان منتظر خبر و نشانی از سارا خانم هستیم. قصد داریم به شهرهای دیگر گرجستان رفته، دنبال خواهر روحانی کریستیانا بگردیم. شاید بتوانیم از طریق او حقیقت را بدانیم و از سرنوشت سارا خانم باخبر شویم و همانطور که به شما قول داده‌ام و به روح مرحوم امیرخان سوگند خورده‌ام تا سارا خانم را نیابیم هرگز برنخواهیم گشت.

بعد از آن نامه دیگر خبری و نامه‌ای از یوسف و تلی نرسید و از سارا هم خبری نشد و معلوم نشد که به سر او و پسرش چه آمد؟ آیا او بعد از مجازات شلاق در اورمیه فوت کرده بود و یا در طول راه تفلیس درگذشته و در نزدیکی ایروان به خاک سپرده شده بود و یا او را به دیر دور و نامعلومی فرستاده بودند و یا این که او را کشتند، هیچ کس نمی‌دانست به سر او در آن دیار غریب چه آمد و او چه شد؟ از یوسف و تلی هم دیگر هیچ خبری نشد. نسترن خاتون سال‌ها با غم و اندوه سارا و امید بازگشت او زیست و بعد از سال‌ها انتظار درگذشت. عمارت باغ ساران بعد از درگذشت او بسته شد و سال‌ها همان طور بسته بود تا این که متروک و ویران شد. اهالی ساران تا مدت‌ها کنار هم بودند. تا این که کم کم پراکنده شده و رفتند و دهکده ساران هم متروک شد و از بین رفت از سارا فقط یک نام ماند و یک تصویر.

متن اول از ۱۱ بهمن ۱۳۷۲ تا ۱۰ آذر ۱۳۸۹

بازنویسی و تجدید نظر کامل اردیبهشت ۱۴۰۱

آثار دیگر از این نویسنده:

نجوای ناتمام
اسماعیل پوردشاهیان
ارومیا

دلباختگان بی‌نام عشق من
اسماعیل پوردشاهیان (ارومیا)

آب‌ها مرا می‌برند
اسماعیل پوردشاهیان
ارومیا

آنجا که زاده شدم
اسماعیل پوردشاهیان
Where I was born
ESMAIEL YOURDSHAHIAN

EN FRANCAIS
La Complainte
Inachevée
Auteur
Esmaiel Yourdshahian
Traducteur
Nader André Dadgar Nowbarian

برای تهیه آثار این کد را اسکن کنید

آثار دیگر نویسنده

شعر:

۱. نیار (منظومه) چاپ زمستان ۱۳۴۹

۲. کوزه (مجموعه شعر)، چاپ تابستان ۱۳۵۰

۳. مرثیه‌های کولی، مجله سخن پائیز ۱۳۵۳

۴. غربت پاییز، چاپ ۱۳۵۵

۵. شب هفتم، چاپ ۱۳۵۷

۶. خیمه در پائیز، انتشارات رودکی۱۳۶۹

۷. آبی در آشوب، انتشارات رودکی ۱۳۷۰

۸. ترانهٔ آبی، نشر یوشیج ۱۳۷۸

۹. اورمیای بنفش، چاپ اول در تعداد محدود ۱۳۷۹

۱۰. در ویرانی صبح، انتشارت قصیده سرا ۱۳۸۰

۱۱. چیزی به خواب زمین نمانده است، انتشارات قصیده سرا ۱۳۸۲

۱۲. آوازهای اورمیا، نشر فرزان روز بهار ۱۳۸۴

۱۳. شب بوی سرخ برگزیده اشعار زیر چاپ

۱۴. یاسمن در باد – انتشارات نگاه – تهران ۱۳۹۲

۱۵. مادرم زنی زیبا بود (انتشارات مروارید بهار ۱۳۹۷)